EDGE
OF
INHUMAN

EDGE OF INHUMAN

THE DELTA TRIAD: BOOK I

ATLAS BLAINE

This is a work of fiction. Character names and descriptions are a product of the author's imagination. Any resemblance to actual persons, living or dead, is entirely coincidental, and any references to real places are used fictitiously.

Copyright © 2023 by Atlas Blaine

All rights reserved. No part of this book may be reproduced or distributed in any form without written permission from the author, except as permitted by U.S. copyright law.

To request permission, contact the author at authoratlasblaine@gmail.com.

First paperback edition October 2023

ISBN: 978-1-962786-00-3 (ebook)
ISBN: 978-1-962786-01-0 (paperback)
ISBN: 978-1-962786-02-7 (hardcover)

LCCN: 2023919910

Cover and book design by Atlas Blaine
Front cover photo by Max Titov

Raven & Quill Publishing
12256 Chorus Drive
Rancho Cucamonga, CA 91739

www.atlasblaine.com

to darkness,
for all it has taught me

ONE

Death is like poison.

The remnants of it seep into your blood and your bones, consuming you, warping you into something unrecognizable. For most, those remnants take the form of grief. For me, however…

It's revenge.

Long story short, my best friend was shot in the head and now I want the man responsible to suffer.

I walk down a lifeless street in Lower Manhattan, silence emanating from my earpiece. The April rain is falling in a soothing drizzle, the distant glow of Midtown's neon lights caught in the haze. I can vaguely make out massive words being projected into the sky, rotating through various languages. I don't know what time it is, but it's a strange enough hour in the night that the City That Never Sleeps possesses an eerie calm, apart from a few broken trash robots driving around haphazardly. The only people I pass are the rotting bodies of those who likely overdosed on sugarpills.

They barely register in my mind, however, because retribution is finally within reach.

For once, tonight will be for me and not for the GUARD.

"Make a left at the next street and it'll be about a block away," a voice says through my earpiece. Holbrook.

I roll my eyes because I already know where I'm going. I've memorized and mapped the entirety of Manhattan within my mind: every subway route, bus route, street, decayed park, and sector.

Turning the corner, I gaze up at the dilapidated apartment building that is my destination, praying that my target is ensconced there. In the few weeks since my previous assassination attempt, all I've been able to think about is beating his pale face bloody.

"Don't kill him. We need to get information out of him."

Holbrook, Head of the Manhattan Division, can practically read my mind, and I hate it. He knows me too well.

Normally it'd be Keating in my ear, as leader of the Field Department, but this mission is quote-unquote "different." I don't know much, of course; bare-bones information is typical when you operate on a need-to-know basis. For some agents, not knowing the details makes the job more mindless. In my case, it often makes it harder to follow orders.

Honestly, I've always resented the control my job imposes upon me, but I'll admit it has its perks. Primarily the detachment from society, because I never belonged there. Undoubtedly I live in a dark world, but I have a home and a life and a relatively sane mind. There are worse ways to live.

"He deserves it," I reply tightly, lacking the sort of politeness with which I'm expected to address my superiors. "I should torture him a bit, at the very least."

This anger I've been feeling has burgeoned like a fire, inundating me to the point that rather than being reasonable, the only thing I want is to hurt someone, to balance the scales of pain.

"Kai."

"I know," I cut Holbrook off. I'm sure I irritate the hell out of him, but by now he must be used to it. What's the worst he can do? I've proven to be valuable enough that I think he'd be hesitant to fire me, though I probably shouldn't tread too close to that line.

He doesn't respond at first, likely trying to rein in his vexation. The street grows darker as I near the hideout, the quiet disrupted only by the faint hum of my scout drone overhead, the faraway moan of a siren, and the rustling of a skeletal cat as it digs through a garbage bag. I continually monitor my surroundings for adversaries, but find no one.

Eventually, Holbrook sighs, then continues, his tone calm. "I'm trusting you to get your job done and do nothing more, otherwise I wouldn't have assigned you to this after what happened. I am giving you an order to take him captive as unharmed as possible. Is that clear?"

No, I'm too stupid, is what I'd prefer to say, but I hold my tongue. "As unharmed as possible" leaves some wiggle room.

"Yes sir," I mutter.

"Good. I know you've eliminated many of his known associates already, but don't make the mistake of expecting him to be alone."

Last time was a goddamn death trap, and I'm almost certain this time will be no different. But that kind of danger simply comes with the job.

"Should something happen," Holbrook continues, "the updated health module in the back of your neck will tell us if and how critically you are injured. But with that temper of yours, I know you're the most likely to walk out alive."

That we agree on. The one unquestionable thing about me is that I am lethal.

I approach the front door of the old complex and pull out my omnikey, courtesy of the Tech and Weapons Department. With a tap of the key to a flickering scanner, I'm granted access to an empty entryway where I wipe the rain off my face with my shirt.

Noiseless, I climb the stairs two at a time to the third floor, then creep down a hallway reeking of cigarettes and mold, my eyes locked on the door that supposedly conceals who I am looking for. When I'm about ten feet away, I jerk to a stop at the sound of a dog barking furiously from behind the door.

"*Fuck*," I hiss. The last thing I need is an augmented attack dog.

Animal enhancement is illegal, of course, but people still do it, especially to experiment without risking a human. The GUARD has been using certain kinds of implants—modules—for years now, but Dark Market tech isn't that far behind, on account of everyone's lack of morals and financial motives. Developing tech fast and selling it for the price of an organ is the best way to guarantee your survival as a DM. vendor. Not so long ago the government was cracking down on the DM, because people were killing each other over shit like that, but now it's become unregulated chaos.

I scan the wall for a camera and spot it after a few seconds, blending in with the hideous old wallpaper. Between that and the dog, I don't doubt that my target already knows that I'm here. I wouldn't be able to blend in if I tried, being outfitted with all-black gear, guns, and gadgets. I also stick to plain ink instead of adorning my body with the weird embellishments that everyone is into—lenticular tattoos, metal fish scale limbs, rainbow eyes, the like. Holbrook tells me it's "old-fashioned," and hence makes me easy to spot.

The target's door, unlike others I passed, has no key reader and no handle. It's just blank. But by tilting my head to get a different perspective, I notice that it's shimmering in the dim yellow lighting of the hall, and realize that there's some kind of skin over it. A faint buzzing indicates that it's electrified, which eliminates the possibility of kicking the door in.

I walk up to it and the dog seems to become more enraged, as if it has X-ray vision too. Unlikely, but I suppose I can't rule it out. "If I can't get through your door, I will cut a hole in your wall," I say, nearly shouting over the barking.

"No need," I hear faintly.

The target yells at his dog, who falls silent, and the door glides open.

He is not in my line of sight, so I sidestep to my right. And as he appears I can't help but recoil, even though I've encountered him before. His facade is crisp, cold, accompanied by brilliant white hair and skin, a defined jawline, and venom-green eyes that make me uneasy. He's tall and skinny and wearing a suit as though he is about to attend a lavish event.

In a word, he's intimidating.

He gestures for me to enter his apartment, so I do. I can't exactly stand in the hallway forever.

Apartment, I quickly discover, is not accurate. Walls have been blown out to create one large room, and the only lighting is the blue glow of various technological instruments scattered about, the kind that you might find in one of those secret hacker caves. Suiting, considering that this one man has allegedly been a cyber force to be reckoned with.

Along the walls, there are multiple holographic video feeds, all depicting different locations. Some of the city, some of the front of the apartment building. Some with entrances to GUARD HQs or government buildings around the world. Worse, it looks like there are video feeds *inside* those government buildings. For all we know he's been watching and listening to policymakers and handing off the information.

"It's a little elaborate," I say flatly.

"This is hardly extensive," Venom Eyes replies, waving his hand casually. His dog sits next to him, uttering a persistent low growl, clearly waiting for a cue to rip my face off. "I've been waiting for you, Kai."

I almost flinch at him knowing my name, but it doesn't surprise me. "Great, let's get started."

On cue, four masked men step out of the shadows of the corners of the room. *How cinematic.* Venom Eyes over here likes to put on a show.

"I guess I should take it as a compliment that you need four extra men to take me on," I say to clue Holbrook into the situation.

"Well. I don't take chances," Venom Eyes responds. "Your so-called backup around the block is being taken out by my people as we speak. If anyone else tries to come into this building, they'll be killed on sight." He frowns in false concern. "I do hope they're not making a scene; we don't want the robopolice getting involved, hmm?"

"The police are far less of a concern to me than you."

"I'm flattered."

"Odds," Holbrook commands before I can utter a snarky comeback. The tightness in his tone is a strong hint that Venom Eyes isn't lying about my backup getting obliterated.

I debate whether to answer. Agents are often asked to gauge the chance that they'll come out of their assignment alive so their superior can weigh the risks, and usually it's at a highly inconvenient moment.

Five-on-one doesn't give me great odds, but I'm too fixated on revenge to care about my own fate. The only way this ends is with one of us in the ground.

"You know," Venom Eyes continues, "a young person of your talents doesn't deserve the grim ending you're about to endure."

"I'm flattered," I mock.

With a glance, I make a note of which hand each goon is holding his pistol with. I know these men won't miss my head, and as soon as I take a shot at one, the next will have me dead.

I run through my list of gear. A modular gun, a plasma knife, hyper-shock darts, and a retractable garrote. Nothing spectacular, really—my instincts need to give me an edge.

"All right, I'm pulling the plug," Holbrook says into my ear. But I'm not listening.

Dimly I remember my orders to keep Venom Eyes alive for information, and for a second I consider it, but the vengeful part of my conscience is far stronger.

"Get out now. Before you get yourself killed." Holbrook's voice grows more anxious as he realizes what I'm doing, but it's probably only because I'd be a hassle to replace. "*Goddammit*, Kai."

I tap my earpiece to mute him. There's nowhere I could run even if I wanted to.

One of the men makes a move toward me and I let him. He grabs my arm in a predictable attempt to put me in a lock, but I'm one step ahead. I grab the back of his neck and knee him in the stomach, then yank my arm out of his grasp and shove him backward so that he falls, sending his gun flying. I start forward to kick him in the head but by that time the other three are on me.

None of them have fired, however, which is a cue that they don't want to kill me—yet.

I start throwing punches, countering fists coming at me from all angles. I manage to hold steady for several moments, but then they begin to overpower me. Two of them land a number of consecutive hits to my head and face, disorienting me enough that another one is able to knock me down.

They drag me through a hidden door into a chamber lined with a hexagonal lattice of soundproofing panels, throwing me onto a board and restraining my wrists and ankles with electrocuffs.

I curse myself for losing so quickly, so pathetically. I've trained for this; I should be better. If there's anything I hate, it's being helpless.

"That didn't take long," Venom Eyes says, apparently also disappointed. "And to think that they call you one of their best. Now, you can tell me what I'd like to know either before the waterboarding, or after. Or never, if you'd prefer to die." He smirks down at me.

Shit.

"Suit yourself," he responds to my silence. "But the sooner you start spilling, the less we have to do this."

I scramble to generate a plan, tuning out the questions he's begun to ask me about the GUARD. *Come on.* But my focus on escaping wanes when one of the henchmen holds a cloth over my face.

I've trained for this too, being tortured. It's one of the Field tests required to graduate from the Academy. But nothing's as brutal as the real world.

Bracing myself, I clamp my eyes and mouth shut before the water comes in a steady stream, though it still gushes up my nose. My body panics before my mind can calm it down and I am gasping, uncontrollably inhaling water, drowning. I struggle against the cuffs to no avail. Venom Eyes keeps pouring for what seems like an eon, then his goon rips the cloth from my face. I start coughing up water like my lungs are attempting to expel demons, which prevents me from getting a decent breath of air.

Words are being uttered to me once again but I am not listening, not answering. Moments later the soaking cloth is back again and I tell myself over and over not to scream, not to show weakness, not to give in. *Think.*

Then I feel something against my hip, in my pocket.

The omnikey. *Oh my God, what a lifesaver.* I feel around my right cuff to find the key reader. Judging by its position, scanning the key one-handed will be challenging, but it's the only shot I've got. I pray that they won't notice what I'm doing until it's too late.

I shift my torso and hips to the right as far as I can, attempting to make it look like I'm in pain, and grapple for the key in my pocket. I'm on the verge of panicking before I finally have it. Blindly I smash the key against the scanner, but my wrist doesn't bend far enough and I almost fear that I'm a goner.

Then I find that the handcuff is *just* large enough for me to twist my wrist if I force it, though it burns and cuts my skin. Just as one of the men shouts something at me, I am freeing my right arm. I rip the soaking cloth off my face, spit up water, and whip out my gun, its suppressor already on. The idiots should've taken it from me the moment they had me restrained.

This B-Team barely knows what's hit them. I catch Venom Eyes backing away in surprise, but decide to save him for last. Black spots in my vision, adrenaline in my blood, I shoot one of his henchmen in the head, then another through the heart.

With three more bullets I split the chains attached to my remaining cuffs, freeing myself. I'm on my feet in a flash.

Then I'm tackled from behind, air being forced out of my aching lungs, a gun pressing into my skull as someone kneels on my back. He spews threats to urge my cooperation but I merely reach around myself and shoot him.

Venom Eyes barks a command, and when I get up I see his dog rushing toward me. But in that moment, any hesitation I might have about killing an animal is overpowered by instinct.

I spin around to find the final gunman frozen in shock, with a pistol raised midway. He is about to fire, but in an instant he is dead on the ground and Venom Eyes is running out the door, into the hallway.

It takes one bullet to the leg to make him fall. He rolls over and looks at me with fury as I approach. I can't help but smile. God, the satisfaction. I press my gun to his forehead, wait for a few slow seconds to relish his anger, his fear, and pull the trigger.

TWO

I collapse against the blood-spattered wall and close my eyes until the adrenaline begins to fade. My lungs and throat hurt like hell, my body feels bruised everywhere, but somehow I'm alive.

I take a minute to just breathe, then unmute my earpiece, though Holbrook is silent at this point. Before speaking, I opt to check if any goons appeared to guard the entrance to the building. Leaving the body where it is, I kick down the door to the next apartment, which I anticipate will be vacant thanks to Venom Eyes. Criminals like him aren't so careless as to risk their operations on a nosy neighbor, though this isn't a place where people ask questions to begin with.

Finding no sign of life inside the apartment, I locate a street-facing window in the bedroom and peer out of it. Sure enough, there are two men in predictable positions. I spot one hiding on a balcony across the street, barely visible in the rain and darkness. The other is on the sidewalk below me, illuminated by a few lights.

Quietly I nudge open the window, attach a mid-range barrel to my gun, then aim at the man on the balcony. I pull the trigger in between breaths. In between heartbeats. The bullet hits him in the chest and he collapses forward, falling over the railing and leaving his cohort looking around frantically. I take him out a moment later.

"Send the driver," I say. There is no reply and I suppose that I deserve it.

I haul Venom Eyes down three flights of stairs, glimpsing a triangle tattoo just below his ear, and find my driver, Cole Sheehan, putting one of the guards in the trunk of his car. Some techie back at HQ has dimmed the streetlights to better hide us from view.

"There's another one over there." I point to the crumpled body across the street.

"I was expecting one living person, not three dead ones," Cole says, raising his eyebrows at me.

"There's four more up in his apartment."

He smiles slightly, amused. "I think you'll pass the record for highest kill count in a year."

"They pay attention to that?"

"They pay attention to everything."

I shove Venom Eyes unceremoniously into the back as Cole brings over the other guard, then slide into the passenger seat, exhausted. The car is a sleek black Audi, enhanced by our Tech and Weapons Department. It's equipped with everything a spy could need: weapons, a first aid kit, a tracker, voice control, autodrive, guns on the outside, bulletproof windows, a self-destruct feature, and an AI assistant. It's coded to the ID modules of specific people so that only they are authorized to drive, which, sadly, means I've never gotten to borrow a car for a joyride.

"I suppose Holbrook isn't very happy with me," I say when Cole gets in next to me. The mood lighting morphs from red to blue upon recognizing his ID.

"Well, no. But I imagine he's relieved you're still alive, since your backup was slaughtered."

"Jesus," I mutter. "We should've been better prepared this time. But this guy was in another league. Always five steps ahead."

He eyes the body in the back for a moment. "And now we'll never know what he knew."

I give him a side glance, lacking the energy to be insulted. Killing Venom Eyes wasn't logical from an intelligence standpoint, and I knew in the end it wouldn't make me feel better because I'd still have a dead friend. But I also knew I desperately needed the resolution.

We drive in silence to the heart of Manhattan, into a parking structure, where we pull up to a hidden garage door on the ground level. An invisible sensor recognizes the car, prompting a holographic pin pad to appear in front of Cole, projected from the dashboard.

He enters a code, and a voice emanates from our speakers. "Welcome back. Passengers identified: Cole Sheehan and Kai Thanatos. Please proceed."

The door opens to let us through, revealing a downward-spiraling ramp that leads to more levels underground. But the only vehicles down here belong to the GUARD.

At the end of the ramp there are two guards, because there's no such thing as too much security. Cole rolls down his window and greets the one on his side while the other looks through the trunk and rear seats, using a handheld scanner to search for anything suspicious.

"Go on through," the guard says after his partner has finished, looking me up and down.

We park, and I offer to help dispose of the bodies, not out of kindness but out of some vague desire to see my friend's killer get chucked into an incinerator.

"Nah, I'll handle it," Cole responds. "I need to hand off the blonde one to the Medical Department anyway, and you... look like you need some rest."

That I can't argue with. "Probably. All right, see you around."

I take an elevator down to where the Manhattan Division is situated, far beneath the subway system. It opens to a hallway lined with black tiles, and at the end is the last security checkpoint, where two more guards stand on either side of a metal archway. I step through without setting off the alarms, and approach a door that slides open when I'm within a few feet, having sensed my ID module.

Then I'm through to the Pit, the high-ceilinged hub of the Manhattan Division that acts as a cafeteria, social lounge, and tech center. Stamped in a huge circle on the floor is the GUARD logo—a minimalist wolf head. Currently, the Pit is void of any activity, illuminated only by soft pathway lights and distant stars dotting the ceiling display. All the false windows and skylights throughout the division are synced via a lighting system designed to provide a sense of time.

Beyond the Pit, the rest of the headquarters is divided into unequal thirds with living spaces, one for each department. The largest is the Field section, where I spend the majority of my time. It's outfitted with a shooting range, a combat center, a gym, and a pool, the last two of which sound nice until you learn they're not really for luxury.

The Medical Department is the smallest, with a morgue, an infirmary, and research labs. There are counseling offices too, but I tend to avoid those, against Keating's recent wishes.

The Technology and Weapons Department, lastly, has exactly what its name suggests. Techies can do everything from hacking and tracking to designing weapons and defense tech, rendering T&W the backbone of the GUARD.

I turn and head into the Field section. It's a maze, but I know the corridors of this place like I know the veins of Manhattan, so even though I zone out, my feet still take me to my apartment. It's been home for a few years now since graduating from the GUARD Academy.

The door slides open for me, and I find Camden Adler lounging on my couch.

"Hey babe," he says with a smirk.

I give him a look. "What the hell are you doing in here?" I ask flatly, unsure how he even got in without my authorization.

"Nothing. Waiting for you, I suppose. I usually don't go to bed until six in the morning, mate. I'm basically nocturnal." He says it like it's an accomplishment.

"So you decided you can just... hang out in here."

"Yeah, pretty much."

"Whatever. I don't care."

"Good. We're going to be such good friends, Kai."

Camden is a transfer from London, though I don't know why he chose to leave. Some people transfer just to get away from the only place they've ever known, some because they have international assignments, others because they want change. Camden hasn't told me anything, and I get the sense he is avoiding the subject. Not that I'm one to pry.

I suspect that my general indifference is why he took a liking to me, because he feels like he can be himself without consequence. All it took was a day of training together and now he won't leave me alone, although I suppose I like him too, even if his endless humor is annoying.

"You walk around this place like a badass," Camden says as I strip off my wet shirt and walk into my bedroom. Detecting my arrival, the lights turn on and brighten to their nighttime radiance. "Your reputation is accurate, that's for sure," he continues. "I mean look at you, blood on your face and all. Bruises. Death glare. The whole package. I bet people don't fuck with you."

I hadn't even realized there was blood on my face.

I wash it off, change into sweatpants, and dig through my medicine cabinet for healing painkillers, courtesy of the Med Department. My lungs and throat and head still hurt, and I feel, overall, like shit. I want to throw up but I can't. So I swallow a couple of pills that I probably take too often.

Just as I'm rejoining Camden in the living room, there is a knock on my door. "I'll get it," he announces, jumping up.

I sigh, irritated that someone else has the nerve to come over at this hour. I had been expecting to come home, crash on my bed, and mull over what just happened to me.

"Calm down, it's just Shay."

"Why can't you hang out at your own place?"

He looks at me like I'm stupid. "*Because* we're supposed to socialize with people who aren't just transfers. They say it'll help us fit in, so technically I'm just doing what I was told."

I shake my head at him. He opens the door and Sharanya Sarai smiles at us, lifting a bottle of wine. Camden has taken a liking to her, too, but I suspect it's a different kind.

If the rumors are true, I hear she's quite deadly, but you wouldn't know at first glance. She's on the skinny side for an assassin, with gentle brown eyes, a metal choker, and long hair that's a gradient from black to purple. The choker, according to Camden at least, is where she keeps all her poisons.

"Come on in, Kai just got back. The party's just getting started," he tells her.

"Hi Shay," I greet her out of politeness.

"Hi. How are you?"

"Terrible."

"You're the best killjoy I've ever met," Camden says, smiling. "Let's open that booze."

"If I'm being forced to socialize, one bottle of pinot noir won't cut it," I reply.

I lead them to my (admittedly substantial) supply of alcohol, to which Camden says, "Jesus mate, do you need help? Aren't you twenty?"

What a strange world I live in, where I can't legally drink alcohol, but I can kill people as an occupation.

"I had a techie make me a few fake IDs."

At one point in time, I actually worried about breaking the law. But ultimately the GUARD cares about itself. The only rules truly enforced are those of the agency, the most important of which are: 1) don't use unauthorized weapons or technology, and 2) no outsiders can know anything.

"Damn. Do you generally drink alone?"

"No, I don't *generally* drink alone, Camden."

He raises his hands in placation. "Well I sure as hell know you're not throwing parties."

I give him a look. "Liquor isn't my vice. It's more of a… hobby."

Camden laughs as he picks a couple bottles at random. "That's what I should call it."

In the morning I wake up far earlier than I would like. While Shay and Camden are still knocked out on my couch, I change into training clothes and study myself in the mirror.

I look awful. Feel awful too, worse than last night.

After I muster the courage to get on with my day, I nudge Camden awake. We spent most of the night watching him do impressions and listening to his crazy stories, and I'll admit, he has a knack for taking my mind off everything else. Shay, meanwhile, is unexpectedly kind for a GUARD agent. She's quiet, but she's also the type of person who can befriend anyone. Make you feel comfortable, lighten your mood. They're the kind of friends I've never had.

Groggily Camden looks around, his eyes eventually finding mine. A smug smile appears on his face. "You're not so bad drunk."

"You, on the other hand, are nearly intolerable."

"Don't hate me because I'm fun, love."

"Don't call me that," I respond tiredly.

"Sorry. Sweetheart?"

"I didn't know we were a couple."

"Okay *fine*, we won't use any terms of endearment."

My phone buzzes just as Shay starts to stir, and a message pops up instructing me to come to Holbrook's office immediately, like he knows that I just woke up and wants to ruin my morning. I groan, because I already know he's going to chew me out for last night.

Leaving Cam and Shay, I walk back out of the Field quarter, across the bustling Pit, and into Holbrook's office.

"You're firing me," I say as I enter.

"No," Holbrook replies without looking up, sitting behind an ornate black desk with two curved computer screens on it.

"You're demoting me."

"No."

"You're sending me to a shrink."

"No. Stop." It's then that he finally meets my eyes. His gaze is dark, but he doesn't intimidate me in the slightest, and he never has. I think it irks him a bit. He's used to having power over everyone. "You... you not only killed someone we needed information from, you almost got *yourself* killed disobeying direct orders. You're lucky I'm not suspending you."

"I had no idea. I'm so sorry, sir."

His face remains emotionless. "Being a smartass isn't going to get you anywhere."

"It's for my satisfaction, not yours."

He ignores that. "I really don't want you stupidly risking your life. Next time I *will* suspend you. Put you on house arrest. Revoke privileges. Make your life hell, more than it already is."

I brush off the threat, though I know he means it. "That's my job, isn't it? To risk my life."

"I can't afford to lose you." He says it not as though he's truly concerned about me, but like I'm valuable property. I'm not sure he feels anything about anyone.

"We're all just killing machines to you," I mutter.

"No, Kai. I care about you and all of my agents."

I scoff at that. "Bullshit."

He frowns. "It's not, actually. And I know it's a bit soon, but I'm assigning you a new partner. One I trust to keep you in line and keep you alive."

"I don't want one."

He sighs. "I know you don't."

"I don't need one."

"Oh yes you do."

"Have you picked them already?"

"Yes, I have."

"Camden, I assume?"

"No. Mr. Adler and Miss Sarai will be working together. They're quite compatible."

"You're putting two transfers together?"

"They're only new to the country, not the job." He looks me dead in the eye. "I know what I'm doing."

This time there's an underlying threat in his voice that makes me halt. I have to remind myself that he has more control over my life than I do.

"Your partner's name is Harley," he continues. "Harley Stone. She is very talented. You two will make an excellent team, if you can work together. And, frankly, she was the only one available."

"The only one available," I repeat. "Why, exactly?"

"She recently completed training, and everyone else has partners."

"So she just turned eighteen? Great."

"She's around your age, actually. Started training a little late."

"Still, inexperienced." I was in her situation not that long ago, but a lot has happened to me since then. And I'm not going to be a handholder.

"Not as much as you might think. Don't underestimate her. Now, I'm moving her to the space next to yours."

I feel myself tense up. *That* hits a nerve—my old partner lived in that space. My closest friend for nearly a decade. Sometimes it feels like he was ripped from my life only yesterday.

"Is this your way of forcing me to move on?"

He purses his lips. "I can't dwell on your partner's death, and neither can you, but I'm not as cruel as you believe. Harley would've joined the Field Department regardless of your tragedy."

I feel a flare of anger. My fists clench, my jaw clamps. This wound is still too raw.

"I can't *dwell* on his death?" I repeat, struggling not to raise my voice. "God, you're cold. I don't have a family, or friends. He was all of that for me. You cannot replace him with some rookie."

His eyebrows raise, as though he's daring me to challenge him further. Which is exactly what I plan to do.

"Again," he says tersely, "what I'm doing is strictly for work purposes. You should not be one to let emotions get in the way."

"Jesus," I exhale, barely maintaining my composure at this point. "You know I always get the job done. But I'm not a goddamn robot. Did you not just tell me you 'cared' for me?" I throw air quotes up to augment my bitter display.

"Caring for someone and letting emotions affect your work are different things," he replies plainly.

"So I can care about someone, but then I have to get over them if they die."

I can tell he wishes he could punch me, and one day he might, but for now he holds steady. "All I'm saying is that you need to accept having a new partner. I think you should go meet her—she's supposed to be moving into her new quarters."

"Fine." I spin and walk out.

THREE

Camden is still in my room when I return. I shove my way through the door, fighting the urge to scream.

"Damn. What happened?" he asks, looking at me with wide eyes. I don't think he's seen me like this, seen my temper. "Mercurial" is what Holbrook used to call me back at the Academy, before I learned how to control it. Sometimes it still slithers out to bite.

"Holbrook is a sociopath, is what happened. I'm getting some new girl as a partner, because apparently I can't handle anything on my own, and now she's moving in next door."

He suddenly acts like he's oblivious to my irritation. "Hold up. There's a new girl?"

"Yes," I snap, exasperated.

"Is she attractive? This is important."

I shake my head. "What? I've never even met her."

"Gotta inventory the prospects here, mate."

I stare at him. "What is wrong with you?"

He raises his hands in defense. "Whoa, don't be so disgusted, I'm only joking. Just trying to ease the tension."

"Right," I mutter.

"Seriously though, maybe you could invite her to train with all of us later. I can see you're not thrilled, but you can't avoid her forever, and I'm an obvious candidate to help break the ice."

I have no desire to do anything that the GUARD expects me to, especially since I didn't get a break in the wake of my partner's death. I just feel so dead. Dead emotionally, dead physically.

But Camden's right. I can't avoid this forever.

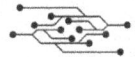

I take a breath before knocking on Harley's door, which feels weird to me now. I've barely even looked at this door in the last few weeks.

A few moments later it opens and there stands a girl, one I've never seen before, with wavy platinum blonde hair and bright purplish-blue eyes. That description alone would suggest that there's nothing atypical about her.

No. She looks like she could kill me. And wants to.

The clothes she is wearing are tattered. Is it fashion? I don't know. Her arms, neck, and thighs—and probably other places I can't see—are decorated with a handful of small tattoos.

She locks eyes with me and doesn't look away. I can't tell if it's sexual, or a power move, or both.

Shit. I didn't expect to have my breath taken away.

I stand looking at her for a few moments before I realize that I should speak. "I'm assuming you're Harley. Or whatever."

"Yeah. Kai, right?" She says it like she knows who I am. Which I suppose isn't unlikely, seeing as we overlapped at the Academy. And, as Camden has made me aware, my reputation seems to precede me.

I catch a vague wariness in her eyes, too.

"That's me."

"I've heard a lot about you. Holbrook had many positive things to say."

"Really," I say flatly.

"Not personality-wise."

"Oh, that makes more sense."

"I can see why people call you Dickhead."

"Yeah, get used to it, I guess."

She raises her eyebrows. "What do you want?"

"I don't *want* anything. I came over here to tell you that I'm going to the training center with a few others if you'd like to join. You can meet us there when you're ready."

She clearly wasn't expecting that. "Oh. Sure."

I nod once, then turn and walk away without saying another word.

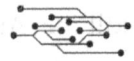

"Did you meet her?" Shay asks when I show up at the training center, where I realize more than a few people are staring at me. Word sure gets around here, apparently.

"Yes."

"And? How'd it go?" She exchanges a glance with Camden, who obviously told her about my earlier outburst.

"Is she attractive?" he adds pointedly.

"Unfortunately," I respond, to which he can't help but smile gleefully. "Maybe you've seen her. Blonde with purple eyes. Looks like she was meant to murder people."

Shay grins at that. "Well, I suppose that's suiting. You invite her here?"

"Yeah. We'll see if she shows up. But I only talked to her for like ten seconds so... jury's still out on what she's like." I shrug, eager to change the topic. "In other news, I heard you two are partners."

Shay nods, attempting to hide a faint smile that suggests she has no complaints about the situation. "Indeed we are—just got out of a meeting with Keating."

"Holbrook was there too. Told us to 'look out for you,'" Camden says, mocking Holbrook's deep voice.

"What does he want you to do, hold me when I cry?" I retort.

"More like encourage emotionless killing," Shay responds dryly. "He's trying to get us to keep you in line. I think he felt like he could manipulate our loyalty to him, being recent transfers."

"Good to know I'm not the only one who realizes he's an asshole," I mutter.

I catch sight of Harley making her way toward us, and fail to suppress a sigh of disappointment.

Camden is immediately embarrassing. "Hmm... blonde, check. Looks like a murderess, check. Hey, I think this is the one Kai was talking about!"

I shake my head at him in exasperation as Harley comes to a halt in front of us, and he responds by flashing his classic smirk. He then introduces himself in his most dramatic, dashing voice, but she remains unimpressed.

"I didn't know Dickhead over here had friends," she says.

"Keep calling me that and I'll shoot you," I snap. "Can we get to work?"

"In case you haven't noticed, Kai hates fun," Camden murmurs to Harley, pretending that he doesn't want me to hear.

"I don't hate fun, I hate *you*."

"I know, and I love it. Now then, what first?"

Our training center comprises a few different components for developing physical and psychological prowess. The combat practice section, for one, is a large area covered with black mats, where weapons are disallowed. It's where I spend the majority of my time since I see punching people as a form of anger management.

The obstacle course, meanwhile, is exactly what its name suggests, but it's dangerous to the extent that people have almost died. You have to run through the whole thing as though you are fleeing, dodging gunfire and attackers. I've scaled fences, run through a fake subway system, and leapt over vehicles, all the while getting shot at. The only mission is to survive.

The Tactical Operation and Reconnaissance Simulator, lastly, is a simulation where the situation and scenery inside change daily. It can be anything from a building to an entire city, where in pairs or groups you are given a time-bound objective to complete. The GUARD never makes it easy, of course—often the level of danger is beyond anything

I've faced in reality. Everything feels entirely real, too, which is what makes it so psychologically rigorous. It's gotten to a point where I can't recall who I've killed in the real world, and who I've killed in a simulation. And if you get shot, it's going to hurt like hell. Some people have even died in a sim and woken up convinced they're in the afterlife.

While the TORS is my favorite, I choose combat practice so I can see what Harley is made of.

"New kids first, Harley Quinn," I say, raising my eyebrows at her as we approach the mat for trainer one-on-ones.

"Wow, you're so creative," she responds to my nickname. "And it's not like it's my first time, you know."

"I've never seen you here." I talk over Camden, who had begun to crack a dumb joke about virginity.

"Not very observant, are you?" Harley says coldly.

"When it comes to people insignificant in my daily life, no."

"Hey, be nice," Camden interrupts. "Harley, too bad, you're going first."

"Fine," she replies, walking onto the mat as the last agent walks off.

The current trainer, Leven Akana, dries his face on a towel before discussing with Harley what she wishes to work on. His primary role in the GUARD is as a T&W engineer, and I've never been sure whether this side gig is to get a taste of field work, or a means of occupying his mind.

"I can see why you're single," Camden says to me.

I scowl at him. "I don't think my personality is the main factor."

"Really? You're tall, dark, and relatively handsome. What else could it be?"

"Oh, I don't know. It could be the fact that I spend all my time killing people or training to kill people. But no, you're right—let me go get a girlfriend."

"Bitter sarcasm is a turnoff, love."

"So is obnoxious, unrelenting humor, along with everything else about you."

Both Shay and Camden laugh, causing Leven to shoot us a look. We all fall quiet as he and Harley take their stances.

She throws the first punch with her left hand. Leven blocks it with his forearm, but she anticipates it and lands a hit to his jaw with her other fist. He counters, she blocks and elbows him across the cheek, but she doesn't see his kick to the stomach coming. It knocks her backward, knocks the wind out of her. She rolls to avoid another kick and scrambles back to her feet.

She's quick, that's for sure. Quicker than Leven, quicker than me.

She grabs him by the shoulders and knees him in the groin, using his loss of balance as an opportunity to kick his legs out from underneath him. He falls forward and in the next second Harley is kneeling on his back, pinning his arms. Leven concedes the round.

Not too shabby.

"Good," Leven exhales. "Again." Harley releases him and they take up their original stances once more. Leven doesn't wait for her to prepare herself any further before he makes a punch to her cheek. I catch her cringe for a split-second and then something changes in her eyes. Focus morphing into anger.

She blocks the next few hits with skill, then counters with a cross to Leven's right cheekbone. He ducks a split-second before the next one comes, then straightens an instant later to return the cross. She elbows him in the mouth this time, then attempts to make another punch but misses, giving him the chance to throw her to the ground. He quickly grabs her wrists and pins her down, a nearly inescapable hold for someone half his size.

When he lets her go, she sighs angrily.

"You're pretty tough shit," he says, wiping blood from his mouth. "Couple things to improve, but Kai will help you." He smirks at me.

"That's your job, not mine," I respond.

"Well yeah, but I'm not the guy who escaped getting waterboarded by like four men."

"He's more likely to be distracted by my tits than teach me anything," Harley counters.

"Good one, sweetheart. That really hurt," I say.

"Sexual tension," Camden whispers behind me. I'm about to lose my mind.

"Shut up," I say, exasperated. This has made everything a lot more awkward, and I hate it. I want to go train by myself and pretend that I don't have a partner or new friends who get a kick out of annoying me.

Leven gives Harley some advice before he invites Camden to have a turn, then Shay goes with a different trainer. They're good, both of them. But not better than Harley, as much as I wish I had another excuse to dislike her.

As I am waiting for Shay to finish, I catch sight of Cole talking to some instructors on the other side of the training center. A few pairs of eyes drift my way again, which I attempt to ignore.

When it's my turn, I defeat the trainer both times, despite the ache in my lungs and pretty much everywhere else. But my body is on autopilot, because my mind isn't entirely in the present. I am reconstructing the events of last night in my head when I realize that I've seen that little triangle tattoo somewhere else before. At the time I noticed it on Venom Eyes, I didn't really pay attention to it. Now I'm attempting to remember where I've seen it, and I'm getting a hunch.

Cole. It's tattooed on him someplace, I'm almost sure of it. I don't know when or where I saw it, but I do know what it could mean for his future.

Sure, it could be a coincidence; a triangle is nothing distinctive.

Or it could be a symbol. A symbol of a crime syndicate. And if Venom Eyes is any indicator…

Perhaps a powerful one.

FOUR

That night, I meet Camden for dinner, at his insistence.

"So?" he says with an eager stare as I sit down at the table he grabbed, setting a plate of food in front of me.

"What?"

"What do you think of her?"

"She's... I don't know."

"Let me answer for you. You're perfect for each other."

"I can't say I feel the same."

"Do elaborate. You were impressive together in the battle zone today. I mean, you located the target and carried out an assassination like you could've done it in your sleep."

"I don't like her," I respond simply, though I don't disagree with him. I mostly don't want to admit that maybe Holbrook *does* know what he's doing.

"That's your brain talking."

"As opposed to what?"

He takes a bite of bread and speaks through a mouthful. "Your dick, love."

"I swear to God." I get halfway up to leave and Camden starts laughing.

"No, no, please stay, I'm sorry! Forgive me."

"We're not going to be friends if you keep making the same joke."

"Fine, I'll make fun of you for something else."

"I'll slit your throat."

"I'm so scared." He's still smiling. "Oh—there's a party of some sort tonight, and I expect you to come. T&W is throwing it in an empty lab, and I can assure you all the fun agents will be there. It'll be a great opportunity to meet girls, per our earlier conversation. Or boys, if you prefer. But from what I've gathered, it's a bit unlikely." He smirks and winks.

"Sorry to disappoint you."

"You're not my type."

"Thank God. How'd you find out about a party already?"

He shrugs. "Shay and I got invited because we're friendly. I would really recommend it to you."

"Don't condescend, asshole."

"I'm not!"

"You are."

"Okay, a little."

"Well, thanks for the invitation but parties aren't generally my thing."

"Have you ever been to one?"

"Yes, believe it or not. My partner and I used to go to them, but it's not like they're a regular thing around here."

"And did you have fun?"

"Sort of."

"Just get intoxicated. I promise you'll have a good time."

"Camden."

"Kai. Live a little."

"I am living."

His expression grows solemn, which unnerves me. "We aren't living, Kai. We're just killing. We're hiding underneath one of the most amazing cities in the world and we don't get to experience it like normal people do. And we have no escape."

"I know just as well as you do."

"So have fun for once. We have to make the most of the life we have."

He has a point. "Fine."

"Good. See you at eleven."

It's probably around three in the morning when I find myself to be extremely inebriated, thanks to some poor choices. Eventually, after dropping Shay, Camden, and some other random people off at their apartments, I manage to make it to mine. But my door doesn't open. Confused, I wave at it, as if that would help, then attempt manually unlocking with the palm scanner.

I'm in the process of slurring a bunch of cuss words when an irritated Harley opens it. She's not wearing much, and of course I can't help but notice, even in my current state.

"What the hell?" I say, a bit too loudly. "Why are you... Oh. Oh shit. I'm so sorry. I'm so fucked up. Sorry."

Not your room, idiot.

"It's fine, Kai, don't worry about it." Her voice is less harsh than I expect it to be. "Do you need anything? Water?"

"No."

"Okay."

"I'm sorry."

She laughs and watches me as I unlock my own door, making sure I'm successful. When I get inside, I fall onto my couch and pass out in an instant.

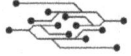

The next morning, while I still feel drunk, Keating calls me to his office. Harley is already there when I arrive, as if the world wants me to pay for having fun.

Amos Keating is nothing like Holbrook, in every sense. He's a Black ex-Navy SEAL, now our man behind the curtain who coordinates Field operations. He's a bit more chaotic than Holbrook, not as orderly and meticulous. Even so, there haven't been many operative deaths under his watch. He's incredibly smart, and has quickly obtained power and admiration in the GUARD. If Holbrook weren't in his way, he'd be leading the Manhattan Division.

I respect him more than almost anyone, and though I wouldn't say that we're overly close, we might be getting there. He's pretty lenient with me, which drives Holbrook insane. I think he knows that despite my tendency to break a few rules here and there, I'm a good agent.

"Ah, Kai. Hello," he greets me. "Rough night?" Wink.

There's a hint of a smile on Harley's face. I can't say I'm not a bit embarrassed at myself for already looking like a dolt in front of her, especially since she's clearly amused by it.

"Nice to see you too, *sir*," I reply bitterly.

"Not as rough as the other night, I suppose. I do hope you've swung by the Med Department for a checkup after all that—I was worried we might lose you. Quite the escape you made."

"Gotta keep things interesting."

He smirks. "I had to convince Holbrook not to suspend or demote you due to your 'insubordinate actions.' I generally trust you to get the job done, and I do hope that you'll uphold that trust. I can't continue to support you when you're reckless." He gives me a look. "Now then. I'm sending you two on your first mission. I need you to kill the CEO of Viper for us. Mikael Johansson. To put it briefly, he's a human trafficker. Owns some of the more... *heinous* sex houses here in Manhattan."

I nod once, but don't ask any questions.

By now I know that anyone the GUARD deems worth our time is worth assassinating. These people aren't good people. They're spies, drug lords, arms dealers, terrorists, cyberterrorists. Many of them have the money and resources to do whatever they please, to finagle their way out of anything. It's why traditional avenues of justice often fail. Which means, by extent, that the law itself is failing. That's when we step in, because it's easier than changing society.

The part that can't be justified is the trauma we bring upon a target's loved ones. It's something that the GUARD wants us to ignore, and for the most part, I've been able to, because I know having empathy in this job is dangerous. But there's always something there, in the back of my mind. Something more human than I've been trained to be.

"He's had a history with alcohol and pills, so you'll make his death look like an intentional overdose," Keating continues. "We're leaking a scandal in a few days while his wife Nari is gone, so you'll have to slip him the Liquid Death the night before in order for it to appear connected. Leven will be working with you on this one, so you three can get together and decide on a course of action. Any questions?"

Harley and I shake our heads.

"Good. Next, you likely saw the memo, but for your awareness, I'll be scheduling your physical and mental evaluations soon, as a result of some modifications to the procedure. Your aptitude scores will be adjusted accordingly, but it's nothing to worry about. Otherwise, Harley, you can go; I just have to discuss something with Kai before he leaves."

As she exits the office I look at Keating skeptically. "Is this about Holbrook nearly demoting me?"

"No." He pauses, as though he is debating whether or not to actually say whatever he's thinking. "There's something that I think you should perhaps know about your new partner. Holbrook was insistent that I not worsen your reluctance toward working with her, but I feel this may help you understand her better."

"What? Why would Holbrook not want me to know?"

"Well, I think he underestimates your maturity. He's worried that—"

"That I'll throw another fit about who my partner is?"

"Basically. Or at least that's what he said. But you don't have a reason to, in my opinion. Harley Stone is no worse than any of the rest of us. I think Holbrook is more paranoid than she is."

"That's... odd."

"Harley does have a past that's... more tragic than most. Which, around here, says a lot. Her story is hers to share, but I just want you to be aware. I think you'll have to work a little harder than usual to gain her trust."

I nod.

"However, I'm sure you'll have no problem tomorrow, and you certainly won't need me in your ear. It's mostly a test mission to see how you two work together. Good luck."

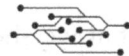

On my way back to my room, I pick up a small black box from the Medical Department containing the vial of liquid that will be responsible for stopping Johansson's heart. The compound has been engineered to present like an overdose, but it only takes a few drops to do the job. He'll be gone in a matter of twenty-four hours. He'll feel normal while it takes effect, and then suddenly he won't. He won't have enough time to call for help.

Honestly, it's a much gentler way to go than a bullet through the brain or a snapped neck.

Executions of important figures are carefully orchestrated in order to avoid their deaths looking like murders. It could be an apparent suicide, or an accident, or a prick of poison to the back of the neck. The more brutal—and easier—methods are reserved for criminals that the general public is not aware of.

The box reminds me to message Leven and Harley about meeting, but I find that they've already worked out a time and place. I arrive a bit late, naturally, and walk in on them talking quietly about something, but the conversation falls dead upon my arrival. I immediately get the sense that they are close, judging by their body language toward one another. There's nothing romantic from what I can see, but I can't help but feel like they're more than just acquaintances.

"Am I interrupting?" I say, too coldly.

"No you're fine," Leven responds, studying me as I sit across the meeting room table from them. Harley looks at me too, but only for a moment.

"Did you have time to skim the briefing?" she asks.

"Yep."

"Well, my initial thought is that we should go about this by being as innocent as possible. We need a way to get to Johansson, and I think his wife's line of work is how we do it."

"She's involved in a lot of charity work, yeah? I saw that Johansson's company Viper donates to nonprofits she works with. Probably to maintain a favorable public opinion."

"Right. I feel like something in that realm would be easiest for us to fake."

I think for a moment. "We could maybe pose as members of a new nonprofit. Perhaps we're seeking sponsors and advisors, and want Mrs. Johansson to be involved. The hard part is that she's gone, so it doesn't make sense for us to be meeting with just her husband, even if we're seeking a partnership with Viper."

"She had to go out of town on relatively short notice, so it *would* make sense if we had arranged a meeting but weren't able to reschedule. We don't have to be local. We can reach out to Mr. Johansson directly, but it'd be wise to run Mrs. Johansson's messaging data through speech pattern analysis in case he decides to confirm our legitimacy with her."

Leven nods. "I've set up a filter so that we'll be able to send our own responses."

"Okay," I say, my eyes shifting to Harley. "So imagining that he either agrees to dinner or an evening meeting at his penthouse, Leven is going to have to spoof security cameras, one of us will be responsible for distraction, and the other will be responsible for slipping the Liquid Death into his drink. Any preferences?"

"I think I can be a pretty good distraction," she responds.

"Why's that?"

She shrugs. "Given his profile, it wouldn't be hard to leverage sexual attraction here."

I clap my hands together once. "Great, let's dress you up as an escort. You can suck his dick while I do the rest."

I know I'm being a piece of shit, but mutual disdain is my goal. I just don't know how else to protect myself from loss after it nearly broke me the last time.

She throws a glare at me. "Don't be a demeaning asshole. I'd much rather take the easier job of poisoning him, but the chance of *you* getting his attention is minuscule."

"I'm sorry, I was under the impression you're fresh meat around here. How the hell have you proven anything?"

"All right you two," Leven snaps, before Harley can utter a comeback. "I think we have what we need for now. I'll draft a message for our target and once we receive his response we can determine our final course of action."

"Sounds good, captain," I say dryly, ignoring the fact that Harley is still eyeing me. "See you later."

FIVE

Harley, Leven, and I sit in a parked car a few blocks from Johansson's Uptown apartment, hazy dusk sunlight quickly fading to darkness. Leven has already hijacked the building's security system to ensure we're not going to be on camera.

Harley is wearing a chic business dress with metallic accents, and heels with concealed knives. In my pocket I have the vial, and beneath my jacket is a pistol.

"You ready?" I ask her. If she's at all nervous about killing someone for the first time, it doesn't show.

She nods once. I get out and hold the door open for her as Leven bids us good luck. I can't help but look her up and down, and in a moment of weakness I say, "You look nice, by the way."

She raises her eyebrows. "Thank you."

I cringe at how awkward that was, and she notices. I want to kick myself.

We walk the rest of the way in silence, through a sector that is nothing like Venom Eyes's neighborhood. Here the streets are immaculate, the robots functional, and the sugarpills purified to limit their damage. There are chromefaces getting chauffeured around in Lucids with neon underglow, and gliding silently somewhere in the haze above are the levitating superways. The only thing this sector has in common with the others is the perpetual immersion of its citizens in their AR worlds, whether it's for work or gaming or gambling or porn.

We enter a grand lobby outfitted with white marble and silver accents, then successfully get past the doorman, who appears to be in a state of numbing boredom. He notifies Johansson of our arrival, and we are allowed up to the very top floor after two security guards verify our IDs.

I hear faint classical music emanating from the penthouse but it stops once Harley knocks on the door. Johansson lets us in, already aggravated. True to his class, he's wearing two pieces of chrome metal fitted to his temples. Other people choose pieces that line their eyes or eyebrows, but all have a retractable screen for blocking out the world. AR contacts are far less popular among the affluent—they don't let you put your wealth on display. Tech in the form of jewelry ensures no one mistakes your status.

"I'm Lydia Sinclair, and this is my colleague Ellis Escher," Harley begins, shaking Johansson's hand. "Thank you for meeting us, Mr. Johansson. Apologies for the poor timing—it's a shame that Nari couldn't be present, but she assures us she's interested in our newly established nonprofit."

I'll admit that Harley puts on a convincing mask.

"It's not an issue, I'm happy to meet with you," he replies, but the bitterness in his tone reveals the lie.

"We're in the city visiting various prospective donors and partners, but Nari's work is definitely some of the most impressive," I say as we move to his living room. From so high up, you can still see the sun on a regular basis. It's just about to disappear over the horizon of haze, and I can't help but relish this sight that has become such a luxury.

"We think having a relationship with Viper would be beneficial for both companies," Harley adds. We both scan, as discreetly as possible, for a drink that he has out.

Johansson studies us warily, and I already notice that he spends more time looking at Harley than me. Maybe she *should* do all the distracting.

Hell, *I'm* distracted by her, though I'm trying not to be.

"I usually leave these matters to my wife. But I'll do my best," Johansson says. "Care for a drink?"

It's with these words that I smell the alcohol on his breath. Addicts are predictable. He has to be buzzed at the very least—on a bar cart is a tray with a bottle of scotch and a nearly empty glass.

"Oh, I suppose I wouldn't mind one, thank you," Harley replies. He makes his way over to the bar cart without giving me a chance to respond.

Harley gazes around at the penthouse as if she were comparing it to her own. "I admire your art choices. Is that Ansel Adams?" She gestures to a black and white landscape photo on the wall, and Johansson looks up from pouring a glass, surprised.

"Indeed it is. Are you into photography?" I'm impressed that Harley has already detected one of his passions, something that is key in distracting someone. I would be hard-pressed to say a single meaningful thing about art.

"I love it."

"It's not every day I come across someone who can recognize specific photographers. Do you know Berenice Abbott? Nari loves her photos of old New York. We have some more modern pictures of course, but we both really enjoy black and white."

"They're lovely photos. I wish I had such a collection." Harley walks away from me, toward another picture. "Who is this one by? It's beautiful."

Johansson is about to pour himself a glass, but stops and heads over to her. That's my cue. While he isn't looking, I slip the Liquid Death into his whisky bottle.

When Harley eventually turns around and looks at me, I give her a slight nod.

I catch Johansson checking Harley out, and I feel a twinge of annoyance. Even if he thinks she's twenty-five, it's still obvious she's less than half his age. *Creep.* "I can show you a few more if you'd like," he offers. "Then we can get to business. I don't want to keep you here too long."

I'm instantly suspicious, but I don't intervene.

"Sure. I'd love to see them," Harley says, giving me a look to signal her displeasure. Johansson pours himself more scotch and takes a gulp, subsequently telling me that I can "help myself." Otherwise, he's begun to completely ignore me at this point. They disappear into another room, so I just wait in the living room, irritated, studying pieces of decor that probably cost more than I make in a year. Only a few minutes later, I hear a thud, so I go to investigate.

And find Harley being strangled on the floor.

My instincts cause me to start forward, my hand reaching for my gun, but then I stop. A part of me wants to kill the guy here and now for putting his hands on her. I wanted him dead just for looking at her the way he did.

But another part of me wants to see what she can do, a rite of passage kind of thing. Proof that she's a force to be reckoned with. This is what we've been trained for, but not everyone can handle the real world and all its violence. If she can't, I'll take action, but something makes me doubt I'll have to.

Am I being an asshole for not helping her? Yeah. I mean, this is what partners are for.

The seconds passing feel like hours as she struggles for air. Then she grabs his forearm with one hand, and just above his elbow with the other. In one quick motion she dislocates it, using his sudden lack of focus to lift her lower body and roll both of them over. Impressive, considering the man is almost twice her size. She whips out her poison case and flips the sedative needle open, then pricks his neck to knock him out.

Catching her breath and clutching her throat, she glares in disgust at the man on the ground, as if she's restraining herself from hurting him. I admire the impulse control and the foresight not to damage the body.

When her gaze finally shifts to me, I see that her eyes are a bit wild.

"Thanks for the help," she exhales.

"You had it handled."

"You're my partner."

"I know. But you were fine. We might not always be able to come to each other's aid every time someone tries to hurt us."

"Whatever." She kneels to pop his elbow back in place. "Come on. Help me get him to his bed."

"Are you upset?" I ask as we haul him to his luxurious bedroom.

"I just have to know if you're going to actually be there for me if I need it. Otherwise I might as well be on my own."

"Of course I will. I'm not that horrible of a person, I just wanted to see you in action, that's all."

She eyes me, like I've seen her do several times. Like she's making some sort of judgment. "You're a douchebag, you know that?"

"Yeah." We dump Johansson on his bed.

"Good. Let's get the hell out of here."

"Let me see what he did to you."

She approaches me, jerking away as I try to touch her neck, but then she changes her mind. She lifts her chin and I gently run my thumb over fresh bruises while she gazes at me, her eyes unreadable. Suddenly I feel nervous. She lightly places her hand over mine, but then I pull away and lead the way out. *Don't get attached to your partner.*

"Everything go all right?" Leven asks as we get in the car.

"Apart from getting strangled, yeah," Harley mutters. "It'll make an excellent footnote in our report."

He turns around from the front seat, alarmed. "What?"

"The son of a bitch strangled her," I repeat.

"Why?"

"To get off? I don't know," Harley responds. "It happened so quickly. I knew he wanted to fuck me, but maybe he's a necrophiliac."

"Are you okay?"

"I'm fine."

"You had to escape from him, then?"

"Yep. Had to knock him out."

"Where were you while this was happening?" Leven addresses me.

"Oh, Kai spectated," Harley answers.

"What do you mean?"

"She means that I stood by and watched," I mutter.

A look of irked disbelief falls upon his face. "Jesus, Kai. What the fuck is wrong with you? Why didn't you help her?"

"She's not a damsel in distress, Lev. She didn't need it."

"He's right, I didn't," Harley says. "We don't need to make this an issue. I trust that he won't let me die."

Leven raises his eyebrows. "I wouldn't be so sure. He sure as hell didn't save his last partner."

I stiffen. "Fuck off. Is that really what you think of me? That I don't care about anyone's life? That I don't regret my partner's death every single day? That's a lie and you know it."

"Well, I don't know what to think of you. And you don't need to raise your voice."

I don't bother to lower it. "Where the hell is this coming from?" But I think I know the answer. He's protective of Harley. I saw a glimpse of it yesterday, and I'm seeing it now.

"Stop arguing. This is ridiculous," Harley intervenes. "Calm down, both of you."

Leven and I both relent, and sit in silence as we head back to HQ.

When we reach the Pit, Harley pauses to say goodbye to Leven before he heads back into the depths of T&W, but I continue on toward the Field Department.

Then, as I'm nearing my apartment, I hear from behind me, "First you let me get strangled, and now you're ignoring me? I feel like *I* should be doing the ignoring."

I halt, sigh. Squeeze my eyes shut. I sense Harley come to a stop as well, at which point I finally turn around.

"I'm sorry," I say. I mean it, too.

"I don't believe you," she responds quietly, her violet eyes piercing, pinning me in place. And it's in that moment that I realize just how stunning they are.

"I know."

She studies me once again, and I hate myself for wanting her to like me.

"You... want to come over for a drink?" I suggest, surprising myself.

Harley is just as taken aback. "Really?"

I shrug. "Well... If 'sorry' doesn't help then at least accept a cocktail or two. I won't brag, but I'm a pretty decent mixologist."

At that, I finally see her lips quirk in a faint smile, and I exhale. "Fine. But the second you're a jackass again, I will punch you across the face. That's a promise."

I smirk in return. "I don't doubt it, Harley Stone."

She follows me into my apartment, where I suddenly feel nervous. *What the hell am I doing?*

I start inventing some concoction at my wet bar while she sits on the edge of my couch, eyes darting around the living room.

"So, your last partner..." She drifts off, but I still hear the question hanging in the air.

"Yeah," I say, my voice growing quiet. "He died on the job. Couldn't save him. But God knows I tried. Sometimes I still feel his blood on me."

"I'm really sorry," she responds gently. "You were partners for two years?"

"Yeah, but we were friends at the Academy before that. Best friends, really."

I see her shake her head out of the corner of my eye. "I can't imagine losing someone like that."

I've run out of things to say about this, so I remain quiet for a moment, pouring two glasses of a drink I seemed to have zoned out making.

"I hear you went against Holbrook's orders and killed his killer," Harley continues as I join her, sliding a glass in front of her, unsure how much distance to put between us.

"I wouldn't have been able to live with myself if I didn't."

She ponders for a second, taking a sip. "I would've done the same thing."

I tilt my head. "Are you telling me you're a bit of a rebel, then?"

She shrugs. "There comes a time where morality should supersede the rules." Her gaze shifts from the floor to meet mine. "But don't worry, I'm not so rebellious that I'd let *you* get strangled."

Shit. "I truly am sorry about it."

She shakes her head. "You were testing me."

"I was," I admit. "But I was still a dick. You could've been injured a lot worse."

Her eyes are still locked onto mine. "And what was your conclusion about me, Kai Thanatos?"

I hesitate for a moment, searching my mind for the answer. "That as much as I want a reason to despise you… I'm not going to get one."

SIX

After a night of very little sleep, I stand on a street corner at seven or so in the morning, impatiently waiting to cross without getting run over. My mind hasn't been able to stop mulling over Harley. How I feel about her. How she might feel about me. My plan to avoid any sort of connection is failing, and failing fast.

My old partner and I used to go out and grab coffee nearly every morning, just to escape for a bit. I figured it might clear my head today, but it's not the same.

Above me, the sky glows a dim orange, buildings and holographic ads disappearing into a thick fog about twelve stories up. There are people stumbling home, still strung out from the night before, and others are already heading to some protest, probably also strung out. A handful of *corpses* (very obvious corporate employees) are making their way to work, uttering demands at their AI assistants while masterfully skirting chaos. As has become routine, I see robopolice tranquilize a few of the more confrontational protestors, human police stationed on corners with rifles drawn.

I always adjust my route to avoid them. People have been able to outsmart the robopolice—you can hide in plain sight if you know how to trick a robot's beliefs about its environment. But you can't hide from the increasingly militarized human police forces. People rarely step out of line when they're patrolling, because they'll gun you down and let your blood fill the streets so everyone can see.

That doesn't mean violent crime rates are lower, though. The opposite, in fact. The police aggressively patrol places they deem worthy of protection—places where the wealthy live and work—but everywhere else is descending into chaos. Their logic seems to be that lower-class people are more likely to come into upper-class neighborhoods to commit crimes than the opposite.

But in my line of work, I can attest to the falsity of that. While crime is rising across the board, the lack of attention to and support for struggling communities opens the door for those with power to take advantage. So, as wealthy areas become more and more controlled, poor areas become more and more lawless.

I don't think it would be unreasonable for the GUARD's lens to impact politics, but we have little sway. Ultimately we operate at a higher level, revolving around national and international security rather than politics. Still, every time I leave HQ and see a crumbling society, I wonder if it hasn't *become* a security concern.

"Excuse me," I hear from behind me. I don't turn around.

The person then taps me on the shoulder, but I still don't look at her. It's best to avoid the sugarpill junkies.

"Do you have—"

"No." I look for cars and start to cross the street, but she grabs me by the wrist. My other hand reflexively jerks and I almost spin around and put her in a hold before I stop myself. I halt and turn to look at her. "What the *hell* is your—"

My words are stopped dead, my anger dissipates because I recognize her, and I'm fairly sure she sees that. *I know her.* I know her from somewhere, and I strain to remember. Dark pink hair, dark eyes, brownish-olive skin, early twenties. Nose ring, oversized jacket. She's short and skinny. Too skinny. She looks worn, with a maturity far past her age.

I don't think I've ever seen her at HQ, but I don't know any outsiders, not anymore. The GUARD only recruits the family-less so that we have no one to influence us. I am staring at her, and she at me, for several seconds before I say something, confused at why she hasn't.

"What do you want?"

A look of concern crosses her face. "We should get out of the street."

I sigh and move to the sidewalk. "Who are you?"

"Are you... Are you Kai?" Her voice wavers.

Great. "How do you know my name?" I hiss.

"Do you remember me?"

I hesitate. "No."

She presses her lips together. "You're lying."

"Answer my question," I demand.

"I'm Reiya."

Reiya.

I just stare at her, because that's impossible.

My sister and I were separated when I was seven. She died when I was eleven. So... how is she standing in front of me?

I shake my head in disbelief. "Reiya died a long time ago."

She tilts her head. "So did you, apparently."

And yet... here we are. It feels too good to be true.

"Prove it," I say, crossing my arms. "Prove that you, somehow, are my long-lost sister."

She takes a breath, pausing for a moment to collect her thoughts. "All right. Our mother was an addict, our father died by his own hand. We were given up not long after that and ended up in different group homes despite all of our desperate pleas to stay together. I remember bawling my eyes out over it. I mean, we were best friends. Inseparable. It was us against the world, and then all of a sudden it wasn't.

"One day my caretakers told me that you'd gotten into a brutal fight with the older kids you lived with, and didn't survive. Basically had your skull kicked in. I went there, to your group home, to see if it was true, because I didn't want to believe it.

"*They* told me that you'd been taken away to a private school and that they'd lost the data on where you went. I begged them to dig up anything they could find, but it's like you disappeared. So I've been looking for you ever since. I haven't found any records of you anywhere, and believe me, I've done a lot of searching, much of it illegally. You don't exist."

My eyes narrow. Everything she's said about me not having digital records I know. The GUARD takes every measure it can to hide its agents. "Then how did you find me, exactly?"

"By using an aging algorithm. I gave it a picture I had of you as a child, genetic data I gathered on our parents, and photos of myself across the years given our resemblance. It predicted variations of what you could look like and I used the resulting images to search for you in various camera feeds and databases in the city. It took years, of course. But it turns out you're a creature of habit. You walk this street a lot. This is the first time I've seen you do it alone, though."

My first instinct is to be wary, and I am, yet for some reason I believe her. Maybe I'm just desperate for this moment to be true, but I can't deny that she reminds me of the Reiya I once knew.

"Jesus," I exhale after a few moments of silence, my mind reeling. "They told me you killed yourself."

She shakes her head, something like sorrow in her eyes. "Why? Who would do such a thing? To us, of all people?"

I have not a single inkling of doubt that it was Holbrook. He ripped my sister and me apart so that he could use me, because that's what he does. His agents are merely gears in the machine that is the GUARD.

"I know the answer to that," I respond slowly, "but... I can't tell you."

Reiya's eyebrows go up, yet she doesn't seem that surprised. "Because...?"

"Because they'll make me kill you."

Her face doesn't even change as she stares at me. "I've gathered that there's secret shit going on."

"That's one way to put it."

Her eyes search mine. "I suppose we're too exposed here then. Is there a way we could see each other again? If you want, of course."

See each other? The thought hadn't even crossed my mind. And one wrong decision could turn this happy reunion into the thing that ruins our lives. The GUARD has almost total control over me, monitoring my every communication, tracking my every move.

But how could I say no?

"Yeah," I say finally. "Where do you live?"

She smiles in a way that eradicates my fear, then pulls out a slip of paper. "My number and address. You free tomorrow night?"

"I'll be there."

"We have a lot of catching up to do." A hint of sadness seeps into her smile as she places her hand on my shoulder for a few seconds, then turns and heads in the direction we both came from.

I stand there for half a minute, frozen, trying to process the surreality of what just happened, still not convinced that this isn't some falsity. Everyone I've ever cared for has left me, in one way or another.

Abandoning my previous objective, I head back to HQ to search for the person who can give me what I need.

I find Q in his office, the door ajar, which I take as an invitation to enter. The head of T&W is a forty-something English man, with a deadpan wittiness and an unrivaled intelligence. He's the designer of our impenetrable security systems, the smart modules embedded in Field agents, the TORS. I wouldn't hesitate to believe that he could somehow destroy the world from his tablet.

He's sitting in the middle of a bunch of weapons holograms filling his office space, telling his personal AI what alterations to make to the designs, when I walk in without knocking. With a snap, the images disappear.

"Ah, Thanatos. Good to see you," he greets me, spinning in his chair to watch me approach.

"You too, Q."

"I got your message. What do you need? Something off the books?"

"Yes."

"You are aware that my job will be on the line, correct? As will yours?"

"Yeah."

"And you've deemed that this is more important?"

"Yep."

"Wonderful. What is it?"

Q gets a kick out of doing secret things, though he always pretends that he's worried about his job. He is well aware that Holbrook would never get rid of him. Not even if he *did* destroy the world. He's probably the most important, most highly paid individual in the GUARD. He pushes back against the rules because he *can*.

I feel stupid asking him to do this, but I have to be smart if I don't want Reiya to end up as a pile of ashes.

"I need to disappear. For a few hours."

He frowns. "That's it?"

"No. I need you to set up untraceable comms between my phone and another."

"This isn't very exciting."

"Sorry to disappoint."

"Why do you have to disappear? And when?"

"Tomorrow around six thirty."

He narrows his eyes at me. "Do you know you have your evaluation at seven?"

"Ah. I vaguely remember the memo. But why do you know that off the top of your head?"

He hesitates before he speaks again. "This isn't a normal evaluation, exactly. There will be more than one person watching. Me included."

That's unusual. "Um, why?"

He waves his hand. "Don't worry about it. We are and have been watching everyone. It's just a different type of evaluation, that's all."

I just look at him because I know he's not giving me the whole truth.

"It would not do you well to miss it, Thanatos."

"What happens if I do?"

"Well, you'll be rescheduled, obviously. But Holbrook won't be pleased, and he'll be sure to investigate your absence."

"That's the help I'm here for. Disappearing without raising suspicion."

Q sighs. "Right. But you still haven't disclosed why. I may be okay with you bending the rules once in a while, but you know I can't let you do anything that will truly endanger the GUARD. I need a good explanation."

"My sister found me."

His eyebrows shoot up. "Your sister? I didn't know you had one. Certainly not an *alive* one."

"Yeah. Both of us were told that the other was dead when we were children. Though I believed it, she didn't. She's been searching for me for years."

"And she found you? That's... impressive, considering how hard we try to hide our agents. I reckon she's discovered a loophole. Did she tell you how she did it?"

"She had printed pictures of me and data on our parents. It took an advanced aging prediction algorithm, illegal access to city cameras, and a hell of a lot of patience."

He ponders that, not concerned but intrigued, as if it's inspiring some idea. "I'll say. That's dedication."

"I think it's a good guess that Holbrook split us apart. So that I would truly have no ties. He was the one who requested my recruitment."

Q leans back in his chair and folds his hands. "Now that is interesting. I wouldn't doubt that it was him. He was quite the ruthless leader of the Field Department back then."

"So I'm probably not the only one he did it to."

"No. Probably not."

For a few moments we exchange a silent acknowledgment of the cruelty of it, of separating families. But there's nothing to be said about it, because we can't change what's been done.

"So you're going to visit her?" Q says eventually.

I nod.

"And I'm sure you realize how dangerous that is. It changes your future and hers. She could be killed. By you, might I add."

"I know. But I can't let Holbrook have that much power over me. With your help I can protect myself and her."

He inclines his head. "And how can you trust her? Anyone can be a foe, you know that."

I shrug, nonchalant. "I can't think of a reason why she'd be a threat. And if she turns out to be one, then I'll handle it."

"Fine. But I will be looking into her myself."

"Fair enough."

"Now then. You're friends with Adler, correct? I'm going to switch his evaluation time with yours. Your new time will be tomorrow at two; definitely don't miss that one. I'll give you three hours to be gone, and make up false locations for your tracking module during that time. Just to be safe, get Stone to be your alibi. If you wish to remain in further contact with your sister, however, I'd suggest meeting somewhere that won't look strange, away from cameras as much as possible. Holbrook would have us both by the throat the instant he found out any of this, so for the love of God don't do anything stupid."

"No guarantees," I respond, deadpan.

"You're going to get me in serious trouble, one day, Thanatos," he says, half smiling.

"That's the day you're living for, Q."

"Indeed it is… Now, you owe me a few favors."

I nod once. "Whatever you need."

"I want you to keep an eye on Cole Sheehan."

Well, well, well. "The driver?"

"Yes."

"I noticed he has a triangle tattoo like the man I killed several days ago."

Q leans forward, placing his elbows on his desk. "Does he now?"

"I'm fairly certain. I only saw it once though. And I'm not sure why he'd expose it around here if he's part of some organization."

"Interesting."

"Why do you want him watched?"

"One of my techies has noticed some odd behavior. The places he goes, mostly. Please report anything even mildly suspicious."

"I'm on it."

"Excellent. I'll give your phone access to his tracker so that you can follow him." He rolls back to his desk. "And good luck with your sister."

SEVEN

That night I sleep even less. Thoughts run rampant inside my head to the extent that I barely blink, as if my brain has ceased regulation of its basic functions in favor of complex cognition.

My mind wanders through the events of this past week, which feels far longer than a week. My sister's reappearance in my life is the best thing that's happened to me in years, yet I'm seething at the mere idea of Holbrook. Not that I liked him to begin with, but I trusted him, despite our spats. Now I hate him for taking my sister and my life away.

Eventually I wind up at the target range with a gun in my hands. It won't help the anger, but it'll at least distract me, so I unleash bullets on the simulated targets, watching their blood spatter.

As I put down my gun after a third round, someone taps me on the shoulder and I flinch, my fists automatically clenching. I spin around to find Harley, looking at me wide-eyed. She's in sweats and a GUARD tank top like me, with her hair in a braid.

"Jesus Christ. Don't do that." I take out my earbuds, exasperated. I want to be alone and goddamn shoot things, yet I feel my heartbeat quicken at Harley's presence.

"Sorry."

"What are you doing here?" I realize that I'm probably coming across as more irritated at her than I actually am, but she ignores it. Maybe because she sees right through my defenses.

"Same as you, I guess. Couldn't sleep." She sighs tiredly. "Thought maybe I should say hello, seeing as we're partners and all."

"Don't you see enough of me during the day?"

"Yeah, but you don't really talk to me."

I shrug, but the look in her eyes makes me feel guilty. "What's there to talk about?"

"I don't know. I'm just trying to figure out why you're avoiding getting to know me."

We study each other for a few moments before I have to rip my gaze away.

"Did someone tell you how I got here?" she continues. "Is that it?"

"No. Well, Keating did say you had an interesting history. But that has nothing to do with it. It's honestly not that personal."

"Fair enough," she responds, evidently unconvinced.

"Though for Holbrook, apparently, it is. He didn't want me to know anything about you."

She narrows her eyes at that. "What?"

"He told Keating to keep his mouth shut about you. The reasons for which I'll admit I'm a bit curious about."

"Well, if I tell you, then you'd be getting to know me. God forbid." I catch a hint of a smirk, and give her a look in return.

"Dark secrets might be something I'd make an exception for."

"Why would I tell you my darkest secrets if you don't want to know basic things about me?" she counters.

I think for a moment. "Because the deepest facets of who we are tend to impact our decisions far more than the shallow ones. As my partner, I have to be able to count on you no matter what happens to us. I have to know what moves you'll make, what your strengths are, how we can work as a team. It's an intimate thing, and obviously I don't enjoy that, but we'll operate better if we can predict the other's moves. There may come a moment where my life is in your hands, or vice versa."

She shakes her head. "You're so confusing. For days you haven't seemed to give a shit, and now you want me to reveal the worst parts of me? I think you have to know everything about someone to truly understand them. What I say now could make you mistrust me even more than you already do, because you'll fill in blanks."

I exhale, unable to argue against that. I *do* want to get to know her, all of her. Desperately. That's the inevitable verdict I came to these past few sleepless nights. And it's taking everything in my power to fight against that urge. What I need is for her to tell me something that will evaporate it.

She studies me, warily. Then, with a sigh, it seems she gives in. "I'm not sure if I should trust you, Kai Thanatos. But I'll tell you if promise me you won't fill in those blanks."

Her gaze is intense, captivating, arresting. And that's when I realize that I've lost the battle. There's nothing she could say that would turn me away.

"I promise."

She nods. "I was recruited about five years ago, straight from juvenile prison. I was such a wreck, and it's honestly a miracle that I was even alive. I hadn't brushed my hair or eaten a full meal in weeks. The other girls tormented the hell out of me. I was a ghost, barely a teenager and already so... *haunted*. Haunted by the things that had happened to me, but not about what I'd done to end up in prison. That's something I'll never regret."

A pause, in which she musters the courage to utter her next sentence, her violet eyes becoming glassy.

"I killed my parents when I was thirteen."

I freeze, unable to respond. But she keeps talking, despite how much it clearly pains her, to prevent me from generating any assumptions.

"They were... utterly vile. Junkie sadists that beat the shit out of my brothers and me. They'd lock one of us in a room for days with hardly any food or water, and we could never help each other for fear of the repercussions. No one around us would've batted an eye, either, considering we lived in Sector 9."

Sector 9, also known as Morgue Row. Where everyone is addicted to sugarpills or dead because of it. It's a neighborhood that rarely has stable power anymore, a neighborhood that first responders don't bother to help. It's a lawless, ultraviolent place. If you go in, you probably won't come out.

"My entire childhood I was trapped, helpless, scared of everyone and everything. I'm not exaggerating when I say that there were many times when my parents could've killed me. For a while I thought it was just the way things had to be, because I hadn't experienced life any other way."

She gazes at me to gauge my reaction to all of this, but it takes several moments before I can bring myself to speak. "I can't even fathom enduring that kind of hell. And then to get thrown in prison for saving yourself."

She nods, finally looking away. "That was particularly unlucky; hardly anyone living on Morgue Row gets caught for their crimes. But that's how the GUARD found me, so maybe I wasn't as unlucky as I think."

"Can I ask how you did it?" I say tentatively, unsure if I'm going too far.

But she doesn't appear to mind. "I took a kitchen knife and stabbed them while they were unconscious from sugarpills. Over and over. I kept going even after I knew they were dead. By the end of it, I was soaked in their blood."

The image sends chills down my spine.

Any words I could utter get caught in my throat. Now I understand why Holbrook had no desire for me to have this knowledge, this awareness of Harley's torment and gruesome past. But it doesn't make me scared of her, or wary of her. It's precisely the thing I wanted—a reason to avoid her—yet I can't bring myself to shun her. I instead find myself admiring her for her resilience.

She's studying me again, but her expression morphs into a smirk. "Now you're really gonna hate being my partner, huh?"

I exhale, my defenses snapping back into place. "It's not like I have a choice," I respond, avoiding her question.

"Right. I just need to know that we can actually work together. That knowing who I am won't bother you."

I run a hand through my hair. "No. It doesn't bother me. You've been through things that I can scarcely imagine. What I care about is how it affected you and will continue to affect you. That's it. Don't worry about it."

The way she looks at me makes me feel like such an asshole.

"I just had to ask."

"I didn't—" I start, but I'm lost for words again. "Sorry."

She becomes amused by my awkward struggle to apologize. "I like watching you try to be a decent human being."

"Oh do you?"

Her eyes narrow as if she didn't expect me to play along, a slight smile lingering. "Mm. I also kind of like when you pretend to insult me."

"Pretend?" I scoff. "That's a bit delusional of you."

"Well, then either you're a piece of garbage, *or* you're trying to hide how you really feel." Her eyes let me know she's just teasing, but there's something else there.

I gaze back at her. Not many girls have tried flirting with me, and I'm sure it's clear why that is. *I* certainly never flirt. But Harley, for whatever reason, is different.

My eyes drift, of their own accord, just for a second, to look at her figure, but she doesn't seem offended. Maybe because she's doing the same thing to me.

Goddammit. Stop.

"I should finish shooting," I say before I can do anything stupid.

She gets the hint, but if she's insulted by it, her face isn't letting me know. "Okay. I'll leave you to it, then. See you later, Kai."

EIGHT

My evaluation is broken down into two phases: analysis and execution. The scenario is an arms deal sting op, which they've designed a world for in the TORS.

Before entering the simulation, I analyze where the seller will likely have lookouts and snipers stationed based on a 3D map of the area. And when I do go in, alone, my job is to take out any such threats to protect the buyers—fellow GUARD agents, in this case, whose goal is to take the seller into custody. My performance during the execution phase will be graded on efficiency and accuracy.

The world is a bayside city, and the deal is set to take place near cargo docks. There are a few ships, container cranes, and warehouses close by, taller buildings beginning about half a mile away. I annotate a projected 3D scene based on what I would do if I were the seller.

Most importantly, I'd ensure coverage of the entire area with snipers. It's not only important for them to have a clear shot at the buyers, but to be well hidden. The docked boats perhaps provide the former but not the latter, and they'd be trapped if they needed to escape. There are a couple of tall buildings overlooking the docks and the bay that seem like they could provide a good vantage point, so I mark them with a crosshairs symbol. Inside the simulation, I'll be equipped with a rifle and a dragonfly drone that can search rooftops and interiors of buildings for targets to expedite the mission. But I still need to be *right*, within reason, to pass this evaluation.

My plan is to take out the snipers, making my way inward, taking up a posting that will allow me to inform the other agents of any trouble I see. The immediate area surrounding the docks is likely to be swarming with the seller's forces, so in order to get a decent spot I can either keep my distance, or get my hands a little dirtier. The second option is riskier, but in my mind, the closer I am the better I'll be able to react to anything that goes down.

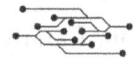

I begin the simulation in the middle of a deserted plaza. It's mid-afternoon, the sky a dark grey, threatening a storm. I quickly realize that it's not just the plaza that's deserted—it's the entire city. The streets are lined with rusting vehicles, the buildings are crumbling, and the plants are gradually reclaiming their land. It's eerily silent.

Not quite what I was expecting.

While an empty city makes my job easier, it has the same effect for my adversaries. They'll spot me in an instant.

I gain my bearings and head in the direction of the docks, toward the nearest building, eager not to be so damn exposed. As promised, there's a dragonfly drone in its case, attached to my harness. At my hip is a pistol and slung across my back is a standard GUARD sniper rifle, collapsed into its carrying form.

Once I'm within a block or so of the area where I anticipate there will be lookouts, I release the drone, commanding it via my phone to perform a multi-building search. It zooms off and I crouch under a worn awning marking the front of an abandoned hotel, watching the video. Upon reaching a target building, it quickly searches for radar signatures of people from the outside.

A couple of my anticipated sniper spots are a no-go, but some prove to be accurate. With the map on my phone, I plan my route to three buildings with adversaries on varying floors, avoiding their fields of view. I'm going to have to take all of them out at close range.

"Command, this is Sniper One. I'm eliminating a few enemy snipers before getting into position."

"Copy."

With forty-five minutes until the deal is set to take place, I make my way to my first stop, rain starting to drip from the sky. I locate an entrance on the opposite side of the building as the target, kick the door open, and head up the stairwell, climbing the steps two at a time. A few rodent skeletons crunch beneath my feet.

When I reach the correct floor I ease open the stairwell door, pistol at the ready, and clear a hallway to the left, then the right. Empty. With a glance at the floor plan, as detailed by a fading emergency placard, I determine a path to my target. By the looks of it, she's staked out in a large conference room.

Most of the offices I pass have glass walls, some shattered and some intact, permitting me to be more confident that she's alone. Still, with every corner I come upon, I expect there to be someone waiting to shoot me.

But there isn't, which makes me even more anxious, because I know at some point in this evaluation there must be a near-death experience.

When I spot her, her back is to me as she scouts the scene at the docks, crouched just beneath a window sill, her elevated sniper rifle aimed out the open window. If she were to turn around, I'd be in full view, courtesy of the glass walls. I creep toward her, soundless. It isn't until I nudge open the door to the conference room that she's alerted to my presence.

By that time I've already fired off two shots, but she reacts quickly enough that the bullets don't enter her chest. One hits her arm, the other smacks into the wall behind her. I curse at myself for missing. She draws a gun on me in the next instant, but while she's fast, she's not fast enough to escape my third bullet.

After confirming that she's dead, I hurry back down a different stairwell, periodically glancing upward to ensure I'm not being followed.

But when I exit the building, I walk right into the line of sight of two approaching SUVs. Black geometric bodies, windows tinted, a block away. A hail of bullets is unleashed from a gun near the front bumper of the lead vehicle. Exposed on the sidewalk, I rush around the corner of the building and press myself against the bricks to minimize my vulnerability. I pull my rifle over my shoulder, and with the press of a button, it expands, components snapping into place.

I load a magazine and take aim.

I quickly discover that the windows are bulletproof, so instead I shoot at their tires. It takes me two tries to blow the driver-side front wheel on the first SUV. The vehicle whirls, coming to a screeching halt. The second SUV narrowly avoids T-boning it, braking hard enough to give any passengers a whiplash.

Doors fling open and out come five goons, heavily armed, each donning the same skull mask. In an instant bullets are flying at me again, barely missing me in a few cases, grazing my arm in one. I dash behind the nearest rusting car for better cover and a better angle. With the barrel of my rifle resting atop the hood, I lock onto the closest person. I anticipate that these men have bulletproof vests at the very least, so I target his head. Tuning out the violent clangs of bullets striking the car and the pain in my arm, I funnel my focus to my eyes and my trigger finger.

With five shots I take all five out.

Cautiously I approach the idle vehicles, expecting another idiot to start shooting at me. But there's only the silence of a dead city. The SUVs are void of people but not of contraband, though I doubt it's the arms supposed to be trading hands in thirty minutes or so. I'm about to head to my next stop when something catches my eye. A tiny, black, rectangular device of some kind, underneath the front seat of the second car.

When I pick it up I realize it's a trigger. And it's probably not the only one.

Shit. We might be the ones getting set up here.

"Command, this Sniper One. What's your status?" I say. "I've discovered a potential bomb threat."

I've heard nothing in my earpiece since the initial exchange, but I wouldn't expect them to contact me except to verify I'm in position for the deal, or in an emergency.

When no one responds, I try again, taking out my earpiece momentarily to ensure it's on.

Nothing.

I consider attempting to make contact via phone, but decide not to take any chances in case our network has been compromised. Given the short time frame I have, I'm left with two options: continue on to take out the remaining two snipers or try to locate my fellow agents and warn them of the threat. The first will be all for naught if everyone is blown to hell, so I opt for the second. Maybe I can still accomplish both if I'm quick.

I send my drone ahead to the location of the deal to scout for explosives. Then, rifle in hand, I jog through the abandoned streets toward the delivery truck where Command is supposed to be stationed, staying close to buildings to limit my visibility.

By the time I make it to their location close to the docks, without encountering any danger, I'm almost certain something is awry. It's a feeling more than anything, but finding a trigger isn't a random detail.

I cautiously walk around to the back of the dilapidated delivery truck, half expecting someone to shoot me. I knock on the rear door using the designated pattern, and hold my breath for a few seconds before it opens. Through the inches-wide crack, I see a gun pointed at my head.

"Sniper One reporting for duty," I say dryly.

They let me in but immediately start cursing me out. "What the hell are you doing here? Why haven't you been responding?" a woman demands. She's the one with the gun, and looks like the one in charge, but I've never seen any of these people before so I don't know for sure. There are two others seated in front of screens displaying live footage of the area.

"Earpiece malfunction," I reply shortly. "I'm here to save your asses. Found a trigger when I wiped out a few goons." I pull out the device as proof, but confirm everything with my drone's discovery of a couple of explosives by the docks.

"Shit." The woman turns to the others. "Pull them out."

They start issuing urgent commands to the Field agents, but my attention is snagged by their aerial view. Based on the location of the agents and the bombs, their escape route leads them right into the field of view of a sniper that I haven't killed. If my memory is correct.

And it always is. Which means they're trapped like fish in a barrel, and we risk losing someone—everyone—if I can't take out that sniper in time.

"Wait," I say, shoving one of the guys away from his computer to pull up the locations I sent. "They're nearly in sniper range."

"What? I thought you were taking care of that," the woman in charge responds sharply.

"Didn't have time. The only way someone doesn't die is if I go back for that gunman before they detonate the explosives. Give me a new earpiece. Tell them to follow our original plans, as if nothing has changed, until I've eliminated the threat. We still have ten minutes until our meeting time."

She nods. "Go."

I maneuver my way to the sniper's location, balancing speed with caution. When I reach him, I push open the door to his hideout and raise my rifle, an instant away from taking the shot.

But when I glimpse the back of his head, I feel a faint recognition.

He turns.

It's not an enemy. It's my dead best friend.

And in that moment I can't pull the trigger.

They're fucking with me—they must be. God knows I've tried to forget that face.

But there's no recognition in *his* eyes as he aims his gun right at me. That's what snaps me out of my hesitation. He's not real. It's just a ploy. *Fuck that.*

He falls dead from a single bullet to the head, and I turn away.

The simulation goes black. When I wake, I rip off the nodes connected to my head. I should be satisfied with my performance, but I'm just angry.

I'm escorted to the watch room, where Holbrook, Q, Keating, my evaluator, and two people I don't recognize have been analyzing me. Those two strangers are probably the only thing keeping me from becoming physically violent with Holbrook.

"Nice curveball," I say, my voice low, my eyes locked onto his. His mouth twitches as if he's trying not to smirk. Because he knows what I'm talking about—hell, I'm almost certain it was his idea.

The animosity dripping from my voice is probably obvious to everyone, but I can't help myself. I don't care if it makes me seem emotional. Using my dead partner to try to throw me off is simply a shitty thing to do.

"Quite impressive," Keating says to break the tension. "You're one of the first to succeed."

"Indeed," Holbrook mutters, as though it pains him I'm so good at my job. Then, speaking up, he says, "Agent Thanatos, I'd like to introduce you to Dr. Adriano Medina. Director of the GUARD, as I'm sure you're aware."

I almost choke. *Director of the GUARD.* He's the real deal. And he just watched my evaluation.

"Pleasure to meet you, sir. I had no idea I had such an audience," I say, shaking the hand of a very stately man. He's probably in his 50s, donning an expensive suit tailored to perfection. He has immaculately groomed hair and an immaculately groomed beard, which only augments his intimidating air. His irises are cold and black and make me feel like he's glaring into my soul. Everyone eyes him, not daring to utter a word.

"I've been eager to see you in action, Agent Thanatos. You're one of Manhattan's best, as I've seen. At the age of twenty. Rather remarkable."

"Thank you, sir," I respond. It's clear that's all he has to say.

"You may go," Holbrook says, wary of me. "You will receive the results of your evaluation within the next couple of days."

NINE

Reiya's apartment is on the outskirts of Sector 7 in Manhattan, a generally lower-class sector, where the streets are filled with vendors and tents instead of cars. I pass a few Dark Market outposts, a handful of overconfident sugarpill dealers with the sunken eyes to prove it, and several holographic naked people offering to satisfy all my deepest fantasies. I despise the degrading marketing of the tech-enhanced sex houses, but it attracts all the chromefaces from other sectors because it's the only kind of place they can do all the weird shit they're into. Any desire can be satisfied with AI-driven AR, so it's big money.

Reiya's eyes light up when she opens her door to me, and she greets me with a hug. "Kai," she gushes, inviting me inside. "I didn't think you'd actually show."

"I couldn't *not* show. If you are who you say you are, then you're my only family."

She smiles sadly. "I was so fucking nervous yesterday, but I'm glad I didn't give up on you."

Her studio apartment is dimly illuminated with purple lighting. Nothing strikes me as unusual, except for an office cove with assorted cameras and screens. I can't help but scan for sugarpills too, but fail to spot any. Thank God.

"Can I get you anything to drink?" she asks as she gestures for me to have a seat on her couch.

"I'm good, thank you." My eyes drift back to her out-of-place gadgets. "What do you do for work?"

She follows my line of sight, sitting casually in a chair next to me, leg hanging over the arm. "I'm an assistant investigator for a PI. That basically entails hacking and following people to get information."

"Damn," I say, impressed. I guess spy talents run in the family. "What kind of people do you work for?"

She shrugs, finger running along what I now notice is a coder band on her forearm. "People who can afford a PI. It's good pay, but I'm just getting started. I was actually working as a waitress until a few months ago. Hopefully I can move out of this hellhole of a sector when I have enough money."

"How'd you get into PI work?"

"Pure chance, really. When I aged out of the home, I had no skills, no money, and no place to go. Serving kept a roof over my head, but I wanted to climb the ladder. There was a hacktivist cave below the restaurant where I worked, and it piqued my interest. The robbing and exposure of public figures is a bit extreme for my taste, but I saw an opportunity. So I taught myself to code, and invested in the equipment I'd need. It took a while, but I finally made something of it."

God, I wish I could reverse time. The two of us have forged our way alone, but doing it together would've made a far better life. It's hard not to be resentful about having that ripped away.

"But I want to hear all about you," Reiya continues, then hesitates. "What you can tell me, I guess."

I deliberate over what to say next, debating whether to lie or simply withhold the truth. But Reiya doesn't deserve dishonesty, after all this time.

"I was recruited into an elite program shortly after I was informed of your death," I begin. "The organization is more or less an international intelligence agency. I took an aptitude test and subsequently trained at an academy upstate until I turned eighteen. At that point I completed a final evaluation before entering the field."

Her eyebrows raise in surprise. "So you're an agent."

"Yes."

"What kind of agent?"

I purse my lips. "An assassin."

I brace myself for her reaction, but she barely falters.

"An assassin," she repeats, more intrigued than judgmental. "Jesus. That's kind of suiting, actually."

"You're not horrified?"

She laughs. "I've seen some shit on these streets, Kai. Having morals around here makes you vulnerable. But I also prepared myself for something like this. It would've been dumb to think you did something normal."

I study her in an attempt to determine her level of authenticity. To determine if I've misjudged her, if I've let my mind become clouded with the emotions of our reunion. I've been analyzing her gestures, her words, her eye contact, knowing I'm either too paranoid or not paranoid enough.

I'm almost frustrated when I don't come up with a reason for suspicion. A part of me is always trying to reject anything good, and more often than not, that's the part I give in to. But maybe this time will be different. Maybe this time *has* to be different.

We spend another hour or so just talking. For once I forget about my job and experience a taste of living a normal life—a calmer, simpler life, one without knowing what's behind the curtains. I know I'm not built for that kind of life, certainly not anymore, but I've been craving it all the same. It's taking a lot of restraint not to let that fantasy get the better of me now that Reiya is in my life.

It's when she shares pictures of us as children that I truly realize what I've lost. One shows both of us flipping off the camera while sitting in a kiddy pool, toys scattered across the yard, my hair an absolute mess. Back then our father was still alive, and our mother still wanted us. It looks like the happiest I've ever been.

Maybe one of the last times I was happy at all.

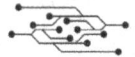

After getting back from Reiya's, I find myself plagued by insomnia once again, and decide to wander the corridors. It's silent apart from the muffled sounds of someone crying in their apartment.

God, the walls are thin. Everyone knows when you're upset, or when you're having sex. Not sure which is worse.

I wind up at Camden's, and find him sitting outside of his room drinking something. Nocturnal as ever.

"Why are you out here?" I say.

"No idea." He seems a bit dazed, which concerns me.

"Mind if we hang in your place? I couldn't sleep."

He shrugs. "Sure."

I sit on his couch, watching him as he lies on his rug and stares up at the ceiling.

"You okay?" I ask hesitantly.

"Yeah."

"Are you sure?"

"Yeah."

He's drunk, that much I can tell. And being drunk, alone, and somber is not usually a good sign. It reminds me that I know nothing about his past, what he might be trying to escape here in New York.

"How'd your evaluation go today?" I say when he doesn't respond further.

"Pretty good, I suppose. I wasn't able to save everyone, though."

"Did you know that Q and Keating *and* Holbrook were watching all of the evals live?"

He finally turns his head toward me. "Seriously? That's... unusual."

"And guess who else was watching?"

"Who?"

"Adriano Medina."

"You're shitting me."

"I'm not."

"You're mental—that's not possible. He's always been unseen, behind the curtain."

I raise my eyebrows at him. "It is possible, and it happened. I don't know why he was there, and I only said like two words to him before Holbrook got rid of me. There was another man in there too, but I wasn't introduced. Something is going on, and they're not telling any of the agents."

"They're obviously testing us for some reason. Looking for anyone who stands out."

Interesting. "It could be a selection process."

Camden perks up. "I think you're onto something. It wasn't just an evaluation if Medina was there."

"Any ideas what it was for?"

"Not particularly."

"I suppose we'll find out soon enough."

"Hmm. What's your aptitude score anyhow?"

"Ninety-six or something."

His eyebrows shoot up in an instant. "Are you fucking with me?" he says, incredulous.

I shake my head, already regretting mentioning the number. I tend to avoid sharing the score that has labeled me as a Tier 1 agent on account of the unwanted attention it imposes. People around here see aptitude ratings as some hugely meaningful facet of your existence rather than just a number that probably shouldn't dictate much of anything.

He blinks hard. "Jesus. I don't think I've met anyone with a better score than that. What's Harley's?"

"Ninety-three."

"Good Lord. No wonder they put you two together. You're practically superhero-level."

"I don't know if I'd go that far."

"How are things going with her, by the way?"

"Fine, I guess." I shrug, feigning nonchalance in the hope that he'll leave me alone about it. I need to figure out my own thoughts first.

"Personally, I still think you're into each other."

I roll my eyes, trying to wipe any other reaction from my face. "Personally, I still think you're full of shit."

"You just wait. One day I'll get to say I told you so."

"Don't get too excited, Cam."

He sighs, seeming to revert to whatever state I found him in. Something is clearly wrong, but I don't say that. Perhaps it's a one-off thing. Or perhaps it's a hint of a side of him that I wasn't expecting.

"You sure you're okay?"

"I'm okay," he responds quietly. Then, "It must be nice to have a family member again."

"Reiya, you mean?"

"Yeah. I can't believe she found you. I'd give anything to have my siblings magically be alive again. But I watched them die."

That I hadn't heard from him before. "I'm sorry. I had no idea."

"It's okay. It was a long, long time ago now. What scares me is that I'm starting to forget their faces."

I know that feeling all too well. But in my case, I wasn't clinging to memories of Reiya, prolonging them. I was actively shoving them away.

"Does she look like you?" Camden continues. "Your sister. All Spanish or whatever?"

"I mean, I guess, yeah."

"Are you actually Spanish?"

"Greek and Colombian, as far as I know."

"Fascinating. My brother and sister didn't look like me, you see. They took after our mother, and I look like my father. Otherwise... maybe I'd still be able to see their faces in mine. Maybe they wouldn't be fading away into oblivion."

TEN

On my way back to my apartment, with a couple of sleeping pills that Camden insisted I take, I run into Harley. The crying I heard the first time around has given way to a deep silence in the corridors.

"A night owl once again, eh?" she says when she sees me, coming to a halt a few feet away.

I shrug. "Been a lot on my mind, I guess. I just came from Camden's; he's very reliably awake at this hour."

She looks me up and down, and I can't quite read her expression. We haven't exchanged more than a few words since the night she confessed her past to me, as if we'd both made a subconscious decision to avoid the other. Or, perhaps it was conscious. Because whatever the dynamic between us is becoming… it's starting to feel dangerous.

"You headed out?" I ask when she doesn't speak.

"Got a lot on my mind, I guess," she responds with a smirk.

"Me?" I tease, the word slipping out before I have a chance to stop it. *Shit.*

Her eyebrows raise, her lips twitching, her violet eyes threatening to crack my defenses. "I'll never tell."

I bite my tongue. "Mysteries are always far more tempting anyhow," I murmur.

She presses her lips together, a faint smile lingering. "See you around, Kai."

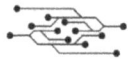

It takes three days to get answers about the evaluation. I'm called to Holbrook's office without warning, but it's not just him there—it's Q and Keating as well.

Harley shows up moments after I do. I don't look at her, even though I want to. Just her proximity to me is distracting.

"Is this an intervention or something?" I say, looking at each of the three men in front of us.

"As you know, most of the GUARD's top agents are occupied with long-term assignments," Holbrook begins, staring at me intensely.

"…And?"

"And it is Medina's opinion, as well as ours, that you two are some of the most qualified agents in the country. As you know, Medina was here a few days ago observing evaluations, but we also examined the

TORS sessions you've completed together. As a team and individually, you are quite exceptional."

"Recently we've detected a major organized threat to national and international security," Keating says. "So what this means is that, based on your recent performances, we've decided to assign you two to a very dangerous, very important operation."

Oh God. All of my naive optimism about a normal life shatters.

"What does this operation entail?" Harley asks, her voice tinged with skepticism.

"We'll inform you more once your other team member arrives."

"Other team member?" I repeat.

"Yes. Medina ordered these evaluations at several divisions," Holbrook answers. "His name is Grant Kohler. He's a German transfer stationed in Washington D.C."

"I'll be accompanying you as well," Q says, which means this must be very serious indeed. "And we'll be breaking an informant out of a prison in Canada. So there will be five of us."

"I'm sorry, what?" Harley interrupts.

"More details to come," Keating says. I shake my head at the lack of clarification, exasperated.

"When do we leave?" I ask.

"Two weeks. Maybe less. Agent Kohler gets here the day after tomorrow. You'll be staying at our safe house in Calgary until you retrieve the informant, but your destination after that is on you to figure out."

Fantastic. Of course this happens right when my sister reappears in my life. A week ago I would've seen leaving New York as a positive change, but now I have someone to live for.

"You're dismissed," Holbrook says, giving us no chance to ask more questions. I exit a bit aggressively, not waiting for Harley. We'd reverted to ignoring each other in the past few days, but I think we both know that we can't keep that up, not now. And it terrifies me to have to face whatever there is between us.

"Kai. Wait," she says from behind me.

I don't.

"Goddammit."

When she catches up to me I don't look at her, I just keep walking. For a few seconds she's silent.

"Are you upset with me or something?"

"No. Why would I be?"

"I don't know, just slow down and talk to me."

"Harley," I snap, growing frustrated. "Can't you see I don't want to?"

"We can't keep avoiding each other."

"I'm not avoiding you," I lie. "I just have other shit on my mind."

Out of the corner of my eye I see her shake her head exasperatedly. "Oh please. Don't act like you don't know what's going on." She lowers her voice. "We've been *flirting* with each other, Kai."

"Don't worry, it won't happen again," I hurl back at her.

We reach my apartment, and I try to slide the door shut after I enter, but she catches it and follows me inside. I have to take a few breaths before I say anything.

"Get out."

"You're a selfish, *miserable* piece of shit," she hisses.

It pisses me off, even though she's right. Or, rather, *because* she's right. "Sounds like there's nothing worth talking about then," I respond.

Harley glares at me as I walk back to the door, intending to hold it open until she leaves.

But at the last second she steps in front of me.

I am inches away from her, so close that I can feel her breathing. Suddenly the ire dissipates. Gone as fast as it came. I look at her for a few moments, trying to read the intensity of her eyes.

"What are you doing?" I murmur, frozen in place. But I'm completely aware of what she's doing.

"I know you're fighting this, and God knows I've tried too," she says, her voice quiet. "I'll leave if you want me to. But I don't think you do."

I feel my chest tighten, my skin grow warm. If I say nothing, it changes everything. It will render me defenseless.

Right now, though, I'm not sure I care.

For five long seconds neither of us moves, the air between us electric, so close it's almost painful. Then she slides her hand up to the back of my neck. And our lips meet in a tentative kiss, one saturated with vulnerability I'd vowed to suppress.

My arms wrap around her, more instinctively than consciously, my body acting on what I want even though my mind would rather resist. There's something in this kiss that is dangerous, something that is utterly captivating. Whatever it is, I've never felt it before. There's something new, something foreign, and God, I need more.

Her mouth moves with mine, heat and fervor growing between us until it begins to inundate me. I press her into the door, hips against hers, as her hands trail down my back. She tilts her chin upward when I move my lips to her neck, tracing my tongue across her throat and kissing her beneath the ear.

"Goddamn." She pulls away, breathing heavily, palms pressed against my chest. "I hate to admit that you live up to your reputation."

"Sexual reputation?" I say, a smile forming. "I didn't know I had one."

"Back when we were both at the Academy, I overheard a girl talking about you. She was having a hard time reconciling your aloofness with your alleged talents in bed."

"And it left you yearning to experience it for yourself?" I tease.

She rolls her eyes, but there's a hint of a smile. "Don't flatter yourself. I had no intention of letting an emotionally unavailable man ensnare me. I don't trust anyone not to hurt me."

I brush my thumb across her lips. "What changed?"

"You're not the person I thought you'd be. You're… something else entirely."

Her eyes are locked on mine as she slips her hand down, fingers pulling at my belt, chest heaving. That's when I think we both realize that there's no stopping now.

In a rush we are ripping each other's clothes off and tossing them aside. I drag my gaze over her, leaving no inch of her unseen.

How this one girl has managed to obliterate my barriers, I have no idea. All I know is that I feel so alive.

ELEVEN

That night I check Cole Sheehan's location on a whim, and discover that he's all the way in Sector 9. Morgue Row. Unless he's buying something on the Dark Market, it's certainly a curious place to go after midnight.

Leaving Harley asleep in my bed, I head out to do a bit of espionage, taking a car with Q's authorization. I park several blocks away from the edge of New York's most dangerous neighborhood, the run-down streets already beginning to feel like I've stepped back in time.

On Morgue Row, you're likely to pass any number of threats at all hours of the day, so it's best to stay in the darkness afforded by power outages. The sugarpills in this part of town will drive even the sanest person to shoot you just for walking by, and anyone under thirty-five is especially at risk of being kidnapped and forced into sex slavery.

I keep one hand on my gun as I make my way closer to Cole, skirting rusted cars and bullet shells, stepping over dead animals and dead people in varying states of decay, carefully avoiding any signs of life. It's not so much the sights of Morgue Row that usually get to me—it's the sounds. The most deeply inhuman sounds I never knew could be uttered. Screams and groans you'd normally associate with a dying animal that needs to be put out of its misery.

The rot of this place, the ultraviolence… it degrades people in ways I can hardly fathom.

My tracker indicates that Cole is in an unmarked building, but I opt not to go in. Instead I wait, hiding in the darkness across the street, to see if anyone comes in or out.

Perhaps twenty minutes go by before I witness a man thrown—literally thrown—out of the door. He writhes on the ground a bit, but doesn't get up. No one else appears.

Gun in hand, I creep across the street, scanning for anyone who might be watching or might accidentally stumble upon us. About halfway there I recognize that it's none other than Cole on the ground, and when I reach him I see that he's been badly injured. Countless bruises, one eye swollen shut, blood seeping from his stomach.

His good eye finds me as I stand over him. He starts cackling, his mouth full of more blood.

"Are you here to kill me?" he warbles with difficulty, breathing heavily, a pool of red forming around him. "I knew… someone would come for me eventually. I… I was hoping… that maybe someone would kill these people."

I debate whether to go inside and find out what this is all about, since Cole is obviously in no condition to tell me. But he doesn't have the health module like I do, so I'm the only help he has.

I sigh, eyes darting up to scan our surroundings again. "I'm taking you back," I say, but when I look down again he's already unconscious.

I lift him, thankful that he's smaller than me, and navigate as quickly as I can back to the car without attracting attention. I dump him in the back seat, then slide in the front to call Q, searching for the first aid kit in the process.

"Kai. What is it?" Q answers.

"I just found Cole beaten up outside of some sketchy building. I've got him in the back of the car but he's unconscious and bleeding a lot." I locate the kit, pull out some bandages and healing spray, and lift his shirt to see the damage. "Shit."

"What? How bad is it?"

"Bad. I'm going to bandage him up. Do you want me to come back to HQ or find out who the hell did this?"

"No, no. Don't do anything until we know what we're up against. Hurry back."

I hang up and examine multiple deep cuts on Cole's torso, staining my hands. I clean the wounds a bit before spraying each one to slow the loss of blood, then wrap bandages around him. That'll have to do.

I drive back a bit haphazardly. One of the guards on duty helps me carry Cole to the emergency room, where Q is already waiting. Nurses attend to him immediately.

"Did you gather any information?" Q asks me quietly as we watch at a distance.

"No. I was there only around twenty minutes before someone tossed him out onto the sidewalk to bleed to death."

He purses his lips. "If these people wanted him dead, he would be dead."

It takes me a second to realize what he means by that. "They wanted to see if someone rescued him."

"Precisely."

"And I just played into their plan."

"Unfortunately so. But until we know more, let's not make any moves. Certainly don't go back there unless I ask you to. When Cole recovers, I'm sure he'll be willing to tell us what happened. You're free to go to bed, or do whatever it is you do at this hour."

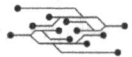

I'm passing by Holbrook's office on my way back home when I hear harsh voices penetrating the closed door. I stop for a moment, debating whether or not to eavesdrop; it's not every day someone has the gall to get into a heated argument with Holbrook. Soon I recognize that it's Harley, to my surprise.

"There was nothing that could've been done," Holbrook says. There's something strange in his voice, a paternal concern, almost, that I've never heard before. I had intended to leave, but that makes me pause.

"*Bullshit*," Harley hisses, rage dripping from her voice. "You were supposed to protect them. That was what I agreed to all those years ago."

"I've done as much as possible, Harley. I can't prevent murder."

A bitter scoff. "Liar. You can, and you know damn well you can."

When Holbrook speaks again his voice has lost all warmth. "Don't forget what I've done for them. I've given them a home, kept them fed, kept them out of jail. Given them a life they never would've gotten after what you did."

"*Fuck you,*" Harley spits, her voice barely audible to me now. "After what I did? If I didn't off my parents like they deserved, we'd all have died long before now or ended up the same as them. You just don't want to admit your pathetic betrayal. Coward."

Seconds later the door slams open and Harley storms out.

But she halts when she sees me. I can almost feel her anger elevate to a new level of fury, and I can't bring myself to make a sound.

"Jesus. It's a dick move to eavesdrop, you know. Where the fuck did you go, anyway?"

She starts to walk past me, and I make the mistake of trying to catch her wrist. She yanks her arm away, seemingly on the verge of punching me, which I wouldn't blame her for.

"Harley—I'm sorry."

But she just glares at me for a few moments, then walks away.

Once I get back to my apartment, I debate for a whole hour whether to go next door and apologize, until Harley knocks on *my* door.

"Hi," I say when I wave it open, studying her. The rims of her eyes are red.

"You gonna let me in?"

I step aside. "I'm sorry about earlier."

Harley shakes her head. "I didn't mean to take my anger out on you." She purses her lips. "Can you make me whatever you made that one night?"

"Sure." In reality, I have no idea what I put in that drink, but I don't have the heart to tell her.

I pull out two glasses and make an educated guess at the ingredients as she slides onto my couch. Though I want to ask her if she's okay, I know she's not, so I instead wait for her to say something.

It's only after I join her that she does, quietly. "Holbrook just told me that my younger brother passed away a couple of days ago." She takes a breath. "Murder, apparently. Holbrook got the three of them out of Morgue Row after I was recruited, but you know New York. This city only spares those who can afford it."

"I'm so sorry. That's awful," I respond gently. "Have you seen them since you joined?"

"I've wanted to, so badly. In hindsight I should've just made it happen, but the GUARD prohibited it, and I found other ways to fill the void of what I'd lost. Leven, who was my mentor, became like family. Nevertheless, there was always that guilt in the back of my mind, about disappearing and never being able to explain why."

Tentatively I take her hand in mine, running my thumb over it. "If you want to see them, I think you should see them. People are irreplaceable."

She takes a breath, and her eyes start to glisten. "I wish I could, more than ever. But one of them is dead already, and I partly blame myself. I can't have the blood of another on my hands because of the GUARD. It's a question of whether I value their safety or being a part of their lives. In that light, it'd be selfish to pick the latter."

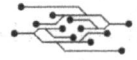

Holbrook schedules a mission briefing on the day our new team member arrives, after which Q has slotted Cole's interrogation. Today, I hope, will be a day of answers.

Harley and I walk together to the designated meeting room, where I reluctantly introduce myself to Grant Kohler, who goes by his last name and has a pleasant German accent. I get the sense that he has a sort of lighthearted evilness about him, for lack of a better way to describe it. Like he's the type of person who could chop someone's head off and completely disregard the severity of it.

"Ah, Agent Kohler," Keating says as he, Q, and Holbrook enter the room. "Welcome to Manhattan." They each shake hands with Kohler before taking their seats at the large, black marble table that consumes the majority of the room. A fake window spans the wall behind them, displaying a clifftop view that I would guess is somewhere in Iceland.

"You three can get to know each other better later, so I'll jump right in," Holbrook says as Kohler eyes him cautiously. Harley, on the other hand, won't meet Holbrook's eyes. "You, along with Q here and Lucien Haddad, who is currently in Devil's Peak Prison, have been chosen to undertake crucial roles in what Medina and the Board have deemed the Delta Mission, codename Operation Labyrinth. The first thing you must know is that the GUARD has been compromised."

Harley and I exchange eye contact.

"From now on," Holbrook continues, "consider it unwise to trust anyone in the GUARD."

"Many divisions have identified their double agents, and almost all of these traitors are part of an organization called Delta," Keating says. "I believe that you've dealt with at least two of their members before, Kai."

Of course. The Greek letter delta is a goddamn triangle. Venom Eyes, Cole Sheehan—they were part of something much bigger. And my partner died for whatever that is.

"They operate deep in the shadows," Holbrook says. "They leave very little evidence and, therefore, are hard to track. Our ally intelligence agencies have given us the reins on this, for the most part, so we've recently sent some agents into Delta to see what information we can gather. But the leaders are quite secretive and quite particular about who they allow to enter their ranks. As of now, the true leaders are unknown. We've only infiltrated the lower levels, and it's evident that there is an alarming amount of order within the hierarchy. Let me warn you now: these fuckers are not messing around. They're unlike anything we've ever faced."

"We know that they're targeting our recruits," Q says. "And we know that they've had help from the inside. There's no evidence to suggest a breach of our cybersecurity, which is comforting, but they're working on it."

"What are the chances they succeed?" Kohler interrupts.

"From the outside, minimal. From the inside, slightly more than minimal. To really understand how our security works, they would need the knowledge of someone who designed it. And there are very few of those people, me being one of them. However, it wouldn't do us well to underestimate their abilities."

"Why are they killing our recruits?" Harley asks. "It's not like that has an immediate effect, assuming they intend to weaken us."

"Ah, the interesting part is they're not actually *killing* all of them," Q responds. "They're making it look like that, certainly, but we've confirmed that the real motivation is to steal talent. Leveraging the work we've already done to identify candidates with exceptional potential."

"So they're kidnapping kids."

"Not so different from the GUARD," I mutter, receiving a glare from Holbrook.

"The GUARD gives recruits a choice," he replies, ice in his voice.

"What choice do orphans really have?" I retort. "Besides, the reason the GUARD even recruits children is that they're malleable. I'd wager Delta had that same line of thinking."

I find that everyone tends to believe that their side is good, that there's a clear line separating them from their adversaries. But in reality, the line is often blurry. It's just a matter of perspective.

"Yes," Keating agrees, to my surprise. "You may find that Delta is like the GUARD in many ways. Organized, intelligent, lethal. Unlike us, however, they are keen on inducing some sort of global rebellion. We believe that they're seeking to overtake or eradicate numerous government institutions, including the GUARD."

"What is their endgame, exactly?" Kohler says.

Keating shifts his gaze to him. "Put simply, they want an empire. They want to be the sole organization governing most of humanity, and they appear to believe quite strongly that they're going to be the ones to prevent the inevitable downfall of civilization."

"And... what exactly is our role in stopping them?"

"Your team will be responsible for finding the heart of this monster. The people in charge."

I run a hand through my hair. "This seems... onerous. If this organization already has the power to eliminate government agencies, to change the course of a nation, and we have very limited information... well, it just seems like we're a little late to the game."

"We have no choice," Holbrook replies, his tone still cold. "We're well aware of what we're asking, so if you aren't up to the job, then *please*, tell us now."

His stab of condescension pisses me off. "You know I'm up to it. It just feels like we may not know what we're dealing with here."

"We have no choice, Kai," Q echoes. "But I think we're capable."

We look at each other for a few moments. Then I nod once. "All right."

"Your first move is to break Lucien Haddad out of prison, and subsequently determine the next course of action based on his knowledge," Keating says.

"What is Devil's Peak, a black site?" Harley asks.

"And more importantly, why is this guy worth our time?" Kohler adds.

"Devil's Peak Prison is no ordinary penitentiary," Holbrook says darkly. "Kept from public knowledge, it houses terrorists and criminal masterminds—valuable ones—that the GUARD has captured, including Lucien Haddad. What we do know is that he was a rather powerful member of Delta who defected. We sent him to Devil's Peak to see what information we could extract, but he has proven to be... resistant."

"Devil's Peak uses specially designed drugs to gain more control over the prisoners' minds," Q explains, casually.

"Jesus," Harley mutters. "Purposely degrading someone's mind? Seems a bit detrimental."

"These aren't good people, Harley. Being humane is not really our concern."

"Yeah, I'm aware of the GUARD's moral stance. What I mean is, he could be completely insane by now thanks to us."

"Frankly, anyone locked in Devil's Peak has likely gone insane."

"That's reassuring," I scoff. "How do we know he'll help us? If he was that high up in Delta, then he certainly aligns with their motives."

"Lucien has critical knowledge regarding Delta, and he'll be invaluable in our quest to terminate the organization, especially its leaders," Q says. "He has nothing to lose, really, but we won't know his mindset until we meet him. If we offer to get him out of that hellhole, he might help us."

"If they can't torture anything out of him, then we certainly can't," Kohler counters.

"Unless he wants to spend his life sitting in Devil's Peak, he'll take this opportunity to get out."

"It seems like we're putting a lot of faith in this," Harley says.

Q is becoming exasperated with us. "We need to know what he knows, and we're not getting it with him sitting in a cell. He's the only solid link our team has."

Harley shakes her head. "But if this is our prison, why do we have to break him out to begin with?"

"As Holbrook said, we can't trust anyone, even the warden. Creating separation between us and his imprisoners will also spawn more cooperation and trust. I've watched a few of his interrogations, and I do think there's still a hint of humanity in him. He's troubled, yes. Dangerous, yes. But evil… maybe not."

TWELVE

Cole sits in the center of a holding chamber made of smooth stone. The stone is interrupted only by a one-way window leading to the adjacent observation room, in which Harley and Kohler are watching the interrogation. There is a drain below the metal chair Cole is in, but nothing ties him down.

"Only hurt him if we really have to," Q murmurs to me in the corner of the room as Cole watches us. He knows it's not in my nature to be any flavor of nice, but I nod anyway.

Q steps toward him. "If you decide that you aren't going to tell us what we want to know, I sincerely doubt if I'll be able to stop Kai from shooting off your limbs one by one."

A lone, empty laugh. "You think you can threaten me? I'm getting my brains blown out whether I cooperate or not," Cole responds, his eyes dead and glaring.

"I mean, if you want to endure a great deal of agony before that, it's up to you," I say.

"Don't get too excited, Kai. I'm not going to be keeping secrets. It's not worth it."

"Great. I'll start by asking you if you're a member of Delta," Q says.

"Yep."

"How long have you been a member?"

"Several months."

"How did you become a part of it?"

"I... They have eyes everywhere. I don't know how they found me, but I was accosted on the street. They threatened to kill me right then and there if I didn't agree to work for them."

Q narrows his eyes at him. "So... you also *continued* to do what they asked for fear of being killed?"

"Yes. At that point in time, being killed by them seemed much more likely than being killed by the GUARD. Clearly I'm about to pay the price for that belief."

Q remains emotionless. "Hm. Did you ever meet in the same place twice?"

"No. They always told me where to go for the next meeting."

"So you can't give us a means of tracking them down."

Cole shakes his head. "No. There wasn't any pattern that I noticed."

"There was no DNA left by the person who beat you up, either."

"He was wearing gloves, and it was dark. I didn't see it coming."

"Do you know why they did that do you?"

"No, I swear. I did everything they asked."

Q purses his lips. "Well, let me tell you. They wanted to see if we were catching on. You did everything they asked, but it seems you were worth more as a sacrifice than as a double agent."

Cole doesn't respond.

"Now, what did you do for Delta?" Q says.

"I mostly gave them information about the agents I drove around."

"Oh, well I hope you put in a good word for me," I retort.

Cole sneers at me. This is a side of him I've never seen before. "You and your casualties were always such a pleasure to chauffeur," he hisses.

"That's your goddamn job."

"He saved your life," Q reminds him, though in another light, you could say all I did was delay his death by a few days.

"I'd rather he left me for dead."

Q rolls his eyes. "Sorry it didn't work out in your favor. What kind of information did you give them?"

"Everything I knew. I observed and talked to people to extract any ounce of information I could, but it was never that much."

"Be more specific," Q says, his voice tight. "What did you tell them?"

Cole sighs. "For every person I drove, it was six things. Their name, their status, what they look like, who they killed, any strengths I noticed, and whether they'd ever mentioned anything related to Delta. But it's surprisingly difficult to get anything out of you elite operatives, and I never really got to drive the same person more than twice."

"Yes, well, that's for a reason. What did they do with this information?"

"They're just amassing data on all our agents. So they can be prepared. And, at some point, find them and kill them. Or so I imagine."

"Why haven't they taken more action?"

"I don't know. They kept me in the dark. My theory is that they don't want to give themselves away just yet by taking out our top agents. It's a hell of a lot easier with people like me."

"Do you know of any other members of Delta within the Manhattan Division?

"No. Like I mentioned, they kept me in the dark."

"Are you sure?" I urge.

"I swear. I don't know anything about any other members. I was at the bottom of the food chain."

"Do you know the names of anyone you worked for?" Q continues.

"No."

"Do you know what they look like?"

Cole seems more uncomfortable now. "No, they always wore masks when dealing with me. Most of them were men. That's all I can say."

"That's all you can say? Jesus, you're not much help are you?"

"I'm glad you found your calling, since working for us was so horrible," I say with a false smile.

"Always have to be an asshole, don't you?" Cole mutters bitterly.

"It's what they pay me for. I hope you've had a nice life."

"I think we're done here," Q says, frowning, turning toward the door. "You're pretty worthless at this point."

I feel Cole's eyes on my back as we exit the chamber into a dim hallway.

And as we leave the thickly secured Brig, there is a lone, muffled gunshot. It doesn't make me shiver like it once did.

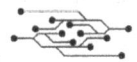

"You think your little traitor was telling the truth?" Kohler asks when our team has gathered for our strategy meeting the next day.

"I do," Q says. "I think he became more afraid of Delta than of us. Unfortunately, it means we're not going to find out much more until we get to Devil's Peak."

Kohler thinks for a moment. "Once we break the defector out of prison, how the hell are we going to control him? I mean, he could probably kill any of us the second we look the other way. I don't want to be a babysitter."

"We are taking a lot of risks, but as I said earlier, he's vital," Q answers. But it's not an answer.

"Not if he won't cooperate," I respond. "It would just be a waste of time."

Q sighs. "Look. Haddad is smart. He'll know that if he kills or betrays us, the GUARD will hunt him down."

"But will that be enough? He'll also know that we're desperate for his help. He may use that as leverage to get what he wants."

"We'll give him what he wants, as long as we're strategic about it. Now, can we focus on how to get him out? I'd like to avoid unnecessary chaos."

"If they notice an inmate gone, surely they'll send out a search party," Kohler says.

Q leans back in his chair. "The thing is, Devil's Peak is sitting in the heart of a mountain in Canada. The only way in or out is by helicopter, so it's virtually impossible for a prisoner to leave the building and survive."

"Are you serious?" I interject. "If getting in and out unnoticed is impossible, how the hell are we supposed to get away with this?"

Q shoots an irritated glance at me. "That's what we're here to figure out, isn't it?"

He asks his AI for a hologram of the prison, and a detailed diagram appears in front of us. Devil's Peak, I see, is a large block with a rather complicated internal structure. A multilevel maze. Q zooms in so that we see the layout of the inside, and highlights Lucien's cell, which happens to be at the bottom.

I exhale, racking my brain for some kind of strategy. "There's no way we can haul him up like twenty floors."

"We can improvise along the way, can't we?" Kohler responds, and I can't tell if he's joking or not.

"I'd rather not risk everything blowing up in our faces because we didn't plan well enough," I say coldly.

"If we can't feasibly go in there and grab him," Harley says, "and we have to do this without involving anyone else, then we need to get him out utilizing more legitimate avenues. The only way a prisoner leaves that place is if they die. So, what if we faked Lucien's death?"

"How do you propose we do that?" Q asks, dubious.

Harley shrugs. "It has to be something we can have control over. We could make him appear dead with a combination of a sedative and a heart-slowing drug. The question is, how would we give it to him?"

Q ponders that. "Each inmate is assigned a single psychiatrist, or analyst, who decides both the medications and the 'influencers' the prisoners receive. I suppose we could use that to our advantage."

"And the analysts are the only ones allowed to perform any questioning?" Harley says. I can practically see the wheels turning in her head as she forms a plan.

"Yes. Unless Haddad has disclosed information to other prisoners or guards, there are only two people who know anything about Delta in that prison: the warden, and Lucien's psychiatrist."

"You said they've been unsuccessful with him so far, yeah? What if we—or Medina, rather—contact the warden and tell him we're sending a replacement analyst? That way one of us can be on the inside."

Q cocks his head, intrigued. "That's... a decent idea, actually. Who do you propose?"

Harley's mouth twists in thought. "I imagine that the rest of the analysts have a substantial amount of experience and education, which might rule out Kai and me based on age alone."

But Q shakes his head. "The GUARD trains people for Devil's Peak, just like anything else. You all received similar training in interrogation and psychology at the Academy. However, in terms of aptitude for understanding the criminal psyche, I think you'd be most suited to the task, Harley. No offense, Thanatos."

Harley looks at me, trying to gauge my emotions, so I look away. Q is certainly right—she'd be the best at it. From what I've seen, she knows how to get through to people, how to read them, how to predict their behavior. I'm just not a fan of sending her into this prison when the rest of us can't be nearby in case anything goes awry.

"It wouldn't be a very pleasant job," Q adds. "Like here, they monitor everything. They record every interrogation and watch your every move, so it's crucial to give nothing away. We can communicate through messages, but anything else is too risky. Do you think you'd be up for it?"

All eyes turn to Harley.

"Of course."

"Excellent. We can give you a few days to learn the ropes before you slip our compound into Lucien's dosage. The nurses will inject him before a scheduled interrogation, and after that, the guards will attempt to bring him to you, the analyst. By that time, if all goes according to plan, Lucien should be unresponsive."

"What will they do with his body?" Harley asks. "Surely they'll suspect some sort of foul play, especially with me being his new psychiatrist. They'll want to determine the cause of death."

"Hm. We'll have to intervene before any tests or disposal are done. The warden is supposed to notify Medina of any prisoner deaths, so as long as he follows protocol, we may have an opportunity."

"Medina could request that the body be preserved for further examination at a GUARD headquarters," I say. "That'd allow us to retrieve him ourselves."

Q nods in agreement. "That'll work."

"Assuming this all goes well, what's our Plan B if Lucien ultimately decides that he doesn't want to cooperate?" Harley says.

"Waterboarding," I suggest. "Or we can just shoot him in the head."

Q thinks for a moment, ignoring my quip. "It may be beneficial, Harley, for you to try to gain his trust while you're in Devil's Peak. That way we'll have a better gauge of who we're dealing with and a better chance at persuasion, should we encounter some resistance. Our only Plan B is gathering intel via our insiders, which currently isn't enough. So I'm betting on Haddad.

"In the next few days, I'll draft for you an outline of all the intelligence the GUARD already has, notify Medina of our plan, and make contact with the warden. In the meantime, it would be wise to continue learning each other's strengths and weaknesses. Learn how to be a team, because the fate of the GUARD may very well depend on you."

THIRTEEN

"I'd like you to meet the mind behind much of our defense technology," Keating says the moment I arrive at his cluttered office for what was supposed to be our monthly one-on-one. "Well, he actually requested to meet you."

"*The* mind? I thought that was Q."

Keating waves a hand. "The second mind, then. He's an outsider, but we were desperate for him to work with us. No one is quite as wildly creative as he is. And he specifically designed a few things for Operation Labyrinth."

We walk to T&W, where the clatter of weapon construction echoes and engineers are crowded around holographic designs, moving and dissecting them with their hands. I follow Keating into one of the design rooms. Standing in the middle of a 3D blueprint, examining a feature of a gun, is the unknown man who had been watching my evaluation.

"Kai, this is Mason Dare."

I halt at the recognition of his name. Mason Dare is the founder of a mega tech company that dabbles in renewable energy, space travel, robotics, and apparently intelligence. It's strange that the GUARD would bring in someone so well-known in the outside world, so I can infer that he must be invaluable for one reason or another.

"World's greatest inventor, at your service," Dare announces dryly, turning to look at me. He's probably in his 40s, with a suiting beard and wild eyes.

"I forgot to mention he's a bit cocky," Keating adds.

"Honest," Dare corrects him, "not cocky." Though I suspect he's joking, it's hard to tell.

"Do you have time to show Kai what you've designed for Minotaur?"

I shoot him a questioning look at the mythical name.

"That's what Medina is calling your team," he explains, before shifting his eyes back to Dare.

He looks lost for a moment, then seems to remember what Keating is referring to with abrupt excitement. "Ah. Yes, yes. I've been eager for him to see."

"Excellent. I'll leave you to it."

Keating departs, and I turn to look Dare up and down. "I've heard of you."

His eyebrows twitch. "Everyone has."

"Why'd they hire you?"

"Well, I can only assume it was my money and my mind, kid, certainly not my personality. Come. I have a few gadgets for you."

He leads me deeper into the T&W Department and unlocks an unmarked door that leads to a storage room.

Inside, there are gadgets and guns mounted on metal tables, along with five metal mannequins, each with some sort of fitted vest. Dare stops in front of five handguns, then spins to face me as he picks one of them up.

"First, as you can see, I have a brand new Ghost pistol for each of you. They'll be coded to your ID modules and handprints so that only your team can use them. The built-in silencing and recoil-diminishing technology will make it the deadliest handgun you've ever had. Q can also track it if you happen to lose it, and if it gets into the wrong hands, he can activate the self-destruct feature."

"I can't accidentally blow myself up can I?"

"No. Virtually impossible."

He hands me the sleek black gun, and I examine it as he continues. "Next—and I expect you'll appreciate this one—I have a more advanced smart gun for you, also coded to your IDs."

He approaches another table and picks up a modular rifle, holding it up for me.

"It's called the Soulbarer," he declares, gazing at his masterpiece with obvious admiration. "It has three barrel lengths, two types of specially designed ammunition, and the same tracking module as the other gun. Please for the love of God try not to lose it."

"What does it do?"

He looks more and more excited by the moment. "Right. Ammunition. The first type is piercing bullets that can cut through most materials. The second is explosive bullets. With just a couple of those you could probably knock down a whole building if you wanted.

"In terms of its 'smart' behaviors, there are four notable ones to keep in mind: person and armor detection, weapon detection, Universal Positioning compatibility, and automatic targeting. The first three funnel into the last one.

"Once you turn it on, if you look through this little transparent screen here, you'll see that people in the field of view are highlighted in blue. If someone is wearing detectable protection, it will show up in silver. Thus, you should be aiming for blue, as it correlates to exposed areas. Any weapons seen in either IR or visible light will glow in red.

"You can use these things to perform manual targeting, of course, but the Soulbarer will always try to detect threats you're aiming at based on whether someone has a weapon. It will account for wind speed and Earth curvature if necessary, and zero in on people's exposed areas, favoring lethal zones. So it'll be very quick to shoot.

"Now. If you have a device with subject tracking, such as one of our lovely insect drones, you can select targets using that device, and subsequently relay the geo-positional information of the target to the gun. I'm sure you're accustomed to identifying people via drone using facial, voice, or gait recognition, or manual selection with a tablet. But now, even if *you* can't directly see your target, your gun can. And it can use that to lock in. No need for targeting systems that are more complex and less discreet.

"Lastly, it learns from your shooting style, like where you aim, when you fire, etcetera, and will become better and better at predicting your moves. It learns to think like you in order to improve its speed. And it works for ranges up to a few miles. Essentially, it's the ultimate assassination weapon."

It takes a moment for all that to soak in. "Goddamn."

"I know." He raises his eyebrows once. "I'll note that we have a vehicle software package for you as well, outfitted with similar target-locking features, remote driving, auto-drive, and Tony."

"Sorry, Tony?"

"Ah. It's the new AI Q and I have designed to assist your team. Tony has so many capabilities that it would take quite a while for me to list them all, but he has access to our entire defense network. He'll be crucial in dire situations."

Next in line are matte black wristband-type devices, about two inches wide. I pick one up and find it heavier than I was anticipating. When I put it on, it forms to my wrist.

"It deploys a shield by voice command," Dare says. "Nanotech, obviously. It also can act as a holographic projector for Tony, in case you want to see something in detailed 3D, such as a map, building, or diagram. If applicable, it will show you your location within the display. Anyone who's wearing one of these bands will appear as white dots, and any targets you identify will be red dots. And of course, you can move the hologram by voice or with your hands."

We move on to a box with five tiny, transparent earpieces and ten contact lenses, Dare's eyes growing even more intense.

"Now… for the good stuff. These will prove to be invaluable. At a basic level, you'll be able to talk to each other, or eavesdrop on nearby conversations. More importantly, they're where Tony will be of the most help. He can use your lenses to provide night vision, readings from your health module if you care to look at them, any data you might want to be displayed, visuals of hostages versus hostiles, messages, you name it.

"It'll be especially helpful in combat because Tony can assist with targeting, discovering advantages you may have, developing strategy, and gathering information about your enemies. If you ever come across them again, Tony will make you aware of any mistakes or habits they are prone to making, in case you didn't notice them the first time around. Since he is connected between all of your earpieces, that means you are all connected, and when one of you is injured, Tony can notify everyone else.

"I know Tony might take some getting used to, but I promise I've designed him not to be distracting so that you can have the visual features on at all times during missions, especially since Tony will be able to protect you by deploying your shield. Everything is automatically recorded as well, in case you want to revisit the event."

Lastly, we reach the mannequins. One is female, obviously for Harley. "These nanovests are the thinnest, most flexible bulletproof and knife-proof vests in existence. As you can see, they've been specially tailored to your bodies so that you can wear them under almost anything, and they'll keep you warm or cool you down as necessary. You can send out a distress signal to your teammates, or if you're feeling rather hopeless, there's also a compartment with a lovely little kill pill. Until I've finished designing your full suits, these will have to do."

He looks around at his work, clearly pleased. "I think that's all I've got for you."

I shake my head in amazement. "I'm impressed. I won't have to do any work."

He shrugs. "Well. I didn't arrive upon my fortune by mistake. Besides, we needed to give you an advantage. I couldn't let Medina send people off to fight a horde of psychopaths without having the proper tools."

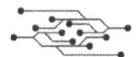

At two in the morning, I'm startled awake by someone knocking on my door persistently, and I'm surprised to find that it's Kohler. He's smiling slightly, which bothers me.

"Is it urgent?" I rub my eyes, trying to get them to focus.

"Well, no."

"What the fuck? It's the middle of the night. What do you want?"

"I want you to come on an... *adventure*." He seems excited, and I'm certainly not in the mood for excitement. I have no intention of becoming friends with him.

"Seriously? No. Leave me alone."

I'm about to shut my door in his face, but then he says, "What if it involved killing someone?"

I stop. "What? Is this something that you were ordered to do?"

"No. We're going to find a murderer and kill him."

I stare at him for a few seconds. "Jesus Christ. How are we going to just *find* a murderer? Aside from half the people in this building."

"Ah, but I already have, see. I've done a bit of investigation and obtained some police data and all that. I think I know where he lives, thanks to a tip that they received earlier today."

"You've been here for like, two days."

"Yes, I'm well aware."

"Who is he?"

Kohler waves a hand. "A serial killer whom the police aren't going to bother catching. Need I say more?"

I shake my head. "But why were you investigating him in the first place?"

He sighs, exasperated. "I look for instances where the police have failed miserably, and I do something about it. We'd be doing the community a favor by getting rid of him. And I find that doing something without the authority to do it is rather invigorating. Win-win."

"You should try something that doesn't involve killing, Kohler."

"It's the only thing I know how to do."

I know all too well.

"What's causing your hesitation?" he continues, shooting me a concerned look.

"We're not supposed to do this kind of thing, you know."

"Well we're not supposed to do a lot of things, but what can they do to us really?"

I think for a moment but don't come up with an answer.

"Exactly," he responds to my silence. "We can argue that it amounts to a training exercise. Besides, they can't be upset with us for killing a killer."

"I suppose not."

"That's the spirit. Get dressed."

"Fine." I'm not sure why I agree to it.

We decide to stop by Camden's to see if he wants to come, which I'm admittedly a little uncertain about also, but I end up not having to worry about it.

He opens the door and I immediately know he's drunk. "Camden..." I start.

"Hey." He numbly looks back and forth between Kohler and me, absently running his finger along the gold crescent of metal behind his left ear. A mood stabilizer implant, as I've learned.

"Are you all right?"

"Yes, darling." I know he's not actually all right, but I don't know what to do about it. Especially not with Camden, who's always so energetic and humorous. I've come to rely on him to brighten my day and now I'm at a loss when he needs someone to do the same for him.

I'm often impressed with my lack of social abilities, for being relatively intelligent.

"Okay. I'm just going to show Kohler around New York."

"Sounds lovely." And with that he shuts the door, not even thinking to say goodbye or ask why we'd stopped by his room.

"I'm a little concerned about your friend," Kohler says as we start toward the Pit, frowning.

"Yeah. Me too."

"If this is a recurring thing, I wouldn't be turning a blind eye if I were you."

I want to defend myself, but I know he's right. I should be doing something.

"I'll check on him when we get back."

"Onward, then."

"Where are we headed?"

"Brooklyn."

FOURTEEN

"Are we just going to walk into this apartment and hope that we see a serial killer as opposed to innocent, sleeping civilians?" I say as we stand on the sidewalk in darkness, facing an old brick apartment building. I'm holding an omnikey in my palm.

"I'm ninety-nine percent sure he lives there."

"How?" I glance at Kohler and catch him rolling his eyes.

"Do I have to describe every detail to you right this instant? Just trust me. It's not that hard to find people with the kind of technology we have."

"I know that."

"Well you asked."

I shake my head. "Whatever. How do you want to kill him?"

"I'll just snap his neck."

I turn and look at him again, but he just looks back, emotionless. "What? I'm being serious."

"All right. And then what? We just leave him there?"

"Yep. You brought gloves, right?"

"Yeah."

"Come on, then."

Inside the apartment, there are no lights on. The living room table is buried under cocaine, sugarpills, and random gadgets, but other than that, there's nothing to hint at what kind of person lives here. Kohler motions for me to come check one of the bedrooms with him.

I hear him inhale, and move around him to see what he's staring at. It's a woman, with a cloth in her mouth, lying asleep—or dead—naked on the floor. Tied to a post. I can't tell if there are bruises all over her, or if the dark is tricking my eyes.

We may be saving her life.

The floor creaks behind me and I spin around just in time to stop a baseball bat from splitting my skull open.

"Ah, there he is," Kohler remarks as I kick a man in the stomach, sending him backward into the living room.

He's nothing spectacular, that's for sure, just average in every physical respect. I duck sideways as he swings at me again, but the third time I grab the bat with one hand, then the other, and shove it backward, hitting him in the forehead. I yank it out of his grip with ease, and he starts to back up.

"Fancy some baseball, Kohler?"

"Why yes I would." I toss him the bat and he walks forward to take a swing at the man's shin, causing him to crumple in agony. "Do me a favor and hold him."

I lift him to his feet, pinning his arms behind his back as he struggles against me. Kohler cocks his head for a second, then rapidly brings a fist across the man's cheek, which is when I notice for the first time that his knuckles are adorned with metal. *Permanent* metal integrated into his hand.

"That's for the woman."

I lose count of the repeated punches, but by the time Kohler is done with him, his face is a bloody, bruised mess of what it once was. Unrecognizable. He's practically slumped against me. I let him fall to his knees.

"This is for all the others," Kohler says calmly as he swings the bat, striking the killer on the side of the head with a sharp crack. He drops to the floor and I kneel to check the absence of a pulse.

Kohler looks down at his work with a smug expression, like a goddamn psychopath. I'll beat the fuck out of someone, sure, but I'm not going to be smiling about it.

"Who the hell are you two?" I hear from behind me.

I turn and jump to my feet.

A girl not much older than me, with golden brown skin and long black hair, looks back and forth between Kohler and me. She's wearing dark lipstick, boots, gloves, and a tank top under a camo jacket, with several piercings and tattoos to complete the edgy facade. If she weren't holding a knife and oddly undisturbed by our bloody body, I would believe that she just happened upon the scene.

"Avengers of justice," Kohler answers, unconcerned. I'm tempted to reach for my gun, but I hesitate.

"I can see that," she says.

"And what are you doing here?"

"I *was* here to kill this man, but I saw you go in first. Apparently you've already done my job for me."

Kohler and I exchange eye contact. "Your job?" I ask. "Who do you work for?"

She tilts her head. "Whoever pays me."

For a moment we all hover in silence, no one wanting to divulge any information.

"Well, I'm Grant. Pleasure to meet you." I whirl and give Kohler a look, but he just winks at me. "Calm down, Kai."

She looks thoroughly unimpressed. "Zahra."

"We should help the hostage, *Grant*," I remind him.

"Hostage?" Zahra repeats, following us to the bedroom, where the captive woman is now awake. And terrified.

I move toward her, intending to cut off the cloth that's gagging her, but she flinches, whimpering. "I'm not going to hurt you," I say too harshly.

"Be nice," Kohler snaps.

She looks at me, wide-eyed, cowering. "Hey. You're safe now, okay? Let me cut off your gag."

With that, I see her relax a bit.

"I'll find her some clothes." Zahra locates a closet and returns a minute later with a T-shirt, sweatpants, and sneakers, just as I'm done cutting all of the ropes.

At this point the woman is on the verge of tears, though whether it's from being overwhelmed or relieved I can't tell. "Thank you," she sobs.

I'm a bit taken aback when she hugs me, shaking. It feels so strange, so foreign, to be saving someone rather than just pulling a trigger and moving on. But I don't feel like a hero. I don't want to be a hero anyway. I'm not made for that.

"You want to go to the police?" Kohler asks her.

She shakes her head. "Home. Can I go home?"

"I'll take her," Zahra says.

"No. We can do it," I say back.

"What, you don't believe me?"

"I don't know who you are, so no."

She crosses her arms. "Fine. We'll do it together."

"Why can't you just leave us alone? Go back to where you came from."

"I also have no reason to trust you, so like it or not, douchface, I'm coming with you."

I roll my eyes. "Whatever."

Zahra turns back to the woman, who has been looking between us trying to figure out who the hell we are, to get an address. She seems a bit horrified at the body of her captor as we go by, but she doesn't utter a word about it. He got what he deserved, in my mind.

After a painful amount of forced small talk initiated by Kohler, we drop the woman off at her home, and Zahra turns to look me up and down.

"So, are you assholes vigilantes or something?" she says.

"I'm Batman, he's Robin," Kohler replies.

"Other way around, sweetheart," I retort.

Zahra is unimpressed. "I'll take that as a no."

"We're definitely not superheroes," I say. "This excursion was... out of the ordinary."

"Oh so it's okay for you to tell her things, but when I do, it's the end of the goddamn world," Kohler protests.

I ignore him. "And you?"

"This is basically what I do," Zahra answers.

"So you... kill people?"

"Not always."

"Can you be more specific?"

"I just get rid of people for other people who pay me to do it, in whatever way they'd prefer. There's quite a few of us."

"Fascinating," Kohler breathes. "You're an organization of hitmen?"

"I wouldn't label it as an organization. There's no hierarchy, no rules. Only one man who keeps it running and finds people to work."

"And someone paid you to kill that guy?" I ask.

"No, actually. Just some community service." She smirks, then raises her chin at me. "How often do you kill people?"

Kohler laughs hollowly. "That's all we do."

I stare at him to signal that he shouldn't utter another word, because we're verging on violating a handful of highly enforced GUARD rules, but he pointedly ignores it.

"We just don't normally deal with lowlife criminals like him," he continues, talking over my attempt to interject. "Everyone we assassinate is affecting society on a larger scale."

Zahra raises her eyebrows, shooting me a glance. "So you're *elite* assassins."

"Yes," Kohler responds excitedly. "We're like you, we just operate on a higher level of the hierarchy, for the most part. Because of that, practically every move we make is monitored."

"You CIA or something?"

Kohler smirks. "Not quite."

I squeeze my eyes shut. "Kohler, shut the fuck up already."

"Does your organization know you're here?" Zahra says.

"No. Well, maybe. We'd appreciate it if you didn't run your mouth."

"Neither of you were here in my mind." Zahra cuts her eyes at me again, unreadable. "Now, as nice as this was, I've got better shit to do."

She turns and starts to walk away, but Kohler stops her. I sigh rather audibly.

"Hey now, don't be rude. It's not every day we run into someone like you," he says.

She raises her eyebrows at him in annoyance. "What, you want to be pals?"

"No," I respond before Kohler gets the chance. "We don't need any secret friends."

"One drink," Kohler persists. "Then we'll leave you alone."

I expect Zahra to say no immediately, but she hesitates, considering the offer. "Fine. You can come to our hangout. But only for one drink."

Kohler grins. "On second thought, I'm feeling a bit exhausted. You two carry on, I think I'll head home." He stares at me, and it takes me a moment to realize that he's trying to set me up with this girl.

Before I can also back out, more out of panic than anything, Kohler is on his way. Zahra gazes at me, amused, waiting to see what I'm going to do. It's probably painted on my face that I'm out of my comfort zone.

"Well? You coming or no?" She gives me a lopsided smile.

And suddenly my hesitation dissipates.

I nod once. "Sure. Lead the way."

She takes me to a sketchy basement bar, where a guard of some sort lets us in. It's hazy and dimly lit with neon, the walls and ceiling painted with graffiti. There are about ten other people sitting at various booths, but none of them pay us any attention, except for one woman who keeps scowling at us. I catch her mutter the word "slut," which Zahra brushes off.

"That's my lovely ex," she explains. "She's jealous."

"Charming."

On one side of the room is a huge holo-board with columns labeled with different names, and more names underneath. Zahra goes over to the list under "Up For Grabs" and crosses out a name, then adds it to her column.

"What is all that?" I ask after she comes back to the bar, sliding onto the stool next to me.

"The top row is the names of everyone who works here, and underneath is the list of all the people they've been paid to handle this month."

"This *month*? Jesus, there are like ten people under your name. And did you just take credit for the man *we* killed?"

She shrugs, lips twitching into a smirk. "April has been a little busy, actually. The guy tonight was someone whose criminal data I came across a few times for other cases, and I was just waiting for a key piece of information to get his location. Even with paid jobs, I only take out people who I feel deserve to die. Abusers, murderers, the like."

"You should put me on your hit list, seeing as I'm a murderer."

"And myself. It's a morality brainfuck."

"Oh I'm familiar with it."

"Find someone interesting tonight, Z?" the bartender asks as he comes over, eyeing me, but in more of a sexual than skeptical way.

"You could say that," Zahra replies. "Could we get two Orgasms?"

"The hell is an Orgasm?" I say.

"Aw, you poor sheltered soul," Zahra teases. "I'll just have to show you."

"I'm sure you wouldn't disappoint," I respond, surprising myself.

And Zahra too, apparently. "So you're not as cold as you seem."

I don't know how to feel about whatever the hell is happening, especially considering my situation with Harley. I do know that if she and I were smart, we wouldn't be getting romantically involved at all, for our own sanity. Not that I should be getting involved with someone like Zahra, either. Unless I were to leave the GUARD, having a meaningful relationship with any outsider is damn near impossible. Even if I did leave, they'd forever be monitoring me to ensure I didn't divulge any secrets.

Some people do opt to run off with a lover, but the GUARD's practices of sterilization and removal from society have killed that motivation in many. So the rest of us are left with just each other, which is often a recipe for trauma, given our line of work.

Zahra pulls out a mist pen and offers it to me first, but I turn it down, as tempted as I am. Technically we can get suspended for drugs, but I've never taken that too seriously, and neither has Keating. I think most of my colleagues have learned to hide their addictions well enough that our superiors generally don't get involved anyway.

"Can I ask why you agreed to get drinks?" I say.

"You intrigue me," she replies simply, her eyes conveying her words as she takes a drag of mist. "I don't give a shit about your douchebag friend, but you seem cool. A loner like me."

"You don't know anything about me."

"Chill. I'm aware of that, mystery boy. And I'm aware it'll stay that way because you probably can't or won't tell me. A bit of secrecy is more interesting anyway."

"I wouldn't mind learning more about you, if you'll indulge me."

She shrugs again. "I suppose."

"You trust me?"

"I don't believe that you care enough to do something to screw me over."

"That's probably accurate."

"I'd shoot you if it wasn't. Right, so this is our headquarters, and over there off of that little dark hallway is Remus's office. He's the one who operates everything, but we're essentially all on our own when it comes to finding and killing our targets."

"You do everything yourself?"

"We do. The investigation, the planning, the execution. The most important rule is, obviously, don't get caught."

"How often do people get caught?"

"Not often. Most of us know this city in and out. The patterns of the police—human or otherwise—become apparent if you watch them long enough. But occasionally someone won't come back."

"Have you ever had a close call?"

"Not on the job. I'm good at what I do."

Something about her makes me believe it. "How would you have killed the guy tonight?"

The bartender slides the two mystery drinks in front of us. Zahra picks one up and throws back half of it before I've even touched mine.

Then her head falls to the side as she ponders, swirling the last bit of her cocktail. "I was hoping that I could sneak in and slit his throat while he slept, but now that I think about it, that would've been too easy of a way out. You and Douchebag had the right idea."

"To be honest, I wasn't planning on being involved in torturing anyone tonight. When Kohler dragged me out to kill that piece of shit, I was imagining something quick and clean."

"Quick and clean should be reserved for when you're getting paid or likely to get caught," Zahra responds, downing the rest of her drink. She nods to mine. "I didn't peg you as so inexperienced. You clearly need someone to show you how it's done."

"You're going to beat that joke to death, aren't you?"

"Hell yeah, it's a good one. Now drink that shit."

I take a sip, letting the sweet taste coat my tongue, before downing the rest in one go.

Zahra's eyebrows are raised by the time I'm finished. "So you *can* keep up."

"You'd be surprised at what I can do."

"Oh I don't doubt it."

I shoot her a glance, struggling to mask my interest in her, especially as the booze starts to hit. The next hour or so goes by in a tipsy blur of banter tinged with vague flirtations. Zahra, with her wit and bluntness and obvious intellect, has me feeling like I could spend all day with her without a dull moment.

When I realize what time it is, I nearly have a heart attack.

"I should leave," I say, exhaling. "Thanks for a good time."

"I have a feeling you're going to disappear into the night, never to be seen again."

I purse my lips. "The more we get to know each other, the more likely it is that we'll suffer the consequences."

Her dark eyes are like the night sky, entrancing yet full of the unknown. "Do you want to? Get to know me, I mean." Her fingers brush against my arm.

My lips part, but for a moment no words emanate from them. So much of me is conflicted, just as I have been with Reiya, with Harley. But the more I throw away genuine connection, the more I realize how much you have to cherish it.

"Yeah," I say. "I do."

She taps her phone to mine, transferring her name and number. "Then get to know me."

FIFTEEN

"Have they finally turned you into a robot?" Camden says as I lounge on his couch, staring up at the ceiling, mulling over ominous messages that greeted me in the morning, delivered to my phone in the dead of night from an unidentified sender.

Traitors aren't who you expect.

Keep an ear out for the name Dr. Rosalie Brenner.

Get to her before she gets to you.

I've been unable to connect any dots, but my gut tells me that this is coming from higher up in the hierarchy. The person didn't give me much to go off of, which has been driving me a bit crazy.

Considering what I've been told about Delta, trying to trace the messages or search our databases for information seemed unwise. Anything could draw attention from the wrong people and end with me in a body bag.

Which leaves me with only one option: outside help. And Reiya's the only person I trust.

"Someone sent me a warning. Anonymously. And I don't know what to do about it."

Out of the corner of my eye I see Camden gesture for me to give him more information. "And? What was this warning? You know I love a good mystery."

"It was about a person who's some kind of threat. Outside of the GUARD, I think. I'm having my sister look into it."

He seems to perk up at that. "Are you now? That's a bold move. What's my role?"

I turn my head to look at him. "What? None."

He frowns at me. "No, no, I want in. This is juicy. And let's be honest, you're not going to have any time running around the world or whatever."

"What do you want to do?"

"Help Reiya get any info she might need. Do some digging myself, maybe."

"Both of those things could get you in trouble, you know."

He gives me the look he always does when I say something he thinks is stupid. "That's why I want to do it, darling. Live fast die young."

I exhale. He's not wrong about me getting sucked into Operation Labyrinth. I could use another person besides Q looking out for my sister, too.

"Fine. Just be careful, or I'll come back here and kill you myself."

"Deal."

"Why the hell are you dressed up like that?" I ask, finally noticing the result of whatever he'd been doing while I was lost in thought. Semi-formal attire, as if he's about to walk a red carpet.

He stares at me, eyebrows raised. "Where have you been, idiot? We have dinner tonight. With Medina."

Shit. In my exhaustion from last night, I'd completely forgotten about the invitation Keating had sent earlier.

I sit up, head cocked in confusion. "I thought it was limited to Operation Labyrinth."

He smirks. "Turns out you and Stone aren't the only chosen ones around here anymore. Shay and I have new assignments carrying out assassinations of known Delta members. Nothing like what I hear your team has been tasked with, but God am I glad for something interesting."

"We're gonna need all the help we can get," I mutter. "Feels like the goddamn world is ending."

"Which is why we're having an epic sendoff tonight before we all die. Clubs on clubs on clubs, baby."

I groan. "I don't remember agreeing to that."

"It's not like I'm giving you a choice."

"You gonna be okay?" I blurt without thinking.

Camden's expression morphs into concern. "Meaning?"

I struggle to find the right words, and I want to kick myself for needing Kohler of all people to tell me how to be a decent friend. "It's just that you're usually a bit desolate whenever I come here at night. That and drunk."

His face falls. "I suppose it was only a matter of time before my mask started to break apart."

"Cam, it's okay. You can talk to me, or Shay, or Harley, or whoever you want because I guarantee you that we'll understand."

"That may be true, but talking doesn't make it go away. It's still there, draining me, no matter what. This is the only way I can blur the lines between what's real and what I want to be real. I have to cope somehow, mate. Whenever I'm alone, my mind goes to the bad things and the alcohol allows me to believe I'm escaping it. I hate that I do it. I really do, Kai."

I don't blame him, really. Our world isn't an easy place to live in.

"I just don't want it to make things worse, that's all."

"At this point it may be, but I'm okay, I promise. I always have been. All right?"

I gaze at him for a few moments, feeling helpless. "Okay."

He studies me in return, recognizing that I'm not satisfied. Then he smiles sadly, and sends me off to get ready. But before I do, I stop by Shay's.

When she opens her door, I can tell that she's surprised that it's just me. Camden's presence has always dominated our trio.

"Hey," she says, her hair half done. "What's up?"

I find myself biting my lip. "You mind if I come in for a moment?"

She steps aside, worry developing in her expression. "Of course."

"Sorry, bad timing, I know. It's just... I'm worried about Camden."

Then I see the shift in her eyes. The understanding. "Ah. About the drinking?"

"Yeah."

She nods, leaning against a wall. "We've talked about it a bit. He still struggles very intensely with the loss of his family, and of his girlfriend back at the London Academy. I don't know if it's survivor's guilt, or if he blames himself, or if it's just too much to bear. I desperately wish I could help him, but he's mostly resistant to my efforts. He refuses any kind of therapy."

"What can we do?"

She looks away, takes a breath, before returning her gaze to me. "I'm not sure, Kai. I think all we can do is look out for him the best we can."

"I'm not very good at it, to be honest."

"I think you have more impact on him than you realize. He truly cherishes your friendship."

At that, I have to squeeze my eyes shut to fight back emotions I'm not ready for. "With Harley and me leaving soon…"

"I know. I'll be there for him, I promise. Okay?"

I exhale. Nod. "Okay."

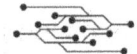

When Harley meets Camden, Shay, and me for our dinner, I have a difficult time not staring. She's donning impressive heels and a stunning black dress with cutouts. Camden starts to ask me if I'm getting a boner but I shush him.

"You look nice," she murmurs to me as the four of us walk through the corridors to the car waiting for us in the garage, receiving more than a few stares along the way.

"As do you." I'm tempted to slide my arm around her waist, but resist for the sake of maintaining appearances. I can tell that Camden and Shay have both noticed the shift in the dynamic between Harley and me, but neither of us wants any rumors making their way to Holbrook.

We arrive at some ritzy restaurant, where someone already knows who we are. She leads us to our own private room with a fountain on one side, metal chandeliers overhead, and a huge marble table in the middle. We are the first to get here, but there are glasses of champagne already awaiting us.

"Is there anything I can get you to drink while you wait?" the server asks us.

"Hmm... we'll have a bottle of your best red wine," Camden replies. "And by 'best' I mean most expensive."

"Of course."

Q and Kohler, followed closely by Keating, Holbrook, Medina, and Dare, show up after some other agents have trickled in and Camden has had time to down a few glasses of wine.

"Ah, the queen has arrived," he says.

We all get up to shake hands with Medina, who seems to be in a rather average mood considering all that's probably looming over him at the moment. He's still got those cold, piercing, unnerving eyes, though.

Holbrook, meanwhile, is his usual moody self. I don't even acknowledge him, which I'm sure he notices. Dare sits across from me, next to Q. He leans toward me, smiling like he knows something.

"I'm eager to see what sort of schemes you have planned for tonight," he murmurs, hardly loud enough for me to hear him.

"What?"

"Well, I just thought you might, you know, take advantage of the fact that for once, Holbrook isn't the most powerful person in the room."

I stare at him as I realize what he's saying. Medina may be more likely to give me something I want than Holbrook, who wouldn't be able to do anything about it. Dare sees that I caught his drift, and raises his eyebrows as he sits back in his chair, smirking in satisfaction.

But what do I want?

"Do you think they have a kids' menu?" Camden asks casually as he inspects the menu, pretending he didn't just hear what Dare said to me.

"I'll ask if they can make you some mac and cheese, Cam," Shay responds.

"Oh, no, I was asking for Kai."

Before I can jab him in the side, Medina leans across the table, staring at me intently.

"Agent Thanatos. How are you feeling about Minotaur's strategy for your first objective?"

I hesitate for a moment to determine the right response. "I won't deny that it'll be tricky, but I'm confident we'll succeed. Too much is relying on it not to."

"Indeed. Please keep in mind that your team has the freedom to do whatever is required to get the job done."

There it is. That's what I want. *Freedom*. Freedom to see my sister whenever and wherever, without someone knowing. Freedom that will give me a semblance of independence.

I choose my words carefully. "Actually, sir... if I'm being honest, I think we would benefit from a bit more liberty."

He scowls. "What do you mean?"

"It probably feels like the GUARD should be trusting its agents less, given the circumstances, but I think we should be doing the opposite. If you don't trust us, our job is a hell of a lot more difficult."

"What are you insinuating?" Holbrook demands. He's been side-eyeing me since the conversation began. "You're well aware that we trust you, otherwise you wouldn't be in Minotaur at all."

I lower my voice a bit so the other agents don't hear. "But do you trust us enough? You still monitor our every move, and have access to our phones, data, and trackers. Our adversary may eventually have that same access. Who knows what they'll be able to find out with their people on the inside."

Q looks at me from across the table with a mixture of respect and disapproval. From Holbrook it's controlled anger, which I get a lot of satisfaction out of. Medina thinks for a few moments.

"So you're suggesting we completely wipe you from our system?" he says.

"Basically. We can't exist. We shouldn't even be using the same pathways of communication as everyone else in the GUARD. If Delta learns anything about what we're doing, we're fucked."

I almost worry that Medina might see using the word "fucked" as a lack of professionalism, but instead I find that, unlike Holbrook, he doesn't have something up his ass. Being a bit brash might instead earn some respect. He turns to Kohler and Harley. "And what do you two think?"

Harley nods. "I'd agree. We can't afford any mistakes."

"Mm. I think he has a point," Kohler answers, though it's clear he doesn't care much one way or the other.

Medina's gaze shifts to me again, and he studies me like he recognizes that I'm one of the only people in this room who isn't afraid of him.

"Fine," he says eventually. "But don't forget that freedom often comes at a cost."

By the time dinner is over, Camden, Shay, and Harley are tipsy, rendering them overly excited to attend an exclusive party Q got us on the list for.

"We need to catch up with them," Kohler says as we climb into the back of a GUARD SUV. "Otherwise we'll be babysitting."

"Never fear, Camden is here," Camden responds, pulling out two flasks and handing them to us.

"What's in these?" I ask.

"Dunno. Stuff Shay and I stole from your place."

"Kai has the best liquor," Shay says with a slight slur as I start pouring whatever the hell it is into my open mouth.

The club, decked out in moody neon lights and booming with bass, is almost packed on every level. Camden's first stop is a glass bar, where he orders us two rounds of shots. I had certainly been expecting him to go wild, but I'm surprised when Shay nearly outdoes him. As she downs the tequila, she gazes at Camden as if she's challenging him, and he's completely enthralled, his mouth nearly agape.

"They're definitely hooking up tonight," Harley murmurs in my ear.

"So are we," I respond, sliding my hand around her waist after resisting touching her the whole night.

I call over a bartender with neon pink eyes and an ornate tattoo between her breasts.

"What can I get you, loves?" she says, eyeing us with interest.

I look at Harley.

"Strongest fucking thing you have," she replies. The bartender ponders for a moment before grabbing a bottle with a vibrant blue liquid and pouring two shots, then sliding them across the counter.

"To sex, saving the world, and not dying," Harley says, raising her glass. I clink mine against it, and swallow, expecting the worst burn of my life. But it doesn't burn. It's sweet, almost sickly sweet. And whatever it is, it's not alcohol.

Then things start to get blurry. Harley takes my hand and leads me into the sea of bodies on the dance floor, pulling me against her and sliding her arms around my neck. I'm dimly aware of disapproving glances coming from Kohler, but I'm too buzzed and too enraptured with Harley to care.

The next thing I know we're kissing, my tongue in her mouth and her hands pulling my hair. The sensation is perhaps the most intoxicating of all.

It takes a couple of hours for the booze and drugs to wear off, and by that time I've lost my shirt, Harley's dress is ripped, and we have no idea where our friends are. We stumble outside, crashing hard, and I call a car for us.

Harley buries her head into my chest as I put my arms around her.

"You okay?" I ask after a few minutes.

She pulls away to look at me, her eyes glassy. "I don't even know. I haven't had the time to think about whether I'm okay. My brother's death doesn't even seem real."

I find myself nodding. This is what happened to me after my partner was killed. No time to process, no time to grieve, no time to *feel*.

"I know," is all I can say.

She exhales. "I want to know what it's like to be happy, Kai. Do you think we'll ever experience that?"

I think for a moment, but I don't have an answer. "Maybe someday."

SIXTEEN

I am walking alone down the corridors of the Field Department when Holbrook's slow, foreboding voice behind me nearly causes me to jump out of my skin.

"I don't know what you're up to, Thanatos, but whatever it is, I'd be careful if I were you. You're lucky Medina has taken a liking to you."

I stop and turn around, but he just stalks past me, reading something on his tablet, turning the next corner toward his office. Doesn't even look at me.

Motherfucker.

"You think you can threaten me?" I say, following him, my voice echoing down the hall. "You can't do anything to me now that I'm under Medina's watch instead of yours."

He halts. Laughs emptily, not bothering to look back. "You know that's a lie. I've seen your TORS recordings. I know your every fear, your every weakness. I could ruin you."

As much as I hate to admit it, he's right. I'm not really free, not from him. His control over me will never wane.

"Remember when you said you cared about me? Still sticking by that?"

"You know that your aptitude for killing is the only reason I've kept you around."

God, I hate him.

"Why did you assign me to be Harley's partner? You obviously care for *her*."

Finally, he turns to look at me. "I knew you'd keep her alive."

To that, I don't have a comeback. I just watch him as he disappears down another hallway, simmering with anger.

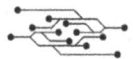

"Is your sister hot?" Camden asks me while we wait for Reiya at a crowded day lounge. I scan for anyone who might be watching us, but all I see are inebriated people who don't even glance in our direction. Between the chatter and the music, no one will be able to hear us either.

I roll my eyes at him. "She's not gonna be interested, Camden. Even on the off chance that she finds you tolerable, she's a lesbian."

"Does she own bulldogs? Ooh, does she have powers? Super strength or the innate ability to fix any machinery?"

"Yes, actually."

We are interrupted when Reiya walks in, and I catch Camden wipe the smirk from his face. He insisted that I introduce him after volunteering himself to collaborate with us on the investigation into Dr. Brenner. Of course, he's been endlessly generating outrageous theories about who the messages were from and what they mean.

I'm glad that I'll have someone else to watch Reiya's back while I'm gone, because I have no idea what we're getting into. However, although I was wiped from virtual existence this morning thanks to Medina, Camden wasn't so lucky. Which means anything that can be traced back to him poses a risk, even with Q's protection of Reiya.

Just as she joins us, my phone buzzes, and I'm surprised to see that it's Zahra. I'd be lying if I said that she hadn't crossed my mind a few times in the last several days, but I couldn't bring myself to text her.

What are you doing tonight?
Are you asking me to hang out? I respond.
Duh. I have to take care of someone, but maybe after that?
You don't want me to come along?
Eh, there isn't room for tourists
Hey now. I wouldn't be a tourist
I work better alone, nothing personal
Fineeeee
I'll message you when I'm done, then you can come to my place?
Deal.

Camden kicks me under our table. "What the hell are you smirking about, dingus?"

"The new girl?" Reiya guesses.

"Yeah," I admit.

"I'm sorry, who?" Camden looks between Reiya and me.

"He met a girl. A goddamn hitwoman, too," she answers for me.

Camden's eyes widen. "You slut," he says, pushing my shoulder. "I saw you with Harley the other night. Save some for the rest of us!"

"Shut up. As if you're any different."

He looks scandalized. "*I'm* not the one stringing two girls along at once. I bet they don't even know about each other."

I exhale. "Look, I have no idea what to do. I shouldn't be getting attached to either of them."

"Listen, monogamy is out. Throuples are all the rage, haven't you heard?"

Reiya laughs, and I give him a look. "Hell no."

Camden shakes his head. "You're denying yourself an incredible opportunity, mate. How'd you meet this girl anyhow?"

"Long story," I respond, "but we crossed paths thanks to a Brooklyn serial killer."

"Just your average meet cute," Reiya quips.

"I don't even know what to make of that," Camden says. "For an asshole of a loner you sure do have game with the ladies, contrary to my initial assessment."

My sister is smirking at me. "I had the same thought."

"Can we please change the subject?" I groan. "We need to figure out how to keep you two safe with all this Delta chaos going on."

Reluctantly they relent, then proceed to brush off my concerns.

"Kai, we'll be fine," Reiya says. "This shit is what we do for a living, right?"

"See? Even Rei isn't worried," Camden says, opening his hands and leaning back in his chair. "Honestly, if I die hunting down some mysterious villain who has it out for you, I'm fine with that."

I don't say it, but I can't help but wonder if his desire for distractions is like all the humor and the booze—another means of forgetting the things that have happened to him. It's difficult to tell whether his nonchalance about serious risks has crossed from confidence into something darker.

Not just a detachment, but perhaps a true lack of concern about whether he lives or dies.

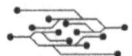

Zahra invites me over around midnight.

My eyebrows go up when she opens the door, on account of the fact that she's a little beat up. One of her cheekbones is red and puffy, like she got clocked, and on the other side of her face are four bloody scratch marks.

"This one put up a bit of a fight," she explains, standing aside to let me in.

"You should ice that."

"It'll feel better after we take a few shots."

"It would help the swelling."

She rolls her eyes. "Thanks, doctor. I had no idea."

I look around her apartment, which is rather chaotic. An unmade nook bed, shelves crammed with tools and weapons, an entire wall covered with pinned pictures and notes of what I assume to be her targets.

"Want anything to drink? I have whiskey or…" I follow her into her kitchen, and she examines a row of bottles. "Whiskey. Sorry, I never have people over."

"Not even the people in your kill club?"

She shrugs. "They're not really my friends. I don't have any friends, for that matter. You'd be one of the first, if we're calling this a friendship."

Zahra grabs a bottle and we climb through her window, stepping out onto a ledge high above the people below. Having been stuck underground for years, I've come to love the feeling of liberty that heights induce.

"You got family, at least?" I ask, inhaling the cool wind.

"Somewhere, maybe." She takes a breath as she pours two glasses, handing one to me. "My brother died when I was young. His schizophrenia got him into trouble because he had no way to get help, and although he wasn't violent, he suffered a lot of violence from others."

More and more I'm reminded that everyone I know has lost someone, or some part of themselves, to violence. To inhumanity. It's an ever-pervasive ghost, leaving wounds that never fully heal.

"I wish I could have saved him," Zahra continues, "because I had no one else. Our dad was out of the picture; he moved back to Korea when I was two. And my mom, well, she was hardly around either. We always had a very strained relationship. She resented me, especially after my brother was killed, and in turn, I resented her. Eventually she kicked me out."

"When was the last time you saw her?"

She thinks for a moment. "God, I don't know. It's been years. After I left I never went back."

"Is that when you learned how to kill people?"

"It was when my brother died, actually. I had a neighbor, probably in his sixties, down the street from where I grew up. He knew what had happened, and he sort of took me in. He taught me how to fight, and how to design and augment weapons. Better than therapy, if you ask me. To this day I have no idea where he acquired all his skills; he'd never tell me. Probably ex-military or something. He was the one who led me to Remus, too. I think he'd been setting me up for this job the entire time, so that I could escape the hell I was born into."

"Where is he now?"

"He died, too. Cancer. I visited him several times but the last time I went, he was gone."

We sit in silence for several minutes, observing the people in the apartments across the street. It's not an uncomfortable silence, however. For the first time in weeks, months even, I feel at ease.

"So tell me, Kai Thanatos. You got a girlfriend?" she says abruptly, smirking at me. "You don't really talk about yourself."

"There's not much to know."

"That's not true. Answer me."

"Well… I wouldn't be here if I was with someone. But if we're being honest, I've been hooking up with this girl who became my new partner not that long ago. Frankly, I like her more than I'm comfortable with. I just know that it has the potential to ruin me, and I don't know if I can survive that."

Zahra doesn't respond right away, just gazes out into the city, a neutral expression on her face as she takes a hit from her mist pen. The smoke curls into the air and drifts away in the direction her hair blows.

"Sounds complicated. But then most relationships are."

"I'm not really cut out for it."

"I'm certainly not. My former partners have been nothing but nightmares. I mean, you saw my ex-girlfriend."

"Guess you have poor taste," I tease.

"Probably why you're here."

"Oh, am I your type then?"

She grins. "Cold and vaguely arrogant? Absolutely."

"Unfortunately for you, this might be the last you'll see of me for a long while."

She raises her eyebrows. "Getting sent on a special mission, eh?"

"Something like that."

"So you really are going to disappear into the night, never to be seen again."

I gaze at her, a wretched feeling starting to descend on my mind as the moment becomes one of those in which I want, more than anything, to live a normal life. "I wish I had more time to get to know you."

Her mouth twists to the side. "Me too. I was starting to like you. Which is saying a lot, because I don't like anyone."

"Maybe one day we'll meet again, on the other side of whatever storm I'm heading into."

"Is it strange that I wish I could come with you? Into that storm."

I cock my head. "What makes you want that? All I do is hunt people, just like you."

She bites her lip, eyebrows pulled together, eyes conveying some sort of yearning now. "I just... want to be something *more*. Be a part of something bigger. Something meaningful. You know? I'm right at the bottom alongside all the pieces of shit I kill."

"Funny, I'm the opposite. I'd happily disappear into the fray and just... live."

She clinks her glass of whiskey against mine. "Well, here's to us getting the lives we want, someday."

"I'll drink to that."

At the end of the night, I have to muster the courage to go home. Because it means saying farewell not only to Zahra, but to my life as I know it. Soon I'll be heading into the unknown, on a nebulous quest to take down Delta.

As she is about to see me out, she stops. Turns to face me, leans back against her closed door.

"I think I might miss you," she says with her crooked smile.

As if there were an invisible string pulling me, I step toward her, closing the distance between us, resting my hands on her waist. "You sound so surprised."

"A bit. And I'm very tempted to ask you to stay just a bit longer."

"I could be convinced," I say softly, lifting a hand to brush her hair behind her ear.

"But as much as I'd like to, I'm not gonna fuck you," she murmurs, smile lingering.

I raise my eyebrows, but can't help but grin back at her. "Oh? And why's that?"

"Because you need to figure out your feelings for this other girl. And if things don't work out with her, then when you see me again, you'll have something to look forward to."

She winks. *God.*

I groan. "You're unbearable. But sensible."

I start to pull away, but then she grabs my arm and pulls me back. We are mere inches from one another now. "I never said I wouldn't kiss you," she breathes.

And then she does. It's lustful, thrilling, barely restrained. I don't touch her in the way I want to, but I don't need to. Her tongue against mine is all it takes for me to be swept away.

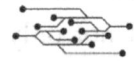

When the time comes to leave Manhattan, Dare and Keating accompany my team to our jet, but Holbrook doesn't bother, which I'm thankful for.

"Now then," Keating begins, addressing everyone as we stand on the tarmac. "Best advice I can give is don't die and don't do anything stupid."

I look at Kohler pointedly.

"I'll be in touch, so don't hesitate to ask for any sort of assistance should you need it. But all tracking and monitoring will be intra-team only, which you can blame Kai for. Now get excited! You're off to save the world!"

"We're thrilled," I respond dully.

"That's the spirit. All right, off with you."

Dare touches my arm as I'm about to board the jet. "If you need anything, let me know," he says quietly, giving me a look that I don't understand.

But whatever he means, it's always good to have another ally. A powerful and rich one at that.

I nod once and climb the steps into the cabin.

Our travels to Calgary are spent mostly in silence until we reach our penthouse, a modern and spacious place that has everything we could ever need. Enough bedrooms for all five of us, a tech room equipped to handle Q's endeavors, fresh food in the kitchen, Wi-Fi and holovision, clothes, toiletries, first-aid materials, and a locker with extra weapons.

As I gaze out the glass walls at the city, I realize how starkly different Calgary is from New York. Manhattan is a place of stacked buildings and neon lights and endless haze, where your wealth is measured by your body embellishments and whether or not you live up high enough to see the sun. They've built the superways—elevated trains that weave through and between buildings—just for the people who live in the above. And the farther out you go, into the other boroughs, the more you'll feel like you're in a wasteland.

Other than a handful of wildfires, Calgary has seemingly escaped most of the environmental catastrophes and pollution that other places have been plagued by, either by luck or by mitigation strategies developed long ago. It's a haven, really. A side of the planet I've never known.

Q calls a meeting shortly after our arrival so we can review the details of our plan for Devil's Peak. Tomorrow, Harley will fly in as Lucien Haddad's replacement psychiatrist. From there, it's up to her to learn the inner workings of Devil's Peak, then render Lucien unconscious after a few days. The rest of us just have to go and get them out after Medina calls the warden.

As we sit around the kitchen table, my attention is caught by the HV in our living area. An American newscast is just starting, the announcer beginning with "breaking news" as usual.

The first story covers a record-breaking spring heatwave in the southwest of the country, which has caused power grids to fail in some areas. People are dying. And in the places that do have power, businesses have shuttered because they can't afford the air conditioning. They roll footage of people and animals struggling to survive, and end with a clip of California's governor avoiding the press, receding into his mansion.

The second story centers on police violence occurring across the nation as people protest a variety of issues, including police violence itself. They slew together countless shots of citizens getting shot, beaten, and gassed, then cut to the president claiming that the police are just doing their job of instilling order.

Officials used to conceal those types of messages within kinder words like "safety" and "protection," but the more people rise up, the more the benevolent facade crumbles. The days of balancing freedom with law and order are over.

The newscast continues relaying disaster after disaster, tragedy after tragedy, painting a picture of a government that's turning its back on its people. War and global power and the comfort of the elite appear to outweigh the alleviation of our own citizens' suffering.

Regardless of how accurate that portrayal is, it's undeniably powerful. Powerful enough to create a revolution.

And the US isn't the only country heading in this direction, by any means.

According to the GUARD, Delta may have a lot to do with it. They're influencing governments and inducing chaos, aiming to exacerbate oppression and poverty to push the world to a breaking point. To make governments vulnerable to a power grab.

People will want radical change and they'll want it fast, leaving Delta an opportunity to swoop in as the saving grace everyone thinks we need.

SEVENTEEN
HARLEY

Q escorts me to Devil's Peak, ensuring I know what to expect as Lucien's analyst, but I mostly zone him out. I gaze solemnly out the helicopter window as mountains grow taller beneath us, the terrain morphing from hills of green grass into untouched wilderness blanketed with snow.

If I weren't headed to a prison for the second time in my life, I'd certainly appreciate this beautiful scenery that has become so rare. Instead, I'm gripping my arm so hard that my nails almost draw blood.

"Look," Q breathes. At first I don't see anything, but then I catch sight of the top of a massive black building nestled into the side of a towering mountain, only sticking up a few stories. According to Q, the exterior is normally equipped with reflectors to make it invisible, but they've retracted the panels for our arrival.

Just based on its external appearance, Devil's Peak is an eerie place. Unforgiving. And I'm preparing myself for something much darker than the so-called correctional center I was thrown into the first time. The sight of the place triggers a deep unease, and I find myself worrying that I'm not ready, wondering why I was even chosen for any of this in the first place. Currently, the entire Delta Mission is resting on my shoulders.

But all I have to do is put on an act and not give anything away. *Not so hard.* I can act. I've been doing it my whole life.

On the other hand, Lucien Haddad is suddenly going to drop dead for no reason. If that doesn't look suspicious, then I don't know what would.

"Q. Can you access their prisoner database?"

"Sure. Why?"

"I think you should change Lucien's health file to show that he has a family history of heart issues."

Q looks at me for a second, then nods. "Probably better than having no explanation whatsoever."

When I don't say anything, he gives me a concerned look. "You all right, Stone?"

"Yeah, I'm fine."

"Good. Keep us updated via text. If anything goes wrong..."

We're fucked, is what I think to myself. "If anything goes wrong, you all are miles away so I'll figure it out. I promise."

Q nods, as though he genuinely believes in me. "Medina and I didn't select you for nothing."

The warden, a grim-looking man in his fifties, is the one who greets me when I arrive. After shaking hands, we immediately head down a stairwell to the top floor, on account of the freezing wind whipping across the prison roof.

The interior of the building is a metal maze, with innumerable corridors and rooms. The chief says nothing of much importance, other than that he hopes that I'll "have luck" with Lucien. But he doesn't seem to expect that I'll succeed. His tone makes it obvious that he's wary of Lucien, unsure what to do with him.

I am introduced to a woman whose job is unclear, and after confirming my fingerprints and retinal scan, she takes me down a few levels to where the living quarters are. My apartment has a tiny kitchen, a tiny bathroom, a bed, plus a chair, holovision, desk, and computer. The decor is as depressing as the rest of the place. It amazes me that people willingly live here, sometimes year-round in the case of Lucien's former analyst, who was one of the few not on rotation.

But maybe they wouldn't let him leave.

"There should be everything you need," the woman says, but she's far from friendly. She hands me a metal ID badge and a phone-like device. "You will be reached using this. All the information about our protocols and your assigned prisoner is on your tablet, but if you have any questions, don't hesitate to ask. We would like you to meet with 481 later today at four."

"Are there any places I don't have access to?" I ask before she can depart.

"A few. You'll know."

With that, she leaves me alone. So I decide to wander to find these forbidden places. I doubt many Field agents of the GUARD have ever been in Devil's Peak; it couldn't hurt to see what really goes on here.

I pass a gym, a grim food court with a bar, and various offices before I find an elevator again. While I see a few people mingling here and there, the prison feels mostly deserted, a vast and cold place of sheer suffering.

In the elevator, I find that all the buttons are labeled except for the last one. I press it first out of curiosity, because I don't think that floor was on Q's hologram, but I'm asked for retinal authorization which gets denied. I sigh and decide on the penultimate level, the last floor of cells.

It's a strange feeling, riding deeper into the mountain, closer and closer to the world's most dangerous criminals.

When I step out of the elevator, two robotic guards check my ID but don't speak. With a quick sweep of my eyes I see more guards, dressed in all black, stationed at intervals or patrolling. None even glance at me.

Down here, the hallways are wide, lined with cells, and the ceilings are high. The cells themselves are relatively spacious, with thick glass from floor to ceiling. No privacy, in other words. And above each one is a nameplate, which means I might be able to find Lucien.

But the more people I see, the more unease creeps down my spine, and the more I want to get the hell out of here.

One woman sits motionless in her underwear in the middle of her cell, her hands wrapped heavily, scratches covering her body. As if she tried to claw herself to death. Another haggard man, wrists shackled together, appears to be attempting to dig a hole in the floor with his bloody fingers. It's almost more alarming to see others staring at nothing, as though they are somewhere other than reality. Whether it's due to drugs or psychological degradation or both, I'm not yet sure.

At the end of the first stretch of cells are two unmarked doors with authentication scanners mounted on the wall. I try to gain access, with no luck. But I can faintly hear what sounds like sobbing, and shudder at the flashback it elicits from the depths of my memory.

I force myself to continue on to maintain appearances, and eventually happen upon Lucien's cell.

At first sight, he's nothing like the other prisoners, because he doesn't seem on the verge of death. He's reading a book, as though enjoying a pleasant day in the park, as though his life weren't draining away. When he looks up and sees me standing in front of his cell, he smiles in a manner that makes my skin crawl. There's something about his eyes, too, something very alive and dangerous within them.

He's certainly not the most unhinged one here, but he may very well be the most insane.

He puts his book down and walks to the glass, standing directly in front of me. He looks to be of Arab descent, tall and skinny, but not gangly. I am immediately intimidated, and I'm pretty sure he knows it. I can see why he's been unbreakable.

"And who might you be?" he asks, his voice seductive and calm. I can clearly hear every word he says, despite the barrier separating us. The guard standing a few feet away from me doesn't even look in our direction.

"Your new analyst."

He's surprised at that.

"Interesting," he murmurs with evident curiosity. "One of the only people younger than me to ever step foot in this building. Assigned to be my interrogator." He studies me and I just stare back at him. "What's your name?"

"Harley Stone."

"Pleasure to meet you, Harley Stone."

"You're not as fucked up as the rest of these people."

He laughs. "That's why you're here, isn't it?"

"Surely they've tortured you."

"Oh, they've tried," he responds lightly. "Psychologically. Physically. It's painful. But they can never get what they want from me."

"Why do you resist?"

"They mistake my resistance as loyalty to Delta, but that's far from the truth. It's because once they get what they need, they'll be able to do far worse things to me. They won't need my sanity."

"What do you mean?"

He looks me dead in the eye. "You must know what goes on in here. They don't just use drugs to get information. They're *researching*. Otherwise they'd just kill us."

I shoot a glance at the guard again. I should've read the fine print of the protocols before talking to Lucien out of session.

"I don't know much, surely," Lucien continues. "I just know that people go into the chambers and are never the same again. Don't feel bad, though. They're in here for a reason."

I stare at him for a moment before deciding that I shouldn't trust anything he says.

"I'll see you later today." I walk away before he can say more, with a feeling that he's trying to scare me. But I can't help but believe him.

The GUARD isn't one to waste resources.

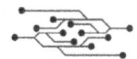

Back in my room, I skim the records of the "treatments" that Lucien's previous psychiatrist had subjected him to, getting sucked into a vortex of disturbing details.

At this point, they've tried just about everything. In the beginning, it was drowning him, shocking him, shocking him while drowning him. Breaking bones, cutting off his pinkie. Beating him senseless to coerce him into caving.

But he never did. So they moved on to other methods.

For each interrogation, they've been injecting compounds that foster loquacity, amplify his susceptibility to fear and suggestions, and slow his brain functioning enough to weaken his deceptive skills. Like a watered-down version of mind control. And, of course, they didn't stop there. They've been giving him compounds *in between* interrogations, inducing hallucinations, paranoia, insomnia, emotional vulnerability, and even amnesia so he might not even remember the last examination.

Yet he endures.

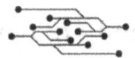

"You don't strike me as a traditional analyst," Lucien says as he sits across a metal table from me. We are in a small room with cameras and no windows, and he is shackled to a chair that is bolted to the floor. He seems a little sedate, but other than that, he's outwardly not much different than before.

"Perhaps that's why they chose me." I remind myself of Q's advice—remain calm, patient, but stern.

"Perhaps. Or perhaps because you're pretty."

I don't let my expression change. "If that's all you think I am, then you're sadly mistaken."

"Oh, no no. I know there's much more to you than what meets the eye."

"Regardless, we're here to talk about you."

"Suit yourself. You won't like what you find."

"You're in here for a reason right?" I echo. He smirks at that.

"Indeed… So, Miss Stone, what would you like to know?"

"Is it too obvious to start with your upbringing?"

"Have you read my file?"

"Sure, but I want to hear it from you. To better understand your emotions about it. And to see if the details match up to what you claimed the first time."

He smiles at me. A sinister, cold smile. It triggers an uncomfortable feeling in the back of my neck. "I am a good liar, actually."

"Is that the only thing you've done since you've been here? Lie?"

"Pretty much. But I haven't lied to you yet."

So you say. "What were your parents like?"

"Abusive," he says shortly. "Well, only my father was."

"There's one thing we can bond over," I mutter. Then I curse myself for breaking character.

"It's strange, though—I think I have him to thank for my ability to withstand what they do to me in here. There's not much worse than being hurt over and over by someone who's supposed to love you."

For a few seconds I can only nod, not trusting my voice not to break if I were to speak. Then I take a breath. "Are your parents alive?"

"My father is, unfortunately. My mom died when I was fifteen."

"When did you start working for Delta?"

He almost responds, but then he catches himself and smiles again. "You're clever. Trying to get me to answer when I'm not even really thinking about it."

"Had to give it a shot. All right. Back to your family. What happened to your mother?"

"Would prefer not to discuss that."

"This is going to be much easier if you share things with me, Lucien."

"I'll take the harder path, then." His face darkens. "I see her daily, anyway."

"Your mother?"

"Yes." His voice is but a whisper. "Hallucinations."

"I'm sorry."

"I doubt that," he hisses with a sudden ferocity. But he immediately collects himself.

"Any siblings?" I continue, ignoring his outburst, deciding it best to deal with his dead mother later.

"Five."

"Five? When was the last time you saw them?"

"When I was fifteen. Up and left after my mom's death. They all hated me anyway."

"Where did you go?"

His head straightens. "Anywhere I could find work." But I don't think that's true. I don't think he wants me to know where he went.

"Lie." His eyebrows go up.

"How are you so sure?"

I shrug. "Subtle cues." I look him in the eye. "Unlike your last analyst, I won't tolerate you wasting my time with bullshit."

When he doesn't respond, I get up to leave. "We'll resume in a few days," I say as I walk out the door.

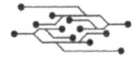

It's not long before the warden questions me about the session.

"I'm impressed," he says as I sit in his office. His desk has a few neatly placed items, including a tablet with Lucien's profile pulled up. "Haddad usually endeavors to mess with people. Get in their heads. But not with you."

"I didn't get any important information out of him, sir."

He purses his lips. "That's not entirely true. We had no idea he was hallucinating his mother. You'll get more, I'm sure of it. He seemed to... *like* you."

I'm not sure if I'm comfortable with that. But I can't deny that something about him intrigues me in return.

Over the next few days, I make my way through the entire building, but fail to find anything interesting that I have access to. I just slip farther and farther into an ocean of anxiety, trapped in this hellhole. I know they're watching me, but no one asks questions and I don't talk to anyone anyway.

Then I make the mistake of visiting Lucien in his cell the night before we are supposed to break him out. It's the middle of the night and he's wide awake, but this time his cool masquerade has vanished. He still smiles when he sees me.

"Ah, Harley," he exhales. "You know what I've come to accept? I'm going to die in this place. But not on my terms. On theirs. I'm going to waste away into a deranged, purposeless collection of blood and bones because every time I try to end it all, they stop me. That in itself is a form of torture."

I stare at him.

And somewhere in him, in that moment, I recognize myself. I nearly wince.

Suicide was once the only means of gaining control over my life that I could imagine. To have even that taken away must be something verging on true hopelessness.

"Have you ever killed someone?" he asks abruptly, before I can bring myself to respond.

"Have you?"

"Not without reason."

"Anything can be said to be a reason."

He is about to reply, but he falters. Like there was a glitch in his code.

There is no warning before his irises shrink and he is shrieking at me, telling me—or himself, rather—that he *has* to give in to "them." He has to give in, or they'll never let him die.

I don't know what to do so I just watch. I watch him unravel.

EIGHTEEN
KAI

It's rather uneventful while Harley is gone, other than receiving her intel about experiments of some sort being performed at Devil's Peak. It doesn't really surprise me, but I'm curious to know what they're doing and why. Could it be a weapon?

Q is unconcerned when I ask him about it—but not even he knows all of what goes on. It's mostly within the warden's domain, and the only person with more power over the prison than him is Medina, who I doubt would be heavily involved. So we don't know much. Harley believes there are inmates suffering quite severely from it, which I know makes her uncomfortable. It's one thing to kill someone, but it's another to torture him for research.

A few hours before we need to leave to pick her up, Reiya calls me. I lock myself in my room to avoid Kohler's eavesdropping ears, assuming she has an update on Rosalie Brenner.

"So... our mother is still alive," she begins, sighing.

My breath catches, and I have to process her sentence for several seconds. That's about the last thing I expected her to be calling about.

"What? You know where she is?" I respond slowly.

"Yeah. A hospital called me. Apparently she has stage four cancer and could drop dead at any moment, not to mention the fact that her brain is fried from years of drug abuse. But she still was able to utter my name when they asked her if she had any family."

"And she thinks that you'd come and see her or something? That's ridiculous. She probably wouldn't even recognize either of us. She always cared more about getting high."

"She never was able to get the help she needed."

"I don't know that she tried."

"Do you... Do you think I should go see her?"

"Do you want to?"

"I don't know... she's still our mother."

"Is she, Rei? I certainly don't think of her that way. I'm not sure I ever did."

"Yeah. I don't know if I could handle visiting her," Reiya says quietly. "But I suppose don't want her last breath to be one of regret. No one should be alone when they die."

"She made her choices. You shouldn't have to feel bad about things you couldn't control, right?"

"I know. But I think it would also give me closure of some kind."

In my mind, my parents are hardly even real people. They're distant, painful memories that could instead be merely a dream I had long ago. But I find myself nodding out of some semblance of understanding.

"Okay. Then you should go."

"Okay." I hear her take a breath before she changes the subject. "In other news, I've found something."

"About Dr. Brenner?"

"Yes. I've been digging nonstop and I think I've uncovered something. Just a small bit of information."

"And?"

"She's connected to some place called Devil's Peak Prison."

Christ. That's not a coincidence.

"She seems to work there," Reiya continues, "though in what capacity I couldn't tell. There are a handful of mountains around the world called Devil's Peak, but none had prisons nearby, so I don't have an actual location."

"I do."

"What?"

"My partner is there right now," I say tightly. "So whoever sent me those messages knew that one of us was going there. But they also sent them specifically to me."

"Seriously? Is there anything you can investigate?"

"Not easily. I'd have to be very calculated about it."

"Damn. All right. I'll keep digging."

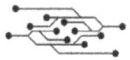

It takes quite a bit of convincing from Medina for the warden to let Lucien's "body" be taken unaltered back to Manhattan. It's evident the warden is verging on panic, if not from Lucien's fake death, then from Medina getting involved. Though I doubt he suspects that Lucien is in fact alive, maybe he has intuited that something strange is going on. But he also knows that he can't go against Medina's commands.

Upon our arrival at Devil's Peak, an expectedly uninviting place, Kohler introduces us as Medical Department agents of the Calgary Division, but the warden is too frazzled to care.

"Medina said that Miss Stone would be returning to Manhattan along with Haddad; is that true?" he says, attempting to maintain a light tone.

"She was brought here specifically for Lucien Haddad, and since he died on your watch, she'll be of better use elsewhere," Q responds coolly. "Besides, we need to conduct an internal investigation to ensure she had nothing to do with it."

The warden narrows his eyes at him. "Hm. Haddad's death was certainly a bizarre event, especially given that she got here only a few days ago. I do hope that Holbrook and his division can unveil what truly happened."

When Harley joins us, we take an elevator down to where Lucien is being kept, first stopping by his cell. Her face is unusually emotionless, numb. I want to talk to her, make sure she's all right, tell her about Dr. Brenner. But I can't until we get out of this hellhole, which is darker and creepier the farther into its depths you venture.

I find the silence of the cell levels to be especially unsettling. All the faces I see are gaunt, lifeless almost, often with unfocused eyes. It's easy to tell which are receiving better treatment than the others based on their uniform alone—some look like they haven't been taken out of their cells in years. Which ones might be research subjects, however, I can't be sure.

Perhaps it's all of them, if the injected compounds are part of it.

"Feels like we're inside a horror film," Kohler mutters as we enter Lucien's cell. It was his idea to put on a more convincing show by examining Lucien's living conditions and personal effects, though I can't say that I hadn't been curious to begin with.

He has a few strange books, a hard bed with no pillow and no blanket, and a toilet. Pretty demoralizing, but I guess he is a world-class criminal. If he's still relatively well-functioning after living in these conditions, not having seen daylight for God knows how long and enduring years of torture, then he's goddamn resilient.

When we finally get to the morgue, Lucien is the only body, lying untouched on a rolling metal table, covered with a sheet. At this point, he's been unconscious only a couple hours, and in a couple more the drug's effects will fade, allowing him to return to normal.

After zipping him up in a body bag and loading him into our helicopter, the ride back is mostly void of conversation, Harley seeming a bit dazed. I know she's avoiding my eye contact, but I can't tell if it's personal or if Devil's Peak wore her down.

Kohler singlehandedly carries the unconscious Lucien from the roof of our building down to our penthouse, and I almost laugh at how strange this whole idea was. Harley retreats to her room, so Kohler and I decide to train against each other until Lucien comes back from the dead.

I find that he's stronger than I am, but not as clever when it comes to hand-to-hand combat. I also find that he's almost certifiably psychopathic. We're almost an hour into our session when he asks, "What's been your most satisfying kill?"

I stop and stare at him for a moment, trying not to believe those words left his mouth. The guy has absolutely no boundaries. "Are you serious?"

"You can't deny that some are more enjoyable than others."

"None of it is enjoyable," I reply curtly, though I'm ashamed that I know what he's talking about.

"I don't believe that you feel that way. No sense in pretending; we're all going to hell," he urges.

I don't respond.

"Here, I'll go first." His eyes get a little wild as he resets himself to tell his story. "I was attending a gala, naturally. Casually I walk up beside one of the only men at the event with no woman at his side, and comment on this fact. He turns, looks me up and down, a little annoyed but also a little intrigued. He was probably twelve or so years my senior, perhaps more, I'm not entirely sure. At first he was wary, as he should have been, but you know how charming I can be, right? I captured his interest."

I feel like I know where this is going, but for whatever reason I let him continue.

"My sexuality is very fluid, so I just go with whatever I feel like. This was one of those moments. He took me back to his hotel room, and I'll tell you, Kai, that man was kinky as all hell. I was pleasantly surprised, actually. I'll keep the details to myself, but long story short, I was on top of him, choking him a bit. It turned into strangling and soon enough he was dead beneath me."

"Jesus."

"I liked that one for its effortlessness. Second place would probably be my first kill due to the liberation of exacting revenge on my tormenter."

"It was off the job, then? Your first kill?"

"Indeed. Something tells me yours was too."

I raise my eyebrows. "Meaning?

He observes me for a moment. "You seem like you've been acquainted with death for a long time."

My mouth opens to deny it, but the truth of it kills my words.

I first encountered death when I found my father with a hole in his head. And again when I accidentally killed a boy at my group home because I couldn't control my anger. And every time I've pulled a trigger since.

In the silence, Kohler eventually looks away. "Well, if it's any comfort, I doubt either of us are as fucked up as the criminal we just released."

"I think you'll give him a run for his money, Kohler." We both turn around to see Harley leaning against the doorway to the home gym.

Kohler gives her a look.

"He's unstable, admittedly," she continues, "but I think we can make him give us what we want. Why don't we go talk to him and see what we can find out?"

NINETEEN

Lucien sits with a blanket draped over him, straight-backed yet dazed, in the exact middle of one of our couches. He's still a bit pallid, like he truly has risen from the grave but could fall dead again at any moment. Harley and Kohler sit across a coffee table from him on another couch, while Q and I stand behind them. I search in Lucien's expression, his body language, for a glimpse of anxiety, but fail.

He is, of course, extremely confused, though not nearly as alarmed as I had anticipated. My first impression of him is that he is complex and intelligent, but not unbreakable despite his current facade. His eyes meet each of ours, no one speaking a word.

It's Harley who utters the first sentence. "How do you feel?" she asks tentatively.

"Horrible," he responds bluntly. "What, exactly, have you done to me?" He has a barely perceptible Arabic accent, a voice that is an odd mixture of rough and smooth.

"We made you appear dead in order to kidnap you," Kohler says.

Lucien laughs humorlessly. His gaze shifts to Harley, and I notice something like fascination in his eyes. "I detected something off about you, but never in a million years would I have seen this coming. Who the hell are you people?"

"GUARD agents," Q responds, folding his arms.

"Let me guess. Your little cohorts at Devil's Peak couldn't get anything out of me, so now you're here to take over."

"Essentially."

"Medina's idea?"

"Partly."

"Delta must be on the move. And now the GUARD is scrambling to save the world."

Kohler leans forward, resting his elbows on his knees. It's a gesture that suggests that his tone is about to grow more serious, perhaps to issue a threat, but Lucien looks at him as though he's irrelevant.

"Here's how this is going to work," Kohler says. "You either help us, or we kill you."

"Then I suggest you kill me now." Lucien smiles pleasantly, but there is no warmth in his face.

"What do you have to lose?" Harley cuts in, giving Kohler no chance to respond. We both know he isn't going to be the one to persuade Lucien. "We're not going to fuck with your brain. We won't even hurt you unless we have to. You'll have food and clothes and a roof over your head."

"I don't want to live as a pawn to GUARD agents. You were the ones who captured me and destroyed my life, my mind, my body. And after you're done with me you'll just execute me anyway."

"We're all pawns of the GUARD," I say. He looks up at me, seemingly caught off-guard by my retracted silence. His eyes are piercing and wide, his gaze curious. "But you're the one who can help us prevent a lot of destruction."

"Destruction was why I joined Delta in the first place," he replies plainly, though his voice doesn't match his expression.

"Was it?" Harley questions with skepticism, and I notice that Lucien's eyebrows twitch a little. *She thinks he's lying and he knows it.*

Then his mouth morphs into a strange smile. "I suppose not. I joined because it gave me what I desperately wanted: power and control."

"When did you join?" Harley asks, taking the opportunity to coax him into sharing information.

"You probably know the answer to that."

Pause. "Around fifteen."

"Yes. Fifteen," he responds bitterly. "There was no reason for me to remain under my father's dominion after my mother died."

"Why would Delta want you?" Kohler says. "What possible reason could there be for a fifteen-year-old to join an organization like that?"

"Delta doesn't spare children. Just like the GUARD. To this day I don't know how they found me, but I'd wager that my father and his criminal empire tripped their radar. Not only did I have the radical mindset they wanted, but I also had the skills they wanted, even at that age. When he wasn't beating the shit out of me, my father was teaching me everything he knew—how to hack, how to launder money, how to manipulate people, how to dig up information. It was free labor from someone he thought wouldn't dare betray him. And after I joined, I amassed more and more technical competency from Delta's experts and rigorous self-teaching. By the time I was nineteen, I was almost at the top."

"And what did you do, exactly?" Q asks, glancing at me with a frown. Lucien looks up at him, then at me, hesitating for a couple seconds, as if he's finally observing us for the first time.

"In the beginning it was very low-level tasks. Before I defected, however, I was overseeing the surveillance and tracking teams. Watching and following anyone who's someone, gathering information about their bank accounts, their travels, their phone conversations, everything."

Q purses his lips. "Anything else?"

"I architected cyber weapons and programs for determining our targets and organizing subsequent assassinations."

"You let AI determine who you murdered and how?" Q asks, failing to hide his intrigue. The GUARD certainly uses artificial intelligence to gather intel and identify patterns, but final decisions are only entrusted to people.

"There was always human input and supervision, but yes. By the time I left, it was heavily guiding every decision from recruiting to political moves. There's no better way to remain logical and calculated. Those programs I designed are why Delta knows more about people than their own families do. Why they own the world."

A few beats of silence in which we all take that in.

"So how far up were you?" Q asks. "In the hierarchy."

"One step from the top. I followed the orders of the creator of Delta herself."

My eyebrows raise. "You can tell us how to find her, then," I say.

"No. I have no idea where she is, or what her real name is, or what she looks like, or even what her voice sounds like. I never gleaned an ounce of information about her."

"Great," Kohler mutters. I see Q press his lips together out of the corner of my eye.

Lucien hesitates before continuing. "I *can* give you her alias. But then I'm done. Kill me or I'll do it myself."

"No," I snap. "You don't get to escape what you've done. You help us, you stick it out until the end."

"Listen," Q says calmly. "There's a lot I can offer you in exchange for your help. I can wipe you from existence, give you whatever the hell you want. No one will have to know anything. The five of us are some of the last people standing in between Delta and its global domination. The world will crumble and people will die in the process."

"I understand that," Lucien responds, bitter. "I know what they're going to do. I know better than almost anyone. If they succeed, tyranny will reign. While I hate the GUARD, I came to hate Delta more." His eyes shift to me. "So you misunderstand why I want to die. The truth is, I don't trust myself, and neither should you. Your friends *damaged* me. I'm not always in control of my own mind and I don't know if I want to live with that."

"We *don't* trust you," Kohler replies sourly.

"We have to take whatever risk you may present," I say. "Whether we're risking you killing us or you killing yourself, we have to take it. This is bigger than any of us. It doesn't matter if you're suffering because you're the best chance we have."

Lucien looks to Harley and I see her nod slightly. "You can help us end it," she says, insistent yet gentle.

We hover in silence.

Then, "Fine." Four exhales of relief.

Harley nods again. "Why don't we start fresh tomorrow? The bedroom at the end of the hall on the right is yours." The finality of her tone prevents the rest of us from questioning Lucien further.

"You trust me to be left alone?" Lucien responds softly.

"You're not a prisoner anymore."

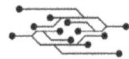

That night I lie awake in my room for about two hours, unable to even close my eyes, my thoughts wandering from Lucien to Harley to Reiya. My life has begun to loom over my mind like an unpredictable and relentless storm—romance and family and saving the world are not things I'm accustomed to. I'm grateful when my sister sends me a message, giving me something to break me out of the prison of my head.

I think Brenner may be related to someone named Elsa Salazar. There are rumors about genetic research Salazar was a part of about four decades ago. I'm gonna hunt down family members and Cam is going to see what data the GUARD might have.

"Who?" I whisper. I grab my tablet off my nightstand, and with a bit of digging I find what Reiya is talking about. According to a few different sites, Dr. Elsa Salazar worked for the US government to develop some sort of genetically enhanced soldiers. Humans with abilities just like in the movies. The stranger part is that she and all her subjects disappeared, never to be seen again. She managed to destroy all the laboratories and data, and no one has since been able to recreate her achievements. Whatever they were.

I don't believe much of it. Sure, I believe Elsa Salazar existed and that she may have been performing experiments, but there isn't much solid information about her. Still, her story is perhaps relevant to Rosalie Brenner. Perhaps Brenner was inspired by Salazar, or is even attempting to recreate these superhumans.

Seems relevant, I respond. *Let me know if you find out anything else.*

Finally accepting that it's useless to keep lying in bed, I leave my room, in search of something else to occupy myself with. Sure enough, I see Harley standing out on our balcony in the darkness, gazing out at the city below.

"We sure don't get views like this underground, do we?" I say as I open the glass door to the balcony. A cool breeze greets me, raising goosebumps on my skin.

"My life may be in grave danger, but I'm certainly glad to be living above ground again," she responds, turning to face me as I join her at the railing. I struggle to read her expression.

"What's keeping you awake?"

"I don't know... Devil's Peak, maybe. The more I've thought about what they're doing to people in there, the scarier it is. I didn't even witness the worst of it."

"It's disturbing, to say the least. But we all knew going into this that they torture people there, right?"

She shakes her head. "These people aren't just being tortured," she replies, and there's a hint of anger in her voice. "They're being reduced to something less than human. It makes me wonder if we're any better than them."

"We aren't the ones doing it."

She rolls her eyes. "You're right. We just kill people instead. For the organization that *is* doing it."

"Now's not the best time for a moral dilemma," I respond, unable to prevent the ice in my voice even though I agree with her point. Before she left for Devil's Peak, we decided to put a pause on our... *fling,* and I'd be lying if I said it wasn't affecting me. But we'd gotten intimate too fast, and we both eventually agreed that our jobs were more important.

Emphasis on *eventually.*

I was stubborn at first, angry that she initiated things only to backtrack a little later. I knew those emotions were irrational, considering how hesitant I was from the beginning, but I guess a part of me still yearned for more. It got a bit heated, and of course, I lashed out and uttered a few insults that I regret.

I can't help but look away as I'm reminded.

"Maybe you can live your life ignoring everything that's wrong," she says quietly, "but I can't. Some of those people in there are in the same situation I was as a child—trapped in a cycle of mistreatment. And just like me, they've almost lost the will to live. The only difference is that they've been numbed by so many drugs that they can't feel the rage that I did."

That hits me like a brick.

"You didn't deserve what you went through. They're different. They've tried to hurt people in ways that we can't even imagine."

"I know that. I'm not defending them; I'm just saying that at some point, someone should stop this endless cycle of pain and dehumanization."

She's not looking at me, instead staring out at the neon city lights as her hair blows in the breeze, hiding her face. I nod anyway. There is about a minute of silence in which I'm torn on how to mend whatever rift has risen between us. But I find it easier to distract us both with more pressing matters.

"I've... got some information that could possibly be connected to this research Lucien told you about."

Harley looks up at me suddenly, scowling a bit. "Seriously?"

I nod. "A little while ago I received messages warning me about someone named Rosalie Brenner. I don't know who they were from, but I decided to investigate with the help of Camden and my sister."

"Your sister?" Harley repeats, eyebrows raised. I can tell there are several points she's trying to make with that question.

"I know. It's dangerous. Hell, I wish Dare's AI could do all of this, but that poses its own risks. I didn't know what I was getting into, so I wanted to keep whatever I discovered away from the GUARD and away from Holbrook."

She nods. "Fair enough. So who is this person?"

"According to Reiya, Dr. Brenner works at Devil's Peak, and is related to some geneticist who led soldier enhancement research decades ago. I think it's a semi-reasonable hypothesis that Brenner could be involved in something similar."

"It's no coincidence that she works at the place we just came from."

"No. It's not."

"Do you have any idea why anyone would want you to investigate her?"

"Not really."

"So... Reiya and Camden are going to keep searching, and meanwhile we do... what?"

"Maybe Lucien has some information, but otherwise I think we just have to wait. Delta is a more pressing matter."

"What if she works for them?"

"Designing weapons for them or something? If she's at Devil's Peak, she's under constant surveillance."

"Not necessarily. She might be the most powerful one there."

"It's possible. Hopefully Lucien can point us in the right direction, assuming he'll actually help us."

Harley thinks for a second. "I think he will."

"Is he as damaged as he claims?"

"In all honesty, what they did to him might be irreparable. I witnessed him having some sort of psychotic break, and it was... like nothing I've ever seen. But now that he's not under the influence of their *methods*, I do think it's manageable."

I nod. "We'll just have to look out for him."

Harley narrows her eyes, evidently not expecting that type of response. "I thought you'd hate him."

I shrug. "I think I might be okay with him."

"Really," she responds flatly.

I give her a look. "*Yes*, really. Despite the way he looks at you." Her eyebrows raise but she isn't confused about what I'm referring to. She takes a breath and looks at me, truly looks into my eyes for the first time in a while. The anger she had minutes ago has vanished, and now her gaze is unreadable, neither harsh nor affectionate.

In that moment, entranced by the purple galaxy of her irises, the distance between us is almost painful. I start to utter a half-formed apology for hurting her, but I'm interrupted by my phone buzzing.

Camden.

"Something wrong?" I answer.

"I think Holbrook is already onto me, Kai."

TWENTY

My heart skips a beat.

But in contrast to his usual demeanor, Camden is practically emotionless. Not worried, not excited. "Either that or they think I'm a Delta agent," he says. "I caught someone following me as I was about to leave HQ, but I knocked the twat unconscious and dumped him in a rubbish bin."

"Anything else happen?"

"No, but one can't be too paranoid, right?"

I exhale. This could get a lot worse. But it's the risk I took.

"We probably need to take some extra measures to protect Rei," he continues. "I know Q is helping keep her safe, but I don't know what

Holbrook knows. So I'll do everything I can, and with any luck, he'll be none the wiser."

"Okay. I'll talk to Q. Be careful, yeah?"

"We'll be fine, promise."

"I should've never—"

He cuts me off. "It's not on you. Based on what Reiya has said so far, I think whatever we find, it's going to be serious. And therefore, worth the risk."

I'm not sure I agree right now, but I hold my tongue.

"I gotta go," Camden says after a few moments of silence in which anxiety begins to flood my mind. "We miss you. Tell Stone the same."

When I hang up, Harley searches my face. "What happened?"

"Nothing."

She knows it's a lie. "Kai," she murmurs, placing her hand on my arm.

"Can we talk about it later? I'm just... tired."

"Sure."

At the brush of her thumb against my forearm, I gently pull her into a hug, closing my eyes as I breathe in the scent of her hair. God, I wish I could kiss her.

"We'll be okay," she whispers.

I'm not quite sure what she means, but I desperately want to believe that she's right.

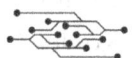

"You look dead," Kohler greets Lucien as he emerges from his room, wearing nothing but sweatpants. The rest of us are gathered around our kitchen table drinking coffee. I study him as he walks toward us, noticing a subtle limp, a missing pinkie, and scarring on his chest. His thinness and paleness suggest poor health, though I had honestly been expecting him to look more haggard than he is.

"I suppose so," he responds dully.

"You sleep at all?" Harley asks, but the atmosphere is infused with a hint of tension. We're all far from being friends with Lucien, considering he's an apparently unhinged ex-Delta leader whom we are almost holding hostage.

"Not much. If I sleep I have no control over what invades my mind. The drugs they gave me had a special way of terrorizing me in my dreams."

"I have some sleeping pills you can try, if you'd like."

Lucien eyes Harley warily. "That's generous of you."

"We need you in the best mindset."

"Right. Well, I'm quite hesitant to take any sort of drug, as I'm sure you can understand."

"Breakfast?" I offer, attempting but failing to relieve the tension.

Lucien seems to glitch for a moment, his face twisted in confusion. "I can't remember the last time I had normal food."

"They ever bribe you with special meals?" Kohler says, smirking like he's proud he hasn't landed himself in prison. But I suppose for him that *is* something to be proud of.

"Yes. It was tempting, of course."

"Maybe we should starve you until you answer all of our questions."

"Let's not be unreasonable, Kohler," Q says half-heartedly. "Lucien has agreed to cooperate."

"So he says," Kohler mutters.

"You couldn't possibly frighten me if you tried, just so you're aware," Lucien scoffs at him tiredly.

"Do I need to hide the weapons?" I say, irritated. The last thing I want is constant bickering.

"Sorry, forgot you were a stone-cold psychopath," Kohler talks over me, challenging Lucien further.

But he doesn't take the bait. "Look, I'm not trying to pick a fight. God knows you need to prove your dominance but I'm just letting you know I won't tolerate being pushed around for no reason."

"Now, now. No one's going to push you around unless necessary," Q says with a twinge of annoyance, giving Kohler a very disapproving stare. "Let's get to work, shall we? Have a seat, Lucien." He takes out a tablet to take notes.

Lucien sighs. "Where would you like to start?"

"Well, our team, Minotaur, was tasked with eliminating the top tier of Delta leaders. You informed us there's only one such individual, so consider our top priority to be getting to her."

"What can you tell us about the person at the top?" I ask.

"Well, she's known as Arachne. And she's... a ghost, essentially. She has an unknown inner circle that exists only to do her bidding, and she never communicates directly with anyone else. I tried on multiple occasions to locate her but never succeeded. She's very well hidden, and even if we did know who or where she was, I'd wager that she'd see us coming a mile away."

"Interesting," Q responds, his fingers hovering over his keyboard. "I still imagine that there's *someone* in Delta who could lead us to her or her 'inner circle.' Could you describe to us how Delta is organized? The GUARD has some idea, of course, but it would be good to have as many details as possible."

Lucien ponders for a second. "It's organized like a business, because at its core, that's really what it is. First there are assassins and spies who work with what they call researchers. Spies gather intel that researchers use as input to algorithms that amass information on everyone they deem important, in order to determine who's a threat, who's useful, and who they still need more data on. On the engineering side, there are people who maintain and design the software ecosystem, including cyber weapons that strive to penetrate the security of corporations and government entities.

"Then there are those responsible for things like political and media influence. Some are members who've snuck their way into positions of power, others shifted their alliance to us at some point in their career. Lastly, there are managers like me who are the brains behind the operation. They pull it all together and train everyone to do their jobs."

We are silent for a moment, taking all that in. Everything Lucien just said makes it very clear that Delta isn't some ragtag group of radicals. It's a highly structured and calculated syndicate.

Q is frowning, though he doesn't show any worry that we may be in way over our heads. "Can you draft a report of specific positions and the individuals who hold them?"

"Sure."

"And from where you stood, what would you say is Delta's core objective?"

"Arachne has always been secretive—vague about her true motives. She claims, however, that humanity is doomed. Plagued with inequality and inefficiency that will lead to extinction by our own doing. Delta's goal, from what I know, is to completely redesign society. They intend to come into power in every major country to create reformation on a global scale. Rid governments of the corrupt, of the people who take advantage of those with less and act with bias.

"It won't be immediate, but don't underestimate them. Arachne has succeeded in recruiting followers who have become nearly religious to her cause. People are desperate for power, and she gave that to them.

Made them feel like gods. Either that or she threatened to kill them or their families. That kind of willpower across the organization will make them onerous to fight against."

"And how do they intend to take over? From what we've gathered, it seems that they are intentionally destabilizing countries."

"Yes. I'm sure you've noticed the pattern of decisions the world's leaders have been making. Things that make a lot of people uneasy, or even angry. Much of it is indeed Delta's influence. Their insiders are reshaping governments to become more radical, more oppressive. They want citizens to revolt. They want to push countries into instability to create a clearer path for Delta to step in with their ideas. Economic and social equality for everyone, they'll say. But that'll come at the price of freedom."

"Christ," Harley mutters, running a hand across her face. "I'm not sure that we or the GUARD are equipped to stop such an immense operation."

"Maybe we should start by protecting our own agents," I respond.

"Where is the GUARD at currently, in detecting Delta's infiltration?" Lucien asks.

"We've been executing a number of suspected and confirmed traitors," Q says without emotion. "Anyone with a goddamn triangle tattoo, certainly. I completely revamped our security system so that only a few key people can bypass it, but it's impossible to really know what intel has gotten out."

"If we can find and break into one of Delta's main bases," Lucien says, "I have a decent shot at retrieving all the files they have on the GUARD, assuming they haven't also rebuilt their security from the ground up since I departed. Alternatively, I can try to do this from outside their network, but it'll take longer."

Q is about to respond, but his attention is snared by something coming across on his tablet.

His eyes widen in alarm.

"The Chicago Division is under attack."

TWENTY ONE

Within ten minutes, we've packed all our belongings and are headed for the airport in a copter.

The GUARD has intelligence that Delta is responsible, but otherwise we're blind—no one in the Chicago headquarters has been reachable since the initial moments of the attack. Medina ordered several agents from New York, the closest division, to head there immediately, but we all know the backup will be far too late.

My team is going to see what's left. We can't miss an opportunity to uncover information about Delta, even if it doesn't help us directly in our quest to identify and assassinate Delta's top tier.

"There won't be survivors," Lucien mutters darkly, gazing out the window of the copter.

Harley looks up at him. "We're not going to sit around while Delta wreaks havoc on us."

"I wouldn't expect you to, I'm just trying to prepare you."

Once aboard our jet, I dig through my duffle bag and pull out my vest, along with my Ghost pistol, Soulbarer rifle, wristband, and contacts that connect to my earpiece. I tuck the Ghost away in a holster.

"Think we can trust Haddad enough to give him a gun?" Q says quietly to me, eyeing him from across the plane.

"No, but at the same time I don't know that we should be leaving him unarmed."

Q nods. "Your call."

I contemplate for a moment before deciding that it's better if Lucien can protect himself. We all know to keep an eye on him, anyway. I move to the front of the plane where he's sitting alone seemingly out of preference. He looks at his designated handgun as I hold it out to him, then at me.

"Coded to your palm print," I say, giving him an earpiece and a cuff to explain how everything integrates.

"Thank you" is all he says, appearing rather dazed.

I gesture with my head for Harley and Kohler to join us. "Right, so… they may be watching for us, but with any luck wiping out the cameras within a two-block radius will keep us safe. Let's get inside the headquarters quickly, where Q can surpass the security. Once we're in, well, I guess we'll just have to see what remains."

Q chooses an entrance inside a hotel, where we take an elevator down to level B4 after he scans a metal card he obtained from the front desk. I'm not sure what he said to the clerk, but she practically tripped over herself to get it for him.

"This division is laid out more like Devil's Peak—many levels," he says as we descend into the earth. "I think it's best that we separate into groups. Lucien and Harley, why don't you take the bottom levels? Kai, Kohler, you can do the top. Look for any survivors, any deceased members of Delta, and anything they may have left behind. I'm going to sync with the Manhattan agents and see if Delta stole any information or technology. Keep your earpieces on."

I'd almost forgotten about Tony, the snazzy AI designed to do my job. I tap my earpiece and the "enhanced vision," as Dare calls it, comes to life. The only thing that gives it away at first is a faint blue glow, but then I hear, "Scanning... No immediate threat."

I sling my Soulbarer over my shoulder and take out my handgun anyway.

Harley catches my eye as our descent begins to slow. "Odds?" she asks me quietly.

What's the chance we walk out alive, is what she means.

"No idea," I murmur.

When the elevator opens, there's nothing. Just a hallway that is a security checkpoint, like we have in Manhattan. We reach a metal door, and I listen for any muffled sounds emanating from behind it, but there is only silence. No gunfire, no screaming. Q disables the security with his tablet and the entrance slides open.

The first thing I see is red.

Blood. Blood everywhere.

I can smell it, too.

Then I see the countless bodies.

We are all frozen for a few moments before stepping through the door and into a dimly lit community center of sorts. I scan the wide room but there is no sign of any living being.

"How many dead, Tony?" Harley asks quietly.

We wait for a few moments as the AI searches the division's RGB-thermal cameras, performing person detection to identify bodies and using heat signatures to separate the living from the dead. "Four hundred eighty-one. No survivors detected."

"Tony, see which members of the Chicago Division appear to be traveling and arrange for their transfer to Denver," Q says.

"Look," Lucien says, pointing toward a ring of bodies, which chairs and tables have been shoved aside to make room for. We approach the display to find three different items placed in the middle of the circle: an apple with a knife through it, a smashed analog clock, and some shriveled cherries with dead flower petals around them.

"How artsy," Kohler mutters.

"What is this?" Harley says.

"A warning," I hypothesize. "I think they're telling us what divisions they're going to strike next. New York, London, Tokyo. The big three." Four heads turn to look at me.

"Why would they tell us that?" Kohler asks.

"Because they want something," Lucien says.

"Let's do a run-through of this place, quickly, then we'll call Medina as soon as we're out," Q says, calm. "We'll discuss this then."

The five of us part, Lucien and Harley taking an elevator down to the bottom level to work their way up, Kohler and I heading to a stairwell to work our way down. I request a hologram of the division, which projects from my cuff, to determine the best route through the levels.

We start on the next floor below, a floor of apartments, by examining a few bodies to determine a cause of death.

I kneel to get a better look at the wounds and blood spatter. "Bullet wounds, close range. Handgun, I think. Probably GUARD weapons."

"What does the AI think?" Kohler says.

"Agent Thanatos's analysis is correct," Tony replies, to which I roll my eyes. Thank God he's here to tell me I'm right.

I gesture at the walls. "This was a very well-planned and coordinated attack, clearly. Not many holes. Each person was killed with a couple of bullets."

"I'll admit I admire their finesse," Kohler responds. "But that probably means we're not going to find much anywhere."

We continue on and search almost every apartment on the floor, finding most of the doors already kicked in. There's nothing of any relevance, just dead agents and the things they left behind. Pictures of friends, cherished trinkets. We even find two people holding each other on the ground.

It's heartbreaking, really.

I imagine a stranger—though not so much a stranger because he knows the life I lived—walking into my room to find me lying cold with a bullet in my skull. He steps over my body and takes a look at the few photos I have. Perhaps he wonders what I was like, and makes a guess that I was a better person than is actually the case. But then he moves on. He'll probably forget me in the span of an hour. My body will be burned and there will be nothing left to prove I ever existed.

A voice in my earpiece makes me jump.

"Possible survivor detected two levels below," Tony says.

Kohler catches my eye, then says, "Show us."

The hologram of the division reappears from my cuff, along with a marker and two highlighted paths to get there.

"Don't kill them," I warn. "Might be one of us."

"Yes, captain," Kohler responds dryly.

In the eerie silence, we descend the concrete stairwell once more, pistols in hand. Opening a door to the designated level reveals two perpendicular hallways, lined with more death that I'll never unsee. Kohler gestures to indicate that he'll take route to the left, and for me to take the one straight ahead.

The corridor seems to stretch farther into the beyond as I make my way toward the target, clearing each open apartment with a glance as I pass, accompanied only by my own breathing.

Until someone stumbles into view.

"Don't. Move," I command, my voice echoing harshly.

He flinches and whirls, and that's when I see that his fist is clenched around the handle of a gun. Bullets are flying at me in an instant. My instincts kick in before my brain processes, and I dash into the nearest apartment for cover.

"Fuck," I hiss, back against a wall. "Where you at, Kohler?"

"Don't you worry," he replies.

I hear a yelp and the hail relents, followed by the clatter of a gun falling to the ground. Peering around a door frame, I see that Kohler has a thirty-something man in a lock. One arm wrapped around his neck, the other pinning an arm against his back. There is blood covering one side of the man's face and body, staining his lips, his shirt, his hands.

I approach and raise my Ghost, pointing it at his head, prompting a smile from Kohler.

"Who... who are you?" he asks as his eyes meet mine, his voice trembling.

"Who are *you*?" Kohler responds, accusatory. "You murder a bunch of people?"

"Tony, who is he?" I say.

"Ryan Colson. The GUARD has nothing on him that may suggest he is a Delta agent."

"I'm no traitor," Colson says weakly, eyeing my gun, which is still only about a foot away from his head. I give him a look to tell him I'm not putting it down.

"What did you see?" I urge. "What happened?"

"I don't know, I swear," he splutters. "It all happened so fast. Gunfire and screaming in all directions."

"How did you survive?"

"I played dead underneath someone's body. All I could see was people running and dying."

I exhale in frustration.

"Ah, they missed one," Q says in my earpiece. I hear a few people in the background—Manhattan agents, I suspect. "Bring the man upstairs, will you, Kohler? We need to get him medical attention before we interrogate him. Kai, head down to the pool—Harley and Lucien found something rather interesting."

I catch a look of disappointment, annoyance almost, pass across Kohler's face before he heads toward an elevator with Colson in tow.

"Any updates from your side?" I ask Q.

"Well, the Chicago agents did their job. Someone was quick enough and smart enough to throw the system into lockdown mode, making it impossible for Delta to break in and steal information in a timely manner, since the only people who can bring the system out of that mode are T&W and division leaders.

"I checked what had been accessed right before they locked everything down, and saw only a couple of unsuccessful attempts at our files on classified weapons and top agents. However, before the whole thing began, someone shut down all the cameras in the building, so we won't be able to see what actually occurred. Tony had to re-enable them when Harley asked for the body count. But I'm still going to search the street cameras above to see who might have entered or exited the compound."

"They're too clean. Feels like we're chasing a ghost."

"Ghosts can still leave trails, Thanatos, don't give up yet. Now go meet Harley and Lucien, then clear out the rest of the place. I've just updated the security so that only a handful of people can access this division, and it goes live in an hour, so finish up before then."

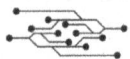

A shirtless Lucien Haddad emerges from the depths of a pool that's tinged red from blood, lugging a body that he brings toward the edge where Harley stands.

"Uh…" I say.

Harley turns and looks me up and down. "You found a survivor?"

"Almost got killed by one, is more accurate. What's going on here?"

"There are about a dozen bodies in there," she responds. "Pretty sure they're Delta. Lucien thought it was odd that they were fully clothed, *and* there are bullet wounds in the sides of their heads, which suggests a mass suicide after finishing whatever happened above. Our hypothesis is that they could be the double agents that were stationed here."

"Interesting. No loose ends, I guess. But surely they didn't pull this attack off on their own."

"I suspect that they had help," she says. "While Delta couldn't risk letting the double agents walk out of here in case we'd track them, others likely disappeared after the job was done."

I go over and help her drag the person out of the water, laying him next to a few others who've been unclothed. Sure enough, there is a triangle tattooed on one's chest.

Kohler enters and is instantly surprised by the situation, exchanging eye contact with me. Upon seeing him, Lucien dives back under.

"I bet he likes swimming in blood," Kohler mutters.

"I thought that was your kink, Kohler," I respond. "You should help him."

"No thank you. I'll let the ex-criminal handle it."

It isn't until the eighth person that we find anything. His pocket contains a scrap of paper in a thin black container, which is clearly no accident. Something left behind for us, perhaps.

Intrigued, Lucien climbs out of the pool, jerking his head to the side to toss his hair out of his eyes. Harley unfolds the paper and her eyes widen.

"Coordinates," she breathes.

"Coordinates?" I repeat.

"Coordinates."

Someone is fighting back.

TWENTY TWO

Tony fails to dig up much dirt on the Delta agents we discovered in the pool, but saves their files in case we find connections later. Though Kohler and I scour the rest of the division, it's void of anything substantial. Delta is too elegant, too smart. It's not only frustrating, but also quite chilling, because now we know they can slaughter hundreds of people and get away with it.

Q takes us to the closest safe house outside of Chicago, the entrance to which is hidden in a dilapidated abandoned building in the middle of nowhere.

Lucien, who hasn't spoken a word since we left the Chicago Division, immediately goes into hiding. I catch Harley's eye and shoot her a questioning look, and she pulls me into the nearest bedroom, shutting the door behind us.

"Something happen?" I ask.

"After you and Kohler left the pool, he had a pretty intense panic attack of some kind," she responds quietly. "They're quite fond of various forms of water torture at Devil's Peak. I think he was barely holding himself together in there, and then it hit."

"He okay?" *Dumb question.*

"I'm not sure. It was... scary." Though she doesn't provide any details, her eyes convey the severity of Lucien's suffering. "I don't know that we need to feel sorry for him, given who he is, I just think it's better if this is something we're cognizant of. There was once a time when I didn't see any way out of my pain other than death, but now I have more good days than bad days. Lucien is still very deep in the bad days.

"Rather than regarding him as a liability, I think we'll be a stronger team if we seek to understand what he's dealing with. What all of us are dealing with. We can't conquer Delta if we're battling demons of our own."

I search her eyes. "Yeah. How are *you* holding up? With... everything."

Her mouth twists. "I don't know. I feel almost... detached from reality a bit. I never expected to spend my first few months of being an agent drowning in so much death and darkness. My brother died, then I witnessed the torture of Devil's Peak, and now hundreds of agents have been slaughtered. Quite frankly I don't even know how I *should* feel."

She leans back against the bedroom wall, then slides down it until she's sitting, knees bent. I sit beside her, tentatively lacing my fingers in hers.

"I don't know either," I say quietly. "I don't know how to do what we're doing and come out okay on the other side."

She lays her head on my shoulder. "I'm sorry I ended our relationship, or whatever we're calling it. I just got too overwhelmed."

"It's okay," I murmur. "I'm sorry I was a piece of shit."

She laughs softly. "It's okay. I still like you."

"What are we now? Just friends?"

"That's all I can really be right now. But you and I both know we'll never truly be *just* friends."

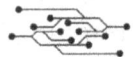

"Oh my God."

I startle at Q's worried voice that breaks the lengthy silence that had fallen over us after dinner, dropping the knife I'd been washing.

I turn around to look at him, sitting at the kitchen table with a tablet.

"Delta just sent GUARD leaders a message," he says slowly.

"What?" Kohler blurts.

Q projects his screen to display a message with an embedded video, followed by a triangle for a signature. He hesitates before expanding the video and clicking the play button.

The screen is black for a few seconds before two figures appear in front of a plain background, one who is standing, her head not in the frame, and another who is kneeling. He is looking directly into the camera, his gaze piercing.

I only get a glimpse of him before the armored woman swings a sword, beheading him in the blink of an eye.

I can't even make a noise; I just need to throw up.

The Delta logo flashes with a skull in the middle of it, then come the words *Stay tuned!* with a countdown below. Roughly thirty minutes until what I can assume will be the next message.

We are all speechless for a few moments.

"That was a GUARD agent," Q says quietly.

"Can you get any useful information out of that video?" Kohler asks as though he didn't just witness a beheading. "Traces of who might have sent it?"

"I'll get my agents on it. In the meantime, I need to connect with Holbrook and the other division leaders. You all sit tight."

The wait for the next thing to happen feels like hours. Harley wanders off toward the room where Lucien is still ensconced, while Kohler and I pace back and forth in the living room, letting Q do his thing.

"We can't negotiate with these psycho terrorists," Kohler says, half to himself and half to me.

"If we don't, we may lose a lot of agents," I respond.

"If we do, that gives them power over us."

"They already have power over us, if you haven't realized."

His eyes shift from the floor to stare at me, a bit wild. "We can't give them more than they've already got. We're too far behind as it is. They're recruiting people as fast as we can hunt them down, and if we don't end this soon, the GUARD is going to fall."

"We're not there yet, Kohler," Lucien says, appearing out of the darkness of the hallway that leads to the bedrooms. Harley is at his side.

"Oh, thanks for joining us," Kohler responds bitterly.

"Calm down," I say tiredly. "Now's not the time to harass your team."

Kohler turns on me, shooting a glare but holding his tongue.

"Did we figure out where those coordinates are?" Lucien asks as he and Harley join us in the living room. He seems a little worn, but he hides his pain well.

"Near D.C.," I reply. "Might be a base."

"Let's pray it's not a ruse," Kohler mutters.

"You should probably all come over here," Q talks over him. "The timer has run out."

Q drums his fingers, watching his tablet's holographic projection unblinkingly as the rest of us gather around him in silence. I don't dare to breathe. Harley has a firm grip on my forearm, but I don't think she even notices in her intense focus on Q's screen. I steal a glance at Lucien, who has his arms crossed, and attempt to gauge his emotions. I wonder if he already knows what's going to happen next.

And then the video comes. The same triangle with the skull appears, fading to reveal a setup very similar to last time, with only one woman visible. Another GUARD agent who's been captured—and likely tortured. She holds a handgun to her own head, and I see her shake slightly, though her face lacks fear. As if she's numb.

Her eyes drift to one side, and she starts reading something.

"Thanks for tuning in," she begins in a monotone. "What we ask from you is quite simple: surrender Adriano Medina. You have 24 hours to turn him in at the coordinates now shown on your—"

She is interrupted by a loud bang off-screen, at which she flinches uncontrollably, squeezing her eyes shut for a second. But then she continues. "On your screen. Medina must be alone, unarmed, and any tracking devices must be removed. We will kill anyone else who comes within a twenty-mile radius. If you do not comply with all of our rules, the New York, London, and Tokyo divisions will be destroyed. Any attempt at evacuation will bring this fate prematurely. Every hour that you delay, people will die."

She pulls the trigger.

Q is on the phone in a matter of seconds, yelling rapidly at people back in New York. "You fucking find these bastards *any way you can*. You hunt these people down and kill them all."

"I thought they'd want more," Kohler says quietly.

"More?" Harley says incredulously, giving a short, almost hysterical laugh. "They want Medina! He knows *everything* about the GUARD, and a lot of other things we probably can't even imagine."

"It's not like he's going to give them information willingly, Harley."

"Delta is very skilled at torture," Lucien counters. "They'll stop at nothing to get what they want out of him."

"Oh, well, you would know, wouldn't you, you spineless psychopath?"

Kohler has raised his voice and clearly intends to carry on, but I stop him. I decide to just punch him the next time around. "Kohler! Chill out. Yes, they could have asked for something worse, but Lucien is right. Don't underestimate the damage this could inflict on us."

"Don't you think they're just going to kill us all anyway? They'll probably destroy our headquarters even if we do what they want."

"Not necessarily," Lucien responds. "If they want the GUARD's cooperation, they'll stick to their word. Until they don't need you anymore. But right now, they do. They need you to give them what they need to weaken you."

"Shut up, stop arguing," Q hisses, and we all turn to find he's brought up a video call with four squares making up the projection. Medina, Holbrook, Kimura from the Tokyo Division, and Byrne from the London Division.

"Evening," Medina says shortly. He maintains an aura of calm even now, when he's been asked to surrender himself. "We have no time to waste. Before any of you begin debating, I think we need to do as they ask. We cannot afford the loss of almost two thousand agents."

"Sir, how do we know it's not an empty threat?" Kimura asks.

"They took out Chicago in a matter of minutes. I sincerely doubt their threat is empty. It'd be a mistake to underestimate them."

"You really think playing their game is the best move?" Byrne says, but Holbrook remains silent, frowning, scowling.

"I think it's the only move," Medina replies gravely. "Until we gain the upper hand."

No pressure.

"We might be able to carry out a rescue operation, at least," Kimura suggests.

"And siphon resources in the process?" Medina says. "It's not worth the risk."

"Handing you over also might not be worth the risk, sir," Byrne cautions.

But Medina shakes his head. "Better to lose me than the people actually stopping these terrorists."

I catch Byrne press his lips together, but eventually he nods, and Medina continues.

"Holbrook, I want you to take over my position. Keating can assume your role."

Holbrook shows some surprise at that. "Yes sir."

I cringe, but then remember I'm on camera and relax my face again. I wish Medina had chosen basically anyone else, though I'm relieved that Keating will be leading the Manhattan Division, as he'll be the one with more direct power over my life.

"I'll meet with you first to devise your next steps. Minotaur, your objective remains unchanged. Any questions?"

I feel like there are a lot of questions I could be asking, but I don't utter a word, and neither does anyone else. Medina has quite clearly made up his mind.

"All right. Good luck, everyone. I have no doubt that you'll succeed. Medina out."

"*Fuck*," Harley breathes after everyone has hung up.

"Indeed," Q agrees. "Now. You heard Medina. We need a game plan. But first, go get some sleep."

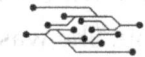

I don't sleep.

Instead, I pace around my room, sometimes thinking, sometimes not.

I jump when my phone starts buzzing in my pocket. Reiya.

"Hey," I greet her quietly, hearing the exhaustion in my voice.

"Hi," she responds, equally tired, her voice already hinting that something is wrong.

"You okay?"

"Yeah, I'm all right. You?"

"Eh. I feel like my world has begun to explode a bit, but I could be worse."

"Want to talk about it?"

"Nah, not really. What's up with you?"

"Well…" she sighs. "I ended up seeing Mom."

I halt. "You did?"

My mom, lying on her deathbed, had completely slipped my mind.

"Yeah. I decided I would regret it otherwise. It felt kind of surreal." She takes a breath. "And... she died only a few hours after I left the hospital."

My brain takes several moments to process that. *My mother is dead.*

"What?"

"She's gone, Kai, just like that."

And all of a sudden I find myself feeling... *something*. For some reason, I care. I care that I didn't see her one last time. I care that I never got the closure I didn't know I needed.

"I wish I could have been there with you," I say quietly.

"Me too. She asked about you. She wasn't sure if you were alive because no one found any record of you, but I told her you were doing well, and I think that made her happy."

"What was she like? After all this time?"

"She wasn't the person I'd constructed in my mind. She was... affectionate, almost. Humble, regretful. But I guess cancer will change you. I still don't know if she ever loved us, but I think she at least cared."

"Yeah. Maybe she did care."

I don't know that I believe those words. And if I'm being honest, it's at least partially because I just don't want to. Warping those who have hurt me into monsters makes it easier to resent them. To forget them.

"Sorry to give you that news right off the bat."

"No, you're fine. I'm glad you called me about it."

"Me too." She exhales again. "It's strange, isn't it? That this happened not long after we reunited. I don't believe in fate, but it feels damn near close to it. Like we'd been separated long enough and the universe wanted us back together."

"I know," I respond gently. "You showed up in my life right when I needed you the most."

"You're going to make me cry if you start saying that kind of shit, Kai Kai."

I smile. "Sorry. We can change the topic if you want."

"Probably for the best. I've got an update on Dr. Brenner if you have time."

"Go for it."

"So… Camden went to visit one of Brenner's family members, who reluctantly spoke to him about her educational background. She's done a lot of genetic research, which fits. According to her family, she broke off all contact several years ago. But none of that information is overly helpful. I did see a name in my search, however, that I thought was interesting. Connected to Devil's Peak."

"Oh really? Who?"

"I'm not sure if you know who he is. Mason Dare? He's famous."

I freeze.

"Mason Dare," I repeat, unfreezing.

"That's the one."

TWENTY THREE

I phone Mason Dare immediately. Either he's colluding with Brenner, or he was the one who gave me her name.

"Hello?" he answers uncertainly. At this hour I hadn't actually been expecting him to pick up.

"Care to explain your relationship to Rosalie Brenner?"

"Kai?"

"Yes."

I hear him sigh. His usual energy and eccentricity have evaporated. "I suppose I should have expected you to find out it was me who sent those messages."

"Why didn't you want me to know?" I demand. I'm probably being more interrogative than is necessary, but I have to find out what the hell I've gotten into.

"Well..." he says slowly. "I needed to keep myself out of it. If Holbrook ever found out I was suspicious of what Brenner is up to..."

Holbrook. Why is it always him?

"What? He has something to do with all of this?"

"I think so. I think he's working with Dr. Brenner. I don't know what kind of role, but I can't imagine it's good. And if he finds out what I know, it puts my family at risk."

"Your family?"

"My son and his mother. They live in South America, and Holbrook is one of the few people that knows they exist. I want to ensure that they remain hidden."

"Hidden from what?"

"Any person or entity who might see them as threats, as weapons, or as subjects."

I'm so lost. "Can you back up? I didn't even know you had a son. Why would he be a threat?"

"He's twenty-two or so now. His mother, Lara, didn't tell me about him until he was six, and by that time I was married to someone else. Evidently Lara left me because she found out she was pregnant."

It's obvious by his voice that he's not over what happened, so I feel like I could be venturing into something that should be private. But still, I have to ask. "Why?"

"She..." He pauses to take a breath, and I imagine him squeezing his eyes shut for a moment. "It was around that time that the GUARD started asking me to come work for them, and she became worried that my involvement would put her—and, as I found out, our son—in danger. She thought that the GUARD would try to use them, and that wasn't the life she wanted. Why she didn't just *tell* me about him... God, I would've gone away with her. But working for the GUARD was huge for me, and she knew that. She didn't want to take that away from me, so she left. I was always a bit of a handful anyway, especially with the fame. Lara would have never been able to live a quiet, protected life with our child, so I can't blame her for what she did."

"But who was she? Why would the GUARD be so interested?"

"It's... it's really hard to explain. I promise I will soon. But not now."

I sigh exasperatedly, but Dare seems firm on this. "Okay. Fine. So you're worried about Holbrook's power to hurt your family."

"Yes. I wouldn't put it past him to take revenge on my child. But there's another aspect, related to Brenner."

"Okay... what about her?"

"We've known each other for a long time. Our families were close, and for a while we were also colleagues. Years ago, she asked me to design technology for her research in synthetic DNA, but I wasn't aware of her true intentions at the time. If I were to guess, I think she had always been planning on genetic enhancement experimentation."

"Genetic enhancement experimentation."

"Yes. And that's something that she potentially would want my son for, if she knew about him, which is why Holbrook's involvement is even more dangerous. Enhancing operatives with technology is something that's been talked about for years, but this is different. This is something darker. Otherwise they wouldn't be hiding it."

I shake my head, my mind struggling to grasp all the information I just received. "But why are you involving me? Not sure if you've noticed, but Delta is threatening to crumble the precarious structures of the world, and I'm at the forefront."

"I think that they've... *chosen* you for this. To be a subject."

"What? How do you know that?"

"As much digging as I could manage. They're tagging the profiles of certain agents."

"Holbrook certainly has it out for me, *that* I know, but…"

"Kai, if I'm wrong, then great. But if I'm not, God knows what will happen to you. Your entire life could be turned upside down, or you could die, depending on what they have planned for you. Whatever it is, it would be irreversible. I'm very serious about this, otherwise I would never have involved you."

I run a hand through my hair. "Who else is connected with this? I need to know how much danger I'm in for just investigating this shit."

"From what I can tell, everything seems to be between Holbrook and Brenner. I'm confident that even Medina doesn't know. I could be wrong, but I think Holbrook's the only person you have to worry about. If you do get caught, you have my word that I'll take responsibility. Okay?"

I don't respond immediately, but Dare waits patiently. "You should have told me a lot of this," I say eventually. "It would've given me a place to start."

"I know. I know. I was… afraid, I guess. I wouldn't be able to live with myself if anything happened to my son. Benson. I couldn't bring myself to risk it."

I sigh, relenting. "Okay. I'll keep searching."

I hang up, unsure how to process, and unease starts to inundate me. Between this and Delta and the chaos descending on the world, too much is happening all at once. And I have a horrible feeling that I won't be the same when it's over.

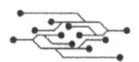

I'm up by seven, but the others are already seated at the kitchen table, conversing about what happened yesterday. Not yet ready to dive in, I grab a banana for breakfast and flop down on the living room couch. I haven't been able to get Dare's story out of my head.

I know now, at some level of confidence, that Brenner is collaborating with Holbrook on genetic research at Devil's Peak. Intriguingly, it's all connected to Dare.

And then there's me. It's not surprising that Holbrook wants to use my body, my genetic material, whatever it may be. It's an easy way to dispose of me. Or to control me.

Kohler joins me and I audibly groan.

"Oh come now," he says, rolling his eyes. "You didn't expect me to leave you alone did you?"

"One can dream."

He takes a seat in a chair across from me, studying me, and I catch something strange within his eyes—a bit of loathing, perhaps? Or wariness?

"Anti-Cinderella and the Anti-Prince seem to have a thing for each other," he remarks when I say nothing further.

"What?"

He sighs, exasperated, but I know what he's talking about. "Harley. Lucien. Bet you don't like their... *connection*."

"It's not like they're sleeping together, Kohler," I reply shortly. I really wish he would stop talking about things I don't want to talk about. Or stop talking to me in general.

"They might be," he says sharply, too loudly. "Quite frankly, you both seem a bit too comfortable with him."

I stare at him, confused at this sudden outburst. He's been a bit weird about Harley and me, and now he's being weird about me *not* being weird about Harley and Lucien.

He continues. "Holbrook and Medina sent us into battle when we hardly know anything about each other. Seems a little careless, if you ask me."

I shake my head. "What, you don't trust any of us? Q and Holbrook and Medina know everything about us. The things that we've never told anyone. The GUARD practically raised us all, for God's sake. We don't need to learn each other's every secret. I'm wary of you, but if Q trusts you, then so do I. And as for Lucien... well, I think we're all still trying to figure him out. Whatever he and Harley have is a probably good thing for all of us."

Kohler frowns. "Every mistake in my life has stemmed from trusting people I thought I knew."

I can't help but roll my eyes. "Well, sorry. I don't know where this is coming from but if there's something you want to ask me, or Harley, then I suggest you spit it out now. Or go have Q show you my entire file if you're so concerned."

"I know you're investigating something, and Harley's in on it. Same with your buddy Camden back in Manhattan. And now we have a goddamn ex-Delta agent among us. I don't know what you're playing at, but I swear to God if—"

"What the fuck?" I cut him off, raising my voice. The others in the kitchen drop their conversation, and I feel their eyes on me, but I don't look at them. Instead, I stare straight into Kohler's eyes. I take a few breaths so that I don't yell, but anger still emanates from my words. I haven't given my life to this organization to be accused of this bullshit. "You think we're traitors? You're out of your mind."

He glares back, his gaze unwavering. It's definitely loathing, which is unnerving. I've never seen him look at anyone like that, and I don't know what to make of it. "Whatever you're doing, Q and Holbrook certainly don't know about it."

"They might. Either way, I'm not trying to take down the GUARD or something. Christ, Kohler."

"Until you can prove that, I'll be watching you." Then he gets up and stalks away to his room.

I finally make eye contact with Harley, who mouths the words, *What happened?* All I can do is shake my head, but when her concerned expression remains, I gesture with my head for her to follow me to my bedroom.

I lock the door behind us.

"What did he say to you?"

"He thinks we're working for Delta or something because we're doing some side investigations."

Her eyebrows go up. "Seriously? He knows about Dr. Brenner, then?"

"No, I don't think so, just that we're looking into something. But I guess I shouldn't blame him for being extra wary."

"It'll probably pass. There's no evidence that we're members of Delta."

"I hope he'll realize that. We don't have time for shit like this, not to mention that it's a dangerous accusation. I mean, you've heard the stories. They're not hesitating to kill suspected traitors."

I exhale, telling myself not to get overworked about Kohler. He's not worth the energy.

"How is Lucien doing, by the way?"

Harley shakes her head, her expression growing grim. "Maybe better than he was yesterday, but he doesn't sleep. I think he's still hallucinating things."

"It seems like you're… connecting with him, at least."

Her expression morphs into concern, worry even. I fear I've said the wrong thing. A truth she doesn't want to admit, perhaps.

"You're right—I have been connecting with him. But I think it's because I see myself in his agony. That doesn't change the fact that he scares me. One moment he acts normal and the next there's this dangerous look in his eye."

I've seen that look. But it's hard to tell if he's truly that dangerous or if it's merely a product of his torment. Being thrown back into the world, into *our* world, is certainly not helping him.

"Do you think we're being too trusting?"

She bites her lip. "I just think we're not prepared for what he might do."

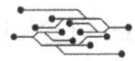

That morning we spend almost two hours talking about our next course of action.

Lucien has provided a document of everything he knows about Delta from a couple of years ago: names, base locations, cyberterror methods, plans for the future, and weaknesses within governments and within the GUARD that have allowed them to trickle in. But there's nothing that can really lead us to Arachne. The best—and perhaps *only*—way of getting anything on her or her trusted allies is via someone on the inside.

Which is what ultimately brings Q to his next plan.

"I've been pondering this for a little while…" he begins ominously as we are gathered in the kitchen. I stop shoving food in my face to listen, already anxious about whatever he's going to say. "I think we need a mole. Just for our purposes."

"Surely not one of us," Harley says, her eyes narrowed.

"No. Not one of us."

"Not *any* GUARD agent," I say. "That might be a suicide mission. They know too much about us."

"Yes. An outsider is what we require." Kohler and I make eye contact at that, clearly thinking of the same person. When I look back at Q, I am surprised to find him staring at me expectantly.

"What?" I demand. "I don't know anyone." But he, obviously, is well aware that isn't true.

"Perhaps I can refresh your memory. I believe you're acquainted with someone named Zahra Kang, yes?"

I freeze.

It takes me a few moments to recover before I nod, reluctant. I shouldn't have ever underestimated Q's knowledge of my life. Nothing is private from him. He likely started monitoring my activities more closely after I asked for Reiya's untraceable phone.

"Right. I've been watching her, and I do believe that she has the capability. From what I've seen, I'm impressed."

Jesus.

My calm has abruptly drained out of my body, but I keep my voice as measured as I am able. Suddenly it's as if Harley and Kohler and Lucien aren't even here, just me and Q and my anger at him for invading the sliver of privacy I thought I had, for being so bold as to think of asking Zahra to leave her life and dive into the depths of Delta.

I hate the fact that no facet of my life is my own. And now Q wants to impose that burden on Zahra as well, someone entirely undeserving of it.

"You're fucking insane if you think we can ask something like this of her."

He leans forward, I lean back. "Would she do it?" he asks quietly, his tone verging on threatening, signaling that he's not going to argue about this. That he's already decided to ruin her life. Which infuriates me.

"That's beside the point," I respond shortly.

"I think she would," Kohler answers for me. I turn and glare at him, finding no apology in his eyes.

"You met her for like an hour," I spit.

"Kai," he begins, gentler. "What if this is what puts us over the edge? What if we can take down Delta with her?"

"But why her? There are more people like her out there."

"She's talented, she knows you already, and she's already on my radar," Q replies plainly. "With a bit of training, she could do the job."

I almost want to punch something—Q perhaps—but instead I sit and seethe in silence.

Lucien, however, comes to my aid unexpectedly. "I've been on the inside. It's an abusive and tense environment, to say the least. I would never wish it upon anyone, so I think we should deliberate very carefully about sending someone with her own life outside of our shitty world into the frays of Delta. She may not make it out alive."

"He's not wrong," Harley says, having also been silent throughout this argument until now. I feel a rush of gratitude for her, for Lucien as well, who despite knowing nothing about Zahra have sided with me. "We have Lucien, who was an insider."

"Yes," Q replies. "We have Lucien. Which is why utilizing Zahra makes even more sense, as he can help her navigate Delta and get the information we desperately need."

"You're not giving us a choice, are you?" I say, my voice dead.

"I'm sorry" is all he says, though I can't tell if he means it.

TWENTY FOUR

I try to talk Zahra out of it to no avail. Q was persuasive to an almost sickening degree, detailing all the horrific things Delta has done and telling her that this could be the most important thing she'll ever do. He's offered her a place in the GUARD at a division of her choosing, and enough money so that she'll live comfortably for most of her life.

But in the end, what she wants is what she told me the night we parted: to do something meaningful for the world and for herself. And there's nothing I can do to sway her.

Maybe I shouldn't feel so strongly about this, but the chances are she's not going to come out the same person she goes in as. And I'm terrified that I signed her death warrant the moment I met her.

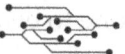

In a day, we are out of the Illinois safe house and onto the next one—Baltimore, this time, on account of its proximity to the capital. Lucien's hypothesis is that the location left for us by the dead Delta member is no coincidence—D.C.'s base allegedly has the most direct connection to Arachne in North America. It's the base that delegates her orders to many of the smaller bases, which also means there's a significant collection of leaders stationed there. And the bigger the base, the better Zahra can blend in.

Over the next several weeks, Q and Lucien will be training her on the ins and outs of Delta. The rest of us, meanwhile, have been tasked with confirming that the coordinates are indeed a base, and subsequently gathering intel. Our job is to find out who's in charge and how we can get Zahra into Delta.

Q has the unspoken expectation that I will not let my emotions affect that job. Emotional restraint was something I'd excelled at before the death of my last partner, because I simply didn't let myself feel a goddamn thing. Now the fortress of my mind has crumbled, and I don't know how to combat the inner battles that have ensued.

It only gets worse when I lay eyes on Zahra again.

"Kai," she greets me as Q lets her into the Baltimore penthouse. She smiles, and I can't quite bring myself to return it.

"Hey," I breathe. I can't bring myself to look at Harley at first; I know she'll see the dynamic between Zahra and me in an instant, and I don't know what to do about it yet. I *do* know that I feel like an ass, even if it's all been relatively casual.

That night, after Q has spent the whole day flooding Zahra with information and everyone has gone to bed, she knocks on my door.

"Hi," she says when I answer, a wry smile on her face, bottle of whiskey in hand. "Mind if I come in?"

I stand aside, unsure where this is going to go. "Of course."

She sits on the edge of my bed, taking a swig of the booze, grin still lingering.

"I thought I'd never see you again," she says.

"I can't say I'm happy that it's under these circumstances."

"What, you don't want me involved?"

"Well, not particularly. I don't want you to get hurt. Or killed."

She holds out the whiskey for me. "Drink this. It'll help. But seriously, I'm not planning on dying, so don't get all emotional just yet."

I sigh, relenting. Her crooked smile makes it difficult to be moody.

I join her on my bed and drink. Though I put a couple feet of distance between us, she scoots closer to me.

"I hope I'm not overstepping by coming in here," she adds. "I don't know if you and Harley are…"

"No, you're fine. Harley and I sort of broke things off for the foreseeable future."

She tilts her head. "Maybe I should go for her. She's very attractive."

"That's not a bad image."

"It'd be better with you in it."

"I'm not the one you'd have to convince."

"Okay great, I'll go get her." Zahra pushes herself off my bed, but I snatch her by the arm and pull her back on, both of us laughing.

We fall silent, passing the alcohol between us.

It's a silence that is permeated with something else, a connection we have that I cannot explain.

"I wish we had more time together," she says finally. "Aren't you leaving tomorrow?"

"Yeah. No time to waste, I guess. You'll be stuck with Lucien and Q."

She sighs. "I can't believe I agreed to this." She doesn't sound regretful, but incredulous at what she's gotten into in a matter of days.

"Why did you?"

She shrugs. "I saw it as an opportunity. To become more."

I only nod. The question that I don't ask is whether it'll be worth it.

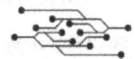

"What happened to your face?" I ask Kohler. He is in the passenger seat next to me, petulant as he stares out the window at the passing towns as we head to D.C. He looks exhausted, with bruises on his hand and his cheekbone. He probably went out to find someone to beat unconscious, the dissolute person that he is.

"Clearly, I got clocked."

"I'm surprised anyone got a punch in," Harley mutters from the back.

"Did you kill him?" I say. I wish that were a crazy question.

"I should have," Kohler responds bitterly.

"What's wrong?"

"Nothing."

I shake my head and glance in the rearview mirror to see Harley do the same. He doesn't speak much more for the rest of the trip, which I'm thankful for, but I know that something is bothering him. Either he still thinks I'm a traitor, or it's something personal that he doesn't wish to share.

We reach our run-down motel about an hour later, where we'll be staying for the next couple weeks apart from occasional trips back to Baltimore. Its exterior neon lighting is flickering, a handful of rooms have broken windows, and a few cars in the lot appear to have been abandoned for years. But choosing a bit of a shithole means there's less of a chance that anyone notices one of us coming back covered in blood, and paying in cash makes us more untraceable.

Harley and I settle into our room, leaving Kohler to mope around in his. Tomorrow will be a scout day to search the vicinity of the coordinates. With any luck, we'll confirm the base's existence and move on to identifying a target suitable for recruiting Zahra.

I worry that we're not making the right move, that this base will be a dead end or a trap and Zahra will pay for the mistake. But our team has nothing else to go on. No visibility as to what happened to Medina, either. Q is hoping we can find out something, anything, while we're here, but we all know that Delta has the upper hand right now.

And if we fail... what will the world become?

Sometimes I almost believe that Delta isn't as bad as we think, that the Earth is going to keep turning no matter what happens, and humanity will be okay. What am I really fighting against? Would changing our stubborn ways be so horrible?

Lucien seems to feel that it's worth it, though, and I suppose that should give me an answer. He lived through Delta, he killed for them, he knows what they're capable of. Even if I didn't give a shit about the greater good, these people took my best friend away from me. That alone is enough for me to want them all dead.

But Delta completely slips my mind when I get an ominous message from my sister.

I helped Camden break into Holbrook's computer. Sending some decrypted files over now. You're not going to like what you find.

"Shit," I breathe, wide-eyed as I sit up straight.

"What?" Harley replies from her bed, concern drawing her eyebrows together.

"Reiya might've just stolen a bunch of files from Holbrook about Dr. Brenner."

Her mouth falls open. "She did? Do you have them?"

I power on my tablet, fingers moving at the speed of light until I open the message from Reiya. Harley sits next to me, looking over my shoulder.

Not liking what I find is an understatement. I'm disturbed, at the very least.

It's genetic experiments all right, gruesome ones. There's a file for each of the subjects, some of which are adults, some of which are children. Inside are pictures, lab notes, and data detailing what they endured.

Many people developed medical problems and either died or were euthanized like animals. Others killed themselves, or effectively lost their minds and were removed from the experiment to live the remainder of their lives in Devil's Peak cells.

I can't determine the specifics of what Dr. Brenner is attempting to accomplish, though I gather that she's adding synthetic DNA to people. *How* she's doing that is beyond me, but it becomes clear that Dare was right—she's trying to make superhumans.

Beings that would make excellent soldiers, excellent agents.

I catch the word *Nyxian* being used to describe the kind of genetic material that appears to be the focus of the experiment. I'm not sure what it means, but it almost seems… otherworldly. Like it's some sort of foreign DNA. But I'd hesitate to believe that. Sure, astronomers have found other life forms, but only very basic ones. None with genes comparable or superior to our own.

I scour the files for any kind of success but fail to find it. The only positive notes I find pertain to a ten-year-old boy, dated a few years ago: *Subject has responded well to treatment thus far. We hypothesize that he may develop abilities over the next couple weeks.* But a few days later, the experimenter logged the boy's sudden death.

I look at Harley, and she looks back at me, speechless, horrified.

"Holbrook is involved in this?" she says in disbelief.

"Apparently."

"And he wants to do this to you?"

"According to Dare."

"Jesus... What should we do?"

"Do?" I echo. I hadn't thought of what I would do once I found out the truth. "I have no idea. Is there anything we *can* do?"

Harley bites her lip in thought. "I'm not sure, but there's no way in hell I'm going to let this happen to you. Look at what it's done to all those people."

"Well... we can't just walk into Devil's Peak and assassinate Dr. Brenner. We can't go to Holbrook, clearly, or Medina now that he's basically dead."

"Dare?"

"I think if he knew a way to stop this before now, he would have already done it. But maybe he can help us. I'm going to send him these files and see if he can tell me what *Nyxian* means. I'd wager that his son has those kinds of genes, whatever they are."

Harley nods, but concern lingers on her face. "What about your sister? And Camden? If they get caught for this..."

I take a breath. "I know. I talked to Q, and he told me he's doing everything he can to hide Reiya from the GUARD, but... Camden's not so fortunate."

"Shay is worried about him."

"Because of this?"

"No. Because of the drinking."

"Ah. I think he's struggling with a lot of things alone."

Harley gazes at me somberly. "Yeah. We all are."

"None of us really talk about it."

"Well, it's a product of being taught to repress emotions."

"But we still cope, somehow."

"By drinking, if you're Camden. By self-harm, if you're me. By hurting others, if you're Kohler."

And how do I cope?

I don't get a chance to answer myself because Kohler lets himself into our room, halting our conversation. I put my tablet to sleep immediately.

"Am I interrupting?" he responds to our silence, raising his eyebrows.

"Nope," I reply. "What's up?"

"Well, I decided to check out the coordinates."

"And?"

"There's some kind of base, all right. I think it might be underground, beneath a large warehouse. The coordinates led me to a hidden entrance a block away, in the back of a restaurant. In their meat freezer. It's likely not the only exit, for safety reasons, but I haven't found another one. There were a handful of people going in and out of the restaurant, but none were known Delta members. So I suggest we do more people-watching tomorrow.

"Main objective is finding a target that Zahra can befriend in the outside world, preferably someone with authority. We'll have to sneak a bug into that base to get more information, because we can't afford to be wrong."

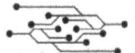

I'm half-asleep when Harley finds her way into my arms, and though she is silent in the darkness, I know something is wrong. I hold her close, running a hand along her back, as I feel my shirt grow damp from tears.

Minutes pass before she finally speaks. "Sorry," she murmurs, her voice muffled.

"It's okay," I respond gently. "What's wrong?"

"I don't know. Having a bad night, I guess. Sometimes I just can't escape the things that haunt me, and my brother's death has made a lot of things resurface. I hate that it will never go away no matter how hard I try to move on, no matter how much I tell myself it doesn't define who I am. But it does, in some ways. I may never know a life without my past trying to suffocate me."

I squeeze my eyes shut.

I know that, as much as I try, I will never truly understand what Harley has endured. My childhood was filled with neglect, hers with violence, which are far from the same thing. And I can't stand that there's nothing I can do or say to fix anything. I yearn for her happiness, almost more than my own now, but that won't change reality.

"You are, without doubt, the most resilient person I've ever met," I respond. "That's what truly defines you, far more than your past ever could."

She hugs me tighter.

"I admire you so much for it. I've admired no one like I admire you, Harley Stone."

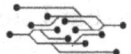

"Should've known you wouldn't be able to keep your dick in your pants," Kohler mutters. I turn and scowl at him as we finish packing a few things for today, Harley taking her turn in the shower.

"Excuse me?" I respond coldly.

"I can smell you guys all over each other," he says, matching my tone. "It seems you have a habit of fucking your partner when there are clearly more important things going on."

This time I do punch him. Right in the jaw. When he recovers I see in his eyes that he wasn't expecting that.

"At least I don't fuck my victims," I spit, ignoring the pain in my hand. "Now grow the fuck up. We didn't even do anything, so you can shut your mouth before I knock your teeth out. What's your deal anyway?"

He doesn't answer. I throw up my hands in frustration and turn away from him so I can pretend he doesn't exist.

Harley detects the tension in the air when she comes out of the bathroom in just a towel, giving me a questioning look to which I just shake my head.

But she doesn't let it slide. "What's going on?"

"Nothing, we're fine," Kohler says.

She crosses her arms. "Clearly not. Spit it out."

"Kohler was being a dick and I punched him," I respond.

"Jesus. Can you two resolve this? What is this about?"

"I have no idea. He accused us of sleeping together—which is none of his business even if we were—but I suspect there's more to it." I look expectantly at Kohler, who is maintaining a poker face.

"Look," he says, exhaling. "I'm just trying to ensure that nothing is going to get in the way of this mission. Sorry."

I roll my eyes at his half-ass apology.

"Then you should probably stop acting like a child," Harley snaps. His gaze grows steely but he doesn't utter a comeback.

We leave the motel at six in the morning to scout Delta members heading into their base. According to Kohler, there's a back entrance to the restaurant that they use, so Harley and I opt to hide out on a nearby rooftop to make notes of everyone we see, leveraging Tony's facial and gait recognition abilities. Kohler, meanwhile, will be remotely conducting background investigations and analyses on anyone Tony can recognize, in order to identify a handful of candidates for Zahra's recruitment.

"There are cameras everywhere around that entrance," Kohler warns us. "We'll be dead the second you're seen, so use Tony to analyze the field of view."

Throughout the morning we only see about forty people going into the back of the graffitied restaurant, mostly men. A couple of known lower-level Delta operatives, but no one who stands out. I have a hunch this isn't the primary entrance, but it's all we've got.

Then Harley nudges me as we are lying with scopes, nodding toward someone who has just come *out* of the diner.

The woman walks with an aura of elegant dominance that's quite noticeable, even at a distance. I zoom in with my contacts and briefly get a glimpse of her face. She's Black, with a shaved head and a noticeable sense of fashion. Maybe late thirties.

"I'm going to follow her," I say. She's different than all the other goons we've seen, and there's something about her that makes her seem like she has authority.

I hurry down to the street and walk along the block, scanning restaurants and shops as I pass. After several minutes of nothing, I almost give up, but then spot her leaving a cafe with a coffee. She heads directly back to the base, preventing me from gleaning any information other than a place that she might frequent.

"Learn anything useful?" Harley says when I get back to our hideout.

"Just the name of the cafe she visited. But I think we should look into her further, yeah?"

Harley nods. "Let's see what Kohler can find out."

TWENTY FIVE
ZAHRA

I jolt awake to the sound of things crashing, and panic for a second before I remember where I am. Some fancy GUARD hideout in Baltimore.

"Oh God," I groan aloud. *Why am I here?*

I can't even answer that question because I'm not so sure I belong with these people. I barely know who they are and what they do. Kai, Harley, and Kohler left last night, but I find Lucien in the kitchen, where I assume the crashing came from.

"Apologies," he says as I walk in, without even turning around to look at me. "Did I wake you?"

"Yes," I respond, a bit annoyed. This is a little weird, probably for both of us, to suddenly be stuck with one another having exchanged only a few words. Both the people we'd rather be with are hours away.

"Ah. Well I made breakfast, if you'd like some. It's ful medames."

"Ful medames, huh?"

"Was I correct in assuming you had Arab heritage?"

I tilt my head. "You were. My mother was born here in the States, but her parents were Sudanese. She used to make this dish for me and my brother when I was small, before our lives fell apart."

Lucien smiles, but there's something off about it. "My mother used to make it as well. She was Egyptian, though, so perhaps there'll be some differences."

"Where's Q?"

"Couldn't tell you. Might be in his room. I suspect he'll appear when he has something important to share with us."

There is an awkward silence for a few minutes before he slides a plate of food in front of me at the kitchen table, then sits across from me.

"So," Lucien begins, staring at me with interest. He's a peculiar one, as Kai warned me. I'm leery of him. "I hear Q has offered you a formal position in the GUARD after your stint in Delta."

I shrug, pausing to take a bite of his dish, which to my surprise tastes pretty good. Similar to how I remember.

"I don't know if I'll take him up on it," I reply honestly.

He raises his eyebrows, cocks his head. "If you could choose to do anything in life, what would it be?"

I laugh once. "I rarely dare to dream of such a world, where I could simply choose to do anything."

He purses his lips. "Understandable. But humor me."

"Hmm. I think I'd be an inventor. I've designed a few custom weapons for my job."

"Well, you could do that in the GUARD. Design weapons and technology."

"Perhaps, but ultimately I want to live for myself and not for some overpowered agency."

"Probably for the best. I don't know about their tech recruits, but Harley tells me the Field exams are quite strenuous. They make you learn at least five languages, torture you, and try to drown you for the swim test. And if you make it far, there's the abduction challenge."

I hide my alarm. "The abduction challenge?"

Lucien smiles again, but in no way does it convey anything positive. "Yes. Someone will kidnap you when you don't expect it, and you have to escape. Evidently many people fail it. But maybe you'd get to skip all that, considering what they're asking of you."

"I certainly feel like I'm sacrificing a lot for people I don't even know."

He studies me for a moment, and I try not to let it make me uncomfortable. Then he sighs and looks away. "At least you have a future. I, on the other hand, may just get executed after I've done my job."

My eyebrows raise. "You think so?"

"I have no doubt I'll be seen as a liability by GUARD leaders. Or anyone who's logical. It's interesting—I practically used to crave death, but now..." He trails off, but he doesn't need to finish. I suspect the recent change in the direction of his life has given him a reason to survive.

"Well, getting shot in the head is probably better than rotting in prison," I reply casually.

He smirks, though I'm not sure if it's because of what I said or the fact that I'm speaking through a mouthful of food. "Anything is better than that."

"Do you have a plan for us?"

"I'm going to teach you everything I know, but I think it's important to decide where you're going to fit in and how you can get us the info we want. How are your computer skills?"

"Decent, but I'm no hacker."

"Right. Well, we'll help you a bit with that, but it doesn't sound like that's an area you want to work in full-time."

"No."

"Can you defend yourself?"

"Yes. Maybe not like Kai, but I'm pretty good."

He thinks for a moment. "That's good. You could be a spy for them. Q and I can teach you some espionage, though they'll want to train you themselves. What else can you do?"

"Improvise weapons. Climb things. Kill people."

"How's your health?"

"Fine.

"Any disabilities?"

"Jesus, is this a goddamn interrogation?"

"I'm just trying to find out everything about you. So I don't get you killed."

I roll my eyes. "Fine."

"Disabilities?" he repeats.

"None that will get me killed."

"Can you tell me more about your background?"

I sigh, exasperated. "I was born and raised in Queens. As I hinted at, I had a bad relationship with my mom and haven't seen her in years. My father was Korean, and he left pretty early on, but my grandparents over there reach out once in a while. I had a schizophrenic brother who was murdered, after which a neighbor started teaching me self-defense. He's the one who helped me get my job."

"Your job as a hitwoman?"

"Yeah."

"This neighbor never encouraged you to do anything else?"

I raise my eyebrows at his judgy tone. As if he's any better, the prick. "What, like get an education? Do good for the world? I certainly wanted to, but I didn't have the resources. I thought if I could earn enough money doing bad shit maybe in the end I could make a better life for myself and do something I actually wanted to."

"Do you still believe that?"

I shrug. "Maybe. Maybe it'll be this job that'll pull me out of my rut."

"When you say 'bad shit,' does that mean you have a criminal record?"

"No. I'm good at what I do."

"All right. Is there any reason at all that Delta might suspect you're working with us? Or that you wouldn't be loyal?"

"I mean, I've been hanging around with Kai, so that connection is an obvious risk. But I assumed Q had already done something about it."

"Indeed I have," I hear from behind me. I turn to find that Q has emerged from his cave. He's also an odd one. But very clearly in a position of substantial power. "Thanks to Kai, he, Harley, and Kohler don't exist anywhere now. All of their digital data has been scrubbed from every database that might've had information or footage. In fact, everywhere they go, they are almost instantly erased from most camera feeds that see them. Using their location we can query for any camera in the vicinity connected to the internet, and overwrite the data before it's stored. I have confidence that Zahra is in the clear."

Lucien eyes him. "Very well."

"I have a few meetings this morning, but afterward we should discuss what's going to happen over the next couple weeks. Yes?"

I nod. With that, he departs again, and I focus back on Lucien, who is sipping his tea. Which is when I notice the tremors in his hands.

"It's the lithium I take," he explains, though I hadn't even realized he'd seen me looking.

"Lithium?"

"For bipolar disorder."

"Ah. Something that arose in Devil's Peak? Or before?"

"Devil's Peak. But it's one of the least frightening byproducts of their methods, in my mind."

"Do you still have episodes?"

"I have various types of what people would call 'episodes,' but I haven't had a bipolar one in a while. They thought the disorder would break me down, but it only made me more resistant to their methods, somehow. I was either too numb or too energized. They started giving me lithium and I haven't had an episode since. But I haven't been as fortunate with the other… *attacks*."

Something in his voice elicits a tinge of empathy in me. "I know I'm a stranger, but it's going to be just us for a while, so if you need something, don't hesitate to ask. I obviously need you if I'm going to survive Delta."

He smiles slightly. "You're nicer than you let on."

"Don't get used to it. I've been informed more than once that I'm an insufferable bitch. I guess most people just don't like someone who takes no shit."

"Except Kai."

I give him a look, and he smirks. "Yeah. We'll see where that goes. I have a feeling that he's head over heels for Harley and there's nothing I can do about it."

"I don't blame him," Lucien responds quietly.

"Why's that?"

"Well… she's the backbone of this team, even if she and the others might not know it. She's an excellent agent and an upstanding human being, more so than anyone else here. She intrigues me in ways no one else has."

"I've noticed."

He frowns. "Is it obvious?"

"Maybe not obvious, but there's something in the way you look at her."

We sit in silence for a few moments before I say what I've been wanting to since this conversation began. To figure Lucien out. "Can I ask you what's stopping you from walking out that door? I mean, yeah, it seems like the GUARD would kill you if you did, but there's gotta be another reason why you're helping these people."

He deliberates for a moment. "A peace of mind, I suppose. I want to put an end to the terrors of Delta, truly. But I had no intention of helping the GUARD until I met Kai and Harley. They've… given me some hope. They're good people." He shrugs.

I find myself hating him less than I thought I would. Probably also less than I *should*. Still, I don't trust him in the slightest. It's weird to me that Kai and the others do.

But then he says, "I also can't physically leave without someone else allowing it. Q has set up the security such that I will literally be electrocuted if I tried."

"Shit."

"It's all right, I'm used to being kept prisoner in some form. Although I hate that Kohler gets so much joy out of it." He can't help but sneer slightly as he mentions Kohler, which I don't find particularly surprising.

"No one seems to like him much."

"No. He's an outcast among outcasts, and he knows it."

"I thought everyone would despise *you*."

"It perplexes me why they don't. Maybe they feel like I'm not the person I was when I worked for Delta."

"Are you?"

He looks me in the eye. "No. But that doesn't change all the horrible things I did. I deserved every second of the torture I endured in Devil's Peak. I probably deserved a lifetime of it."

"Probably," I agree. But I can see unmistakable guilt in his eyes. It takes a special kind of fucked-up person to do what he did, yet something tells me he never sought out that kind of life. I wonder what drove him to do it.

"You're not exactly innocent, either," he responds.

No, I'm not. Not in the slightest. Am I just as bad as him? Maybe it doesn't even matter—a murderer is a murderer.

I sigh. "I know. And it's going to get worse."

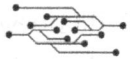

That morning comes the news of a likely Delta assassination: the Prime Minister of the UK. He, along with his wife, died in a car crash deemed an accident, conveniently only a couple weeks before the country's elections, which are a way for Delta—and the GUARD—to interfere.

By no means is it a unique case, according to what Lucien tells me. The public has no idea whose hands their lives are really in.

Delta is influencing elections to put radicals into power, attempting to induce anger of the public toward their leaders. All it takes is a reduction of liberties and a widening gap between the elite and everyone else.

In the US, it has manifested as cuts to government services, increased incarceration and police brutality, and rising poverty levels. As quality of life has decreased, it seems as though humanity has begun to revert to a baser form. People have begun to turn on each other as much as they've turned on their governments.

And it could create the cascade that Delta wants. Uprisings could be all they need to carve a new society.

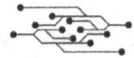

Q analyzes me as we sit gathered around a table, his tablet in front of him. "First of all," he begins, "you are going to have to live and breathe your new alias, Harper Olsen. That starts now. Lucien will teach you who you need to be, because Delta doesn't just take in anyone. I'm going to help you gain more technological proficiency, after which Lucien will be able to detail what their cybersecurity looks like, for when we need you in that area. Eventually, you're going to have to sabotage some of their protocols so that we can come in and take down that base. But until then, your job is to get us any and all information you can, with a focus on identifying or locating leaders."

"You have a lot of faith in me," I reply.

"Yes," Q responds seriously. "We do."

"No pressure," Lucien adds lightly.

"Lastly, Kai will help you with hand-to-hand combat. I'm aware of your existing abilities but it cannot hurt to have more practice. We don't want you getting stuck in training when you're there."

I nod. This is going to be an intense few weeks.

"You can still back out, if you so desire," Q says after a couple seconds, still studying me. For a moment I think about it, but as afraid as I am, this opportunity could be what I need to set up the rest of my life. Being a hitwoman for hire isn't taking me where I want to be.

"No. I'm in."

TWENTY SIX
KAI

A wine collection, an extensive array of philosophy books, and a few black-and-white photos. That's all that strikes me as personal in Diana Parrish's otherwise austere apartment. Frankly, I think Delta is her hobby.

After our day of target hunting, she came away as the most promising candidate, in that her background is similar enough to Zahra's to enable them to connect. And she's clean, which means she knows what she's doing.

I locate her personal computer and stick in a malware drive that'll attempt to download data while I scour the rest of the place. Tony is able to disarm a small safe she has, where I find a pistol, a few fake IDs, and a couple of death certificates. Sister and daughter, according to Kohler's research.

Otherwise, there's not much to see. Nothing that suggests she'd be problematic, and nothing that directly reveals her position in Delta. But her living space, with its air of affluent minimalism, echoes what I felt before: she's powerful. We'll need to sneak a bug into the base to determine just how much.

As I'm leaving the apartment, I glimpse a man sitting in his car across the street, and it's not anything I think much of until later, when I glance out the window of our motel. We are in the midst of discussing our next moves when he catches my eye again. The same guy, the same car.

I shut the blinds, Harley and Kohler abruptly ceasing their conversation and staring at me in confusion. I snatch my tablet and scribble three sentences:

I think someone's watching us.
Black car outside I saw earlier.
Look for a bug.

They don't dare to utter a word, eyes wide. We begin to scour our motel room for a bug that I pray we don't find.

But my prayers don't work.

It takes us fifteen minutes to find the tiny black piece cleverly concealed in an HV remote. I crush it under my foot, fear beginning to creep into my bones. I continue hunting for a hidden camera, or another bug even, practically destroying the room in the process, though I fail to find anything else.

"We're fucked," Harley breathes. Kohler kicks a chair in anger.

"Did we ever leave anything important behind here?" I ask, attempting to maintain a level head. "Anything that would give him any ounce of information?"

"We always took everything of value," Kohler responds, then looks to Harley. "Right?"

"We never left any technology or information in here. Just clothes," she says.

"Okay, good," I say. "We're not total idiots, then. I'm going to find out who he is. This isn't over."

"What are you going to do, kidnap him?"

"Maybe."

Harley gives me a disapproving look. "We can't do that unless we know for sure he's Delta."

"I know, I know. Maybe I can get him to follow me again. If I can't capture him I can at least hold a gun to his head in the hopes he'll share some information."

"Killing him would be easier," Kohler remarks, his arms crossed.

"Don't do anything stupid, Kai," Harley replies warily, ignoring Kohler. "And please don't get yourself killed. He may already know we know, since we destroyed his bug."

I put on my protective vest and my earpiece to stay in touch with Harley and Kohler, who will be tracking me and watching my video stream. My Ghost is tucked into my jacket.

I head out of the motel, driving as though to go back toward Parrish's apartment. Although I'm skeptical that he'll follow me, I see him tailing at a distance. It's dark, but there are people out around town, so I opt to park somewhere it's unlikely we'll be seen, and pull into the vacant lot of a long-abandoned roller rink.

Daringly, he parks into the spot right next to me, which means he's no longer hiding, if he ever really was. I wish I could see his face to get a read on his emotions.

"Wish me luck," I mutter. "It seems he's inviting a confrontation."

My Ghost is in my hand as I walk around to the driver's side of his vehicle and take aim at his head. One of these bullets would go straight through the glass and into his skull. But I want to see who he is.

"Out," I command. He complies, slowly opening his door. The moment I can see the entirety of him I have an arm wrapped tightly around his neck and the gun against his head.

"I would be careful if I were you," he warns, struggling to breathe in my hold. "Unless you want the CIA and MI6 hunting you down."

I freeze. Not what I was expecting.

"Who are you?" I ask.

"Agent Nico Sanchez."

"CIA?"

"Yes."

"Confirmed it," Harley says only moments later.

I release him, and lower my gun. If he pulls one on me I know I'll be a split-second quicker, but I can't threaten a CIA agent. I look him up and down, judging him to be in his early 40s. Muscular, neat beard, suave aura. And here I was thinking *I* was Latino James Bond.

"Congrats on finding the bug," he says. "But I have an audio scanner, so I still heard everything."

"Why are you following us?"

"Well when GUARD agents suddenly drop off the map we have to see what they're up to. You watch us, we watch you. We can't let you people go unmonitored."

You people. What an ass.

"And what did you conclude, Agent Sanchez?" I say his name mockingly, but he ignores it.

"Your team can continue, for now."

"For now? We don't report to you."

"No," he agrees, further ignoring my biting tone. "You don't. Which is why I'm watching you."

"Well, you're not doing a very good job at being discreet."

"I wanted to see how you'd handle this. And it seems the GUARD teaches their agents to resort to violence as the first option."

I don't respond to that.

But he presses me to admit it. "'Kidnap him,' 'hold a gun to his head,' 'killing him would be easier.' Is that not what you all said? You didn't even consider the option of stalking your stalker. Not to mention, you gave yourselves away immediately. I expected better."

I raise my eyebrows. He's not wrong, but we also don't have time to be playing games. "We operate under different rules than you do."

He snorts. "Clearly. I'm not sure if you were made aware, but several intelligence agencies signed an accord to place checks on the GUARD. Medina really had no choice but to partake in the agreement, of course."

That's news to me.

"He failed to mention it," I reply shortly.

"Yes, well, until now you've been running around, unrestricted, killing as you please. I'm here to ensure the moves you make don't endanger the United States or its allies."

He's also not wrong about us having a shocking amount of freedom. But that's the point. The GUARD was a last-resort solution against enemies with few constraints. A remedy for the kind of bureaucracy and political division that had plagued prominent governments to the point of catastrophic failure.

It was intended that the GUARD be dissolved after the threat had been mitigated. However, with the success that manifested, the GUARD instead burgeoned into something bigger and stronger.

"We're fighting a threat that the world has never seen before. Unless you and your pals at MI6 are going to *help* us, I suggest you not hinder our operations because your lives may depend on it. How are you so sure that your little accord isn't Delta's doing anyhow?"

He eyes me. "I can't be. But I also can't be sure that the GUARD isn't being influenced just the same. That's the issue. No one knows what side everyone else is truly on."

"So what exactly do you want? To hover over us and be the reason that information gets leaked to Delta? Sounds like a great way for my team to get killed."

"You're going to have to do a better job of convincing me to trust you if you want me to leave you alone."

Q's voice is suddenly in my ear. "Bring him back to Baltimore, Thanatos. This is going nowhere. Harley and Kohler, you stay there and continue working on Parrish."

I sigh. "All right. Boss wants to meet you."

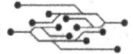

The next day I am back at our safe house after a painful car ride with Agent DILF.

Sanchez looks between me and Lucien and Zahra and then says to Q, "Does the GUARD have any agents over thirty? Jesus, you're sending our youth out to die."

Q regards him coolly. Eventually, he simply shrugs. "They're our best."

"We're tougher to kill than you might think, bro," Zahra adds with nonchalance.

He gives a half smile. "Fair enough."

He and Q spend a couple hours locked in the safe house's office, I assume to try to come to some consensus regarding the CIA's involvement in Operation Labyrinth. If Medina did indeed make an agreement to allow oversight, then we might not be able to stop it. And if Delta's claws are as deep as we think… it could end up killing us. But combined resources could also give us an edge.

The good part about this trip back to Baltimore is Zahra.

I teach her some self-defense at her request, but the whole time I'm distracted by how close she is to me, by the heat of her body against mine. I'm demonstrating a hold and having her break out of it when my lack of focus allows her to nearly snap my arm.

"*Fuck*," I complain. "I need that arm."

She merely laughs. "Fight me."

She's looking at me with a twisted smile, but there's something else there, and it stops me in my tracks.

A few beats of hesitation pass before she reaches her hand out. As I place my palm in hers, she gently pulls me toward her.

"Remember what I said before you left?" she murmurs, gazing up at me.

"How could I forget?" I breathe.

"Well, my offer still stands."

Suddenly I'm nervous. God, I want her, but I also know that it's dangerous emotional territory.

"I can't… get into something serious," I say quietly, worried that she might ask for an explanation.

"I know," she responds, her voice gentle but her eyes still hungry. "That doesn't mean we can't have a bit of fun."

She leads me back to her room, my heart racing faster and faster with anticipation. But she doesn't open her door at first. She presses me against it, presses herself against me, unconcerned about anyone who might see.

My eyes drop to her lips as her hands roam my body. I can hardly stand the teasing, but I don't dare rush it. Eventually she brings her mouth to mine, and my arms slide around her.

That's when there's a shift in our dynamic, an exchange of control.

When I push into her room, our shirts are on the floor in an instant. Her fingers are dangerously low, sliding under the waistband of my underwear to tease me further. My hands have made their way underneath her shirt, around her waist, down her back. Her legs wrap around me as I carry her to the bed and lay her on it.

I grab a half-empty bottle of liquor on her nightstand, spinning off the cap and taking a drink. Standing between her thighs, I pour it into her open mouth and kiss her before the taste dissipates.

She slides backward as I climb onto the bed, holding myself over her. My lips and tongue snake slowly, deliberately down her neck and chest, and she arches her back when I reach one of her pierced nipples. She moves against my hand down below, but only after a few minutes do I finally slip it into her leggings.

And when I take them off, she locks eyes with me like she wants me —or what she knows I'm about to do—more than anything.

I kiss her from her hipbones to the insides of her thighs, teasing her for just a bit longer, and she's practically dying by the time I make it to the middle to taste her. That's when she moans, uncontrollably. God, it's such a turn-on.

She's breathing hard, shaking, by the end of it, but it's only a few seconds before she sits up and unbuttons my pants, practically ripping them—along with my underwear—right off. She pulls me toward her, into her. I can hardly comprehend how good she feels.

The rest of the night is a blur of pleasure until we fall asleep, tangled bodies under tangled sheets.

TWENTY SEVEN
ZAHRA

Let me just say this about Kai Thanatos: that boy knows what he's doing. And the best part is that he's not even aware of how sexy he is. God, that look in his eyes he gets when he flirts. I don't let myself lust for him too much, but he's making it hard. He hugs me goodbye when he leaves again, too, in front of everyone, which Lucien immediately gives me shit for.

"What did I just see?" he asks, a knowing look in his eye.

"Nothing," I reply innocently.

"I certainly *heard* something last night."

"Get to work, for the love of God," Q interrupts, frowning, about to head out himself.

He and the CIA guy are making a trip to Langley, which I had figured would mean Kai would be babysitting. Given that he's not, I decide to take the opportunity to do whatever I want, despite Q telling me not to do anything he'd have to kill me for.

"Hey," I say to Lucien, after Q and Sanchez have departed. "What do you say we go grab a couple of drinks? Sit outside, talk, whatever. I'm tired of being inside."

Yesterday was the first time I witnessed one of his so-called episodes. I found him curled in the corner of his room, having some sort of anxiety attack. Terrified, sweating, talking only to himself. I have no idea what he was actually going through, and I get the feeling he has no intention of sharing.

He looks at me, hesitant. "You want to talk about Delta in public?"

"Not blatantly. But no one's going to pay us any attention, really. We'll go somewhere noisy."

"You know that I can't actually leave, right?"

"Oh don't worry. I convinced Kai to show me how to disable the prisoner protocol."

His eyebrows raise.

"But don't get too excited—I'm sure as hell not showing you," I add.

Eventually he nods. "That sounds nice, actually. Normal." He says the word "normal" like it's foreign, and I suppose it is.

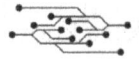

"Can I ask you a question?" Lucien begins as we await our beers at a bustling joint in downtown Baltimore. The city is akin to New York in many ways, with its fair share of junkies, decaying buildings, and street vendors, but you won't find a place quite like Morgue Row here.

"Sure. What's on your mind?"

I think Lucien feels exposed out and about like this, but he tries to shove the paranoia down. He places his elbows on our table and looks at me with his piercing eyes. "I'm curious about you and Kai. You two seem very compatible."

I shrug. "Yeah. We get each other, I think. I never expected it, though."

"Mm. I find him interesting. He has a lot of opposing traits that kind of have me at a loss. He's mean but sometimes kind, cold but caring, tough but not emotionless."

"I think that's what I like about him."

"People seem to be either drawn in or repulsed by his personality, no in between. Which I think gives him a power he doesn't really recognize. He has the ability to alter the atmosphere of a room. And he's the leader of the team, even if he doesn't know it. I will say, though, that I think he has some intense demons."

Ah, the monsters inside. I've sensed their presence, but I haven't seen them. Before I got involved in all this bullshit, we both left our baggage at the door and just existed with one another. We certainly can't do that anymore, and I don't know where that leaves us.

"Yeah. But don't we all?"

He purses his lips. "I can't tell if you do. Which is a good thing. Because it means you're in control of them, and not the other way around."

I study him for a moment, pondering whether his judgment is true before deciding that it has to be.

"Separating one's behavior from emotions that are dictated by past trauma is not something many people do well," Lucien adds. "I get the impression that it's something the GUARD expects from its agents, but doesn't actually teach. Which makes you very valuable to our team."

My mind flits to my late mentor. Over the years I've come to realize how many things he taught me, and emotional discipline was one of them. I came to him in need of an outlet, but he slowly turned it into a means for growth.

I'm going to need that resilience when I join Delta, which is what I suspect Lucien is hinting at.

In a couple weeks' time, I will become Harper Olsen from Detroit, who has witnessed and survived poverty, addiction, and violence, all of which have contributed to her resentment of society. According to Kai, it looks like Diana Parrish grew up in a similar world. But we all have. It's the typical American experience.

Harper participates in the protests but stays out of trouble; she's angry but not too impulsive. Delta does not want people they can't control. Rather, they want people they can manipulate.

They also want talent, the potential to be lethal. So Harper, like me, can defend herself and learn quickly. She knows how to hide, who not to mess with, how to survive with next to nothing. Somewhat unlike me, she's good with words, adept at convincing people to believe her and trust her. She's confident, but not too assertive.

The others are going to spend the next week watching Parrish's every move. It's on Lucien and me to develop a strategy of how best to win her over and prepare for what's on the inside.

But Lucien already knows what awaits me on the inside, for the most part.

He drills into me three things: "Those in power will abuse you. The second you step out of line, they will kill you. So you cannot break. You *cannot* break."

"Is that what you did? Abuse people who were beneath you?" I look him right in the eye. He does not look away.

"Yes." His voice is barely audible. "And then I broke."

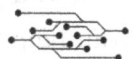

As we are walking back to the safe house, Lucien breaks again.

I'm not clear on exactly what transpires; all I know is that in my peripheral vision I see a man make a rapid movement and then Lucien has him by the throat. A total stranger, whose eyes widen with fear before he even comprehends what's happening.

In the span of a second Lucien slams the man to the ground and is kneeling on his chest. I am frozen in shock for an instant before I yank him off with all my strength.

"Lucien!" I shout at him, holding him firmly by the shoulders. "Stop!"

But he's not there. It's like he doesn't recognize me. His eyes are utterly feral, and I feel my heartbeat quicken in response.

Then, his hands are around my neck.

"You can't hurt me," he snarls, his voice low.

You're strangling me, asshole.

I struggle for a few seconds before I force myself to focus. I pry his one pinkie away from my neck, bending it backward until something pops, but he barely winces. My body, on defensive autopilot, seems to take over as I knee him in the groin, then twist my shoulders and thrust an elbow into his face. His grip loosens just enough to enable my escape.

I stumble backward and gulp in a breath of air.

Then I slap him, hard, across the face. "Lucien!"

When he looks at me again I see that he has returned, confused. *What have they done to him?*

The bystanders just got one hell of a show, that's for sure. I look around at all of them. "Thank God you guys were here. I don't know what I would've done without your help."

They just stare at me. One of them has a phone in her hand like she's about to call the police, or has already.

"No, no," I say. "No police. He has PTSD, it's fine. Carry on with your days, please."

Turning back to Lucien, I see an apology forming on his lips, his eyes bleeding with guilt. "You okay?" I ask before he can say anything. I don't think that he meant to hurt anyone. It's as if a different version of him took over.

He runs a hand over his face. "Me? Yeah... I don't really know what happened. God, I'm sorry."

"How are you so strong? I mean, I have to squint to see your muscles."

I get a weak smile out of him for that. "Adrenaline."

"Damn, I'm gonna need to carry around a taser."

"I'm thinking I shouldn't go out in public to begin with."

"Yeah let's get the hell out of here. Sorry about your finger, by the way."

"Sorry about your neck," he replies.

I anticipate that Q will be irritated with us for this whole fiasco, but it turns out we are the least of his worries.

Rather, it's Adriano Medina.

Q returns close to midnight, on edge. And for the first hour, we are in the dark, though we catch bits of the heated conversations he has with Keating and Holbrook. Whoever they are.

Eventually, Q directs his attention toward us, with Kai, Harley, and Kohler present via video call.

"Medina is dead."

Four seconds in which that information hangs ominously in the air. I see Kai pinch the bridge of his nose. Everyone else is silent and motionless, waiting for Q to continue.

"More importantly, we think Medina gave them something."

"What?" Harley asks.

"We don't know. All we have are vague whispers from the inside, so we're in the dark for now. But you should assume it's whatever they need to try to take us down. I don't think Medina would be dead otherwise."

Q's gaze shifts to Lucien, who nods.

"So," Q continues. "We think they're going to strike, and we may not see it coming, which means we don't have time to waste. Zahra, I think we should accelerate your operation. Get into Delta as soon as possible in case you can get some intel. I'm going to head back to New York to try and get ahead of this."

Wtf happened to your neck? Kai texts me after we've ended the video call. *I didn't think I was choking you that hard...*

Haha no, that was Lucien. Lost his shit for a few seconds, I reply. *But you can choke me harder if you want.*

"Zahra." My head snaps up from looking at my phone.

"What?"

Lucien gives me an exasperated look. "Wipe that smirk off your face and tell Kai to come back and get us tomorrow. There's no sense for us to stay here anymore."

I nod. With Q's orders, we should be working as closely as possible with the others and establishing Harper's life in D.C., starting with an apartment and a job. Q and his team have already supplied me with an ID, birth certificate, and SSN. Harper Olsen is now a real person with records and bank accounts, and Zahra Kang is gone. As if I never existed.

And once I'm done with Harper, I'll have the chance to start fresh as whoever I want to be.

It's that fact that's going to get me through all this.

TWENTY EIGHT

KAI

Zahra and Lucien are outside on the balcony, casually smoking mist together like nothing is wrong, like they've got all the time in the world to just exist. Or maybe it's a means by which to fend off anxiety, because of everything that's going on.

Lucien silently offers me their pen as I join them, but I shake my head. "Not my thing."

"You need it," he insists.

I sigh, debating. It's probably not going to be mist that kills me in the end. "Fine."

I take the cancer stick between my fingers and put it in my mouth. I hate the sickly sweet smell, but God does the first drag feel good, swirling into my lungs and dosing me with dopamine.

"What are you guys doing?" I ask, smoke drifting out into the grey sky and disappearing as the wind disperses it into the cool air.

"Smoking," Zahra responds.

"And day drinking," Lucien adds, pulling out a nearly empty glass bottle of whiskey to take a swig.

"Don't be stingy," I say, grabbing it from him.

I want to ask why the hell he apparently strangled Zahra yesterday, but I can intuit the answer. I figure it's best not to bring it up—Lucien is dealing with the psychological effects of Devil's Peak, and the rest of us were aware of the potential consequences when we agreed to seek his help.

At the same time, I need to know he's not going to kill one of us. Q is occupied with the whole Medina disaster, and we have a few weeks to get Zahra a position in Delta, so the last thing we need is Lucien affecting our work. But he knows that.

He is about to say something but loses my attention to my buzzing phone. Shay is calling, and for some reason I grow uneasy. I leave Zahra and Lucien on the balcony to answer, knowing that Shay is probably not calling because she misses me.

"Have you heard from Camden?" she asks before I even say hello.

It's exactly as I feared. "No, why?"

"He's gone. I haven't seen him for two days. Leven said his tracker is offline, too."

My heart skips a beat, because I know what that means. "His tracker is offline?" I repeat.

"Yes. There's nothing that points to where he may have gone, because his last logged location is his apartment."

"*Shit*. The GUARD must have him detained somewhere."

"Seriously? Why?"

I wince. "He broke into Holbrook's computer to get information I was looking for."

I can practically see her eyes widen at that. "What? They could kill him for that. They might be torturing him as we speak." She's starting to panic, and I am too.

"Let me call Keating and see what I can find out."

I hang up and tap Keating's name in my phone, pacing while I wait for him to pick up.

"Thanatos. What's wrong?"

"Do you know if Camden is being detained?"

"Adler? Why would he be?"

"He—fuck. It's too hard to explain. Can you just find out for me, please?"

He exhales, wary. "Fine. Just a minute."

It doesn't take long for him to confirm my hypothesis—Holbrook has Camden locked up somewhere under the justification that he is a suspected ally of Delta.

Keating is understandably skeptical of my involvement, though he is equally skeptical as to why he wasn't informed about Camden's detainment. I debate whether to tell Keating the truth, but now that I know Holbrook is monitoring us like a hawk... I need to choose my moves carefully.

I decide to take the blame, but spare the details, and bank on Keating being willing to release Camden because he trusts me.

"You're telling me that *you're* the reason we have him detained? What in God's name did you have him looking into?"

"You can't honestly believe that Camden of all people would be Delta."

"It's never the ones you'd expect, Kai, you know that. We're not taking any chances. And you never answered my question."

"I can't say, not now."

"You're not being very compelling."

"You know that I'd never do something that I didn't think was important, right?"

I hear him sigh in exasperation. "Of course."

"So trust me. Please." There is pained desperation in my voice that he must hear.

Eventually, he relents.

"Fine. I'll do what I can. But you know what our policy is with everything going on, and I have to level with you. I may already be too late."

With those words, I nearly stop breathing.

Too late.

The possibility had flitted across my mind, but I hadn't let myself actually believe it could happen. Not to Camden.

My mind reels. *Why did I do this? I knew I knew I knew.*

And if it can happen to Camden, it can happen to Reiya.

I drive with Zahra and Lucien back to the motel, lost in thought. I barely process checking them into their rooms, handing them off to Kohler to get caught up on our plan with Diana Parrish, and retreating to my own room, where Harley is looking through our data.

Then Mason Dare calls me.

I put him on speakerphone. "Please tell me you're going to explain what the hell Rosalie Brenner is doing."

He exhales. "Yes. Those files you retrieved pretty much confirmed my fear. But I have to start at the very beginning."

Harley and I exchange a glance. "All right."

"A few decades ago, a rural rancher in Utah unearthed some peculiar remains in one of his fields. He decided to send those remains to be examined, but the lab that received them was unable to identify them. The creature was subsequently passed around from lab to lab, and eventually, it was determined that *no one* had seen the species before. Not only that, but the genetic material was vastly different than anything on Earth. Thus began the speculation that it didn't actually originate on this planet. While they soon recovered two more of the same species, the thing that confirmed the theory, and perhaps is the more interesting discovery, was a piece of alien *technology*. And that's when the US government started getting involved.

"Scientists realized the device was still functioning, and, either by experiment or by accident, discovered that it allowed near-instantaneous interstellar travel. The device had cached a location on a completely different world, a planet with three moons and human-breathable air that they named Nyx. The animals there had gone extinct, but countless species of plants and bacteria-like creatures had survived whatever catastrophe had befallen the planet.

"Long story short, although we call them *Nyxian*, biologists concluded that Nyx was not in fact the original home of the extraterrestrials discovered by that Utah rancher. They were planet-hoppers, likely trying to avoid their own extinction. While at first they may have been escaping extreme natural disasters such as supernovas or asteroid collisions, we believe that they came to Earth and other life-sustaining planets looking for a cure to something killing their kind. It's no coincidence that we can breathe the air on Nyx, nor is it a coincidence that life has developed on relatively similar planets across the universe.

"All of this, of course, was fascinating but also quite frightening. No one could make sense of a lot of things. Based on the civilization they found on Nyx, the extraterrestrials seemed highly advanced, and showed evidence of incredibly complex abilities we lack. Abilities, it turned out, that they had *engineered* through genetic manipulation. They were quite unlike anything on Earth but still comparable to the mammals that we are familiar with.

"The government soon hired a European geneticist—Elsa Salazar—to lead a research team. And at first it was just that, but in America's continual pursuit of power, the leaders who knew about it saw an opportunity.

"That's when the project turned into a quest to biologically alter humans to see if they could develop some of the abilities that the extraterrestrials had. Really, it was a shot in the dark, because I don't think anyone knew what they were doing. But if we could artificially evolve the human species... imagine what we could achieve. They took thousands of volunteers and prisoners and experimented for years. All the records indicated failure after failure, death after death, but in reality, Salazar was hiding the true results.

"She had been on the front lines of gentech innovation for a while, and she discovered a way to study the aliens' extracted genetic material—something like DNA—to pinpoint the 'supergenes' that allowed their enhancements. She subsequently developed synthetic DNA to mimic the supergenes, and added synthetic chromosomes to her subjects. To this day I am in awe that she ever succeeded. I mean, this was a while ago.

"She knew that her subjects were going to be exploited, so she helped them escape. I doubt many of them came from privilege—one doesn't agree to be experimented on without a strong incentive, which presumably was money. To protect them, Salazar gave them a home on Nyx."

At this point I can't help but interject. *"What?* You mean she basically teleported a bunch of people across the universe to start a life? That's one hell of an escape."

I'm still unsure if I should believe any of this, but why would Dare make it all up?

Harley's mouth is hanging open, her eyes unblinking.

"Yes," Dare responds. "They built a society, called Elysium, as a new species. Then Salazar destroyed her lab, stole all of the superluminal transportation tech that the government has never been able to recreate or understand, and disappeared. However, under the radar, she periodically transported back to receive aid and technology from her connections. That's how I got involved, when I was much younger. They contacted my family and asked us to help."

"So... your son..."

"His mother was part of the original experiments when she was a child—her parents volunteered her without really knowing the extent of what they were getting her into. They were promised money and with the economic crisis going on, that was enough. About a year before Benson was born, she got stranded here on Earth due to political turmoil that resulted in the Elysian society banning contact with humans. We haven't heard from them since."

This is all so crazy but I try to stick to the point. "And Dr. Brenner?"

"She was vaguely involved with the Elysians due to familial ties, but never directly, and I suspect that it angered her to be on the fringe of something so spectacular. She probably wants what she could never have."

"And Holbrook sees it as an opportunity to enhance his agents," I finish.

"Seems that way," Dare says grimly. "And if he sends people after one of you... there may not be a whole lot you can do."

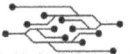

Harley and I spend at least fifteen minutes reeling after Dare has hung up. It's almost too much to comprehend, let alone grasp the consequences of whatever Holbrook is planning.

"Cam shouldn't have gotten involved in this," Harley says quietly when I break the news of his detainment.

"Don't you think I know that?" I snap. "I knew it all along but I didn't know what else to do. He's not exactly one to take no for an answer."

She shakes her head. "For once in your life can you not raise your voice? Don't get mad at *me*, Kai. I'm not blaming you."

I exhale. "Sorry. I'm just stressed out about it. Let's go see what the others have accomplished."

We open the door to the other motel room just in time to witness Kohler slam Lucien against a wall and Zahra yank Kohler down to the ground by the back of his shirt.

Lord help us.

"What the fuck?" I say, looking between the three of them.

Kohler rights himself and wipes blood from his nose, smearing it across his cheek. I can't tell who punched him, though I'd bet on Zahra.

"In case you didn't notice," he responds tightly, "Psycho over here tried to kill our mole. I think it's high time we dump him before he *actually* murders one of us."

"He didn't do it on purpose, you insufferable douchebag," Zahra spits.

"That's the problem!" Kohler snaps back. "He's not in control of himself!"

"Kohler!" I interject. "Calm down." My jaw is clenched and I know that if he says another word I'm really going to lose it. There's too much shit happening.

Admittedly, I had been worried about the exact thing he is; I just resolved it a little differently.

He throws up his hands in irritation and says, "You'll all regret the day you let this monster into our lives."

Then he walks out.

"Well. Now that that's over, did you guys talk about anything useful?" Harley asks.

"We started to, before he noticed the bruises on my neck," Zahra responds. "He already has an apartment for me, a plan for me to meet Parrish, and a plan to sneak a bug into the base."

"Would've been nice for him to mention," I mutter.

"He wants me to get a job at some bar she frequents—do you two know anything about that?"

Harley nods. "Yeah. It's probably not a bad idea. I've spent some time watching her, and from what I've seen, she generally goes there alone and doesn't really speak to anyone. And then she leaves. She likes remaining on the fringes of regular society, but I have a feeling that's not the case in Delta. Once we get that bug into the base, we'll know exactly who she is."

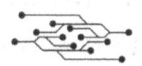

Kohler and I sit in silence in the Audi, parked a block or so away from Parrish's favorite cafe. Harley is there awaiting her arrival, awaiting an opportunity to slip our bug into the bag she always carries. All Harley has to do is stick the bug, which looks like a boxelder, to the side of the bag, and from there I can remotely control its movement as necessary. Once it's inside the base, I can find it a good hiding spot.

Kohler may be a shitty person, but he's good at coming up with simple plans, which I appreciate.

"She's late," he says, his hands on the wheel as though he's preparing for a car chase. "Any sign of her, Harley?"

"No," Harley responds in my earpiece.

Kohler and I both scan the sidewalks.

"There." Kohler throws the car into drive before I've even seen what he has. I don't know how the hell he spotted her so quickly, but Parrish is up ahead, waiting at a bus stop. And the bus is almost there.

"Get on that bus. Harley and I will follow."

He pulls over and I am out the door before he comes to a full stop, racing across the street to catch the bus. The driver looks me up and down like I'm out of place.

He grumbles a price that I can't make out, but I'm already scanning my phone.

With one eye on Parrish, who is sitting adjacent to the back door, I take a side-facing seat toward the front and inconspicuously take out my earpiece so she doesn't happen to see it.

She doesn't disembark until we're in the heart of Washington D.C. I wait for a few moments to give her a head start before following her down the sidewalk, catching a glimpse of Harley and Kohler close behind me in the car. I slip my earpiece back in.

"Any idea where she might be headed?" I ask.

"She might be meeting someone," Harley replies.

"I'm going to drive up ahead to drop Harley off so she can intercept her and get the bug into place," Kohler says. "Kai, you stay behind her."

I watch as Harley gets out of the car, and, pretending to be distracted by her phone, brushes up against Parrish. In the blink of an eye, her fingers attach the tiny bug to Parrish's bag. Even if someone were watching very attentively, it still wouldn't look like anything out of the ordinary.

Parrish eventually enters an office building, but Kohler warns me not to follow her inside.

"It's a government building, and that means there'll be cameras and security galore," he says. "Meet me around the next corner and we'll see what our mic picks up."

As we listen, Parrish utters just a single sentence: "Everything is there."

And a man responds: "Thank you."

TWENTY NINE
ZAHRA

TWO WEEKS LATER

Diana Parrish hasn't even looked at me in the fifteen minutes she's been sitting at the bar, and I'm frantically trying to figure out how to start a conversation without being awkward. It's my fifth night working at Luna, but this being the first time I've seen her here, I'm anxious as hell. Listening to the way she talks to her inferiors has only made it worse, but I least I'm now aware of the kind of human I'm dealing with.

She's tough, takes no shit, and commands any room she walks into. People here definitely notice her, but I think they're too intimidated to say anything to her.

While I'm wiping the bar I casually ask if she wants another drink, and that's when she seems to notice me.

"Yes, thank you," she responds, studying me. Then, by sheer luck or by the grace of whoever may be watching over me, she starts the convo for me. "You new?"

"Yeah." I glance up at her from making her drink to flash a quick smile. "I just moved here from Detroit."

I can't tell if I'm already boring her to death or if she just always exhibits no emotion.

"What made you pick here?"

I shrug. "I guess I've always liked D.C. I wanted to change the way my life was heading, try to make a difference. I figured maybe I'd have a shot at it here, where everything is happening."

I set down her glass in front of her. "It's not a bad place for a fresh start," she says. "I came here myself for exactly that."

"How has it been for you?"

"Life-changing, I'd say. But it hasn't been without difficulty, of course. Nothing good comes easy."

"Any advice? I sometimes feel a bit… stuck. Unable to get where I want to be, despite exhausting every avenue I can think of."

She ponders for a moment. "I often find that being stuck is not a result of failure, but rather an abundance of caution."

"Caution?" I repeat.

She looks me in the eye. "If there's one thing I've learned, it's that sometimes you have to be willing to go to extremes to thrive."

Before I have a chance to reply she downs her drink and gets up to leave. "Nice meeting you…"

"Harper."

She nods once. "Harper."

Then she's gone and I'm wondering if that went well or if I didn't do enough.

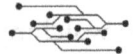

I get back to my new apartment around one in the morning and tell Kai to come over. At this point we are supposed to be separating so that I'm not seen with any GUARD agents, but I can't help myself. Given that I'm now talking to Parrish, this could be one of the last times we see one another, and I have no idea what's going to happen to either of us. Although we aimed for casual, we've gotten closer in the past couple weeks than we should've, and now it's made everything harder.

"Hi," he says when I open the door and pull him inside. He gives me a genuine smile but it's not enough to mask the worry that is always eating away at him. He's worried about Camden, who was recently released and is apparently drinking more than ever. About Reiya's safety and his inability to protect her. About Harley and everything that causes her pain.

Even about me.

I often feel like he has convinced himself that he's going to lose one of us.

And though he cares so deeply for a select few, he lives a life of haunted solitude that those closest to him cannot penetrate. It's mental solitude that I don't think he knows how to escape.

"Any update from Kohler?" I ask.

A couple weeks ago, Kohler opted to break off from the rest of the team to investigate what might have been exchanged between Parrish and a New York senator's aide. We were all relieved, to say the least.

"Nope. But I think he's getting closer. How was work?"

"Well, I talked to Parrish."

His eyebrows go up. "And?"

"I think I have a shot at getting closer to her."

"Of course you do," he says like it's obvious. "There's no one I'd rather bet on."

I find myself smiling at his genuine belief in me, which I often lack. "What did you learn from the bug today?"

"Parrish mentioned Medina's capture and death but didn't reveal anything about their next big move. She speaks in code so it's often hard to determine who or what she's really talking about, but we've learned a couple of base locations and planned assassinations. Names of people who work for her, too. Nothing that has gotten us any closer to Arachne, though."

"So what are your next steps?"

"Harley and Lucien have already left to check out one of the bases Parrish mentioned, one that's under a bit of scrutiny. From what we gathered, there was a request from pretty high up that D.C. watch this base in case they're stepping out of line. I'm heading there soon, at which point we may end up wiping it out."

I nod, taking his hand, and for several moments we are silent.

Then he grazes my cheek with the backs of his fingers. Tilts my chin upward, looking at me with those pained dark gray eyes that are like a chasm that I'll never see the bottom of. And as he parts his lips, I close the gap between us.

Our kiss is different than before—more raw. More somber, perhaps. I knew at some level that deciding to pursue him would likely end in heartache for at least one of us, but I also knew it'd be a heartache that was worth it.

So I pull him into me for one final moment of this, this intimacy that I've never had with anyone, then pull away, exhaling.

"How are you doing?" I murmur.

He holds my gaze for a few seconds, then, almost at a whisper, he says, "I'm okay."

"You don't seem okay," I respond gently. I know it's something he doesn't want me to say, because he hates being vulnerable.

"I'm always okay. Are you okay?" A deflection, as expected.

"Yeah. For now."

He sighs heavily, running a hand through his hair. "I wish you weren't going to be on your own going into this."

"Me too. But I'll be fine."

"I know you will." He takes out a folded piece of paper and presses it into my palm. Written on it is a phone number. "But just in case you need something."

When he pulls me into a hug I become emotional at the fact that I haven't felt this cared about for a long, long time. Then he says, "I'm gonna miss you, Z," and the tears come.

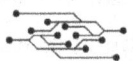

I go a whole week and a half thinking that I've made zero progress with Parrish. Every time I see her I reveal a bit more of Harper, of the person Lucien told me to be. Angered, smart, and strong, yet malleable. But I can't tell if it's working.

I start to panic, on the verge of desperation, before I find out that she *is* intrigued by me.

She pulls me aside after my shift one night, and for a few terrifying moments I think that she's onto me. My heart stops. But I maintain my composure.

"Harper. I know we hardly know each other, but I believe you might be a good fit for where I work."

"...Sorry?"

"Would you like to interview?"

I feign confusion. "What kind of work is it?"

She purses her lips. "I need to know if you can do the job first. Do well at the interview, then I'll tell you."

"That sounds..."

"Trust me," she cuts me off.

So I nod. "Okay. Sure. Just let me know when and where."

"Day after tomorrow. Artemis Cafe, say ten in the morning?"

"I'll be there."

The paranoid part of me still worries that I'm falling for a trap, but the rational part of me knows that Lucien's coaching might have paid off. All those hours of listening to her to analyze what she respects—frankness, drive, resilience—and what she detests—indecisiveness, laziness, ignorance. I made myself into a person Delta would want, reinvented my outward personality and beliefs, ditching my sarcastic default for a hardened, tenacious persona. I bonded with Parrish about the violence I've witnessed and the hardship I've experienced, and not all of it was fake. It wasn't easy but something caught her attention. Maybe it was Harper's ideas, maybe it was her ambition. Maybe it was all because she saw herself in me—Harper, rather—the very first night we met.

When I walk into Artemis Cafe two days later, it's empty apart from one man I've never seen before. Parrish is nowhere to be found; there's not even any staff present. I pause after entering to shove down the uneasiness creeping up on me, then promptly take a seat across from the man.

"Harper Olsen, nice to meet you." I stick out my hand, and although he shakes it he doesn't say anything for a moment.

"I am going to ask a series of questions, and I request that you reply accurately rather than adjusting to what you think I might want to hear. Remember, you know nothing about the job yet."

I nod, and he nods back, maintaining a steely presence. But he's not as intimidating as he thinks.

"Okay. How old are you?"

"Twenty-three."

"Have you ever gotten into trouble with the law?"

"I got a speeding ticket once."

"Would you describe yourself as more present- or future-oriented?"

"Future."

"Do you have many close relationships?"

"Not anymore."

"Are you content?"

I raise my eyebrows. "Not really."

"Are you political?"

"Yes."

"Describe a time when you manipulated someone."

Not a question I anticipated, so I pull something out of my ass. "Well... I used to shower a former partner with affection that I didn't mean in order to get things I wanted. Money, mostly. He ate it all up because I made him feel like a god, and he was too blind to see that I was only around for the benefits."

His expression doesn't change.

"Describe a time when you hurt someone you cared about."

I look at him for a few moments, faking hesitation. "Recently I left my ailing mother with no one to look after her, and no one to pay her medical bills. I wanted to pursue my own goals, and quite frankly, she was in the way. I care about her, but I don't even know if she's still alive."

That part of my fake background is thanks to Lucien—he thought I needed something dark, and suggested I utilize my animosity toward my real mother.

"What is your biggest regret?"

"Hm. I think it would be not having the guts to take a stand sooner. On my life and on the things that matter to me."

"Lastly, Miss Olsen, please describe your skillset. Tell me what you can do."

"Well, I'd say I'm quite versatile. I'm good at reading people, which enables me to work well with various personalities. I'm persuasive when I need to be but can collaborate with others even if we have opposing ideas or traits. I'm fit and competent at self-defense, including with weapons. I also have basic command line skills and fluency in Cobra.

"However, I feel that with my ability to see patterns and absorb unfamiliar material quickly, I'm more than willing to learn something new. Ultimately, my forte is that I can adapt. I can adapt and survive. I know how to make the most of what I have and how to choose allies. I'm trying to *become* the skilled person you might be looking for, and I'm not going to let anything prevent me from reaching my goals."

He doesn't really react, but I'd expected that. "All right, thank you. I'm going to move on to word associations. I will say a single word, and I need you to respond with the first word that pops into your head."

I nod again.

"Human."

"Flawed."

"Secret."

"Protect."

"Family."

"Struggle."

"Technology."

"Opportunity."

"Intelligence."

"Key."

"Adversity."

"Imbalanced."

He says a few more words but I notice he's not writing anything down, which means that he's likely recording me. Hell, these people have probably been watching my every move. They already know everything about me.

"Now then. Miss Olsen, one of the most important characteristics of those we hire is that they align with our mission. I'm going to get a feel of the extent to which you will fit in, and again, please answer honestly."

"All right."

"Regardless of policies and parties, are you, as a US resident, satisfied with the structure of the government and how it functions?"

"Well… I've always recognized that there's room for improvement. At a high level, I think there's a reason we've remained one of the most powerful nations in the world, but there are many flaws. The structure as it is now, and as it has been for a long time, benefits a small group of people. And lately I've noticed how easy it is for those in power to harm those with less. It's safe to say that I've lost a lot of trust in our system because people like me are suffering."

"And how do you hope that change will be achieved?"

"I used to believe that we could create change through the democratic processes meant to provide power to the people. But again, my trust has waned. I think our country is being controlled by powerful individuals who benefit from never solving problems. They don't seem to truly care about the rest of us, and they're not going away any time soon. I'm beginning to think that something more radical will have to be done, but I don't necessarily know what that is. People will need to rise up against the corruption and tyranny, in some form or another. That revolution, so to speak, may be inevitable, actually. I feel it coming."

"Would you want to be a part of that?"

"I already am. But I'm looking to do more, and that's why I'm here."

"At this job interview or in this city?"

"Both. Ms. Parrish didn't give information about your organization, she just seemed to think my ambitions, however unspecific they are, were relevant to what you do."

"Perhaps they are. I'm going to send my feedback to her and someone will be reaching out to you shortly."

I nod once. "Thank you for your time," I say, knowing that's my cue to get out.

I take several deep breaths once I'm outside the cafe to get a grip on myself. I think that went okay.

This time, though, I don't have Kai to discuss things with. I'm on my own now, Q having given me very serious directions to only contact the team with information or in a dire emergency. He set up a portal on my computer, disguised as a game app, over which I can securely send files and messages to everyone in Minotaur. It's really my only connection to them. To anyone.

Being alone has never felt so terrifying.

THIRTY
KAI

By the time I arrive at our Rio de Janeiro safe house, Harley and Lucien have already developed a plan to wipe out the small Delta base on the outskirts of the city. More importantly, however, they have a name—a name of someone who could be an essential cog of Delta. Finally, some progress.

"We've been listening to them nonstop," Harley explains. "It turns out that the leaders here are *also* trying to figure out who Arachne is. I think it's why this base came up in Parrish's conversations—they suspect something. The agents here have been meeting every morning and keep mentioning someone called *Gokiburi*. Means cockroach in Japanese, as I'm sure you know. They think his real name is Takeshi Otsuka, and they're trying to find him."

"He could be the link we so desperately need," Lucien adds.

"You've never heard of him?" I ask.

He shakes his head. "No. Or if I did, he wasn't significant."

"Why are they trying to find out who Arachne is?"

"From what we've heard," Harley begins, "they don't enjoy her power, her anonymity. They're trying to find her because they may want to amass support to dethrone her—they realize that not knowing her true intentions with Delta makes them vulnerable."

"Interesting. So what's our game plan? Should we be wiping out a base that could provide us information we need? Not to mention the attention it will draw to the GUARD. I mean, Delta could retaliate."

"We debated that with Q and the head of the Rio Division. After being here a few days, it seems this lead on Gokiburi is all they've got. Gleaning more information is a possibility, but their members have been infiltrating the police force and killing civilians. Facilitating unrest to destabilize the city and the nation. Everyone agreed we need them gone."

I nod.

"This base is going to be pretty easy to get into," Harley continues. "Nothing like Zahra's base, certainly. Lucien is going to spoof their camera footage and disarm their security so that they won't see us coming, after which he and I will go in and take out Delta members from the bottom up. We've located a good sniper position for you to simultaneously target people from the top down. The leaders all gather for a daily meeting on the top floor, so that'll be your focus, but you'll be able to scan for threats we can't see."

"I'm also going to try to write some malware to steal their data," Lucien says. "Just in case there's anything we missed related to Gokiburi."

"You think it'll be that easy?" I reply.

"I designed a lot of their security, remember. I actually considered attacking their entire network but thought it might be too soon. Rather, we should have Zahra do it after we have a clearer path to taking Delta down."

"Fair enough. Have you two heard anything about Medina and what information he may have given them?"

"No," Harley replies. "And Q hasn't communicated any information either."

"Maybe we should make a stop in New York. Do some research on Gokiburi and check in with Keating before making our next move."

"Holbrook will want an update, too. Especially since he's running the GUARD now."

"He can rot in hell, as far as I'm concerned," I mutter.

"Shay told me he's increased security and takes people—*our* people—captive out of nowhere to ensure they're not traitors. Rumors are that he's approved the interrogation and potential torture of some of them like he did with Camden."

"Jesus. Maybe we should stay away from him," I respond, giving Harley a pointed look. "Let Keating tell him what's going on."

She nods in understanding.

But we both know that we can't stop him from doing anything. If he wants me for Rosalie Brenner's research, then he'll get me.

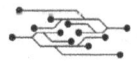

The following morning, in the dim haze of the sunrise, I lie perpendicular to the base on a rooftop a few buildings away, my Soulbarer rifle pointed toward the meeting room that is my first target. I zoom in on everyone through the small screen on top, observing. The weapon is quick to lock onto the person I aim at, and even adjusts for the wind factor, though I won't really need the extra help. If I was farther away, it'd even calculate Earth curvature.

With my earpiece I tune into their conversation, having Tony record it for future reference. They mostly discuss who they're going to assassinate and which Delta branches they despise, but my attention fades in and out as I listen for Harley and Lucien to confirm that they're in the building.

"You ready, Kai?" Harley says.

"Yep. Status?"

"We're just outside the main entrance. No one has seen us yet. Their glass is bulletproof, by the way, but Dare assured me that it'll only take two or three shots from the Soulbarer to break it."

"Got it. Let me know when you're inside."

"Will do." Then she adds, "Odds?"

"I don't think we can afford for it to be anything lower than a hundred percent."

"A hundred sounds good to me."

"Be careful in there, okay?"

"I will, Kai."

It's only thirty seconds before she gives me her confirmation and I fire three bullets in rapid succession toward the top-floor meeting room window. It bursts, and in the split second that the people inside are frozen in shock I've already taken out two.

One person, one shot.

I'm vaguely aware of the screaming in my earpiece, but it doesn't cause me to falter—I don't *let* it. Most of them don't even have time to drop to the ground before I hit them, though a few have the chance to run for cover. One scrambles underneath the table, while another dashes out into a hallway.

By now others in the building must know what's going on, so I start targeting the other rooms on the top floor. One person, in sheer desperation, jumps out one of the windows I broke, at which point I catch sight of the scene on the third story.

"A few heading down the stairs to the second floor," I tell Harley and Lucien.

I switch to the radar imaging mode on the Soulbarer so that I can see people behind the walls of the old building, knowing that my ammunition can cut through. I manage to clear most of the upper two levels, but I don't have a direct shot at those who escaped to the second floor.

"First floor secure, moving up the stairwell," Harley says.

Then, abruptly, it becomes an all-out gunfight, two against at least a dozen.

"*Fuck*," I hear Lucien hiss.

"What?" I say, straining to see what's going on. Tony informs me that a bullet grazed his leg.

While their comrades were taken by surprise, the people on the second floor have had a minute or so to prepare for a fight, and I almost abandon my position to help out. But I know that by the time I get there it'll be over, one way or another.

So I wait with bated breath as the bodies fall, praying that Harley and Lucien walk out of it alive.

Then a bullet whizzes by, inches away from my skull. My heart freezes for a second before I comb the scene for the origin.

"Tony, where'd it come from?"

"Three o'clock, across the street."

It takes me a few seconds to locate her, dressed to blend in with the buildings. Her dark hair is the only thing giving her away. I fall flat against the roof as she starts to fire at me relentlessly, and wait for a window of opportunity.

When she pauses her attack, my brain relinquishes control to instinct.

Gun up, exhale, lock in, pull the trigger.

I don't miss. But she doesn't miss either.

A blinding pain detonates in my upper left arm and I am suddenly gushing blood. My vision flares a bright white for a moment before I can see that the bullet left a hole straight through my muscle.

Cursing, I check that my attacker is down for the count, then dig through my bag for a tourniquet band, healing spray, and some bandages. I patch myself up haphazardly and refocus on the situation down below. There is silence in my earpiece.

"Harley?"

"All good. Almost died, but we're good. Finishing off one more."

I use my Soulbarer to watch as they confront the last man standing, who has begun to beg for his life. But then his words halt, and his eyes widen. Lucien smiles.

"Bet you thought you saw the last of me, didn't you?" he says in Portuguese, satisfaction emanating from his words. He shoots the man point blank.

Ah, sweet revenge.

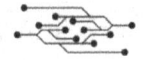

I'm just leaving the roof when Kohler calls me.

"They're going to take out New York," he says immediately.

"What?"

"The files, Kai. From Parrish? They're Delta's plans to wipe out our New York Division."

"Do they have a date?"

"No. But Keating is already discreetly evacuating everyone and sending them to a temporary location on Staten Island. They were going to hack the ventilation systems and gas everyone."

I squeeze my eyes shut.

"I'm headed there now," Kohler continues. "Where are you?"

"Rio. We were going to head back to HQ anyway, so we'll see you soon."

I notify the others and we drive straight to the airport, despite the fact that Lucien and I are still bleeding from gunshot wounds. Harley, however, is unscathed apart from bruises, crediting Dare's bulletproof vest for saving her life.

"It was only a matter of time," Lucien says about Kohler's news, Harley wrapping a clean bandage around his thigh as our jet leaves the city. "They have what they want from Medina, so now they're going to follow through on their threats to start destroying our divisions."

"We have to act fast. Us, specifically," Harley responds. "We got lucky this time but I don't think we can prevent every attack on the GUARD."

"No. The GUARD is going to collapse."

At that, I look up from attempting to dress my own wound at Lucien, who is expressionless. "It's useless for our team to try to protect the GUARD. That's not even our job, anyway. Our job is to destroy Delta."

I shake my head at his nonsense. "We can't do that without the GUARD."

"We don't need the *entire* agency," he counters. "What's most important—technology, data, resources, leaders—will be protected. And that's enough. Therefore, I suggest we not focus our efforts on defense because it wastes time we don't have."

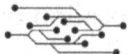

Several hours later we arrive at the makeshift headquarters, which is situated inside a run-down office building. It's nothing fancy, but it gets the job done, even as it becomes cramped as more people file in. Keating and Holbrook, to my relief, are trying to maintain order and don't really have time for my team at the moment.

So I search until find Camden, almost nervous as I push through people setting up beds and computers and weapons lockers. I don't know that I can forgive myself for what he endured. He wouldn't tell me what that was, probably for my own sanity, but I suspect it was waterboarding.

When he sees me he breaks into a grin. "Oh my God, look who it is."

"Hey Cam." When I give him a one-armed hug I can't help but blurt out an apology. "God, I'm so sorry. I feel horrible for getting you involved."

He pulls away and holds me at arm's length, without a hint of seriousness in his face. "Are you kidding me? You've made my life far more interesting, mate. Holbrook had his fun with me but you've got nothing to mope around about. Tell me what you found out."

I glance around to see if anyone's listening. "Dare told me some crazy shit. Harley and I can tell you later but Holbrook probably has eyes and ears everywhere right now."

He sighs exasperatedly. "Fine, fine. Everything's so damn strict around here now. Rules and more rules. I feel like I'm living in a dystopia within a dystopia."

"So I've heard. Anything noteworthy happen since I've been gone?"

"Well, I don't know if you know, but Holbrook told the whole GUARD about Delta when he released a statement about Medina's death. People are scared, confused, and angry. It's been chaotic, really. Lots of drama, etcetera. But I don't pay attention." He waves his hand casually.

"Fair enough. Let's go find Harley. You can meet Lucien, too."

The four of us, plus Shay and Kohler, manage to find a relatively secluded corner room and some alcohol to make the night a little better. Oddly, everyone is happy. Happy to just exist together for a bit.

But then we hear an explosion, and our laughter drops dead.

Then another, and I lock eyes with Harley. We already know what's happening.

"We need to get out. Now!" I start grabbing people's arms and pulling them to their feet.

"Left! There's an exit that way," Shay says as we are out the door of our room and running through the hallways as the place becomes an inferno. The explosions are growing closer and the building begins to tremor and crumble. Alarms are blaring.

There is a series of blasts to my right, and I witness bodies being thrown, burning, drawing lines across my vision.

The detonations are deafening and people are screaming and I am trying to keep an eye on all of my friends but somewhere in the madness I lose track of Shay and Camden.

Lucien, Harley, and I stop in hesitation for what must be only three seconds, debating whether to go back and risk death to find them or to push on. And in those seconds, Kohler, who is ahead of us, is blown to hell.

His body severed into pieces.

I throw my arms in front of my face just as the rest of us are flung backward. The horrid agony of burns is instantaneous, but I ignore it, scrambling to my feet to help Harley. Then everything seems to collapse around us, and a massive slab of building comes crashing down directly onto her legs, nearly crushing me with her.

Her scream is piercing.

In a flash Lucien and I have shoved it off of her and he is lifting her now unconscious, bleeding, scorched body. He leads the way through the destruction, the smoke, the flames, but there is no clear path of escape. The adrenaline coursing through my veins prevents me from noticing the chunks of debris embedded in my body and keeps me focused on survival.

Then everything goes black.

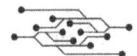

When I wake, I'm not sure that I'm not dead.

I am almost disappointed when I realize that I'm very much alive.

My eyes are blurred for a minute, but when they clear I see I'm in some sort of cell. Four grey walls. There's a toilet, a tray of food on the floor, and a bed, where I am lying now. There is a steel door across the room, but no bars and no windows.

I try to move but every muscle of my body aches, so I give up and just lie there, immobile. The burns on my arms have been bandaged, along with my shrapnel wounds.

As much as I would love for this to be a GUARD hideout, I know that's not the case, and I dread that I have been kidnapped by Delta, who could've utilized all the chaos they caused when they destroyed our base. Who else would it be?

My only hope is that Harley is alive. The chances seem slim, but that hope may very well get me through the torture I'm likely going to endure here, wherever I am.

I look around again and find that something seems... familiar. Horribly familiar. Maybe I'm still delirious from everything, but I feel as though I've been here before.

And then, it hits me.

The only time I've ever been in a place with cells like this... is Devil's Peak.

Devil's fucking Peak.

My breath catches when I hear muffled voices outside, and my heart begins to pound. In a few moments, I could finally come face to face with Dr. Brenner. Face to face with fate.

When the door opens, however, it's not her.

It's Q.

THIRTY ONE

I know almost instantly that he's not here to rescue me. No, his eyes are malicious.

My first instinct is to believe he's working for Delta, but then I catch sight of several bruises and burns that indicate he was caught in the chaos. Yet if he's responsible for my kidnapping…

I squeeze my eyes shut. I have no idea what happened to me, no idea how I made it out of the explosions alive. It's a horrible feeling, knowing that there's a large chunk of time missing from my memory.

"What have you done to me?" I groan.

"Nothing," Q replies simply. "Nothing yet, anyway."

"How long have you and Holbrook been planning this?"

He laughs coldly, still standing in the doorway as though he knows I'll strangle him if he gets too close. "Holbrook had nothing to do with this. Everyone was so easily fooled."

Goddammit.

How did I never see who Q really was?

"He certainly wouldn't have selected you for Operation Labyrinth if that were true," he continues. "I pushed back on it, of course, but ultimately was overridden by Medina. So I was forced to keep you safe."

"You didn't do a very good job," I mutter. "Almost got obliterated."

He purses his lips. "Yes, well, Kohler failed me there."

"Kohler?" I repeat, surprised. "What does he have to do with it?"

He shrugs. "I needed someone to protect my investments. Kohler fit the bill. He was in a vulnerable situation, and so I made a deal with him. Well, technically I made *Holbrook* make a deal with him. He would join Operation Labyrinth to protect you and Harley, give his life for you if he had to, in exchange for the GUARD letting the person he loved live."

"What?"

"Kohler made some grave mistakes. Mistakes that the GUARD would've eventually hung him for, right after making him kill his lover. He desperately needed a way out."

I exhale. No wonder Kohler had begun to hate my guts.

"Where's Harley?" I ask, voice wavering.

"She's alive. Lucien, too, actually. They don't have a clue where you are, though. They'll assume it was Delta, of course, which is why I took the opportunity to get to you as soon as our headquarters began to explode."

"Why are you doing this?"

"I'm a visionary, Kai. Medina and Holbrook were never able to see the danger looming. Delta is merely the beginning of a new age, a new *breed*, of conflict. You will be part of a new league of weaponry to arm the GUARD for the future."

One word makes me hesitate. *Were*. "Is Holbrook alive?"

Q eyes me for a moment, but there's no concern, no remorse. "No. And I know you'll be surprised to hear that one of his last acts was getting Harley and Lucien to safety." He pauses, but continues when I don't respond. "Byrne is acting as interim director, scattering all our agents to keep them safe while Sanchez coordinates CIA protection. But it won't be long before Delta makes another catastrophic move. And that's why we're here."

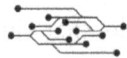

I'm not allowed to leave my cell for three days.

During that time, I scour for any way to escape but come up empty-handed. The constant solitude is enough to drive me crazy, but what's even more unbearable is being completely unable to contact anyone. I fight the urge to punch a wall out of frustration, but I'm going to need my fists in good shape so I can beat up Q when I finally get out of here.

On the third day, my door abruptly bursts open in the middle of the night, and two guards come rushing in to put me in cuffs. Disoriented, I'm dragged out into a hallway, past several unmarked doors, to another room. There's a hell of a lot of equipment and monitors, and what looks like an operating table. In the corner stands a very rigid-looking woman, with straight, prematurely grey hair and thin lips.

She smiles at me without warmth as I am strapped down to the table, my wrists and ankles being shackled. "Hello. I've heard so much about you."

"I'm thrilled to be your lab rat, Dr. Brenner."

She's not surprised that I know her name.

"Patient," she corrects me. "You'll be my patient, Agent Thanatos. Not a lab rat."

"Really? Doesn't seem like you've succeeded thus far."

"Oh, but I have. Yes, my attempts at recreating the Nyxian supergenes were largely fruitless. But I've moved on to something better. Bigger. You will be the most powerful person on the planet."

"That's a hell of a claim," I reply flatly.

Despite what Dare has revealed, I'm having a hard time believing that this operation has any legitimacy. This lady is out of her mind if she thinks she can make science fiction a reality.

But I could be wrong. Then what?

"It is," she replies seriously. "And I intend to live up to it."

"Why did you pick me? Because I trusted Q with my life?"

She cocks her head. "Partly. It was simple to get to you, certainly. But the *primary* reason was that you are the kind of person who is easy to turn into a weapon."

"Pretty sure the GUARD has already done that."

"You're lethal; that I know. But right now you're a tool. Not a weapon."

She approaches, coming to stand beside me as I lie helpless. Gazing at me ravenously, she strokes the side of my face with the back of her hand and I jerk away.

"Strip him," she commands.

The same guards step forward and start cutting off all of my clothes, ignoring my writhing and cursing. They start to hook me up to the machines, jabbing things into my arms and taping things to my chest. I try to break out of my restraints but I'm not going anywhere.

"Sweet dreams."

And everything goes black again.

Only this time, I'm not completely unconscious. There are bits and pieces, flashes of red beneath my eyelids, flashes of pain rippling across my body.

I swear I can hear myself scream.

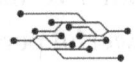

When I wake, I'm in a different room than before, lying on a cot in my underwear. The walls are stone, and there are only a few dim lights dotting the ceiling far above me.

"You're alive," someone says.

I turn to see a woman, probably in her mid-twenties, staring at me from another cot across the room. She has bright white hair and iridescent circuit tattoos on her arms, and although she is in underclothes like me, it doesn't seem to bother her.

"Who are you?" I ask.

"Nastasia."

"GUARD agent?"

"Yeah. Denver Division."

"New York. I'm Kai."

"Come here often?" she teases.

"Surprisingly, I've been in this place before," I respond dully.

"Oh? I honestly have no idea where I am."

"Deep inside a prison in the middle of nowhere."

She presses her lips together. "No one's coming to rescue me, then."

"Probably not."

"Well, at least you're here."

"Why don't they give us any clothes?"

She shrugs. "Humiliation, I suspect. They want to break us down. Although… being forced to be half-naked with you is kinda turning me on."

I ignore that. "How long have you been here?"

"Dunno. A week? I've been alone until now."

She comes over to sit on the edge of my cot, and it's then that I notice her turquoise eyes. They're so… *strange*. Bright, inhuman.

"What?" she says, concerned at my reaction. "Am I that ugly?"

"No… your eyes are, like, glowing."

She shakes her head in confusion. "They don't glow; they're brown."

"Not anymore they're not. They're turquoise. Honestly, it might be a side effect of the experiments."

She laughs once. "Change in eye color as a side effect? That's a new one."

"I'm serious. What Dr. Brenner is doing is… alien."

Nastasia just stares at me for a moment, skeptical.

"How do you feel?" she asks.

"Like my insides are burning and my head is spinning. On edge, to say the least." It's difficult to articulate the sensations, but what I do know is that something is wrong with me. As though I'm not in my own body.

"Your strength and senses are going to heighten, most likely. That's what happened to me. I could see all of your scars from across the room."

"Seriously?"

"Yeah. It's crazy. My brain is still adjusting to all the input, so it feels like I'm constantly being overstimulated."

"God knows who we'll be when we get out of here."

Not ourselves, that I'm certain of.

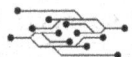

That night I dream about my old partner. The dead one.

The details are vague, but it's a warped version of one of our last assignments together. I'm staked out in an office building, waiting impatiently for him to return from a surveillance check on our target. When he does, he's grinning about something.

"What?" I say.

"We're really good at this shit, Kai," he responds, gazing at me eagerly.

"Uh… yeah, and?"

"So I think we could do it. We should just fucking leave. You and me. Kill everyone they dare to send after us."

I stare at him. He'd been by my side since we were at the Academy—the one person I'd thought of as family. We had occasionally joked about going AWOL, surviving on our own. But I never seriously considered it.

He steps toward me, placing his hands on my shoulders, smile lingering. "We have nothing to lose," he says gently.

Then a gunshot rings out. His blood splatters across my face. I snap awake.

I exhale, running a hand over my face.

"Bad dream?" Nastasia murmurs.

"None of your business," I respond half-heartedly, rolling over on my cot to face away from her.

"What was it about?"

"An old friend."

"Where is he now?"

"Gone."

"I'm sorry."

I groan. "Leave me alone before I clock you."

"Eh. I could use a good punch. Maybe it'll wake me up from *this* nightmare."

"I think there's a bigger nightmare outside of this place," I mutter.

"Delta, you mean?"

Reluctantly I turn back over. "A few days ago they blew the New York Division to dust. It won't be long before they kill us all."

"Apparently that's why we're here. Though I can't tell which side Q and the doctor lady are really on."

"I think Q is trying to take matters into his own hands. He wants the GUARD to be a force to be reckoned with. An army. And he wants to be in control of it all."

Nastasia isn't convinced. "Did he say that?"

"No. It's just the way he was talking. It's almost as if the deaths of Holbrook and Medina have paved the way for whatever he's been planning. By now the Board and the other leaders of the GUARD have to be pretty desperate for a way to stop Delta, so if Q shows up with enhanced agents to save the day, they'll start looking to him to make decisions. Hell, maybe they'll elect him director if that's what he wants."

"So he's on a quest for power. He probably promised Brenner a fortune and a half."

"Yeah. But I think she may have her own motives—"

I'm cut off by guards busting the door open dramatically. Four of them come in, splitting into pairs and dragging both Nastasia and me out into the concrete hallways. She looks at me, wide-eyed and silent, as they take us in opposite directions.

I need to do something.

I break out of the grip of Goon #1 and punch him across the face, but the other one is quick to clout the back of my head with a heavy baton. My vision goes black for a moment.

"*Fuck,*" I hiss.

I turn and slam Goon #2's skull into the wall as hard as I can, my bullet wound sending a sharp bolt of pain through my arm. He slumps, and Goon #1 hits my back with his own baton, right on the spine. I am a second away from reaching for his head, intending to snap his neck with a sharp twist, when I hear, "Enough."

I halt. Q is ominously standing farther down the hallway.

I hate that I just listened to him like a dog.

In the second that I hesitate, I feel a needle stab into my neck.

As I regain consciousness again I slowly become aware that something is happening to my head.

I am lying face down, and although I try, I'm unable to move any part of my body except my eyes, which doesn't help because all I can see is the floor. The area around the base of my skull is numb, but I can still feel someone doing something back there. *Are they cutting me open?*

"Don't worry," Dr. Brenner says calmly. "You won't notice it's there. Not physically, at least."

That only makes me panic. They're embedding something into my head.

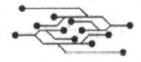

They spend two more days injecting me with things, running biological tests, and putting me through hell to test my endurance. I'm kept in a single chamber, but I'm too unstable to attempt an escape.

My body feels like it's been filled with a poison that's warping me into a monster. My brain does not recognize the foreignness. I feel sick, yet somehow I've become stronger.

They lower the temperature of the cell to one that should kill me, then raise it so that I'm practically burning alive. They slash my leg open to observe my neural response to pain and see how fast I heal. They send in a dozen trained fighters (who try to kill me) to assess my reflexes and strength. And for the entire forty-eight hours that all of this goes on, they force me to stay awake, with little food and little water.

By the end of it, I feel dead, but not as much as I should, which scares me.

Dr. Brenner enters, guarded heavily, her thin lips curved into a chilling smile. She looks at me with the same hunger as when we first met, although this time it's mixed with pride. She is Doctor Frankenstein, I'm her creation.

"Come," she says. "We still have much to do."

I'm escorted by goons, with tranquilizer guns pointed straight at me, to a room with a glass divider. I'm shoved in alone, the six-inch-thick door locking behind me. I can't see what's beyond the glass more than a few feet—the other side is pitch black.

Then a sole light flickers on, illuminating a kneeling figure.

It's Reiya, gagged, wrists tied, bruised. She's shaking. My heart quickens, and I immediately rush to the glass, at which point her eyes snap up to meet mine. What I see in them is not relief, but worry—no, terror. It makes me falter.

"Now then," Brenner's voice echoes through the chamber. Just as she begins to speak, I glimpse movement in the darkness behind Reiya.

She's not alone in there. "You have thirty seconds to break through that glass before your sister meets her demise."

I don't have time to panic, to think. Brenner's not joking.

I just start punching the glass over and over, so hard that the bones of my hand should shatter, but there's no way it's going to work. A glance around the room tells me that there's nothing here of use. It's just me and my body.

But my body fails me.

A figure steps out of the shadows and drags a knife across Reiya's throat.

THIRTY TWO
BENSON

I'm not a violent person, I swear. I just prefer that people get what they deserve, and it doesn't help that I can more or less make that happen whenever I want. Maybe my methods *are* a bit violent, but that's beside the point.

Today I let the impulsive part of my brain take over for the the first time in a long time, and it sure as hell felt good. Worth it? Probably not. Do I regret it? Hell no.

My mother opted to raise me in a small coastal town in the Middle of Goddamn Nowhere, South America, and quite frankly, it's been suffocating. I've never truly fit in, and never will. I'm quite literally a different species. So rather than making friends, I like to entertain myself by lightly antagonizing the scum of the town, which usually makes me some enemies.

Long story short, I pissed off one of these so-called enemies to the point where he tried to start a fight. In my defense, he pissed me off first. I was just minding my business at the local bar when he started drunkenly talking shit, calling me a bastard child because I appear biracial, calling my mother a whore who got knocked up by an "American chromeface." It was a low blow. Far lower than I'd go. Not much gets under my skin, but insulting my mom is pretty effective.

He expected me to take a swing at him, which I did consider, but only for a moment. That's far less fun. Instead I decided, after years of suppression, to liberate the power lurking inside me.

It's difficult to express exactly how I do it, but it's like my brain is hacking someone else's. I trigger their pain receptors, and their body will explode into agony. Every inch of their insides feels like it's being incinerated, or at least that's how my mom describes it.

A few seconds of that usually does the trick for me. Any longer and I start to feel bad; the writhing around is just pitiful. It's a nice (albeit brief) break from hiding, and luckily I have an understanding parent who has swept some mistakes under the rug.

Now that I'm reasonably mature, however, she expects me to have a better handle on things. But she tends to overestimate me.

By the time I had reined myself in with the drunken man-child, leaving him shocked and panting on the floor, I realized that another bargoer had been recording the whole exchange. He was probably expecting a fight but didn't get what he bargained for.

I'm replaying all this in my head, still undecided on whether to inform (and disappoint) my mother, when she returns home from a night shift at the health center.

"Ah, mother dearest. You're getting younger every day, aren't you?" She ignores my sweet talk, like always. There's still a hint of a smile on her face, though. "You have a nice day today?"

"Old Anita died finally. Other than that, sure." She glances up at me for a moment as she puts down her things on the kitchen counter.

"Well, it was about time, don't you think?"

"Is that how you're going to treat me when I'm old?"

"Probably."

I take a breath. A few feet in front of me is a wooden trap door that leads to our bunker, where we keep all our tech. I need to get down there to erase the video if it's online anywhere. It doesn't really show anything that could give my abilities away, but you can't be too careful. This isn't the first time it's happened, and it won't be the last, knowing me. The first few incidents had been accidents, but now it's just my inability to control my emotions.

It's better if there's nothing out there to get me into trouble.

"Um..." I start. My mom gives me a look, knowing that I'm about to tell her something she won't like.

"What?"

"I may have briefly lit a guy's insides on fire."

"Benson." Her eyes grow dark. In this house, and in this house only, we speak English, and she calls me by my real name. Everywhere else in the town, I am Andrés.

"Someone caught it on video. I was just standing there, but..."

"It's still gonna look like you're the devil or something."

"Not something that should be forever preserved online, I suppose. But I kind of like it."

"I know it's difficult to keep things in check, Bense—I don't expect you to be like these humans. But we wouldn't be allowed to live a normal life if everyone knew what we were."

"It'd be nice if my capabilities weren't so... *violating*. So I could use them under the radar."

There are three things I can do with my mind: trigger extreme pain, knock someone unconscious, and induce hallucinations. All of which would be useful if I wanted to be a criminal.

My mom thinks for a moment, biting her lip. "Maybe you could."

"What do you mean?"

"I took us away from the States for a reason, but confining you to a simple life goes against everything in your nature."

I have no idea where she's going with this. "Are you saying there's another option?"

"There is now. The GUARD could use our help."

"The what now?"

"The Global Underground Agency for Reconnaissance and Defense."

"The hell is that? Sounds stupid."

"They're a hybrid intelligence and R&D agency. Basically a secret, international organization of spies and engineers, without a lot of the structural and legal restrictions that normal government agencies operate under. They develop weapons and technology, and strive to maintain global security. There's a lot of assassinations that go on."

"That doesn't sound like a very moral organization."

"Not really. The GUARD was founded a few decades ago, primarily for defense against the West's biggest cyber adversaries, but evolved into much more once that threat dissipated. They were originally what I ran from when I learned I was pregnant with you, and I still stand by that decision. But they've changed. Some recent information has made me rethink how we should be living our lives."

"What recent information? You think we should work for them or something?"

"We could. Your father works with them, actually. He was the one who reached out to me, and it sounds like they're up against a pretty powerful threat."

"My father."

"Yes."

Now this is getting interesting. But I can't read my mother's expression.

"You never talk about him."

"I know."

"Why not?"

"It's selfish, I know. I think it's just the difficulty of accepting that I left him when we loved each other most."

"Damn, heartless. Does he even know about me? You told me we could never contact him."

"He does know about you. Though I didn't really tell him until you were around six."

"And what has he done about it?"

She looks down. "He practically begged me to see you. I think he's been keeping eyes on you somehow, if I'm being honest. It's just that I know the GUARD watches his every move. I didn't want us to be exposed, to be turned into weapons or experiments."

"So you've kept me from my father for my entire life. Someone who seems to want to know me."

Her eyes plead with me to forgive her. Sure, I'm upset about it. But my mother always does what she believes is right. I can't hold that against her.

"I'm sorry, Benson. I really am."

"I know. Will you at least tell me his name?"

Her expression returns to its unreadable state. "Mason Dare."

My mouth falls open. "Are you shitting me? Mason Dare? Billionaire inventor?"

"That's the one."

Now I know where I get my volatility from.

"Jesus Christ, my father is a celebrity? Damn, Mother, you got some serious game."

She merely shrugs.

"Okay, I'm coming back to that, but moving on for now. What did he say?"

"He told me that one of Elsa Salazar's relatives is attempting to recreate her work. Essentially, what I tried to prevent from happening to us is happening to others."

That surprises me.

"Seriously?"

"Unfortunately. Mason is investigating it with a few GUARD agents, because he believes there's someone in the GUARD that's working with her. Off the books."

"So you want to help stop it?"

"I do. But that's not all that's going on. To put it briefly, the GUARD is struggling in a battle against an insurgent organization that seeks to upend the world. And that's where you fit in. Mason says there's an elite team that would benefit from your abilities."

"Wait, you want me to go into the field? I'm not an agent. I don't have their skills."

"Benson, I taught you how to fight, didn't I? You're stronger and faster than humans. You could probably learn how to shoot a gun fairly quickly. What are you worried about?"

"Jesus, you were just telling me to lie low and not use my abilities, and now you want me to go off to save the world with some assassin squad? Take it easy, Mother. I don't even know if I can think well on my feet. I could be a total dipshit."

"Honey, you're not a dipshit. I'm not forcing you, I just feel like you haven't realized what you can do. I don't want to keep telling you to suppress the Elysian parts of yourself when I know there's an opportunity for you to use them."

I run a hand over my face, overwhelmed. Suddenly I have a chance to get what I've wanted for my whole life, and I don't know that I'm ready.

But I'd be an idiot to waste this.

THIRTY THREE
LUCIEN

For several days and nights I don't leave Harley's bedside. I don't eat, I don't sleep. I just hold her hand.

At first no one was sure if she'd make it—she lost a lot of blood before we ever got her to safety. Both of her legs had to be amputated below the knee, though I can't tell if she has really become cognizant of this. Only yesterday did she actually begin to have conversations again.

I certainly don't tell her that Kai is missing. Dead or captured. Every day I expect Keating to tell us that they finally found his body. Camden and Shay, on the other hand, have convinced themselves that Delta kidnapped him, but I know that deep down they fear the worst.

Mason Dare is—conveniently—letting us and a few other agents stay at his secret island villa off the northern coast of Africa, a place that feels like it's in a time of its own. A place somehow beyond the reaches of political chaos and pollution and death. Not, however, beyond the reaches of Delta. If they want to find us, they'll have a way.

I am staring out the glass wall of Harley's room, at the sun descending over the ocean, when Keating finally calls a meeting. For the sake of safety, he's not permitting GUARD agents to know where he and the other leaders are stationed, nor is he giving out locations of agents themselves. Every division has split its people into smaller groups and spread them across the globe, though in some cases Delta was one step ahead. In the long run, however, it's likely a good move. The downside is that it's a lot more difficult to work as a unit, especially with the sudden increase in secrecy. The leaders of the GUARD will have to be absolutely meticulous.

"Where's Q?" I ask Keating as his hologram joins Camden, Shay, and I at Dare's dining room table.

"He hasn't told me precisely where he is," Keating responds tiredly. "All I know is that he's trying to help fix this mess."

I wonder, silently, why no one seems to know anything about where he is or what he's doing. He's watching everyone, but no one's watching him.

"Any word on Kai?" Camden says.

"No." Keating sighs. "But I guess that's good news—maybe he's still alive."

"Yeah, and being tortured, probably," Shay retorts.

"We need to find him," Camden urges. I glimpse him placing a hand on Shay's knee beneath the table, a subtle gesture of comfort. Perhaps a suggestion of something more than friendship between them.

"I know," Keating says. "I know we do. That's what I'm about to discuss."

He takes a breath again.

"First off, Lucien, I'm bringing in some help. Benson Moreno, Mason Dare's son, is flying in tomorrow. You and him are going to be tasked with finding Kai, to start. Shay, Camden, hunt down Gokiburi and get as much information on him as you can."

"And what about Harley?" I say.

"Dare is designing new legs for her. She'll be safest there until she can fully recover. And when she does, well, we're going to need her. In whatever way she can help."

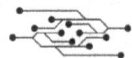

"Lucien." Harley's sharp voice wakes me in the dead of night, though I'm surprised I actually dozed off to begin with. Usually I'm too afraid of what I'll see when my eyes close.

"Yeah?" I respond, making my voice gentle.

"Are we... are we dead?"

"Surprisingly, no. Well, at least I don't think we are."

"Where's Kai?"

Shit.

"...I don't know."

She grabs my forearm suddenly, the abrupt movement causing me to flinch. Her fingers dig into my skin hard enough to bruise me, but I don't pull my arm away. "What do you mean you don't know?"

I sigh. "Somehow... I lost him trying to escape the explosions with you. His tracker is offline but they haven't recovered his body, so... there's a chance he's being held prisoner by Delta."

She stares at me hard for a few seconds, then shifts her gaze to the ceiling, no words leaving her lips.

"How are you feeling? Do you need anything?" I ask.

"I need my damn legs back."

"You'll be able to walk again soon. Dare has a team on it. You'll actually be able to test your legs out in a simulator to get used to walking with them."

Her eyes remain fixed on the ceiling. I know that she's frustrated about being so helpless, especially when we need her the most.

"How many people were killed?" she says quietly.

"Roughly sixty-eight percent of the division. The number is up to five hundred fifty or so."

"Jesus. So whatever plans Kohler recovered, those were fake? Or did he fucking set us all up to die?"

"We don't know. Do you think he'd have returned to New York if he knew what was coming?"

"Maybe. Maybe he wanted to die, for all we know. He had been acting weird."

"It also could've been Medina. He could've easily given Delta Manhattan's secondary location. But we may never find out the truth, with both of them dead. All we can do is keep on."

She turns her head to look at me, study me, read me.

"How did you live with yourself? When you were in Delta? Destroying lives, murdering innocent people. How'd you do it?"

That takes me off guard. I feel the memories from that time nearly break out of the prison I put them in.

The first couple of years after I was promoted to a second-tier leader, dictating which people should die, I felt nothing. Not for the people whose lives I was ruining, not for the people underneath me who I put through hell. But eventually, seeing firsthand the destruction I'd initially been so indifferent to broke me. I could sit and code cyber weapons until the end of time and not feel guilty about it, even now, but the pain, all the pain, is what got me in the end.

I was supposed to be heartless. My father tried to instill it, Delta tried to instill it. But I turned out to be their worst nightmare.

"Well..."

"I ask because I want to understand. This... this battle we're in with Delta, it's not as simple as good versus evil. I mean, we just wiped out an entire base in Rio. But the GUARD doesn't slaughter the blameless like Delta does. Most of the agents I know would raise hell before doing that. So what drives the people working for Delta to utterly abandon their morals?"

"I'm curious myself," another voice chimes in from behind me, in Arabic. I can't help but startle, though this happens all the time. I thought I would escape it after departing Devil's Peak, but I was sorely wrong. My theory is that my mother shows up to act as my mind's reminder to itself of what I once was, of all the horrible things I did.

I ignore her presence. My hallucinations will drown me if I let them.

Harley waits patiently as I formulate an answer to her question.

"There are many factors," I say finally. "Fear is a significant one. People will do anything when they're afraid for the lives of those they love. Anger is another. Many are so frustrated with society that they're willing to go to extremes. Both of these things you're aware of. The less obvious factors include, for one, agents simply not knowing who they're killing and why. Delta is very hierarchical, so you never question a directive from higher up in the chain. Then there's the culture. It's very cultish, as I'm sure you can imagine. People believe, religiously, that they're doing the right thing for the world, as if it's their destiny.

"For me, however, it was control. For my entire childhood I never felt that I had power over my own life, my own body, my own mind. When I joined Delta, I was suddenly on the other end of things, and over time the influence that I amassed became addictive. Frankly, I became the exact kind of person I swore I'd never be. The kind of person my father was. I hate myself for it.

"But... what's most interesting is that both Delta and the GUARD recruit people who have faced adversity. They both feed off—*exploit*—people's trauma. The only difference is how. Many people in Delta truly are *bad* people, probably including me. Not everyone, though. Some just got swept up in the madness and never escaped."

Harley's eyes are gentler now, though she's still wary. "That doesn't entirely excuse their actions."

"No. Of course not. I'm just trying to elucidate the psychological magnetism of Delta."

Harley nods, taking a breath. "They're certainly a force we didn't see coming. I worry that the GUARD will become more like them in our efforts to impede them."

I've been thinking about the same thing lately, but I'm not convinced it's not inevitable. Unless we can continually outsmart Delta, we may have to use their own methods against them.

"Speaking of Delta, have you checked in with Zahra at all?" Harley asks.

"Q told me he's been in contact with her. Said she was accepted into the organization, and that she's adapting. I don't know if he informed her of what happened, though."

"Maybe there's been word around Delta."

"Yes, but only in the upper tier. Things like this are often kept secret from the lower ranks. And, of course, Delta has an impressive unseen influence over the media, so the attack hasn't even been in the news."

Harley shuts her eyes for a moment, sighing. "I'm starting to think we're a little too late in this fight."

I could say something optimistic, but that would be deceitful. "Yeah. We are."

"Is Q still gone?"

"Yeah. He hasn't really told us anything, so I don't know if or when he'll be rejoining us."

"He's busy trying to save the world, I guess."

"Maybe, but it seems like Keating is the one doing all the work. I don't know if anyone told you, but he found us a new team member."

"Really? Who?"

"Benson Moreno. He's Mason Dare's son."

At that her eyes widen. "What?" she says in disbelief.

"Uh... you know him?" I respond, confused at her reaction.

She debates what to say for a second. "He's... somewhat related to the experiments going on in Devil's Peak. His mother was part of genetic research that happened decades ago, and Kai and I think someone is trying to recreate that research. Dare was legitimately worried for Benson's safety, but I suppose losing hundreds of operatives will change your outlook."

I stare at her. "I didn't know you were investigating that."

"The whole thing is insane. If the stories are true, Benson may have... *abilities*."

My eyebrows raise involuntarily. "As in superhuman abilities?" I say dubiously.

"Basically. I guess we'll find out. What's the plan once he gets here?"

"Camden and Shay are heading to Tokyo to follow a lead on Gokiburi, thanks to the information we recovered in Rio de Janeiro. You, Benson, and I are going to try to find and rescue Kai. How, I don't know. It's like he disappeared into thin air, and any evidence back on Staten Island was probably burned to ashes."

"Well there's only a few possibilities that have any merit. One, he could've died. But they've combed through the bodies and haven't found any sign of him, right? So we can't focus on that. Two, Delta could've taken him. I guess we haven't even confirmed that the attack was them, but it's pretty likely. Are there any other agents unaccounted for that you know of?"

"No. But that would make it seem like Kai was targeted specifically. Delta would have to have known he'd be in New York. Considering that there were very few people who had that information…"

"That's true. However, it could've been Kohler. So we can't rule it out."

"Fair enough. What's another possibility?"

She thinks for a moment. "Holbrook died… right?"

Saving us, I think. But I decide not to mention that yet. "Yes. Why?"

"Based on what we know, Holbrook may have been planning to subject Kai to those experiments."

Interesting.

"Are you sure it was Holbrook?"

"Fairly sure. Camden and Reiya broke into his personal computer."

"I think there are many people in the GUARD who could pull off planting fake evidence in order to throw you off their trail."

Harley looks at me for a moment. She and Kai were likely too blinded by their animosity toward Holbrook to consider other people. "You're not wrong. In that case, it would likely have to be someone also on Staten Island at the time of the attack."

"Well, we can rule out five hundred fifty."

I know who I think it could be, but I don't say it, because things wouldn't look good for me if I were wrong.

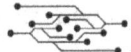

The second Benson gets off Dare's private jet, I immediately know he's a punk. He's around the same age as Kai and Harley, but he's more immature. Probably hasn't faced the kind of shit the rest of us have, though I shouldn't assume.

His mother is with him, but she soon heads to the US, wherever Dare needs her.

He awkwardly introduces himself to me and Harley, who has started wheeling herself around in a wheelchair. I'm amazed at how quickly she's recovered, but I guess I shouldn't be. If there's one thing I've learned about her since we met not so long ago, it's that she's strong in every sense of the word.

"So," she says to Benson after he's settled in, crossing her arms. "What can you do?"

His golden eyes shift between the two of us; he's clearly out of his comfort zone here.

"You guys know I'm half Elysian?" he responds, surprised. "Or… are you just asking in general?"

"We know who you are. I want to see what you can do that we can't."

"Uh… okay. I need a volunteer."

He looks at me.

"Just because I'm crippled doesn't mean I can't handle it," Harley says. "Show us what you've got."

Benson nods once. "All right. Here goes."

Suddenly I'm not standing in Dare's house.

I'm in the arctic, nothing but snow stretching in every direction as far as I can see. I can even feel the frigid wind, smell the clean air that's like ice in my lungs.

The only thing that ties me to reality is Harley's voice. "Holy shit."

It takes me a second to grasp what is happening. For once, I'm not hallucinating on my own—Benson is *causing* it.

Then it's gone, as fast as it came.

Harley and I are both silent in astonishment for a few moments.

"Incredible," she whispers finally. "What else?"

"Yeah… this one might hurt a bit. A lot, actually."

I narrow my eyes, but gesture for him to continue.

In the next second there's a flash of horrendous pain, as if all of my nerves have caught on fire. My body practically seizes from the shock of it. Before I can utter a sound, however, it disappears.

Benson is cringing. "Sorry. I've heard it's bad."

But Harley is smiling. "Jesus. That's intense. I even had phantom pain in my nonexistent lower legs."

"Is there more?" I ask him.

"I can also knock people unconscious, but I don't know if you want me to do that."

"I'll take your word for it."

"How can you do all that?" Harley says.

"It's hard to explain," Benson responds. "It takes a lot of energy, but it's as natural as moving a muscle. I have what we call synthetic morphing DNA, in addition to human DNA. It's a recreation of something a far more advanced species developed. Two extra pairs of chromosomes, coded to give me those abilities. Most ability genes are silenced, actually. Occasionally *all* of them, for some people. The genes that *aren't* silenced depend on the rest of your genome, and your environment. Sometimes people can gain or lose abilities with time."

"So… the morphing DNA is passed down to offspring?"

"Yeah. Often parents and children will have similar abilities, but not always."

"I don't understand how you can trigger sensory experiences in others without even touching them. That seems impossible."

Benson shrugs. "Hey, it's a mystery to me too. It has to do with the amplified electromagnetic radiation my brain is emitting, I think. It's like sending a signal. I have to be near people, unimpeded by walls, for it to work."

Harley shakes her head in incredulity. "I'm impressed. Welcome to the team, Benson."

THIRTY FOUR

ZAHRA

God, Delta is a fucking nightmare.

The indoctrination period bears an eerie resemblance to historical cults. It's all about forming a movement together, to eradicate the elitist structures of society, no matter the cost. They're convincing people that they were chosen for a reason, that they have the power to change the world. And there's no time to waste. Honestly, I can see why that kind of message captures people. What most of them *don't* know is that many of the issues driving them to seek radical change are actually part of a mechanism of manipulation. One that has been crafted by Delta itself.

Shit's confusing, but it works. Delta is creating the demand to thereby create the supply.

And what's the endgame? Hell if I know. We can overthrow leaders and governments, sure, but what then? All these people who so blindly follow their orders around here don't have a clue what the post-rebellion world would truly look like.

They don't control us just by trying to brainwash us, of course. They make us feel guilty about our unspoken urges to report the operation. In the words of one of the leaders, "You might feel that what we do is extreme, and you'd be right. But the world needs extreme right now. We can't depend on the system. The police are corrupt. The government is corrupt. You were brought here to change the world. To *save* the world. Don't waste it. Because people are suffering, and it can't go on any longer."

In reality, there have probably been numerous people who have tried to stop Delta after getting involved, or at least that's what I'd like to believe. I guess I can't be sure that anyone has broken away from the conformity and taken a stand. So either everyone is a coward, or the rebels have all died for their bravery.

My days consist of working around twelve hours in the industrial maze that is the base. Parrish is a tough boss, but she takes a liking to me, which is probably going to save me. After orientation, I make it clear that I want to work in the government infiltration division, and she sends me into rigorous training for it almost immediately. Delta has several different tracks, some focusing heavily on physical dexterity, some on technical expertise, and others on psychological cunning. My track has three components: a martial arts and improvised weapons class, a stealth class, and a whole slew of classes on lying, manipulation, and persuasion. I test out of a lot of it though, thank God, otherwise it'd be months before I could concentrate on getting information for the GUARD.

I do as much eavesdropping as I can with the invisible earpiece Q gave me, but I don't get much for the first week. Nothing about the GUARD. I don't hear from Minotaur, either.

Nevertheless, I focus on fitting in. In training, I manage to make a friend, Sena, who was born in Seoul but grew up in Singapore. Everyone else has been relatively cordial, but there's serious pressure to conform and perform. It might not be long before we're competing against each other. Some people even drop out, probably because they see what's coming.

I don't know what happens to them, but I can be fairly certain that Delta doesn't let them simply walk away.

Naturally, I also make an enemy, though not because of anything specific that I did. One of the martial arts instructors—Markham is his name—and I just don't align. He's a real douche, to say the least. But what's interesting is that I've caught him checking me out, which Sena makes sure to point out to me.

At first it seems like we're just going to agree not to get along, but then he starts to target me. I'm already good at martial arts, way better than some of these idiots, but he tries to make me feel like I'm worthless by embarrassing me in front of everyone else. Forcing me to make mistakes. My ability to brush it off only drives him to do it more—he wants his games to break me down.

I know that if I'm not careful, he could easily end my career here. He holds a position of power, that's for certain. Still, I end up punching him in the jaw while he's using me as part of his demonstration, to my satisfaction of course. It was more of an instinctual reaction to his moves than it was an attempt to get back at him, but he doesn't know that. He perceives me as a threat.

I see rage flash across his face just before he returns the favor, almost knocking me to the ground.

Jesus, that hurt.

"Watch it, Olsen," he hisses.

Sena comes to my rescue, raising her hand to be a smartass. "Uh, I thought you wanted us to defend ourselves."

Markham turns to glare at her, but he doesn't have a comeback. He just sneers. "Off the mat," he says, his voice low. He doesn't look at me.

I have a feeling he's going to make my life hell.

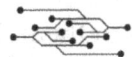

Parrish calls me into her pristine, grey office at the end of my first week, and I can't help but think she's going to rip me apart. I've seen her do it multiple times to other people; she accepts nothing less than your best, and sometimes even that isn't enough.

I quickly glance around to get a gauge of where she might keep important files or hard drives, even though I know that the chances of me breaking in here later, unnoticed, are next to none. I wish I still had the bug for eavesdropping, but we wanted to eliminate the possibility of anyone finding it.

"Harper. Sit." She smiles at me briefly, which is a good sign. Probably means I'm in the clear. "How are you doing?"

Her eyes are boring into me, trying to read every aspect of my body language, and I struggle to maintain eye contact. Her entire aura is one of power. Her clothing, her shaved head, her poise. She may be a member of Delta but I can't help but admire her. "I'm good. Everything has been unexpected, frankly, but I think I belong here."

"You can be honest if you have concerns. I know this place is tough, and I want my people to feel like they have what they need. I also want them to feel that it's all worth it."

I know that the wrong thing to do here is complain. Normally, I'd make a few polite suggestions about improving upon the toxic culture here, but Harper wouldn't do that.

"I'm someone who appreciates a challenge, if I'm being honest. As you've said, anything that's truly rewarding doesn't come easy. With this job, I have more than I've ever had, and that will drive me. I'm part of something meaningful for the first time in my life, and I don't want to give that up. This feels… like an opportunity of a lifetime."

Parrish is satisfied with that, though I'm unconvinced that I'm even good at bullshitting. "Good. You'll do great things serving our mission," she says, her tone vaguely menacing. She issues orders, not requests. "You're dismissed."

I head back through silent corridors to my desk, where I'm supposed to be reading the lengthy onboarding documentation in my apparently copious free time. It mostly covers basic information that Lucien has already made me aware of, but one thing it doesn't mention is how Delta really makes its revenue. How can they afford to continually build these secure bases, pay their people, and provide resources? I know that there are numerous wealthy people backing the organization, somewhat ironically, but there must be other sources of income. Perhaps it's weapons deals, or drugs. God knows everyone is addicted to sugarpills these days.

The GUARD seems heavily focused on taking out Delta's members, especially the leaders, but I'm wondering if we need to target their revenue streams as well. I guess that's my job: figuring out Delta's weaknesses.

It's well past the dinner hour on a Friday night, and many people (of my status, anyway) have gone home, so I'm alone among the rows of desks. I put in my earpiece to see if I can pick anything up, and it scans for conversations. For almost thirty minutes I barely hear anything, and certainly not anything important.

Then I do.

"... the United Kingdom is becoming more unstable. The parties are at odds, the people are outraged. London Headquarters has been in contact with Arachne. They're making a move."

The UK has been in chaos after Delta killed the Prime Minister. He was a moderate that seemed to temper the majority conservative Parliament, a voice of reason that held the country together through recession and disaster. For a week or so now there's been violent riots—and riots to protest those riots—in reaction to the new leader that the Conservatives have chosen. Many MPs were either influenced by Delta or are Delta members themselves. The new leader, of course, is beyond conservative. He's a fascist.

In reality, the sudden outburst in the UK is not solely due to the new PM. It's been a long time coming. Tension has been building for years now as a result of political, environmental, and economic turmoil, both domestically and globally. The death of a beloved figure was all that was needed for people to snap. Any hopes of turning the country around were shattered in an instant.

Another voice responds. "Excellent. It's only a matter of time before the rest of Europe follows."

To my disappointment, the conversation ends, leaving me with no idea as to what "move" Delta is going to make. Whatever it may be, they believe it's going to trigger an international chain of events.

I'm not sure that the GUARD is ready.

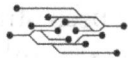

Sunday morning it begins.

First is the news of high-casualty rebel bombings across South America and the interim PM's announcement that, after a long period of strategic inaction, the United Kingdom will be backing the governments to quell the uprisings. The London rioters retaliate almost immediately, outraged at their country's support of tyranny.

Then in turn comes the police involvement in the riots. Rather than simply taming the crowds and arresting only when necessary, as they've been doing, they suddenly change tactics. Now they're gassing people, beating people, even shooting them in a few instances.

It only exacerbates everything, which is what Delta is gunning for. It's a perfect time for a new figure to step in.

She's skinny, crisp, well-dressed in a stylish but modest pantsuit. Dark hair, brown skin. Probably mid-forties. She has a tattooed maze on one side of her neck, extending to her ear, and long, pointed black nails. Red eyes. But not just red, *glowing* red. Not who I'd expect, but she stands out among the sea of people younger and wilder than her. And, as I soon find out, she's a mesmerizing speaker.

By the time the cameras start to focus on her, she's already atop a vehicle at the forefront of the protest outside of Palace of Westminster, megaphone in hand, standing against a backdrop of smoke and haze. It's evident that no one is listening to her, at first. She's not the first to try to rile everyone up.

Then, slowly, order unfolds, because riling is not what she's doing. Instead, she wants the opposite.

It starts with the people closest to her, which I can't help but suspect are members of Delta that have been strategically placed to facilitate a movement. They're the first ones to settle down, to lower their fists and turn their eyes upon one woman. Though it takes several minutes, it cascades like a wave through the crowd as she speaks.

To me, it looks artificial, but to everyone else, it likely looks like she's miraculously captured the attention of the masses. It takes awhile for the broadcast to get audio of her, and even when they do, I have to up the volume because, unlike everyone else, she doesn't shout.

"Citizens of London," her voice echoes, "we must harness this anger, this *momentum*, to achieve the change we deserve. Our leaders cower in the face of hardship, abandoning morality and turning a blind eye to the suffering of those not like them. And so I ask you: how much longer will we tolerate their injustice? How much longer will we allow them to abuse the power that has been bestowed upon them in trust? The people of the United Kingdom are not, and have never been, ones to back down.

"We must rise against a system that has betrayed the commoner. *Cleanse* our government of the corrupt, who have, for as long as we've lived, painted a falsity. A false sense of hope, of justice, of equality. All designed to hold us down. Is it not time for them to be knocked off their thrones?

"You've watched, through crisis after crisis, as they did *nothing*. So now it's time for us, the people, to do *something*. And not back down. Because it's the only way forward."

It's a dangerous message. One that connotes unity to mask encouragement of hatred and violence. On the surface level, I agree with her. A lot of people probably do. The question is whether they'll see that she wants to radicalize their anger and warp the riots into an overthrow.

Right now it seems ludicrous. But far less ludicrous than it did yesterday.

Over the following week or so, British lady goes viral. The riots continue. People die. The government doesn't relent, but everyone anticipates that a breaking point is imminent. Citizens have started barricading roads and lighting shit on fire, and they're certainly not returning to work. It's not only thrown the country into a state of emergency, but ignited a response across Europe as well. The entire continent is waiting to see what the resolution will be.

I send a message to Minotaur to pass along what I know but don't receive a reply. I actually haven't heard from them at all, which worries me because Kai would check in. But there's nothing I can do, so I just keep on.

After finishing training, I endure a stressful evaluation. And of course, Markham is a straight-up dick during the whole thing. It's up to him, Parrish, and a few other leaders to score me and decide whether I'm ready to enter the field.

First comes the self-defense and hand-to-hand combat test.

I fight against a handful of people on mats, Markham circling and throwing insults. He calls me weak or pathetic at least half a dozen times throughout the evaluation, which wouldn't bother me if Parrish weren't watching. As if that weren't enough, he also forces me to repeat the last segment—escaping from being pinned down by a man twice my size—so many times I almost collapse from exhaustion.

"Again," his sharp, sadistic voice rings out, over and over and over. As though my reality has become a loop.

When he does finally stop I don't even realize it, and Parrish has to intervene. But she only gives me a short break before the stealth test, which consists of espionage and B&E. Luckily, it turns out to be nothing I'm not comfortable with already, and before I know it I'm onto the final test.

Manipulation. The one I've been dreading the most.

"Here's the hypothetical situation," Parrish briefs me. "We need the expertise and skills of a particular individual and would like him to join our cause. Thus far, he has declined our offers, so we've brought him in for one last interview to show him we're worth it. Your job is to persuade him. Persuade him that we are the only way forward."

I know she's not talking about the standard techniques an employer would use to bring someone on. This is the *work for us or we'll kill your family* kind of shit that Lucien warned me about.

I need to find this man's weakness and exploit it.

Parrish opens the door to a room with no windows, indicating that I'm not going to get any more information. Inside is a metal table, with two metal chairs opposite each other. A man (an actor, I guess) sits in one, hunched over, his head in his hands.

His head snaps up and he looks me up and down like he's trying to gauge what kind of person I am. I wonder if I look even remotely intimidating. I know that it'll be clear to anyone that sunshine and rainbows aren't my thing, but if I'm going to crack this guy, who's at least fifteen years my senior and a whole foot or so taller, I'll have to pose a threat.

But not at first. First, I need to gain his trust. While a person like Markham would come in here guns blazing, I need a more calculated approach.

I take the seat across from him. "Hi. Harper. Nice to meet you."

"Percy," he responds warily. "Who are you, exactly?"

"I'm here to give you an idea of what it's like to work with us."

He merely looks at me.

"Do you have any questions that I can answer?"

"I don't have questions."

All right then. This guy's not giving me anything to work with. "Okay. Well, then let me provide a glimpse as to how you'd be making an impact for our cause. Just so I know what department you'd be in… what is your area of expertise?"

He stares at me with confusion. "Don't you know? After all, you guys have been…"

As he drifts off, I swear I see a flash of fear in his eyes. *The hell?*

I pretend that I didn't notice. "Sorry, no. I haven't been a part of your recruitment."

I think he debates whether to believe me, and he eventually decides that he does. His shoulders relax a bit. "What happened to your face?"

It takes me a second to remember that I'm covered in bruises from the first test. I shrug. "Self-defense training."

That lie he doesn't buy.

"Fucking convince me, Olsen," Markham barks from invisible speakers, his voice echoing through the chamber. I grit my teeth. He's trying to make me lose focus, crumble under the pressure.

Percy jumps at the noise, his eyes searching the air above us as if he would see the sound waves. He has no idea what's happening.

That's when I know for sure that this is real.

Initially I thought his doubt would ruin this, but then I change tactics. I force false terror into my eyes, my face. I force my hands to shake. And I let him see.

We share a moment of eye contact in which I try to convey that I'm as much a terrified prisoner as he is, and in return I catch a glimpse of his understanding.

Now that he knows there are people listening to us, he leans forward to utter words at a whisper. He's so quiet that I have to read his lips to help my brain understand him. "You're not really one of them, are you?"

Almost imperceptibly, I shake my head no. "They're going to kill me. If you don't agree to work for them." I pray that Markham and Parrish don't hear me, because I shouldn't even know about Delta's murderous talent acquisition schemes. Not yet, at least. "They have my baby," I add.

God, I wish a tear or two would fall dramatically down my face.

Percy squeezes his eyes shut in empathy. "If I had any family, they'd do the same to me."

Shit. That rules loved ones from the list of possible means of exploitation. And I doubt he's going to make any sacrifices for me, a stranger.

"So they kidnapped you?" I ask.

"After their blackmailing failed, yes."

"They can't get you to crack."

"No. But neither of us are getting out of here alive unless we do what they want."

The next sentence he says almost to himself.

"I told my students I was coming back today…"

Ah. A professor.

He may not have family, but he does care about something—his students. Why would he think about them at a time like this, in a life or death situation, unless they truly meant something to him?

"Your students," I repeat, louder, sitting back in my chair, all emotion drained from my face and voice. "They're like a family, aren't they?" It's not really a question.

He's frozen, his eyes wide. I think he realizes he made a grave mistake. The sheer betrayal in his eyes almost breaks me.

"It would be a shame," I continue, "if something happened to all of them. If another awful massacre were to take all those brilliant minds from the world."

"You... you can't do that," he breathes.

I scoff. "This is America. No one would bat an eye."

This is fucked up, I know. But while it's real for him, it's not like Delta is actually going to go out and kill his students just because I threatened it. I hope.

His mouth is open, but he doesn't utter a word.

"I trust you'll make the right decision."

With that, I get up and leave.

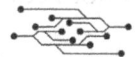

At the end of the day, by which time I've convinced myself that I'm going to get my brains blown out by Delta at any second, Parrish brings me into her office.

"We were... impressed today," she begins. But there's some sort of skepticism in her voice. "You did very well. I found it intriguing, however, that you resorted to violence so quickly on your last test. I just want to understand your thought process."

I feel sweat on my back, and tell myself to calm down and take a damn breath.

"Well... you asked me to persuade him. I first considered convincing him to believe in our mission, but I gathered that he was quite averse to joining based on what both you and he said. Thus I felt that approach would be fruitless and concluded that I needed to be a bit more extreme, especially after he claimed he'd been kidnapped. It dawned on me that you were likely not testing me on how much I could fluff up the organization, but rather how well I could adjust tactics when a situation calls for something drastic. I would never condone or threaten anything that extreme unless absolutely necessary; that's just inefficient."

Parrish maintains eye contact for several seconds, then nods. "Interesting. Again, I'm impressed."

"Thank you."

"I suppose you deserve to know that your last test was not in fact hypothetical."

That admission was unexpected.

I feign confusion.

"Sorry?"

"The man you talked to was not acting. Thanks to you, he's started to cooperate."

"So... you actually kidnapped him?"

Parrish's expression doesn't change. "Not me personally, certainly. But yes. And let me tell you why." She folds her hands. "Delta was founded on the idea that the world needed to change, hence the name. Society has long been stuck under the rule of the elite and privileged, and look at the damage it's caused. War, famine, poverty, genocide. Humanity will continue to repeat its mistakes until we destroy our species. Unless *we* prevent it.

"America itself was designed to enforce the power of the people, yet here we are, with CEOs and legacy politicians pulling all the strings. 'Power of the people' is an illusion. Most of those who have tried to initiate a movement have ultimately gotten trapped—by scandals or smears, by the slow cog that is the government, by the majority party, you name it. America's founders failed. Delta is going to create something new, this time on a larger scale.

"Now. I'm sure you've noticed that in your lifetime, especially in the past decade, the world has grown more... unstable. Chaotic, even. What you should know is that much of this was a result of Delta's strategy."

I feign more confusion. Internally, I'm rolling my eyes. "What do you mean?"

"I mean that we're the ones inducing the turmoil, to an extent. And we have good reason. The world would've reached this point organically, just as it has in the past. The world has never needed an entity like us to push it into chaos, but it *does* need us to help break its cycle. We're going to be the ones to provide an avenue for change. We've only accelerated and exacerbated the tumult to allow for that. Delta's leaders saw that they had the ability to change the world, and they took it."

She is silent for a few moments as I pretend to ponder something deeply. "Instability is a catalyst for change."

An almost villainous smile. "Precisely."

"But how did Delta amass so much momentum? So much influence?"

"Through the diligence and determination of our people regarding our mission. Over time, we attracted many people like you and me, with a variety of skillsets and backgrounds, and we formed connections to different institutions. Simple as that. It was only once we had those connections that we started getting backed financially by individuals who understood the benefit our organization could provide to them and to the world. After all, we are not waging a war against the rich. We are waging a war against those who use their status to oppress. And more importantly, we're igniting the people.

"But make no mistake, Harper. We understand the cost of it all. Sacrifices are necessary for there to be good. Whatever it takes, yes?"

I nod. "Yes."

"So you understand, then, why we kidnapped the professor."

These people are fucking psychos. "I do."

"Good."

THIRTY FIVE

KAI

I fall to my knees.

Reiya and I are mirrors of each other, for just a moment, before she drops, her head hitting the stone beneath her like a rock.

I choke on my scream.

Suddenly my body feels like it's going to detonate, like there's heat, energy, accumulating near the surface of my skin.

Then, a burst. But I don't feel the pain. The glass shatters, I black out.

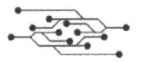

I swear to God, if I fall unconscious one more time I'm going to lose it.

This time I wake up in some sort of hospital bed, machines monitoring my vitals. It looks like the prison infirmary. I start ripping off the things hooked up to me, the act making me aware of how hazy my brain is, how weak my body feels.

"Kai." I nearly jump out of my skin. Q is standing in the corner, watching me. Suddenly everything comes back to me in a rush.

I curse at him. "I'm going to kill you."

"We did what was necessary."

I scoff incredulously, on the verge of crying, screaming, or vomiting. "Necessary for what?"

"Seeing if we were successful."

"Well, clearly you weren't. You wanted me to break the glass, and I couldn't."

"Ah, but you did. Remember?"

"What do you mean? There was some kind of explosion."

"Yes. That was you."

He raises his eyebrows as if he expects me to understand, but I just stare at him. I'd call him a lunatic, but that's the one thing I know he's not.

"You released a large amount of energy," he continues. "It's why you passed out."

"How?"

"It's a complex interaction between your neurocomputer and how your modified cells store energy."

"Neurocomputer."

"Yes. Embedded into your brain. We can now code different skills for you, such as knowledge of another language or an instrument, or even a martial art. It can reduce pain. Drain you of emotions. It can even leverage your specialized synthetic DNA to give you new abilities. The computer can help control almost any part of your body, both subconsciously and consciously."

"Meaning that I can tell it what to do?"

"To an extent."

"Is this 'specialized DNA' the same as Elsa Salazar's research?"

"For the most part, no. Whereas Nyxian abilities lie completely within their genetic material, yours mainly lie within your neurocomputer. Unlike the Elysians, we couldn't replicate their morphing DNA, which was the invention that allowed the extraterrestrial species to artificially augment themselves and pass it on to offspring. Instead, your DNA has synthetic modifications that we designed from scratch. Not only do those modifications enhance your cells, but they enable your body to respond effectively to the advanced algorithms in the neurocomputer. Your energy burst being one of them. Think of it as an external tool without which the neurocomputer wouldn't be able to execute its protocols."

"How can I hear more? See more?"

"We implanted tiny amplifiers and enhanced your brain's sensitivity and ability to filter input. Your senses are still limited by the physical properties of the human body, certainly, but the plasticity of the human brain is quite remarkable."

"And my strength?"

"That part *is* thanks to the Nyxians. It was the portion of their genome, specifically for physical enhancement and distinct from the morphing DNA, that we could recreate. Simply put, your muscles are constantly getting more fuel. More importantly, however, they're actually more... *pliable*. That's the thing we couldn't code—muscle memory and capability. Your brain may know what to do, but if your muscles can't compensate, then it's all for nought. So we made it easier for your muscles to adapt to what your brain expects."

It's all too much. "Jesus," I breathe. "What am I?"

It's a question directed more toward myself than Q, but he answers anyway. "A new species, essentially. You probably couldn't have children, but seeing as that's already been taken care of, no need to worry."

The snideness in his voice sparks my rage and I'm on my feet in an instant. For a second or two, dizziness threatens to make me lose my balance. Then, slowly, I approach him, ignoring the shaking in my hands and knees. "Fuck you. You *murdered* my sister, all so I could be your goddamn super soldier."

He frowns. "A small price to pay for what you've been given, and for what you'll do for the world."

I lunge, and in an instant my hands are around his neck. I want nothing except for him to suffer. And, in this moment, I feel like I have the power to cause it. I could crush him if I really wanted to, but I'd rather he have some time to think about his impending death. He struggles to no avail.

But then at the edge of my vision I see him tap his earpiece, and suddenly I've collapsed on the ground, unable to move.

Q collects himself, his irises cold and dark as he gazes at me. "Don't think I didn't prepare for your emotional outbursts, Thanatos. I've designed blackout protocols for those moments of weakness."

He leans down before uttering his next words, face inches from mine, eyes unblinking. "I can immobilize you. I can knock you out. I can *kill* you—stop your heart cold."

And that's when I realize that my life as I know it is over.

My mind and my body are no longer my own. Q can decide to revoke my free will whenever he pleases.

"That's the beauty of your technology. The hybridity makes the capabilities... *endless*. Delta won't know what hit them." He straightens. "Now then. Since you've proven to be untrustworthy in your current state of mind, I'm putting you in a holding cell again. I'll be running tests and monitoring your brain activity remotely until we perform physical evaluations of your specialized skill set. In a week I'll take you back to the GUARD, where we'll demonstrate what you can do."

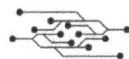

I'm kept in the same cell as before, only this time Nastasia isn't there. It's dead silent and nearly pitch-black.

In that solitude, I finally mourn Reiya, sitting with my back against the cold wall in a state of shock. I can't even cry, but my body is shaking, though I'm not sure whether it's from weakness or anguish.

Having a loved one ripped from your life is a pain like no other, and I can confirm that it's not any easier the second time. No—knowing I could've saved her makes it far worse. It's almost too much to bear.

And I don't even know what to do about it, because Q's so-called blackout protocols present a problem for getting revenge. I decide that it might be best to wait and see exactly what I can do, and what he can control. I need to play my cards right.

Over the next couple days, I don't eat or sleep.

Those days become some of the most surreal in my life as things... *happen* to me. There are times where I'm in immense physical pain, to the point where I can't stop myself from screaming, and others where everything is numb. There are times where I feel void of emotions, and others where the intensity of my grief and anger and loneliness nearly break me.

It's almost torturous. Just the idea of Q controlling my neurocomputer, an invisible force, is enough to drive me insane. He claims that he's just testing everything, that it will automatically know when to reduce my pain, when to filter sensory input, when to calm me down.

When to take control, is what he means.

I'm terrified of it.

I don't even have time to process it all before Q continues on to test physical abilities that I didn't know I had.

He brings me to a high-ceilinged chamber with a strange sort of climbing wall designed to emulate a building. A man is standing in front of it, arms crossed, looking bored out of his mind.

"When he scales that wall, I want you to copy him exactly," Q says simply.

I almost respond but falter. He's speaking to me in Russian, yet I understand him.

Which is odd, considering I didn't know Russian a few days ago.

He smirks at my realization.

"What the hell?"

"No English, please."

I repeat the phrase, mockingly, in Russian.

It's a bizarre sensation, knowing how to do something but lacking cognizance of that knowledge. It's like I have another mind informing my own, which I suppose is somewhat accurate.

"Adding another language to your repertoire was extremely simple, seeing as you have a talent for it. Because you know several already, most of the neural connections were already there."

"Cool," I reply flatly. On the inside, I'm losing my shit.

"Now. Like I said, mimic him." Q gestures with a nod of his head to the other man, who scales the wall with remarkable speed and precision. Effortlessly. I can climb, sure, but not like that. And especially not in my current physical state.

Yet somehow I do it, kind of. I'm slower and clumsier and it exhausts me, but I make it to the top, using similar technique—technique which I've never been taught. Far above Q, I look down at him in disbelief.

Even from here I can see his satisfaction.

"It's a mimicry protocol," he explains, though I didn't ask. "Rather than having to specify each skill, I thought it'd be more elegant if you could attain them on the fly. Your neurocomputer analyzes visual input to generate a movement pattern. Again, you must actually be physically capable—it's not like that would've worked if you were out of shape. As you practice more and more, you'll gain more finesse, but be careful not to strain yourself. You're not quite indestructible."

"Seems like you could've put in a *little* bit more effort to make me indestructible," I respond. "You've already hijacked every part of me."

"Well, let's see just how close to indestructible you are. I want you to jump. As you land, some of that kinetic energy will be absorbed for you to use later. In fact, you can absorb a few different kinds of energy, but too much could potentially be lethal."

I have the urge to just fling myself off this ledge head-first.

Down below, there's no mat, no cushioning of any kind. I'm going to break a goddamn bone.

"*Jump.*"

It's a command this time—a command which my mind wants to obey. There's a switch that's flipped, and the neurocomputer takes over. I only have a second to panic at the loss of control before I'm falling.

When my feet meet the ground I feel an upward rush through my body, but there's minimal pain. I don't even have to roll upon impact, just bend my knees.

"What the *fuck* was that?" I breathe.

Q cocks his head, fully aware that I'm not talking about this energy absorption ability.

"Well. Voice command is far easier than entering a command via UI. Would've used it last time, but seeing as you were strangling me…"

Then I finally throw up.

Q can control me with his voice.

THIRTY SIX
ZAHRA

Until now I'm not sure I really understood the full extent of Delta's power. I mean, an external entity controlling multiple governments across the globe? It's inconceivable. It should be nearly impossible.

Yet, here we are.

Delta is like a cancer. It took a couple decades to spread, but now it's ready to kill. Somehow, I ended up on the front lines, and it's utterly terrifying.

My first shadowing assignment is on an operation that, of course, Markham is a leader of. The good news is that it's an operation related to the turmoil in the UK, which seems to be a prime opportunity for gathering intel. My job is to help oversee the actions of the government and suppress any motions to resolve the riots peacefully. Delta is urging both sides to not back down so that the country reaches a breaking point, after which the people will presumably prevail.

I'm going to do what I can to prevent it, because it would mean that Delta is one step closer to their goal. Their power will expand, especially since one of their own is the leader of the movement.

Talia Bellona is her name.

When I ask Parrish about her, she claims that Bellona is "just a face, a voice." Someone trained to persuade, to stand out. But Delta choosing her is not as insignificant, in my opinion, as Parrish makes it out to be. I think she's more than a symbol.

While the London base is handling their country's representatives, my team is primarily responsible for managing the US response to the situation, including media coverage. Markham assigns the US ambassador to the UK to my partner, Lex, and me.

The US ambassador. Someone who's representing our entire nation. I'm just shadowing on this one, but I'm still nervous as hell.

Lex is in her thirties, and a well-established member of Delta. She already knows the ambassador, too, by which I mean that she's long been responsible for ensuring that he does what Delta wants. She introduces herself, but for the most part ignores me. After all, she doesn't need me—I'm just someone who might get in her way in an operation that's pretty significant for her.

We have our first team meeting in a vault, where Markham gives each of us a high-level overview of our objectives. Most of us will be departing to London in a few days. For Lex and I, all we have to do is coach the ambassador on how to reassure the UK's government of the US's support and willingness to help subdue the retaliations. This is going to be our government's stance, thanks to Delta's invisible puppeteering, but we still need to manipulate him into putting on the right show. Lex already has him on a tight leash, but we can't afford for him to break loose now.

Markham's animosity toward me doesn't fade, but around our more senior coworkers he keeps the insults to a minimum. I do notice, however, that he eyes Lex more than me. He's into her, that much is clear, but he's not ogling, he's a predator assessing his prey. He's targeting her, like he did with me.

The rest of the men in the room are totally oblivious. Or they don't care. But if it's obvious to me, it's probably obvious to Lex, yet she doesn't show it. I feel like I should mention it, but I worry she might not take it well. God knows everyone around here either turns a blind eye to harassment, or endures it silently.

It all comes to a head on a Wednesday night, two days before we're scheduled to head to London. Markham is forcing us to work late, to detail again and again each person's role and backup strategies. The man is absolutely relentless. I can tell Lex is reaching her limit, as is everyone, but he wants perfection. Delta *needs* perfection right now. So he digs in. He enumerates every possible scenario that could play out with the ambassador—every reaction, every stance—even though we're confident that he'll be loyal.

When he finally lets everyone leave, he still holds Lex back.

I pause on my way out, assuming that he wants to berate the both of us.

Then he says, "Get out, Olsen."

But I'm sure as hell not going to leave Lex alone with him, so I stand outside the vault's open door, hidden from sight. The base is mostly deserted at this hour, anyway.

"You know, a lot is riding on this operation for you," I hear Markham say. As usual, he's being patronizing, menacing. But I can tell he has even darker intentions.

"Yes," is all Lex says.

"What I mean is, if I don't put in a good word for you, you're not going to get the promotion you want."

"I know that."

"Good. So why don't we make a deal. I'll do you this favor, if you do me a favor."

Jesus. I can't imagine that he has a particularly friendly favor in mind.

I hold my breath, ready to act if he tries to hurt her, but debating what kind of intervention isn't going to get me killed.

"And what favor would that be?" Lex responds coldly.

I don't really hear what happens next before she makes a noise of disgust. "No. I'll take my chances."

Then she breezes out the door, not looking back, not even aware of my presence in her rush to get the hell out of there. But I'm not spared from Markham.

"*Fuck*," he hisses, gathering his things in anger before leaving the vault.

When he sees me he halts. Sneers.

"Eavesdropping, are we, Olsen?"

"I don't think she's interested," I respond plainly, maintaining my calm. "Maybe you should leave her alone."

He glares at me, draws a pistol, points it right at my head. "Is that so?"

I glare right back. My heart is nearly beating out of my chest, but I can't let him see how terrified I am.

In an instant I could be dead, but something tells me he's not going to pull the trigger, so I decide to make a move. I know I can't fight him. I probably can't run from him. To take control of this situation, I need to exploit his weakness.

Slowly, slowly, I lift my hand and gently nudge the gun away from my face, stepping a few inches closer to him.

He is silent as I place a hand on his chest, almost bringing my lips to his. I want to vomit, but I hide it well. I hesitate to see if he'll close the gap, and after a few breaths he does.

But a minute later the gun is back, cold against the side of my head. I freeze, lips still touching his, hand down his pants.

He's so hard. Maybe it's embarrassing him.

"Go ahead," I murmur. "But my corpse isn't going to suck your dick very well."

I swear his eyes blacken.

"You bitch," he hisses.

He punches me across the face, my vision going black for a moment. Then comes another hit, and another.

"Markham!" I hear someone bark. Reeling, I spit blood out of my mouth as I turn to see Parrish, the sight of whom causes Markham to back away from me. She's got a gun of her own pointed at him. "Drop the gun. Kick it away from yourself," she orders while beckoning me with her other hand. "Let's sort this out, shall we?"

Reluctantly, Markham sets his gun on the ground, pushes it away with his foot, and raises his hands slightly, clearly under the impression that Parrish is going to let him walk away.

Maintaining a steady glare at Markham, she hands her pistol to me. "Shoot him," she says calmly. I look at her in disbelief, then at him, who's about to piss his pants in shock. "Don't hesitate."

I raise my arm and aim, but still I falter, and I don't know why. I can't count how many abusers I killed when working for Remus. Markham is no different, so why is this so hard?

But I know I have to do it. If there's anything Lucien taught me it's not to be soft: *You cannot break.* So I walk up to him, and spit the last thing he'll hear into his face.

"Rot in hell, you revolting pig."

He doesn't even plead with me, because he knows it's not worth it. He just stares down the barrel of my gun like he finally realizes what he's done.

Then, eyes locked firmly onto his, I pull the trigger.

He didn't even deserve such a nice fate.

With drops of blood on my face, I turn around to face Parrish. All she does is nod.

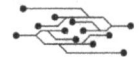

That night plays out like an edgy HV show as I attempt to cope with everything that's happened via indulgence.

I go to a club, I drink, I get hit on. I drink more, the pain ebbs and suddenly I'm drifting in a sea of induced bliss.

A woman takes me into the grungy, dimly-lit bathroom, and we do a line or several.

She goes down on me, I go down on her. We go to her place to do it all again.

I feel myself craving to live like this forever.

Then it fades, and I hit the ground hard.

In the moment, drugs and booze and meaningless sex can make everything better, but in the long run, it only exacerbates things. I want to talk to Kai more than anything. I need to just hear his voice and then I'll be okay.

I stumble outside, taking out the piece of paper that he slipped me before we parted, with the number to a burner phone. *In case of emergency*, it says on the back.

For when shit gets rough, is what I know he meant.

But it's not Kai who answers.

"...Lucien?" I ask hesitantly.

"Jesus, Zahra?"

"Yeah."

"Are you okay? What happened?"

I suddenly feel kind of stupid, because this is not a dire situation. It's probably four or so in the morning, too. "I'm okay. I just... I'm fucked up."

"I know the feeling," he says gently. It comforts me because he does know, he knows all too well what I'm dealing with. "I'm sorry we ever sent you into that hellhole."

"Where's Kai?"

"Ah... he's not here." His words are saturated with anxiety and I start to panic. Suddenly I feel very, very sober.

"Tell me. What happened?"

"I thought Q had been informing you of everything."

"What? No, I haven't heard anything from you guys in weeks. What happened?" I repeat.

"He... we don't know. We have no idea where he is. They blew up our base in New York, but we never found his body. We think that he's been kidnapped."

"Oh my God." *No no no.* "By Delta?"

"Maybe."

"Well are you looking for him?"

"Of course, Z. We're doing everything we can. We'll find him, I promise."

"If he's not dead!"

"We'll find him," he repeats, grim and tired. I'm not sure he believes what he's saying. "We're just a little understaffed. Kohler's dead, Harley is still recovering from losing her legs. So right now it's just me and some new guy."

"Jesus…" is all I can say. It's horrible. It's all so horrible. I squeeze my eyes shut as though it'll block everything out.

"I know. I'll tell you the second we find Kai, dead or alive. Okay?"

"Okay," I respond quietly.

"Do you need anything?"

"No."

"Okay. Take care of yourself. We can't lose you too."

I don't distinctly remember making it home, but somehow I end up sprawled across my bed, fully clothed. I stagger into the bathroom the next morning and see a disheveled—no, utterly wrecked—girl in the mirror, her makeup smeared all over and her hair in knots. Not to mention the hickeys and the red eyes, and the bruises from Markham. Lord help me. I look like I've been ran over by a train.

In my head, yesterday feels like merely a nightmare, but my appearance is convincing evidence that it all actually happened. That I shot Markham point-blank, that I did a hell of a lot of coke, that Kai is missing. *Kai is missing.*

I don't know how I'll be able to do my job knowing that.

But I also feel more compelled to continue. If these people are going to hurt someone I care about, then I'm going to hurt them back. Whatever it takes.

I tell myself to get my shit together. Because this is only the beginning.

THIRTY SEVEN
HARLEY

Living without legs is honestly one of the hardest things I've ever done. The GUARD's medicine has helped me heal quickly, but I'm still weak. I'm trapped on this goddamn island, dependent on Lucien to help me with the daily things I never gave any thought to. Unable to do what I'm good at.

But it's not so much due to the physical challenges as the mental ones. Although Mason Dare is designing a set of prosthetic legs for me, it's not going to be the same ever again, and knowing that has left me feeling lost. Paranoid about the unknowns of my future.

I've been pinching myself again, digging my nails into my skin again, sometimes subconsciously. It doesn't hurt; it alleviates my anxiety, my fear, my emotional pain. Sometimes I just need to make myself bleed.

But I'm also happy to just be alive after what happened.

For me, that's a relatively unfamiliar sensation—pain and anger are quick to consume any semblance of a positive emotion. But after days of staring out at the waves, I've come to accept that persistent happiness is unrealistic. Happiness is fleeting, far more than sadness. I think that instead, I can be content if I have purpose, and if I have human connection. For most of my life I had neither, and now I have both.

Nothing can hurt me anymore.

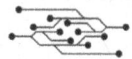

"What are the chances that Q nearly drops off the map at the same time Kai does?"

I look up from reading Keating's daily report at Lucien, who has his head bowed in thought, his hands gripping the back of Dare's living room couch. The past couple days he's been acting a little… manic. He's hardly slept, hardly eaten, hardly sat down.

"He *lied* to us about keeping Zahra in the loop," he continues. "Why wouldn't he just tell us to reach out to her? It implies that he didn't want us talking to her."

"Maybe so as not to worry her?" I suggest, though I share his skepticism. "I mean, the GUARD is in chaos. She needs to focus on her part, not on us."

Lucien shakes his head. "Don't you think she deserves to know Kai is missing?"

"Of course. And now she does. I'm just trying to give possible explanations. I don't want us jumping to conclusions."

"We don't exactly have time to mull things over. God knows what's happening to Kai."

"I know, Lucien. But I trust Q with my life."

"That's the problem," he snaps, wild-eyed.

I cross my arms. "What's your theory, then?"

"I think he's the person you should've looked into instead of Holbrook."

"Based on what?"

"It started as a hunch, really. I went along that line of thought and hacked into Kai's sister's computer."

Christ. "You *what?*"

"Hear me out. Reiya was investigating Dr. Brenner, and she eventually led Camden to Holbrook. Camden was the only one who took the fall for it. I didn't find any hard evidence on Reiya's machine, but it looked… tampered with. A lot of her security protocols had been disabled or modified, which was why I was able to gain access so easily. There was clever monitor viewing malware hiding out as well, which I'm sure she wasn't aware of. She's good, but she's no match for Q."

I shake my head. His brain is clearly going a thousand miles an hour. "What are you suggesting?"

"That Q used her. Holbrook seemed like the most logical person to shift blame onto—he was easily unlikeable, held tremendous power, and might've been standing in Q's way. Reiya's investigations provided a means for Q to get more false evidence into our hands. And he could've protected her from Holbrook ever finding her in case he needed to leverage her relationship with Kai again. But he *didn't* protect Camden because he didn't have a reason to. In fact, he may have intentionally set Camden up to be interrogated because it only further solidified everyone's beliefs about Holbrook."

"That's…"

"A lot, I know. Granted, I don't know Q that well, but I truly think it's a possibility we should explore. He knew we were in New York. He was the one with unlimited access to our every move, not Holbrook. And now Reiya's computer hasn't had any activity for several days, which means she could be missing same as Kai."

I deliberate in silence, unconvinced but willing to admit to myself that Lucien being an outsider gives him perspective that I'm too blind to see.

"All right," I say finally. "Say you're correct. Kai could be anywhere, but it probably makes sense to start with Devil's Peak."

"Yes," Lucien agrees, his tone growing grave. I can see him tense just at the mention of the place that robbed him of himself.

"Devil's Peak?" Benson repeats, chiming in for the first time. "The hell is that?"

"A fortress," Lucien responds. "An impenetrable prison."

Benson grins with excitement. "Excellent. When do we break in?"

"Tomorrow."

I look for some sign that Lucien is kidding, but there is none. "We can't manage that."

"Sure we can." He looks at me with feral, sleep-deprived eyes. "We have to fly halfway across the world to get to Canada. That'll give us enough time to develop a game plan."

I scoff in disbelief. "We're going to need more than just us to pull this off."

"We have Benson. You've seen what he can do. He can literally just knock everyone out as we go along."

Ah, right. The guy with the superpowers. Makes things a bit easier.

"That's true," I respond. "We just can't afford for anyone to get killed."

There is a spike in the intensity of his eyes. "I'll be damned if I die in that place now."

I sigh, relenting. Lucien's right—there's no time to waste, and we have no other leads. It's probably worth it to rule it out. "I'll inform Keating. You two pack our shit."

When Lucien's expression morphs into one of pity, I already know what he's going to say. "Harley... are you sure you should come?"

It makes me see red. "Yes," I snap. "I'm not going to sit here and wait for you to rescue *my* partner. Just because I can't go into the field doesn't mean I can't help. You both need a level head anyway."

Benson shrugs. "You're not wrong there. I have no idea what the hell I'm doing. And Limp Dick over here, well…"

I can't help but smirk at his nickname for Lucien, which arose from the fact that he has a limp and, at times, acts like a dick.

I'll admit, having Benson around has actually helped. Lucien is usually very serious, and Benson is, well, not. Like his father, he's chaotic. He's the type of person who can make himself at home anywhere. Every so often he'll make fun of one of us or crack a joke, and it'll yank me out of my chasm of anxiety. Unexpectedly, Lucien is getting on with him, as if their opposite personalities create a strange harmony.

We're a band of misfits, yet somehow still a team.

Lucien holds my gaze for a few seconds longer, then nods.

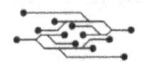

The implications of our second Devil's Peak operation are far greater than the first. If Lucien and Benson are caught, it wouldn't be unreasonable for the warden to suspect that the GUARD is behind it, since the last time he saw Lucien we were taking his corpse back to New York. I suppose that conclusion could be interpreted as either good or bad—Devil's Peak is essentially the GUARD's prison, so either this'll be easy to sweep under the rug, or it'll add to the chaos.

With access Keating reluctantly agreed to provide, Lucien will be hacking the prison network to spoof their security cameras like he did in Rio. On top of that, he'll be giving Tony authorization that will enable the AI to unlock doors, alert us of threats, and identify individuals. From the Calgary safe house, I'll be using Tony's intel and monitoring non-spoofed cameras to guide Lucien and Benson in searching for Kai, Q, and Dr. Brenner.

We're under orders from Keating not to kill Q if we do find him, but I have no idea what'll come of it. Hell, he could have a reasonable explanation for all of this. And if not, I doubt that he would face the consequences he should.

Throughout the whole flight to Calgary, I debate whether to ask Lucien if he'll be okay going back to Devil's Peak. When I study him I find not fear but tenacity in his eyes, as if he's planning something beyond the potential rescue of Kai.

I recognize it. It's the same thing I once witnessed in my own eyes as I stared at myself in a bathroom mirror, gripping the sink, plotting the murder of my parents.

Revenge.

Benson's plan is to go in and harm as few people as possible, apart from the occasional, brief infliction of intense agony. Lucien's plan may not align with that.

Given that he feels that he deserved what he endured at Devil's Peak, it's a little ironic to me if he wants to exact revenge on his tormenters, but on the other hand, cruelty is cruelty. Tormenting a bad person doesn't make you a good person.

Still, would I be comfortable with numerous people dying? While I wouldn't sit around crying about it, I'll admit it would nag at my moral compass, like everything my job entails. Rio was no different. But thus far I've continued to believe that what I do is making an impact for the better.

Who knows, maybe I'm delusional. The issue with the *greater good* philosophy is that it's difficult to predict whether the benefits will outweigh the catastrophe you've caused.

But I shove all of that to the back of my mind. Right now all I want is to get answers about my partner, whether they're the answers I want to hear or not. I can't really explain why, but Kai has become the most important person in my life. And I don't know what I would do without him.

THIRTY EIGHT

KAI

A cacophony of agonized screams and gunfire jolts me from my shallow sleep. I hold my breath, struggling to understand what is happening, but moments later the door bangs open in a burst of light that penetrates the utter darkness of this cell, as if someone is arriving (ungracefully) from the heavens.

"The fuck is it so dark?" A voice I do not recognize.

I am frozen, unable to make a sound, my back pressed hard against the wall in the hope that it will absorb me.

"Kai?"

I exhale. That voice I do know—it belongs to Lucien Haddad. He flips on a flashlight and shines it at me. God, it's good to see him.

"*Jesus,*" he breathes, coming closer to kneel beside me as I shield my eyes from the light. "You don't even look like you're alive."

"Harley," I whisper.

"She's okay. Lost her legs, but Benny's daddy is building her new ones."

I don't even have the energy to ask who he's referring to. Suddenly he flinches at some unseen source of pain, swearing.

"Don't do that," he hisses at the other person, who snickers in response. "This is Benson Moreno. Mason Dare's kid."

"We can do introductions later, man, we need to get out of here," Benson says, coming forward to lift me off the ground. I almost collapse but he holds me up with surprising strength.

Lucien, pointing with a Soulbarer, scouts for any threats before leading us out of my cell. Disoriented, I look around at all the bodies of my guards. Some of them have been gunned down; others, I notice, look like they simply dropped dead. Something tells me Benson was the cause.

Then, as if reading my mind, he says, "Most of them aren't actually dead. I just knocked them out. Lucien did kill a few though, he just couldn't help himself." He smirks.

"Oh, piss off," Lucien responds from ahead of us. "These people tortured Kai, clearly. They torture everyone in this place."

"I bet they loved you coming back to fuck them all over," I say, weakly smiling.

Lucien grins back at me. "Felt good. I wish I could've given them a taste of their own medicine, though. They're all getting off easy."

"How's Zahra?" I dread his answer.

"She's alive."

Not okay, but alive, which is all I could hope for.

Then Lucien halts. Benson too. I look around in confusion, but there is no threat. Then I notice their earpieces—probably someone saying something on the other end.

"Reiya is here," Lucien says. "Harley sees her on one of the cameras."

My heart freezes. "That's impossible."

Lucien whirls, narrowing his eyes. "Meaning?"

"She's dead. I saw it."

He stares at me. "Don't be so sure. Let's go double-check the cell Harley says she's in."

Numbly I follow him, Benson still holding onto me. I'm not sure what the hell Harley sees, but it's probably not my sister. I know what I saw.

And yet, I'm wrong.

Reiya rushes up to me, throwing her arms around me. *"Oh my God. You're okay."*

When she releases me I have to touch her face to make sure she's real. "I thought… How are you alive?" My eyes dart to her neck to look for a wound, but there is none.

She looks at me in confusion, but before she can respond Lucien is hurrying us along again.

"Talk later. Let's go," he says.

"Where are Q and Dr. Brenner?" Reiya asks as we make our way through the prison maze. I watch in awe as Benson knocks people out—without touching them, even. It makes me question whether this is reality, but at this point anything seems possible.

"Not here, as far as we can tell. We think they saw us coming," Lucien responds, guarding us from the back now, gun always at the ready.

"They're not our priority, anyway," Benson adds.

I'm so dazed that I don't really process what happens before we make it to the top of the prison, where a helicopter is waiting. I just hold onto my sister.

It's when I lay eyes on Harley that I cry.

I crumple to my knees in front of her, unable to hold in the emotional trauma of these past couple weeks any longer. Not just my trauma, but that of everyone who matters to me.

My head in her lap, she bends to embrace me.

And for minutes we stay like that. Until I lift my head again and our lips meet in a kiss that conveys far more than we could utter in words.

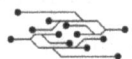

We spend the rest of the day exchanging grim stories. Reiya and Lucien think that when I saw her die, I was experiencing a simulation of some kind. When she was first brought to Devil's Peak, Q obtained full imaging and recordings of her to generate believable gestures, postures, and expressions.

I have a haunting suspicion that the simulation emanated from my neurocomputer, which would mean that my reality can effectively be altered. As if everything weren't shitty enough already.

"Kai... this is insane," Harley says. "He's changed every fiber of your being, literally. God knows what he's planning."

"Nothing we can do to reverse what he did," I respond bitterly.

"What if we could hack it?" Reiya says. "Disable some of the protocols."

That hangs in the air for a moment.

"Hack it?" Lucien repeats.

"Yes. It's bound to have some vulnerabilities."

"Q will have implemented nearly impenetrable security, I imagine. Not to mention that us messing with this... this *thing* that can control Kai biologically is quite dangerous. We could damage his brain, his body. We could kill him."

"I know. It's up to Kai whether it's worth the risk."

"It is," I reply. "I want my own mind back. But... that can probably wait. First, we need to figure out what the hell we're doing. With Q and Dr. Brenner, with Delta, with the state of the GUARD. We're all in disarray."

"According to Keating," Harley says, "Byrne is pulling resources from other assignments and focusing almost everyone on stopping and eradicating Delta. Zahra and our other moles will be working nonstop to help us get ahead and prevent another tragedy. Our team, meanwhile, is still tasked with finding out who the leaders are. Cam and Shay believe they have a solid lead on Gokiburi, which will hopefully lead us to Arachne.

"However, Zahra has given us information regarding a new figure—Talia Bellona—who has gained popularity in the UK and even in other countries across Europe. I put her on Keating's radar but I'm not sure if he recognized the significance. He has a thousand other things on his mind."

"And what is the significance?" I respond.

"Zahra's intel suggests that the movement Bellona has started is intended to create political upheaval. Overthrow in the near future. If the

United Kingdom, one of the United States' biggest allies, falls to Delta..."

"It'd be hard to come back from that," I finish. "What's Byrne's take? Can't he send one of his agents to kill her?"

"It's not that simple," Lucien says. "Delta protects its assets at all costs, so taking her out is going to require a bit of work. Byrne already ordered a hit but instead lost an agent. Other than that, there's no one in the GUARD tracking her in all the chaos."

"So you think we should?"

"Some of us, at least. The rest can assist Shay and Camden. It doesn't particularly matter who goes to London and who goes to Tokyo, but I think Reiya and I should be split up since our skills are comparable."

I sit up straight. "Uh... Since when is Reiya involved in this?"

"I think we need her."

I look at my sister.

"I don't know that I should just go back to my life," she says, her eyes gentle. "And besides, someone's gotta learn how to control that thing in your head."

I'm not sure where she's better off—in New York City, where Q can kidnap her whenever he pleases, or with me, where she'll be on the front lines of this battle we're in.

Eventually I nod. Lucien's right—we do need her. A few weeks ago I would've never agreed, but my perspective has been forced to change. I need to savor whatever time I may have with her.

Then I look to Harley, desperately hoping she'll be by my side through all of this, especially after we almost lost each other.

She looks back at me, and for some reason I know she feels the same.

"Help me dress, would you?" I turn around to find Harley topless, in the process of removing her sweatpants that have been knotted at the knee. We'd spent the night next to one another, holding one another. But nothing more.

I can't help but just stare at her.

She gives me a look. "Come on, it's not like you haven't seen my tits. Or did you forget we used to fuck?"

I flush. "It's not that, I just…" I exhale, running a hand through my hair. God, I want to touch her.

Her expression morphs into a smirk. "Hm. Well then stare all you like."

Here we are, stuck between being friends and being lovers, unsure if we should move in either direction.

Not to mention how Zahra complicates the matter. I like her more than I want to, but, if I'm being honest, not in the way I like Harley. The fact that my emotions about Harley are lingering, perhaps even growing deeper, leaves me in a difficult position.

But I push my anxiety over this aside. This is no time to fret over my love life.

While I'm helping Harley I instead mull over what Benson has told me about Nyx. Nyx, the planet where an advanced species once dwelled, where Dr. Elsa Salazar sent her creations to live. They established a civilization called Elysium, utilizing the buildings and technological inventions left behind. There, they survive on plant-based food, given that no other animal-like beings exist. It's just them, several thousand of them, alone, galaxies away from the nearest humans.

Benson describes it as a haven, but not without conflict. Around the time he was born, a tyrannical, radical leader came into power and banned travel to Earth, disconnecting our worlds. Kyrios, as he's known, proclaimed that the Elysians were a superior race who had no place interacting with the species that created them to fight their battles. Since then, to the best of everyone's knowledge, no communication between the two planets has been made. Given the political unrest before the interstellar travel ban—unrest that Benson's mother was trying to evade—he's not convinced that we'll reconnect with Elysium.

I'm not sure if he meant in the near future, or ever. Either way, it might be for the best. I can scarcely imagine the danger of Delta acquiring this information. We're going through enough shit on Earth as it is.

Reiya, Harley, and I will be heading to Tokyo to meet Cam and Shay, making a pitstop in California at DareTech HQ so that Harley can get her custom bionic legs. Benson and Lucien, meanwhile, will be following up on Zahra's information and working with her in case they need insider knowledge.

At this point we're not really taking orders from anyone, merely maintaining steady communication with Keating and Byrne. And I suppose it's what I've wanted for a long time, but I didn't expect it to come with such weight. The leaders of the GUARD have decided to put trust in their agents to make the right decisions, make no mistakes. At a time like this, either it'll bring us down, or we'll prevail.

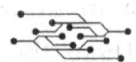

DareTech is a futuristic campus with a minimalist vibe. There's a handful of thin, winding solarglass buildings, surrounded by gardens of foliage engineered to be resistant to drought, heat, and wind. Engineered to capture more carbon dioxide than natural trees. While Dare has made his fortune off technology—the things people care about—he's remained one of the world's most prominent advocates for the environment. Even the GUARD's jets have been designed to use renewable energy, thanks to him.

A secretary takes us to a twenty-fifth-floor lounge to wait for Dare, with views of the Southern California desert on one side, a distant grey ocean on the other side. There's fancy whiskey set out on a tray, so I pour us all a drink—God knows we need it.

Dare is taken aback when he sees us. I'm not sure if it's because of how exhausted we are or how many wounds we have collectively or both. "Jesus. You all look like wrecks."

I can't help but run my fingers over the fresh scar at the base of my skull.

"Better pour more of that," he continues, gesturing to the drink in my hand.

"You can count on it," I mutter.

He looks at me apologetically. "I'm sorry I never suspected Q. If I had, perhaps we could've prevented what happened to you."

"He manipulated you just the same as he did the rest of us. I don't blame you."

He almost responds, but stops himself, instead merely nodding once.

"I hear you've got something for me," Harley says.

Dare's eyes suddenly get that same wild glimmer I noticed the first time I talked to him. "Yes. I request that you stay here for at least a day so that I can ensure everything works as expected. And that everything fits your desires." He turns to Reiya and me. "I'll take Harley to get fitted with her legs. Meanwhile, one of my engineers has a few things to show the both of you."

He whisks Harley away, leaving Reiya and me alone for the first time since being reunited. I'm grateful that Q left her alone after getting what he needed from her, but I think being imprisoned still took a toll on her.

"You look different," she says. "Your eyes are more… metallic almost. Your skin is smoother."

"Really? I hadn't noticed." Then again, I don't think I've really looked at myself in the mirror in a while.

"Didn't you say the girl you were with had turquoise eyes?"

Nastasia.

Harley never saw any white-haired girls when she helped us escape, but I still dread that I left Nastasia in that hellhole. We spent very little time together, but shared trauma has a way of creating bonds.

"Yeah, she did. So I guess it would make sense if mine have changed."

"Benson doesn't have weird eyes."

I shrug. "He has Dare's eyes. Plus, I don't know how much what Q and Brenner did mirrors the Elysians. He said they only copied the muscle enhancement aspects."

"Could be related, considering the iris has muscles in it. What about your neurocomputer? Has it done anything since leaving Devil's Peak?"

I exhale. "No. But I keep expecting it to."

"If I can get behind a terminal I can try to access it and figure out its patterns."

Turns out Dare is one step ahead. One of his engineers gives Reiya a coding tablet, outfitted with holographic visualization features, all kinds of simulation and analytical tools, and an AI assistant for hacking and code development. I've seen a few of our techies with these, but only our very best—you have to know what you're doing to be trusted with a powerful tool like that.

Reiya is ecstatic. She figures out how to use it almost instantly, and it reminds me who was always the smarter sibling. I, meanwhile, basically just know how to beat someone up. It's why I'll always be under someone's command and she won't.

The engineer gives me a nanotech suit, emblazoned with a circular maze logo, equipped with black holsters, gloves, and boots. Not just me of course, there's one for everyone on Operation Labyrinth, even Reiya. They'll replace the vests that Dare had originally provided, with the same temperature adjustment abilities and protection against knives and bullets. However, this time there's a computer embedded in each, one that can change the physical properties of the suit, including color and breathability, and unfold a stronger armor layer overtop. It even has, to my amusement, deployable wings under the arms.

The computer will know when to change the suit based on the environment, using sensors for body and external temperatures, as well as body position in terms of orientation and global location. But Dare has also designed the suits such that Tony can control them, either using visual input or direct voice command from us.

My question is whether it will be able to withstand my new energy expulsion capability.

"You should try it," Reiya says, looking at me intensely. "I think if you tell your suit to loosen, thereby increasing the distance between atoms, your energy release is feasible. But—and I know you won't like this idea—I also think we can train your neurocomputer to control your suit for you. It'll know when you're about to use one of your superpowers and can change the suit accordingly. That way you won't have to think about both."

I groan. She's right, I don't like that idea. I don't want the stupid implant to have *any* control over anything.

"I thought you were going to help me disable it."

"The malicious portions, yes. It's dangerous. But that thing also makes you *powerful*. If you could truly harness its abilities while limiting how much thinking it does, you'd be unstoppable."

My immediate reaction is vehement disagreement. I hate what Q and Brenner have done to me. I hate that Reiya sees it as an opportunity rather than as a violation of my mind and body.

Yet, if I'm going to live with this, I should make the most of it. While the last thing I want is to be the weapon that Q envisioned, I can still be what he tried to prevent—uncontrollable.

"Fine," I respond. "But they're not *superpowers*. I'm no hero."

THIRTY NINE

Tokyo is all neon lights. Blue and pink and purple. Holographic projections of people talk at you, trying to sell you things—or, if you're in a seedier part of the city, trying to entice you to come into a sex club. A lot of people are wearing pollution masks, which, similar to Los Angeles, have become necessary enough that they're now fashion, like jewelry. Those without masks are assumed to be poor.

We arrive at Camden and Shay's hotel suite around ten at night. Camden, being who he is, gives me shit for getting kidnapped by Q.

"Always have to be so dramatic, don't you?" he says, already handing me a drink. "*God*, ever the attention whore."

I roll my eyes but can't stop myself from smiling. "Missed you."

"Oh I know. You barely function without me, clearly."

After a night of drinking and catching up, I'm awoken at five in the morning by Harley coming in, though I didn't even know she went out. In her wheelchair, too.

Thus far she's been able to stand and walk around on her new legs, which she credits to quick healing and bionic simulation training. Dare's prosthetics lab has designed limbs that can generate artificial neural impulses, which means that if they're fully integrated with the body, your brain can be tricked into believing you have real appendages. Essentially, Harley's legs appear and function almost exactly like real ones; it's just a matter of growing accustomed to the feeling and developing synapses. But right now she can't feel the ground.

"Where'd you go?" I murmur as she pushes herself out of her chair and onto the circular bed where I'm lying in a pile of blankets. It's dark, but she's still illuminated by the soft blue lighting that lines the ceiling of the bedroom like a halo. It's then that I realize that her legs look... robotic. Like I'm seeing the innards of the technology. Earlier they matched her skin tone.

She follows my gaze and grins. "I kind of like it."

"How'd you change it?"

"Get this—I can change their skin with my *mind*. I've been trying to do it all day. Eventually it'll take the same amount of thought as moving a muscle."

My eyebrows raise. "That's pretty badass."

"I know. Anyway, I went to get a new tattoo."

She turns her back to me and pulls her shirt over her head.

I expect to see something small, like everything else she has. No, it's a snake that winds and curves all the way across and down her back. She rotates herself and it begins to morph, causing my mouth to fall open. When looking at it from the left, it appears as a regular snake, but as you move to the right, its skin seems to dissolve in patches until it's a mechanical skeleton.

Like her legs.

"Thought I'd celebrate becoming a hybrid robot-human."

I sit up, against the headboard. Tentatively I trace my fingers along the tattoo. Her back straightens in response but she doesn't move away.

I would be lying if I said we hadn't developed some kind of intimacy over the past several weeks, something beyond sexual intimacy. And then we almost lost each other.

It's clear to me now that losing her is not something I could survive.

"Kai," she whispers, turning again to face me. "I know I decided to be just friends. But… we don't have the luxury of assuming our futures."

My heartbeat quickens. The words I want to say get caught in my throat.

She places her hand on my arm, thumb running along a vein. "You and I, we're *good* together."

Still, I can't utter a sound, immobilized by her violet gaze.

"I'll understand if you and Zahra are…"

"No," I breathe. "No. It's always been you. I want you, more than anything."

Anxiety evaporates from her expression, replaced by something far more intense. Desire.

She strips off her sweatpants. I feel my body flood with heat as she puts a knee on either side of my hips, my back still pressed against the headboard.

God, is she beautiful.

Slowly she leans toward me, arching her spine, my hand sliding up to the back of her neck, the intensity of her eyes locking me onto her.

Then, she kisses me. It's heavy, sensual. Hungry and raw and emotional.

My hands are light on her waist, but then she murmurs, "Don't be gentle. I want all of you. All of your strength, all of your desire."

So I surrender, gripping her hips as our lips collide again. She tugs at my shirt, pulling it over my head, but I barely bother to breathe before bringing my mouth to her chest, leaving a trail of kisses. She inhales sharply when my tongue grazes her nipple before I continue the trail, her fingers wound in my hair.

With my tongue roaming her body, she leans her head back, lips parted, eyes closed, breath catching with each tease.

Then, "I need you inside me." She says it into my ear like an exhale, her fingers already guiding my sweatpants down.

With one palm on her spine and the other slipping down to the back of her thigh, I pull her against me, onto me. And everything else fades away.

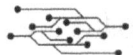

"So the Rio branch learned about Gokiburi via a couple of informants who had direct contact, as you know," Camden begins a briefing in our suite's kitchen the next morning. "They were able to identify and roughly locate one of his bodyguards, which is what Shay and I followed up on."

"We watched and followed the guard for a few days, and we think we've found a hideout," Shay says. "With your help our next move is to identify Gokiburi himself, and subsequently bring him in for interrogation."

"Did we find out what he actually does?" I ask. "I'm still a little out of the loop."

"Based on the intel we got from Rio, it seems like he doesn't have an official position, which is why they didn't really know who he was. Rather, he's likely Arachne's right-hand man, or within that realm. As far as we can tell, he monitors her employees, oversees money laundering, and carries out deals, both for financial purposes and gaining allies."

"Got it. Do you have a plan for getting into his hideout?"

"It's in a hotel on the outskirts of the city," Camden says. "So we can't exactly go in there guns blazing. We first need Reiya to access the security footage to see if we can determine where their lair is. If that doesn't pan out, one of us will follow the guard in. Next, we watch and see who comes and goes to determine who's being guarded, and who's doing the guarding. Lastly, we go in, take out the guards, nab Gokiburi, interrogate."

It takes Reiya an hour or so to do her part, using Dare's coding tablet. She inputs an image of the guard to continuously scan for him in the security feed, while Cam and Shay are waiting a couple blocks from the hotel to send in two insect drones. Our goal is to get them both inside the hideout to get a better sense of what we need to prepare for.

Harley, meanwhile, is pushing herself to gain back the ability to walk. And then run. She falls a few times but doesn't let me help her back up, forcing herself to fight through it. By the end of the morning she's able to make it across the entire hotel suite, having gained some sensation in her new legs. By mid-afternoon she's practicing self-defense moves. And by tomorrow, maybe she'll be beating me up again.

"You should take a break," I tell her, watching her from the kitchen with Reiya. "This kind of thing would normally take people a couple months."

She gives me a look. "I don't have months. I don't even have weeks. I can't sit here while you all are out there fighting. And besides, I'm not normal, and neither are these legs I have."

"Fair enough. I just don't want you to exhaust yourself."

"You'd be doing the same."

"Yeah, and you'd be telling me to sit down. I don't think you got much sleep last night, anyway."

I get a smirk out of her for that.

Reiya soon identifies a fifth-floor room as the hideout, and controls the hotel elevators as the others fly in the drones, streaming their video feeds to us. Then they wait, almost two hours, for the door to open to route them inside.

But inside, there's nothing. Nothing out of the ordinary. It's a hotel suite like any other, not a soul in sight.

"Are we wrong?" Reiya says in confusion.

Harley narrows her eyes, scanning the live stream being projected by Reiya's tablet. "Where's our guard? The guy who just walked out isn't him."

"I'm guessing there's a hidden room," I say.

Then, two cleaners come in, pulling a towel cart, and head through the living room toward a window wall. Sure enough, the cityscape scenery blurs and fades to reveal a grey wall and a door that slides open. Camden and Shay are quick to guide both drones at a safe distance behind the cleaners, who push the cart through the door.

On the other side is a large chamber outfitted with minimal black furniture, several computer displays on one side, and no windows. I notice something that looks like a laundry chute embedded into one wall. There are four additional people, three standing motionless, one sitting.

That alone gives away who's important.

"You think that's him?" Harley asks.

"Maybe," I reply. "I guess I was expecting more. This isn't a fortress, that's for sure."

"I don't think he needs one."

The instant after the chamber door shuts behind the cleaners, both of them have a bullet in their skull.

It happens so fast that I barely catch it.

"*Jesus,*" Reiya exhales.

The guard who shot them, the one who led us there, doesn't approach the bodies. He just re-holsters his weapon. Then, the other two tip the cart, and another body comes tumbling out. At first I think the person is dead, but the guards roughly lift her to her knees, tearing off the bag over her head. Shay nudges one of the drones to get a better look at her face, and Tony identifies her as an English journalist.

That's when the sitting man finally stands.

It's quickly apparent how menacing he is. There's something about him, not about his physique but about his mannerisms, that makes him intimidating. He knows he has power, and he knows how to use it.

He talks for a few minutes, pacing back and forth in front of his captive, delaying what we all know is coming. Then in one swift movement, a twist of the arms, he snaps the journalist's neck.

He's not just a deal-maker. He's an executioner.

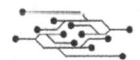

We carry out our next course of action in the early hours of the following morning, opting to use their vault for our interrogation rather than taking Gokiburi to a new location. All we need to do is take control of the hideout. He has 24/7 guards that monitor the hotel's cameras and protect his bedroom while he sleeps, but they're not as lethal as us.

After we're done, we'll dump the bodies down the chute, destroy the computers, and disappear.

Camden is excited about the operation, naturally. I'm laying out roles for him, Shay, and me when he interrupts.

"I think we should just improvise."

I give him a look. "This isn't something we should improvise."

"Mate. They're not going to see it coming. We have every advantage. We get in there, we get everyone into the vault, rough 'em up a bit, execute them. Simple as that."

I'll admit, it is pretty simple. I just think I'm more cognizant of what's resting on our shoulders than Camden is. Or more affected by it.

"No Delta agent is walking out alive with you there," he adds.

I'm reminded that this is the first time Reiya will see me kill someone, and the thought makes me uneasy. I don't know if I want her to see that.

"I know," I say quietly. "Killing is easy. We just have to be smart. This is our only solid lead on Arachne."

Right now, we have no leverage over Gokiburi other than torture, which I think we'd all like to limit as much as possible. If that doesn't make him talk, it's up to Reiya to do as much digging as she can to find a weakness. She and Harley will be working remotely, spoofing and watching camera feeds as needed.

Shay, Camden, and I throw on civilian clothes over our DareTech suits, arm ourselves with Ghost pistols, pack backpacks with essentials, and head to the hotel. Reiya guides us to a service entrance, where we scan a keycard she provided access to. We head to a stairwell and climb to the fifth floor, pausing before exiting into the hallway. Gokiburi has his own cameras set up, so the moment we step out the door is likely the moment that one of the guards will spot us. Which means we still need to look like civilians up until we break into the suite.

"From what we see with the drones, as of now there are two guards in the hidden room, one right outside the bedroom door, and one near the door to the hallway," Harley says in our earpieces.

I make eye contact with Cam and Shay to check that they're ready, then pull open the door. And when we reach the designated suite, the split second they draw their weapons, I scan the fake keycard and shoulder inside.

Shay shoots the closest guard with a tranquilizer dart. She and Camden head left toward the hidden room, while I head right toward the bedroom. The guard there pulls a gun on me but I knock him out before he pulls the trigger. I kick open the bedroom door, where it's nearly pitch black.

But in the next instant, my eyes adjust, the room coming into focus as though lit by moonlight. I'm shocked at how well I can see, but forget about my new supersenses when I realize the bed is empty. *Shit.* I hold my breath and scan the room, but it's my ears that save me.

There's a rush of air from my eight o'clock. I turn and block a knife strike with my forearm, my suit protecting me. I glimpse confusion in Gokiburi's face as I kick him backward. He regains his balance with surprising speed, taking up a stance once more. I could just tranq him now, but that takes out all the fun. I mean, Gokiburi seems more capable than his damn guards.

He takes another swing at me, but at the last moment he tosses his knife from one hand to the other and makes a jab to my stomach. I sidestep, but it still catches me, just barely. Not that it has any effect of course, thanks to Dare.

I counter with a punch to his cheek, and it knocks him to the ground like he weighs nothing.

When he looks up at me again I finally see a bit of fear. "Who are you?" he asks in Japanese, spitting blood from his mouth, as I stand over him.

"Your worst nightmare." I point my tranq gun and shoot him in the chest.

By the time he wakes, we have him and all four of his guards restrained in their lair.

Depending on how much watching each other die encourages our captives to spill information, we could be here for hours, or we could be here for days.

Reiya and Harley are alternating remote guard duty, in case anyone decides to visit. Meanwhile, Camden, Shay, and I are going to take turns interrogating in pairs while the third person sleeps. Shay and I opt to start, but Cam refuses to miss out on the first round.

We have Gokiburi in a chair in the center of the room, the guards in a corner.

"Takeshi Otsuka, right?" I ask as he comes to, speaking his native tongue.

He spits in my face as a response. It makes me want to punch him again, but I resist. Calmly I wipe my face with my sleeve.

"You're just going to make this worse for yourself."

"What do you want?"

"The identity of your boss," Shay says. "*Arachne.*"

His eyes shift to her, but he probably doesn't gauge her as a threat. I didn't, when I first met her. That's what makes her such a dangerous agent. Shay has been the most caring and kind in our friend group, but when she's in the field, she's a force to be reckoned with. She's made more kills than Camden. And she's not afraid to be brutal.

"I'd die before talking," Gokiburi says.

Shay grabs a bucket of ice water and dumps it on him. "Let's test that belief."

"Would your guards die before talking?" I ask.

"No," he responds after shaking off the shock of cold. "That's why I cut out their tongues."

I don't let my face show my internal reaction.

"Cam," I say, but he's already checking Gokiburi's claim. He grabs one of the guards by the jaw and yanks his mouth open.

"He's not bluffing, mate."

"Well," Shay says. "Just because they don't have tongues doesn't mean they can't write."

"Maybe we'll spare them more pain and let them live. If we get what we want," I add.

Gokiburi sneers. "I don't believe you."

"We're only monsters if we need to be."

"You're GUARD agents, aren't you?" he says, his voice venomous. "You're all under the delusion that you're saving the world, but all you do is murder."

"Could say the same about you," I reply indifferently.

Shay turns on a fan and faces it toward him. Her preferred method is slow-burn suffering, drawn out until it becomes unbearable. Being cold, wet, and sleep deprived can drive a person mad.

I, on the other hand, tend to get physical, and Camden likes to play mind games.

We'll see which one breaks Gokiburi in the end.

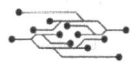

He remains resistant for our first rotation. Silent, for the most part, even as he begins to shiver violently. So for Camden's turn, we move on to his goons. Using facial recognition and the databases of the GUARD and the Japanese government, Reiya has been able to get us information on familial ties. It took her a few hours to narrow in on the family of only one guard, so we try to stall to give her time, without looking like we're stalling. What's interesting is that she had to go a couple *years* back to find anything, which might be when this particular guard got involved with Delta. I can't help but wonder if he's actually seen his family since then.

Camden hauls him to the center of the room, shoving Gokiburi roughly into a corner with a gag in his mouth. Blasts a fan on him for good measure.

"This your kid?" Cam asks casually, holding up a picture on his phone to the guard. It's a photo of a boy who looks about seven. Then, he turns his phone around to look at it himself, feigning pity. "Looks like a sweet kid."

No response.

He continues, switching to Japanese. "Don't worry, we won't hurt your little boy unless we have to." With a swipe on his phone, the photo changes to a forty-something man outside a suburban residence. "This is your spouse and home, is it not?"

I catch a glimmer of fear in the guard's eye. We have no intention of harming anyone who's innocent, but he doesn't know that.

Camden leans in, dropping his voice to a murmur.

I can hear him, but I doubt anyone else can.

"You have three options. One, you can answer our questions truthfully. If your answers differ from those of your cohorts over there, we'll shoot you in the head. Two, we can torture you until you agree to number one. Three, I'll pay your family a visit and torture *them* until you agree to number one." Camden leans back again with a pleasant smile. "Which would you prefer?"

Still, no response.

Good thing we have a tiny camera drone waiting outside his family's house to elevate our threat.

Camden brings up the video feed as a projection. "If you don't decide, I'm going to have to pick for you, and to be honest, I kind of like number three. Look, they're home together."

Get closer to the window, I message Harley, who is piloting.

The guard stares at his partner and child, who are watching HV, so completely unaware.

"I'll ask again, for the last time," Camden says, more insistent now. "Which option do you prefer?"

Wrists bound together in electro cuffs, the guard shakily uncurls a sole finger from his clenched fist. Camden grins.

"Excellent. First question. Do you know the identity of Arachne?"

He shakes his head no.

"Has this man," Camden points, "Takeshi Otsuka, ever met with her?"

Nod.

"Have you seen her?"

Shake.

"Can you tell us where they've met?"

Nod.

"Can you tell us approximately *when* they met at each location?"

Nod.

"And if I ask your friends over there, will they tell me the same thing?"

Nod.

I hand Camden a tablet and a stylus, and unholster my Ghost, taking aim at the guard's head.

"One wrong move and you're dead," I say as Camden releases him from his cuffs and gives him the tablet. He's still bound to the chair, but it can't hurt to have a gun pointed at him just in case.

I take back the tablet after he's done writing down locations and dates, skimming over the list. There are cities all over the world, but most recently is London. It makes sense, given what Delta is planning there. Arachne may even be there right now.

I send the list to Reiya to see if she can find anything. GUARD divisions overseeing the locations might have data that could prove to be useful—photos, flight records, credit card transactions. None of it will connect back to Gokiburi's real name, most likely, but we might be able to do a face search like we've been doing to get information on the guards. Thus far Reiya hasn't been able to find anything on him—like Lucien said, Delta protects its assets at all costs. The guards, however, are disposable, replaceable.

But that was their mistake. That's what led us here.

I get some sleep while Camden repeats his method with another guard, who eventually ends up giving us a fairly similar list, but nothing else useful. So Shay and I give Gokiburi another round.

Shay circles him as he sits, still shivering, slowly losing feeling in his fingers and toes. "Is she a lover? Is that why you're so protective?"

"She doesn't need my protection," he spits.

"Yet, here you are. So tell me. What is she to you?"

Silence.

"Because, as far as I can tell, to her, you're just an obedient dog. She says jump, you ask how high."

"Bitch."

Shay stops in front of him and punches him sharply across the face. It splits his lip, bruises his cheek.

"What has she done for you?" She pulls out Gokiburi's own knife, then resumes circling, dragging the flat side of the blade across his back. "Do you think your death will mean anything to her? Or will she rampage on?"

"Your tactic is pathetic."

Shay drags a chair over and takes a seat across from him, her face only inches from his. "Yeah?" She trails the knife up his leg, all the way up to his crotch, pressing it into him ever so slightly. "Maybe I should cut your balls off, hmm?"

She digs the knife tip in a bit more, and I see him start to wince. Then, she relinquishes. But the next second she drives the knife into his thigh. He lets out a guttural scream.

"No," she hisses over his groans, "I think we'll save that for last."

She stands once more.

"Have a go at him, Kai."

"Oh, are you the muscle?" Gokiburi says in between breaths. Even when he's bleeding out he's still an asshole.

So I punch him. Twice.

"No, I'm just too impatient for anything else," I respond, this time in English, pressing my hand against his wound. He glares at me through the agony. "Now, all you have to do is give us her name, and this can all be over."

"Fuck you."

"Where does this loyalty come from?"

He looks me in the eye. "I believe I'm doing what's right for the world, same as you."

"What, going around snapping journalists' necks and selling drugs and weapons?"

"Our mission will save the world from itself."

I can't help but roll my eyes. "Oh right, the *mission*," I repeat harshly. "You know, your *cult* has killed hundreds of my people. And thousands of others. If not directly then by the chaos you've caused. You're not saving the world; you're lighting it on fire."

Delta took my partner from me. They almost took Harley, too. Camden, Shay, Lucien. Next time they might just succeed.

I throw several hits to his gut, followed by a few more to his face, my hands covered in blood from his thigh.

"She in London, right now? Pulling all the strings from the shadows?"

No response.

That's when my anger breaks loose. And I lose control.

"Tell me!" I yell in his face. I catch him flinch for the first time.

In a flash I've broken his restraints, picked him up, and thrown him to the ground. In his eyes I see that the instinct to survive is kicking in, and that's what I'm counting on. In the end, people usually fight for themselves.

I can't stop myself as I kick him. Over and over.

But I halt when I realize he's trying to speak again.

"The shadows..." he begins to utter, struggling, "are in plain sight."

FORTY

"Who else could it be?" I say, debating with Camden over whether Gokiburi has actually given us what we need. He's continued to refuse to give us a name, so all we've got is his cryptic message. But that message isn't an insignificant one, in my mind. I think he was telling us that Arachne has finally stepped out into the public eye, even if most of her own people don't even know it.

Camden thinks I'm reading into it too much. "Kai. He gave you a fuckin' riddle. That's not a name."

"If it gets us a name, it's as good as."

"Look. This random lady leading the uprising in the UK is undoubtedly Delta, but for the top dog to put herself out there like that? I don't think she'd risk it."

I turn to Shay. "What do you think?"

She debates in her head for a moment. "I think you could be right. If what Zahra says about these riots being the beginning of a huge movement is true, it'd make sense that Arachne would want to be in complete control. Why would she give the reins to someone else?"

"Exactly," I say.

"However," Shay continues, "I don't want to kill Gokiburi until we can be pretty confident that we're right."

"I know. But I think we're getting pressed for time here."

"You're right about that," Camden agrees, running a hand over his face. "Is your gut telling you that it's her? Talia Bellona?"

God I hope I'm not wrong. "Yes."

He exhales. "All right, then. I trust your judgment."

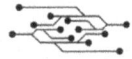

Shay is the one to kill Gokiburi, with a bullet to the head. He didn't even beg for his life, which I kind of respect.

We decide to let his guards go to repay their cooperation, with the threat that the GUARD will always be watching them. I'm a little wary of just letting them walk free, but the relief on their faces when they realize we're not going to kill them diminishes that doubt.

When we're back at our hotel, we video call Benson and Lucien.

"How's it going?" Lucien says wearily. He looks like he hasn't slept.

"We think the person you're following might be Arachne herself," Shay says.

A few seconds of silence.

"Seriously?"

"Seriously. What's your status with her?"

"I injected a tracker," Benson says. "But we keep losing her for varying chunks of time. It's weird."

"How'd you manage that?" I ask.

"I used a Wasp. Something my dad invented. It's an insect drone that looks like a real wasp, and the sensation when it implants the tracker is designed to mimic a sting. The drone contains fake hemolymph in case it's crushed, so no one would suspect a thing."

"But it's faulty? Or do you think she's going somewhere that could jam it?"

"We're not quite sure," Lucien responds. "Could be a vault, given that her location will drop completely; there's no intermittency. Like she's... teleporting in and out of existence."

Benson's face falls suddenly.

"Wait... Can you pull up an image of her?"

Lucien's brow furrows. "Uh... sure."

Next to their video, another panel pops up with a close-up of the red-eyed woman.

"How often do you guys see enhanced eyes like that?" Benson asks.

"People change their eye color all the time," Harley says, shrugging. "It's not unusual, but I will say that I haven't really seen that luminescence effect."

Luminescence effect.

My eyes widen. I know where I've seen *that* before.

"Oh my God," I breathe. "What if..."

"She's Elysian," Benson finishes.

"What?" Harley blurts. "How can you possibly know?"

"Her eyes," Benson says. "Most of the Elysians have eyes like that. And she keeps *disappearing*."

Harley shakes her head. "I don't quite follow."

But I do. "The transporter."

"Yes," Benson agrees. "Well, not *the* transporter. *A* transporter. She could be traveling to Nyx as she pleases."

"Okay, hold on," Lucien says. "Let's not let our imaginations get the better of us."

Benson sighs. "I know, I know. It's crazy."

"How could you confirm it?" Harley asks.

"Unless we see it, we can't. We could try to send in a drone, but in order to follow her through things like doors, it'd have to maintain a riskily small distance."

We all think for a moment.

"I think we should come to London and go from there," I decide. "If this is Arachne, she's planning something big, and we need to be there, regardless of whether she's Elysian."

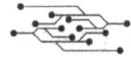

When we land in Bristol, on account of all the London airports being shut down, we get a call from Dare.

"I talked to Benson's mother, Lara, about your theory regarding Talia Bellona," he begins after I've put him on speakerphone. "She agrees that she looks Elysian. She also agrees that the interstellar travel thing, albeit a bit unlikely, is plausible. The technology undoubtedly still exists. However, the connection between Delta and Elysium is what's difficult to explain. Twenty-some years ago Elysium's new leader sought to separate from humans, not take us over."

"I think there's a lot we don't know," I reply. "Twenty-some years ago is also when Delta was formed. Maybe there's a bigger picture. Or maybe there's not. It's still important to get to the truth, because we may not know what we're in for."

"I know. I'll dig into Bellona as much I can to try and get you some answers."

"Thank you."

"Hang in there, all of you. Oh, and uh… you should check the back of our hangar. I left something for you."

What we find is a sleek, black electric motorcycle. Attached to it is a little note from Dare: *For Harley. It's self-driving, weapons galore, etc. Send it a location, and it'll navigate to you. Just try not to crash it.*

"Are you shitting me?" Camden says, incredulous. "Is it because your name is Harley? I want one."

Harley traces her fingers along the bike as though she's stunned that someone would give her something like that. Frankly, I think it's perfect for her.

She decides to ride it to London while the rest of us pile into an SUV with our weapons and tech. I watch as she slips on leather gloves and a helmet, climbs onto the bike, and speeds off ahead of us.

"You're hitting that, right?" Camden asks from the driver's seat.

I give him a look.

"I'd be disappointed if you weren't."

I notice, even amidst his incessant joking, that he seems a little off today. Part of me wonders if coming back to his home is difficult for him.

We discuss our game plan with Lucien and Benson as we drive—it'll take us two hours to get to London, accounting for Camden's speeding. We intended to act immediately on taking out Talia Bellona, but the tumult here alters our course.

"They're bringing in the military to subdue what is now effectively a rebellion," Lucien says. "The citizens are arming themselves. From here on out, it's basically war."

"What?" Camden says, disbelieving. "The government is going to use military force against its own citizens?"

"Yes. The police haven't been able to contain it. People have started dragging representatives from their homes. Murdering them in the streets. Both sides are more vicious than ever. Delta has poisoned everyone's minds."

"That's all it takes," I mutter. "So what do we do? Does anyone know what the hell London Division is doing?"

"The GUARD was not designed to handle national emergencies like this," Shay responds. "We're an intelligence agency. I don't doubt that Byrne is trying to push back on the government side, but there's not a whole lot his division can do aside from kill Delta agents. And besides, everyone is spread out. The majority of London agents might not even be in the country."

I nod. "Fair enough. Let's discuss our priorities, then. One, probably damage control. That means removing as much of Delta's threat as possible. Two, Talia Bellona. Without her, things might crumble."

"Kai… we're not equipped for this," Lucien counters.

"I know we're not," I say. "But we'll do what we can."

A few seconds of silence. "Okay. What do we do, then?"

I expect someone else in the car to start throwing out ideas, but I realize they're all looking at me.

"Well… Let's split into teams. Benson, you should lead the assassination of Bellona. Especially if she is who you think she is. Cam, Shay, you go with him. Harley and I will be on the streets to try and temper this storm. Reiya, Lucien, you be our eyes and ears. Call in some surveillance drones, watch city cameras and news broadcasts, listen in on comms. Anything to get us ahead of what's going on. I'll talk to Byrne and see how much backup we can get."

When we arrive in the heart of the city, we find that streets have been barricaded, stores have been broken into, car windows have been smashed. Holograms flicker. A lot of people are making their way, by car where possible and by foot otherwise, toward *something*. The Parliament building, maybe. Some have clubs and mallets, some even have guns. That right there is a wake-up call.

Camden looks around like he doesn't even recognize the place.

I don't know what the people are planning, but with Delta in the mix, and with the military, it's going to get violent.

We meet Benson and Lucien at a GUARD safe house in an unremarkable grey high-rise. They're still staring at Harley in disbelief by the time the rest of us get there.

"Were you not wheelchair-bound about a week ago?" Benson says. "Jesus, my dad can replace your legs in a matter of days but he can't even visit his own child. Classic."

I think he's joking, but I can't really tell.

"Now's not the time for your daddy issues, Benson," Harley teases back. "You have two parents who give a shit, the rest of us have zero."

"Fine. Paternal abandonment aside, we think we have a good idea where Bellona will be today. From what we know, based on Zahra's intelligence and our own, her plan is to make a brief appearance in public before dipping. She doesn't want to be caught in the midst of a battle. Her people—well, *armed forces* is more accurate—are going to escalate the riots, which is where you two come in." He gestures to Harley and me.

"Zahra is here in London, actually," Lucien adds. "She's going to do what she can to continue to get us information, but in all honesty, this is going to get messy pretty quickly."

"Zahra's here?" I repeat, my heart skipping a beat. "Where?"

I've tried so hard not to think about her, but she's always in the back of my mind, another person that I've fallen a little too hard for. Another person I desperately wish I could protect.

"Not quite sure. She's working an ambassador for Delta. But it's too risky to see her."

"I know. But if *she's* here, that probably means that a lot of bases have sent their people here."

Lucien nods somberly. "This is big for Delta. It's the turning point that they've been striving for since the beginning. It's what was always in the back of my mind. Revolution."

I study him to determine how he's feeling. "Do you think we can stop it? Sincerely."

He returns my gaze, his eyes communicating his belief before he says it. "No. But we have to try."

I nod once. Look around at my team, these people who are my friends. None of them are afraid. "Let's get to it, then."

"Try not to die, darling," Camden patronizes me as he, Shay, and Benson break off to plan their strategy.

"See you on the other side," Shay says with a crooked smile, sliding her hand into Camden's. He glances at her, just for a moment, with what I can only describe as adoration. I don't know how the hell I didn't pick up on it before. I mean, I know they've had a thing for each other, but I had no idea that they'd fallen in *love*.

Harley and I make our way separately toward the riot, the epicenter of which is indeed the Palace of Westminster. Given the threat, I doubt any MPs are actually there, but it's at least symbolic. I ditch the safe house car a few blocks away and start pushing through people, heading toward Parliament Square Garden. Rows of military officers have managed to hold a decent radius around the building, forming a human wall. But I can't imagine it'll last.

A single command echoes through loudspeakers: "Disperse immediately or risk arrest."

It doesn't seem to be inspiring anyone to turn around and go home. Instead, a chant begins reverberating through the crowd: "You did nothing, so we'll do something."

"How's it looking on your end?" I ask Harley, who's on the northern side of the park.

"Nothing crazy yet," she responds. "Right now it feels like it's just a protest. But something is coming. I think they're... waiting."

"I think you're right. Let's meet in the middle."

With our trackers we manage to find one another in the massive crowd. We stand on the street near the southwest corner of the park, Big Ben directly ahead. I slide my arm around her waist as I scan for threats, feeling the Ghost tucked into her jacket. Slung over our shoulders are our Soulbarers, hidden away in a retractable sleeve.

"What's our plan?" she asks, also scouring the scene, our earpieces allowing us to hear each other over the chanting.

"I don't really have one," I respond honestly. "I think we're going to have to react to the hell that breaks loose. The two of us can't de-escalate anything at this point, so let's try to take out anyone who's gunning people down. Military, civilian, doesn't matter."

In the periphery of my vision I see her nod. "What did Byrne say?"

"He's sending some agents out to help us, but he has a lot of them on guard duty for MPs and government officials that we're pretty confident aren't working with Delta, and thus need protection. Upper tier damage control, I guess."

"So we're on our own."

"Looks like it. How are you holding up?"

"Considering I learned how to walk again only days ago, pretty good. I'm not at full strength but I can run if need be."

Truthfully, I don't want her to be here, caught in a firefight when she hasn't gained back her full physical dexterity. But I need her. The GUARD needs her, these people need her. She's not going to sit on the sidelines, anyhow.

"Anything interesting from the street cams or drones, Lucien?" I say.

"Not yet. I'm using facial rec to search the crowd for any known Delta agents."

"Keep us posted."

And then, the palace explodes.

FORTY ONE

By instinct, Harley and I drop lower, but everyone else is momentarily frozen. For a few seconds, they gaze at the spectacle. We're far enough that no one around us is injured, but close enough for the explosion to rattle my bones.

Then the crowd surges forward with a roar.

We're shoved from behind as people start to rush toward the armed forces and police.

In an instant, it's chaos. And it doesn't take long for guns to start firing up ahead. All of a sudden we're in a war zone. Harley and I may be wearing Dare's suits, but we're not invincible.

I look at her. "Odds?"

She takes my hand. "Minimal."

But we both know that it doesn't matter. So we get to work.

I unsheathe the Soulbarer that's attached to my harness, and it constructs itself. I keep the trigger beneath my fingertips as Harley and I make our way through a maze of people toward the front lines, where civilians are clashing with law enforcement, batons meeting bone. I have no idea who's Delta and who's not, but there's no time to worry about it.

Tony helps me pick out those who are heavily armed, highlighting them in my vision and suggesting moves to make. I focus on the man closest to me. He's big, tattooed, vicious. In the span of several seconds, I see him shoot two people in the head and fight others hand-to-hand, using his gun for blunt force. With ease he grabs an officer's upper arm, pushes downward and twists until he's in a hold, then knees him in the stomach. He throws him to the ground, then shoots him.

I find myself analyzing his technique. He's trained, that's for sure. Maybe even more than I am.

Thanks to my neurocomputer's mimicry protocol, however, technique matters less. It'll come down to strength and wits.

I see another goon close by.

"Eleven and one o'clock, you see them?" I ask Harley.

"Yep."

"I've got eleven, you get one."

There's no clean shot from this distance, so I opt for a close-range attack. I run at my target, fully intending to get his attention so he'll stop killing people left and right.

Just as I reach him is when he tries to shoot, but I'm a step ahead. I deploy the circular shield in my wristband and block a bullet from hitting my heart, then knock his weapon to the side. That alone seems to enrage him.

I retract the shield and kick him backward, causing him to stumble. I'm raising the Soulbarer but he's on me again with speed that almost rivals my own, impressive for his size. I block his right hook with my gun, pushing out and down against his arm to break his stance. Then he throws a punch to my gut, the impact lessened by my suit, and an upper cut to my jaw, throwing me off my pattern.

The hits keep coming with ferocity that I underestimated, every movement designed for maximum injury. I stop a few but not enough—he's been aiming for my head, the only part of my body not well protected. Blood is running from my nose.

So I readjust. I sling my Soulbarer back over my shoulder and counter with rapid, precise punches, matching a few of the strikes that worked on me. He doesn't expect it. Then I press forward, grab him, plant a foot behind his, push him. He falls backward. I stand over him, unholster my Ghost, and shoot him before he can get up again.

I look to my right and find Harley nearby, raising her Soulbarer and taking out a soldier before he can do the same to her. Another attacker, not unlike the one I just killed, approaches her and yanks her weapon out of her hands, the harness buckle giving way, as designed, so she doesn't get pulled forward. He sneers with satisfaction at his successful disarm, but he doesn't know that the weapon won't fire for him.

Harley doesn't miss a beat. As she moves toward him I see small blades extend from her feet. With one kick to his side he yelps in surprise, but he doesn't go down. She kicks him again, this time in the stomach, with her heel. He tries to pull the trigger of the Soulbarer, his panic at its defiance allowing her to take it back. Then he's down with a single bullet.

We kill several more like him. Arachne's army, I suspect. But some are just people. People not like him or me, people who want to take matters into their own hands, ignited by Talia Bellona. Or maybe by their own rage toward the world.

I run over to Harley and we crouch behind a nearby abandoned car to momentarily avoid the anarchy. There are a few nasty bruises on her face but it seems she's otherwise unharmed.

"You okay?" I ask.

She nods wearily. "I'm fine. A bit unbalanced. Slow. But I'm fine."

"Let's stick together, yeah? Watch each other's six."

She wipes blood from my face. "Yeah. We should—"

"Kai, Harley," Lucien says suddenly. His voice wavers. "We think there's going to be coordinated bombings. NCA, MI5, and MI6 headquarters, residences of MPs. And more. Zahra confirmed it, but she doesn't know when it's going to happen."

Shit.

"And the royals?" I say.

"Less likely they'll be attacked, for now. They're all relatively safe up in Scotland."

"What do we do?"

"Reiya and I are sending out evacuation messages, but we also might be able to jam the—"

Even over the gunfire and screaming I hear it. The city has begun to detonate.

We're too late.

In the span of a few seconds, thousands of people die.

I'm still trying to process, mind spinning to come up with a course of action, when Tony alerts us to another wave of people approaching, based on our drones scanning the scene above.

My eyes snap up, head whipping around. Behind us is a horde of people equipped with gear and guns and anger.

"Round two," I say, my hope dwindling. Of course Delta is not going to lose this battle. Thus far the military has been able to stand their ground, being better protected and better armed, but I don't think they can hold much longer. There's just too many people to fight.

After that, who will be left?

Delta has organized the murders of countless elected representatives, intelligence agents, and soldiers. There's no one else to defend the institutions of the United Kingdom, so once they all fall, Delta has won.

Harley and I scramble to the other side of the car, exposed to the battle now behind us but well-positioned to attack the army ahead of us. I prop my Soulbarer up on the hood, she props hers on the trunk. Through the view I aim at the hearts and heads of those highlighted as targets. The gun has algorithms that seemingly predict where I'm going to shoot based on what's in the view, making the targeting speed remarkable.

We take out a good number, especially after I tell Tony to target people from the drones, but when we start receiving return fire, we're forced to take cover again. That's when I hear the beat of blades in the sky, growing closer. Copters, no doubt, but the question is which side they belong to.

"There's an onslaught of people coming toward the park from every direction," Lucien says. In other words, we don't stand a chance. "You should get the hell out of there."

"No," Harley responds, leaving it at that.

She grabs my hand and we run toward the middle of the park, the epicenter of the bloodbath, where the ground is stained red and littered with bodies. We weave through people, dodging attacks and weapons.

We approach a military officer, who initially assumes we're a threat, but Harley disarms him in the blink of an eye. She relays Lucien's information, pointing in the direction we came from. The officer's eyes widen, as though he hadn't seen the second wave because he'd been so immersed in fighting off the first.

"Tell your superiors," I add.

"It's okay," he says, a bit dazed. "We've got help." His eyes raise to the sky, and I follow his gaze to the approaching copters.

When I look back down, the horde of people, now forming something like a semicircle around the western edge of the park, is rushing at us. Harley and I, accompanied by whoever is left on our side, start shooting. But the dent we make isn't enough.

I see Harley re-sheathe her Soulbarer.

"Harley?" I say, confused.

"I'm going to try something," is all she says.

She runs *toward* the army, then jumps before she reaches their front line. I hardly believe my eyes as she reaches a height that must be over twice as high as is humanly possible.

And, when she lands, there is what I can only describe as a small earthquake. The ground seems to roll outward from her in every direction, accompanied by a gust of wind, like a seismic wave. Everyone in a fifty-foot radius is thrown to the ground, apart from myself. Instead, I absorb the energy, just as Q claimed I could.

But I barely pay attention to the fact that I'm still standing.

"You failed to mention that Dare gave you superpowers," I shout at Harley.

She resumes shooting at close range. I start to move forward, to take advantage of the fact that our adversaries are down, but then I catch movement at the edge of my vision, to my left.

I turn my head. It all happens in the blink of an eye.

A region of air just above the ground twists into a blur, as if space-time is being warped. Then, somehow, it morphs into people, and the air returns to normal, as if nothing strange had occurred.

For a moment I almost think I'm hallucinating because I can't comprehend what I just saw. Then my breath catches as sudden realization dawns on me, and I brace myself for Talia Bellona to be revealed, followed by an army.

But it's not her. It's five people I've never seen, dressed in black.

Out of habit, I raise my Soulbarer, zeroing in on the heart of the first one, a black-haired girl not much older than me. Her eyes lock onto me. An immediate detection of my threat.

She throws out her arm and there's a flash of light like a bolt of lightning. I seize with the electricity, and crumple to my knees, but it's not enough to knock me out. A mild burning sensation spreads through my body, but in an instant, my neurocomputer diminishes the pain to tingling.

The girl cocks her head in confusion—or curiosity, perhaps—as though she had intended to do more harm. As though she tried to kill me.

Is this a death squad?

Arachne must be sending people over. Elysians.

The other four start taking in the scene, but my attacker is still focused on me. She begins to approach and I raise my gun once more, still on my knees and unable to stand. But then I realize that she's not approaching with the intent to kill—that motive has faded, and my perplexity at it makes me hesitate.

"Are you human?" she asks as she stands over me, a strange weapon in hand but not aimed at me. She looks at the maze logo on my suit and narrows her bizarre ice-blue eyes.

"Well I'm not whatever you are," I respond warily.

"You're certainly more resilient than the average person. I meant to—"

"Kill me, I know."

"Are you Delta?" she demands.

I pause, unsure which answer is going to get me killed. She's Elysian, that much I'm fairly confident of. Logically that'd mean she's fighting for Arachne. But I don't know if I'd be alive if that were true.

"No. Are you?"

"No. Amaia."

"Kai. Who are you guys?"

She sticks out her hand to help me to my feet. "Tartarus. At your service."

Tartarus. The opposite of Elysium.

As she runs off to join her comrades in the battle, where Harley is in the middle of all the action, the black copters descend behind me. There are three of them, bearing the logo of the British Armed Forces, landing in sync. Across the street behind them burns the Palace of Westminster.

Sounds of relief echo through the ranks of the armed forces.

But they're silenced by machine guns. A bullet whizzes through the chest of the officer Harley and I talked to. Tony deploys my shield before I realize what's happening.

The copters are Delta.

And we're completely encircled. People around me start to drop like flies and for a few seconds I have no idea what to do other than protect myself.

That's when I feel the neurocomputer begin to take over. I feel my mind slipping, losing control of my body. But this time, I fight it. I strain against the movements it wants me to make, not with my muscles but with my brain.

When it relinquishes control once more I think I've won.

But in my next moment of consciousness, I'm standing in front of the copters. Or, rather, the burnt *remains* of the copters. The grass beneath my feet has been incinerated, or something close to it, in a large radius around me. There are charred bodies, some of which belong to allies.

What just happened?

It only takes me a few seconds to piece together the answer.

I caused the explosion. And the neurocomputer knocked me out to do it. It didn't just take over, it *became me*.

I have no idea whether it was programmed by Q to shut off parts of my brain, or if it *learned* because I fought back.

"Kai!" Harley yells frantically in my earpiece. "Are you okay?"

"I'm okay," I breathe, my voice raw, my knees weak, my mind reeling.

I turn and scan the scene for her blonde hair, but she's already running to me. She practically throws herself into my arms.

"Thank God. I thought that explosion killed you. You weren't responding."

"That explosion *was* me."

She pulls back, disbelief on her face. "What? You mean…"

"Yeah. The neurocomputer took over. Couldn't stop it."

"Jesus."

Over her shoulders, I scan the scene which has now, to my surprise, calmed. People are dropping their weapons, raising their hands. People on our side.

"What's going on?"

"The military is surrendering. I don't think they know that those copters weren't actually theirs." Harley takes a breath. "Delta won."

Delta won.

I knew they would, but it doesn't make it less devastating.

I squeeze my eyes shut for a moment. "What do we do?"

"It's over, for now," Harley responds grimly. "We need to get out of here before someone realizes who we are. I called your car to come get us."

I spot Amaia coming over to us, and finally get a good look at her. She's dressed in some sort of sleek sci-fi armor, with tattoos on her neck and dark makeup. She looks human enough, but there's definitely something inhuman about her, and I can't quite pinpoint what it is.

"You sure you two are human?" she says, more intrigued than wary.

"We come with a couple of enhancements," I respond.

She cocks her head. "Interesting."

Harley looks between us in confusion. "Who the hell are you?"

"Amaia Hale. I'm sorry we arrived a little late to the battle. But I think we should talk."

"They're Elysians," I tell Harley.

Her eyebrows raise. "Seriously?"

"Seriously," Amaia replies. "But we're here to help you."

"What exactly is Tartarus?" I say.

Amaia's eyes shift to me. "A resistance organization. Just as Talia Bellona is seeking to overthrow your civilization, we're seeking to overthrow *her* on Nyx. If you have a secure location we could meet, I'll answer all your questions."

"How do we know you're not going to kill us?" Harley says, shaking her head.

"Well, we wouldn't need five of us to do that," Amaia responds.

"Five?"

"Yes. Location?"

I wish I had more time to make a judgment, but we're beyond out of time. Anyone who's willing to fight Delta is an ally to me. So I give her the coordinates of our safe house.

"Excellent. See you there." With that she spins on her heel and jogs back toward the rest of her people, who are eyeing us from a distance.

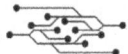

Harley and I are mostly silent on our drive back to the safe house, both from exhaustion and from the weight of what just happened. The car reroutes itself to avoid any barricades or explosion debris, so I just gaze out the window at a burning city, avoiding any thoughts about the thing in my brain or the fact that we failed.

I check in with Lucien to see if he's gotten any word from Benson regarding Talia Bellona, but then Camden calls.

"Cam?" I answer.

"She's gone," he says, his voice hitching. "She's gone, Kai."

My heart stops. "What? Who's gone?"

"I didn't—I couldn't—"

"*Who's* gone?" I repeat.

"Shay. I saw it happen."

My heart stops. *No no no.*

I haven't even processed it before he continues. "We couldn't stop her. We couldn't—Benson's abilities don't work on her."

It takes me a second to realize he's referring to Arachne.

"Cam, slow down," I plead, but it's no use. He's not listening to me.

"I'm—I'm gonna kill her. I'm gonna fucking *kill her.*"

"Camden *wait.*"

The other end goes dead. *Goddammit.*

"Tony, where is Camden?"

"Just a moment..." the AI says. "Location for Camden Adler not found."

"Lucien," I yell, growing frantic. "Can you get eyes on Camden and Benson?"

"On it."

I hold my breath.

"I... I can't see them."

"What? What does that mean?"

"Their trackers are offline. As are their earpieces."

"How?"

"... I think they transported to Nyx."

FORTY TWO

Q

I replay the footage from Thanatos's contact lenses for a third time, eyes unblinking as I align the timestamps with the logs uploaded by his neurocomputer.

Pinpointing the exact moment it took control.

I'd initially made the assumption that Thanatos had remained conscious, even if he'd been resisting the loss of autonomy. But closer inspection of the logs, and a slight difference in his movements, indicate something rather intriguing.

It rendered him unconscious, then brought him back without so much as a twitch.

The behavior aligns with my intentions, certainly. But, if I'm being humble, it's not something I knew how to design manually. So the fact that it adapted so quickly, so effortlessly...

It means my creation is more capable than even I thought it could be.

Had I known Minotaur was going to thrust themselves into battle, I might've been inclined to monitor Thanatos's feed and send commands myself, and thus never made this discovery. But now I can be confident that I need not fret about babysitting.

Now I know that if we want to stand a chance against an Elysian military and whatever weapon Medina might've given Delta, I should be embedding a neurocomputer into every agent I can.

Finally, a decade-long vision coming to fruition.

Elysium first revealed its existence to me during a thorough background investigation I performed on Mason Dare long ago, which subsequently spawned my clandestine research. And while I did not develop suspicions of Delta's connection to it until much later, after I'd already hired Brenner to assist, it was that revelation that solidified the direction we were going.

With the downfall of the United Kingdom, it's only a matter of time before the rest of the GUARD inevitably sees the need for the future I've been guiding them toward: a hive mind of elite agents, evolved through technology, empowered by AI, data, and logic. Unbounded by nature.

Fighting the mind of chaos.

ACKNOWLEDGMENTS

Writing this novel was a long, lonely, mind-body-and-soul-consuming journey. I wrote it, rewrote it, gave up on it, rewrote it again, then decided to publish it myself because it's my dream, dammit.

But of course, there are several people who I wouldn't have made it across the finish line without.

First and foremost, to my amazing partner (in crime): thank you for being my go-to alpha reader, my dream supporter, my everything. Thank you for enduring my rants about publishing, marketing, social media, and humanity as a whole. Thank you for inspiring some of the technology and villainous motives in this story, and thank you in advance for powering through all the future books I will undoubtedly make you read. I love you.

To my beta readers: you truly helped make this story what it is. Your input was invaluable and a gift I can never repay. Thank you for supporting me and helping me grow as an author.

To all the other readers who have taken a gamble with an unknown writer (me), and all the readers who will take that same gamble in the future: you are who I hope will fall in love with my art. But even if you don't, thank you for reading it anyway. You, whoever you are, are what motivates me through the hardest parts of being a writer.

Lastly, thank you to my dear friend of a decade, Ariel. I was so excited for you to read this novel one day, to read about the badass character you inspired (arguably one of the best characters, of course). I'm devastated that you'll never get to do so, but it was so wonderful to know you, and I will always find inspiration in you.

ABOUT THE AUTHOR

Atlas Blaine is fascinated by the human condition and all its complexity. She writes stories that often explore what that means, with a particular fondness for science fiction and thrillers. She draws inspiration from her education in computer science and psychology, and finds herself intrigued by tales that are evocative, cerebral, and tinged with darkness. She lives in Southern California with her partner, where in her free time she enjoys playing music, cheating in The Sims, and generating outrageous ideas for her next novel.

Learn more and join her mailing list at **www.atlasblaine.com**, or find her on social media (**@atlas_blaine**).